Chris Nyst was b[orn in]
Queensland, in 1953. [He studied]
and obtained a Law d[egree in]
Queensland before [becoming a]
solicitor in Brisbane, a[nd later]
As a lawyer he has been involved in some of
Australia's most sensational cases. Recognised as
one of Queensland's most experienced criminal
law advocates, Chris has been a regular speaker
and guest lecturer on criminal law and advocacy,
and has made a prolific contribution to a range of
legal publications. His first novels, *Cop This!* and
Gone, received excellent reviews, and in 2003 he
won the Lexus IF Award for Best Script for the
film *Gettin' Square*.

Chris lives with his wife, Julie, and their four
children on the Gold Coast, where he conducts
his legal practice.

Also by Chris Nyst

Cop This!
Gone

CROOK AS ROOKWOOD
CHRIS NYST

HarperCollinsPublishers

*This is a work of fiction. No resemblance is
intended to any real person living or dead.*

HarperCollins*Publishers*

First published in Australia in 2005
This edition published in 2006
by HarperCollins*Publishers* Australia Pty Limited
ABN 36 009 913 517
www.harpercollins.com.au

Copyright © Chris Nyst 2005

The right of Chris Nyst to be identified as the
author of this work has been asserted by him under
the *Copyright Amendment (Moral Rights) Act 2000*.

This work is copyright.
Apart from any use as permitted under the *Copyright Act 1968*,
no part may be reproduced, copied, scanned, stored in a retrieval
system, recorded, or transmitted, in any form or by any means,
without the prior written permission of the publisher.

HarperCollins*Publishers*
25 Ryde Road, Pymble, Sydney, NSW 2073, Australia
31 View Road, Glenfield, Auckland 10, New Zealand
77–85 Fulham Palace Road, London, W6 8JB, United Kingdom
2 Bloor Street East, 20th floor, Toronto, Ontario M4W 1A8, Canada
10 East 53rd Street, New York NY 10022, USA

National Library of Australia Cataloguing-in-Publication data:

Nyst, Chris.
    Crook as Rookwood.
    ISBN 0 7322 8057 5.
    ISBN 978 0 7322 8057 4.
    I. Title.
A823.3

Cover design by Darren Holt, HarperCollins Design Studio
Cover image (woman) courtesy of Corbis/Australian Picture Library
Cover image (skyline) courtesy of Shutterstock.com
Typeset in Sabon 10.5/13 by Kirby Jones
Printed and bound in Australia by Griffin Press on 50gsm Bulky News

5 4 3 2 1   06 07 08 09

*To my beautiful sons and
my darling daughters*

PROLOGUE

Old Tommy Attwell had lived at number fourteen as long as anyone could remember. He'd hoisted his young bride across the threshold in two strong arms, he'd mowed the back yard (what there was of it) a million times, fixed the gate a thousand more, painted the fence, weeded the garden and hosed the path. He'd raised three children in the street outside, umpiring cricket games and kicking footballs; he'd cried bitter, private tears slumped across his workbench in the shed on the night his eldest died, proudly toasted his daughter at her wedding underneath the back-yard marquee, and flogged his useless druggie son-in-law on the footpath out front. He'd got drunk at all the neighbours' barbecues, done a lifetime's work and watched his old friends move out one by one to the new, more fashionable estates. And eventually he'd seen his life's companion pass away, leaving him alone where he had lived as long as anyone could remember, at number fourteen.

Tommy wasn't going anywhere. It might be old and a little weather-beaten, but he knew every nail and washer in the little terrace house, and every nook and cranny held a story. The unmatched pane where Danny hooked a six straight into the upstairs bedroom window, the rose bushes Dawn had planted, the missing tap handle that none of the kids knew anything about. It was home, and he was happy there.

The developers were moving into Marrickville, buying up the neighbourhood, pulling down the old places, replacing them with flash unit buildings, all brick and tile and brand new. They were splashing lots of money about, offering the world to anyone who'd listen, and plenty had. But Tommy Attwell wasn't interested. Where would he go? Where else would he live? Not in some brick unit up three flights of stairs, and not in some new place out the back of Woop Woop, that's for sure. He was happy where he was. Number fourteen was his home and it had all he needed: room for the kids to visit when they wanted, a tool shed out the back, and Dawn's roses out the front. The developers were driving him insane, knocking on his door all day, sending around young estate agents dressed up in suits and fancy ties. They just couldn't seem to get the message. Tom was staying put. The day they took Tommy Attwell out of number fourteen he'd be in a wooden box.

'Bob! You there, Bob?'

The fat old tabby waddled out from behind the couch and meowed appreciatively as Tom set the saucer down. 'Get into it, son.'

Tom settled back into his armchair and listened to the comforting sound of Bob lapping up the milk. Bob was the last of the family, the only one who'd stuck around. Dawn and the kids had picked him out, a playful little ball of fur that was always underfoot or hanging off the lounge-room curtains. But he'd become a fixture through the years, and now he was a mate.

It was late, almost midnight. No wonder poor old Bob was hungry. He'd probably been waiting for hours for Tom to wake up and get him dinner. Tom opened up the television guide and leafed through, trying to work out what it was he'd woken in the middle of. It looked vaguely familiar, a re-run of a re-run of some Yankee show he'd probably seen a hundred times before. He'd have to watch it one more time unless he could find something better; he had no chance of getting back to sleep.

Tap, tap, tap.

The light knocking startled him. For a moment he sat silently, listening, his mind now more alert. Was that a knock on the front door? He wasn't expecting any of the family, and it was too late for visitors.

Tap, tap, tap.

It was someone at the front door. Tom groaned out of the chair and Bob stepped his rotund body sideways to make room, still lapping rhythmically at the milk. The wooden floorboards creaked softly underfoot as Tom lumbered down the hallway.

Tap, tap, tap.

'Yeah, righto. Coming.'

He flicked the front porch switch. As he fumbled with the lock he didn't notice that the light hadn't come on. He clicked the door open and drew it back towards him.

Whack!

The door hit him like a battering ram, slamming him brutally against the wall of the narrow hallway. Suddenly there was someone there in front of him, standing over him, grabbing at him, wrenching, pulling. It was a man, a big man. He filled the shadowy hallway, grunting, grappling, until he had Tom Attwell in an iron grip around the throat. A huge fist smacked loudly against the old man's face, smashing his nose and splintering the bone around his eye. It was pulled back quickly and then came crashing down again, throwing the old man against the wall and down onto the floor. Blinded by a thick red film of blood streaming from his eyebrow, Tom tried to get up on one elbow but images were moving round him in a crazy pattern and he could feel a nauseous blackness descending upon him. He fell back on the wooden floorboards and watched the distant shadows on the ceiling fading with his consciousness.

Roger Baston walked into the kitchen and emptied a jar of coins into one hand. As he stepped back over Tommy Attwell's limp body he pushed the coins into his pocket.

'Nice doing business with you, sport.'

He left, closing the door behind him.

* * *

'Fred. It's Roger.'

Fred Hunter was expecting Baston's call. 'G'day, Rog. How are you, mate?'

'Pretty good, mate, pretty good.'

'What's the news, son?'

'I hear that old bloke run into a bit of strife tonight.'

'Is that right?'

'Yeah.'

'Nothing too serious, I hope.'

'No, mate, no. Just a bit of a shiner, that's all. But I don't think he'll be too keen to hang around much longer.'

'Well, it's a rough neighbourhood as you know, Rog. No place for an old bloke on his own like that.'

'No, that's right. I'd say he'd be a lot more willing to talk right now.'

'Yeah, righto, Roger, thanks for that.'

'No worries, Fred. I'll catch ya.'

'Good, mate.'

Fred Hunter dropped his finger on the phone to disconnect the call. Then he punched in a set of numbers and waited while it rang.

'Hello.'

'Sharpey, it's me. Apparently that old bloke got a touch-up tonight.'

Gary Sharpe knew Fred Hunter's voice immediately. It was about as smooth and silky as eight miles of gravel road.

'Yeah?'

'Yeah. Someone's broke into his house and flogged him. Probably some junkie looking for loose change to whack up his arm.'

'I'd say so.'

'Yeah well, as you know it's a rough neighbourhood.'

'Yeah, that's right.'

'Anyway, it might be timely if you get someone around to renew that offer in the next few days.'

'Could be very timely, yeah.'

'Alright, I'll leave it with you, ay?'

'Yeah, righto, mate.'

'Oh listen, you'll look after that other thing for Roger too, won't you.'

'Absolutely, mate. I'm having lunch with Donny Bollard tomorrow.'

'Good. Righto, son.'

Gary Sharpe couldn't help smiling to himself as he put down the phone. He loved the way old Fred did business, understated, talking in riddles out the corner of his mouth. Just like a gangster in an old-time movie. Who knew what the truth of it might be, what was going on? Whatever it was, he was sure Fred Hunter had his finger on the pulse. If Fred reckoned now was the time to back up with another bid, now was the time. And if they could get the old bloke to sell, they would have the whole site tied up.

Sharpe opened up the liquor cabinet and poured himself a Scotch. He was in a celebratory mood. This was the deal he'd been waiting for. He'd snagged a guernsey as silent partner in Michael Wiltshire's new-unit site development in Sydney's inner west, and he was about to hit pay dirt. He and Wiltshire were old mates from way back, but Gary Sharpe wasn't kidding himself. Michael Wiltshire didn't cut him in on the project out of the goodness of his heart. Sharpey was there for his Labor Party connections. Everyone in Sydney knew Gary Sharpe had enough good mates to get whatever he wanted through the local council and that made him the perfect partner for any astute real-estate developer wanting to push the limits in the inner west. And Wiltshire was nothing if not astute. He knew that with Sharpey's contacts on the local council they'd get the whole block rezoned for multiple dwelling, provided they could stitch up the site.

It was Sharpey's contacts and pure rat cunning that were going to get this one across the line. Michael Wiltshire could never have done it without him. He might know how to pick the sites, get all the fancy consultants together and put a swish set of drawings on the table, but no one could grease the wheels of local government in this town like Gary Sharpe. And not too many, least of all Mick Wiltshire, understood that sometimes you had to get your hands dirty in the process. There should be close to half a million in the deal, and half of it was Sharpe's. He chuckled quietly at the very thought of it.

Who would've guessed the old bloke would hold out so long? In the end they'd had to call in Fred Hunter. Sharpey hadn't wanted to, because sometimes Fred's associates could be a little heavy-handed. But things had definitely gone on too long, and there was much too much at stake to walk away. The developer had offered that old bloke top dollar but he wouldn't budge. Stubborn old bastard. There was always a hard way and an easy way to do anything.

* * *

When the estate agent dropped in at number fourteen two days later Tommy Attwell didn't look himself. The left side of his face was bruised and swollen and he was moving feebly and tentatively, seeming even older than his advanced years. As Tommy told the young man how he had been mugged in his own home two days earlier his voice cracked sadly, the old strength and confidence gone. The agent listened attentively, as agents do, not interested in much except opportunity, and then he talked again as he had before about how Tom might well be better off out of the house and in a unit somewhere, with all the modern conveniences available, including a fully integrated security system. This time Tommy listened carefully to what the young man had to say. And when he left, Tom rang his daughter down in Melbourne and talked some more, and then he rang the agent back. After nearly fifty years in number fourteen, Tommy Attwell was moving out of Marrickville.

CHAPTER ONE

'Mate, I'll tell you what ...' Don Bollard cracked another claw and probed the stringy white flesh within. 'I'll tell you bloody what,' he went on, stuffing a new load of crabmeat into his mouth, 'this is still the best bloody joint in Australia to get a decent muddy.'

The New South Wales State Attorney-General was enjoying himself, that much was clear. The plastic bib over his shirt front was wearing enough crabmeat to choke a small dog, his sleeves were rolled up and he was hunched over his meal as though he meant real business. He was chuckling as he chomped rhythmically on the white flesh and cracked and crunched the shell.

Gary Sharpe looked across the table at Darryl Beane and felt a flush of pride as he caught his old friend's knowing glance. Darryl was impressed, Sharpey could see that. Darryl was a top solicitor and a very clever fellow, and he'd been a Labor lawyer long enough to know everyone in Sydney, including big Don Bollard. But Darryl couldn't have set things up as sweet as this. He was a legal Mr Fixit but he didn't know how to swing a deal like Gary Sharpe. No one knew how to get the best from people the way Sharpey did. Sharpey was the master. He'd told his lawyer friend just how they'd get the attention of the State Attorney-General: there was nothing Donny Bollard enjoyed more than diving into the bowels of a good muddy. And nowhere served better mud crab than this place.

'So this bloke Baston ...' Don Bollard washed his mouthful down with chardonnay before assuming a more serious expression. 'What did you say he's charged with?'

'Grievous bodily harm.'

'What'd he do?'

'Well Jesus, Donny, he didn't do any bloody thing, that's the point!' Gary Sharpe erupted into his trademark staccato cackle and the others chuckled warmly as he splashed more chardonnay into their glasses. 'It's over some blue in a nightclub down the Cross last year. Some bloke's given a couple of bouncers a bit of a touch-up with a lead pipe.'

'What sort of injuries?'

'Couple of broken bones, that's all. Bit of skin and bark off here and there. They originally charged GBH because one of the bouncers had a fractured skull, but it turns out he's okay.' Bollard had a troubled look about him, so Gary Sharpe kept talking. 'When it first happened they were saying it was Baston, but both the bouncers are now conceding they didn't really get a decent look at the bloke, and they don't want to testify.'

'Is there any other evidence?'

It was time for Darryl Beane to chime in with his reassuring legal wash. 'One patron, Don. A very weak identification. He saw the assailant in dim light and only for a very short period of time. Difficult circumstances, fleeting glimpse. Highly unreliable stuff at best. It's the sort of thing most judges wouldn't even let go to the jury.'

'Darryl's done a detailed written submission setting it all out in full,' Sharpe added. 'I've read it — it's all dead set. They've got nothing on him. The charges should be dropped. Darryl'll get the submission in to you tomorrow and all you've got to do is no bill it.'

Don Bollard was still frowning. By ordering a 'no true bill' on the Baston charge, he could end the prosecution with the stroke of his ministerial pen. But he wasn't convinced. He was still thinking. Sharpe didn't like it.

'Jesus, look at that, will you.' He held his wine glass towards the gleaming waters of the harbour stretching out towards the Opera House. 'Isn't that the *Marlin 44*?'

It wasn't, but it was close enough, and Gary Sharpe couldn't believe his luck. The appearance of the sleek white cruiser couldn't have been better timed if he had orchestrated it himself. He hadn't, but he almost wished he had, it was so sweet; and the beautiful thing was, he knew Darryl Beane would always wonder whether he had set it up.

The significance of Fred Hunter's *Marlin 44* was lost on none of them. It was Gary Sharpe's famous fishing trip out to the Heads on Hunter's luxury cruiser that had saved Don Bollard's bacon and averted an electoral backlash that would have driven Labor into the political wilderness for at least a decade. The 'Broker Boat Affair' had become Labor Party folklore and had cemented Gary Sharpe's reputation as the Labor Right faction's number one deal-cruncher and chief power-broker.

Like all good factional shit-fights it had blown up at local council level when the campaign director of the New South Wales Labor Party announced that a Left faction councillor had lodged an official complaint with party headquarters that Big Don Bollard, the state Labor MP for their area, and the party president had threatened to have him stripped of his Labor Party endorsements if he didn't back the party line to block a new town plan that was before his local council. The proposed changes to the town plan would have killed off a multi-million-dollar development site controlled by one of the party's new friends from the 'big end' of town, a corporate giant that had been pouring huge donation dollars into Labor's re-election slush funds. The councillor claimed he could support his story with a tape-recording of Don Bollard offering him fifteen thousand for his local election campaign coffers if he voted in council to postpone the new town plan. It was a very serious allegation which, unless handled delicately, could land at least two prominent members of the New South Wales Right in court and plunge the Labor Party into a very public and very messy inter-factional brawl that would almost certainly drive it from office in New South Wales, and perhaps even federally.

Within hours someone had leaked the story to the press, and it soon became apparent that the whole thing had been cooked up by the campaign director in an effort to kill off the party president, whom he had hated with a passion ever since their uni days. One of them just had to go. The worry was that Donny Bollard and the Labor Right were about to get caught up in the crossfire.

The campaign director had counted on the support of his young friend and staffer Gary Sharpe, and most believed he would have got it if he hadn't stooped to the unthinkable and unforgivable: doing deals with the Labor Left.

Sharpey had moved quickly and decisively. The press broke the story on the Wednesday. On Thursday night he rifled through his boss's office and photocopied enough documents to make a case for him having rorted his expense accounts. On Friday he mentioned to the campaign director that he'd had the transport company heavyweight Fred Hunter's cruiser for the weekend, and suggested they take a spin on the harbour.

On Saturday morning the campaign director climbed aboard the *Marlin 44* in a celebratory mood, cradling a six-pack of stubbies under one arm, only to be met by the party president and a group of the state's most influential right-wing trade-union leaders. In the midst of them was Sharpey, a report to the finance committee detailing the expense rorts in one hand, and a resignation letter in the other.

The trip round Sydney Harbour took an hour or two, long enough for them to drink the six-pack and a few more, and to air a bit of dirty washing, and for everyone to see a bit of sense. On Monday morning the campaign director publicly announced that he felt he had achieved his personal milestones in the job and he now wanted to look to new horizons outside the party structure. A week later the administrative committee reluctantly accepted his carefully worded resignation and the press was inundated by glowing tributes from his colleagues in the Labor Right. Within a month he had accepted the plum job of trade commissioner in London, about the same time Gary Sharpe was settling in behind his new desk in the campaign office. The newspaper rumours about Don Bollard and the party president soon disappeared, and no one in the Labor Party, particularly the local councillor who had recently accepted Labor pre-selection for a state seat, had anything at all to say about the matter.

The 'Broker Boat Affair' had pulled Big Don out of the fire, and Gary Sharpe knew the name *Marlin 44* would always hold a special significance for the State Attorney-General.

'Look at that!' He sat back in his chair, basking in the collective admiration of his guile, while pretending to be oblivious to it. 'It's a bloody ripper, isn't it!'

During the general discussion that followed on the proposition that they should all be out there on the water, making the most of the glorious weather Sydney was enjoying at the moment, history rolled around in the back of Don Bollard's mind and he grappled with the issue that he well knew remained firmly on the table. *There's no such thing as a free lunch.* Gary Sharpe was pitching for a favour that he wanted done for Roger Baston and, one way or another, Don was going to have to deal with it.

'Getting back to this Baston thing,' he said eventually, as Sharpey knew he would. 'Can I pull the charges, given that there's independent identification evidence?'

'Course you can, Donny! You're the bloody A-G for Christ's sake!' The line set Sharpe off on another round of machine-gun laughter and splashing of chardonnay into glasses.

'Good luck,' he added convivially, holding his glass up and drawing them both in. As Bollard clinked his glass and wished him cheer, Gary Sharpe could see the lingering discomfort in his smile.

'Listen, Gary, if it's such a weak case why not just let it go up to the judge and he can throw it out?'

Sharpe took a sip of wine and gently set the glass down on the snow-white linen cloth. Now he was deadly serious.

'Because to do that is going to cause unnecessary gut-ache to some good people, Don. You should understand that.'

They both knew what he was talking about, but there was more to this than old time's sake and doing the right thing by a mate.

'Baston's got a big reputation, Gary. The press are all over him.'

'The press have been all over all of us at some stage or another. That's never stopped us from doing the right thing, has it?'

Don Bollard didn't like it. He didn't know much about the assault case facing Roger Baston, but he knew enough about Baston to realise there was a lot more to it than Sharpey and Darryl Beane were trying to make out. Baston was an ex-police detective who had left the force under suspicion over the ransom-kidnapping of the teenage daughter of a millionaire Sydney businessman. He had since established a high-profile inquiry and collection agency which had developed a dubious reputation for heavy-handed 'mediations' and debt-recovery, and was rumoured to be an intermediary in unhealthy liaisons between certain Sydney detectives and the criminal classes. Baston and his heavies had been called in by the developers of several inner-city sites when the militant Builders Labourers Federation had joined local residents and student radicals to try to stop the demolition of the grand old terraces. They had spilt a lot of blood smashing the green bans and breaking through the union picket lines, and had made a lot of enemies. No one was ever going to shed too many tears for Roger Baston. There was a bad smell about him, and anyone who jumped into bed with him was liable to come up smelling pretty nasty too. An operator like Gary Sharpe knew that, and he wasn't taking the risk of going into bat for Baston out of some overwhelming sense of justice. There had to be a better reason.

'Why's it the right thing?'

Sharpe shook his head and sighed painfully. Sometimes trying to bring these clowns along was like herding cats.

'Listen, Donny, let me spell it out for you, okay.' He sat forward in his chair and lowered his voice to a confidential murmur. 'Roger Baston is Fred Hunter's man, and Fred controls the inner west. Marrickville's going the same way as Balmain and all the other inner-city suburbs. You've got the yuppies and the trendies moving in and doing up these old joints and what-not; the whole feel of the place is changing, and the Left is getting a real foothold down there.'

He paused for a moment, holding Don Bollard's unflinching gaze. He could see he had his interest.

'Now Fred Hunter and his mates have still got real clout with the workers, and Fred can control the Marrickville branch, and Enmore and Balmain too. That means he controls three Labor local councils, two Labor seats in the New South Wales state parliament, and two federal Labor seats. That's the jewel in the bloody crown, Don, and Fred Hunter's got it tied up for the Right.'

He paused again, waiting for the message to seep home.

'If that sort of power base goes over to the Left, you can forget the Attorney-General's portfolio or anything else. The lefties'll have their own blokes in there before you can blink, and then it's only a matter of time until we're back in Opposition.'

Don Bollard nodded thoughtfully, raised his glass and gulped down a mouthful.

'Now Fred Hunter and his mates can stop that happening, but they need a bit of support, and I think they're entitled to it, don't you?'

Sharpe paused again, this time long enough to allow Don Bollard to reflect on history and to contemplate the future.

'Roger Baston is Fred Hunter's china, and Fred wants to get him on the council in the next elections. If he does, that'll give Fred the extra grunt he needs to push things through in Marrickville. But you know and I know that if this assault blue is still hanging over Baston when the council elections come around, he's no chance, and it won't help much when the judge turfs it out of court after the bloody event.'

There was no doubt Sharpe had identified the problem perfectly. But did he have the right solution?

'Sharpey, listen, mate. Fred Hunter's one thing, but that Baston's red bloody hot. Should we be getting this close to blokes like that?'

Sharpe's eyes narrowed to a lethal slit and he leaned so far forward that his silk tie trailed across his empty oyster shells.

'Now you know the answer to that question, Donny, so don't you shit me.' His voice was hushed, conspiratorial. 'We should be doing exactly what it bloody takes, that's what we should be doing, and you know it.'

He sat back and sipped his wine.

'Exactly what it takes.'

CHAPTER TWO

'Do you drink?'

'Not much.'

'What does that mean?'

The diminutive brunette sitting opposite Michael Wiltshire pursed her crimson lips and squinted at him like a small dog sizing up the postman.

'Not much. I don't know.'

Kirsten Foster didn't enjoy answering questions, particularly idiotic ones. But she wanted this job, so she was working hard to keep a lid on it. He could see it, and she could see that he could see it. He was sitting back with a satisfied expression on his face as though he'd somehow caught her out.

'What about you? You drink much?'

His eyebrows jumped a little and he shifted uncomfortably in his chair. 'I'm not the issue here, Ms Foster.'

It felt good to make him squirm even just a little. This guy was a control freak, she could see it, and you couldn't afford to give a guy like that an even break. He'd walk all over you. In fact, you couldn't afford to give any guy an even break. If you did they were going to walk all over you, get into your pants or break your heart. Or all of the above, not necessarily in that order. This one didn't seem too interested in option number two. It was a pity really, because judging from the house he was definitely rich, and he wasn't exactly the ugliest guy she'd ever laid eyes on either. But she could see that option number two just wasn't what was on his mind. If it was she would've had the job already. She'd worn a nice tight skirt, not too short, but short enough to remind him that these pins went right up to the top, and a plunging neckline that wasn't leaving anything unsaid. If this guy was a pants man she wouldn't be sitting here listening to his idiotic questions.

But no, this guy was no pants man, he was a control freak.

'I don't want anybody bringing drugs or alcohol into my house.'

'I don't do drugs.'

'What about grass? You smoke any pot?'

Kirsten breathed out slowly and reminded herself how much she wanted this job. But this guy was testing her patience and involuntarily her eyes narrowed again. She glared at him so venomously that he sat up and drew his feet in under him, as if he feared she might suddenly nip at his heels.

'What are you, a cop?'

Michael Wiltshire snorted his amusement and shook his head. There had been precious few applicants, most of them too old to keep up with a seven-year-old boy or too spaced-out to even contemplate. This woman was the right age, she had good references and she had a pleasant look about her. He'd hoped she might be the one. But the interview had been hard going from the start. It was as though they were in some sort of contest, one she was adamant she wasn't going to lose.

'Fair enough.' He folded up her references and held them out to her. 'Listen, I don't think this is going to work out, do you?'

She didn't take the papers. 'Why not?'

If it wasn't desperation there was at least determination in her voice as she held his gaze. She was a pretty girl, her features soft and fragile, but he could see a tough resolution in her eyes.

'Look, I don't do drugs, okay? And I don't drink much. If I'm at a party I might have a glass of bubbly — I might have more than one. If I have any more than about three I end up shit-faced and if I'm lucky I have a real good time. So what? That's a party, that's not work. I don't gamble and I don't lie unless I have to. I'm over twenty-one, I'm a good Catholic girl, I still go to church at Easter and Christmas, and I hardly ever swear, except when some dickhead's really pissing me off asking stupid fucking questions. Okay? So what more do you want to know?'

She was leaning forward now, ready to jump down his throat. His eyes dropped to her cleavage and then instantly bounced back. He could see she had noticed.

'Listen, I've got a seven-year-old son.' He was looking firmly at his hands now as he folded her references again and placed them on the table. When he looked back up at her his eyes were sympathetic. 'I need someone reliable, someone who'll be there on time to pick him up from school and have his dinner on the table for him every night. Someone I can depend on.'

'So how do you work out whether you can depend on this someone if you don't give her a chance?'

He smiled gently. 'I don't know. I guess I ask stupid fucking questions.'

One corner of her mouth curled into a cautious smirk as she reached into her bag, pulled out a cigarette and lit up without asking for permission. He glanced briefly at her crossed legs as he retrieved an ashtray from the wall unit and set it down in front of her.

'I wouldn't want anyone smoking in front of my son either.'

'Really?' She blew out a stream of smoke. 'So are you this paranoid with him too? You must drive the poor kid crazy.'

It was true. He did drive Simon crazy at times, he knew that. But when you couldn't be around every minute of the day you had to make a lot of rules, and you had to make sure they were adhered to. Now that Jane was gone, Simon was all he had.

'He's got no mother to care for him. I look after him.'

There was a waver in his voice that made her feel uncomfortable.

'But you need some help. And I need a job. And I'm real good with kids.'

He sat back in the chair, his arms and legs crossed and his brow furrowed. She didn't like the body language: he was back in inquisition mode.

'Are you married?'

'Divorced.'

'Any kids?'

'No. My brother's got three boys and we get on great.'

'What's your husband do?'

'Ex-husband.'

'What's your ex-husband do?'

She paused again, her eyes narrowing back into the squint and her red lips pursed distrustfully. This guy was so full of shit.

'You are a cop, aren't you.'

Michael Wiltshire breathed a frustrated sigh and rubbed his forehead. Why was he wasting both their time?

'I don't want any husbands, friends or lovers around here.'

'I told you, we're divorced.' Now she had her arms and legs crossed too and they were sitting opposite each other like two chess players waiting for the other one to make a move. She slid to the edge of her chair, ready for more action. 'Listen, Mr Whatever-your-name-is ...'

'Wiltshire.'

'Yeah, right. You know you're barely offering the minimum wage here, don't you?'

'It's less than twenty hours a week and it includes evening meals thrown in.'

She nodded silently and waved a painted fingernail at him. 'You're a tight-arse, aren't you.'

He smiled despite himself. It was true. Michael knew the value of a dollar. He'd worked hard for what he had and he wasn't known for splashing it around.

'Some people have said that.'

She sucked hard on her cigarette and nodded sagely, as though she was now the interviewer and had just discovered a dark skeleton lurking in his closet.

'Yeah, like that's all I need, to be arm-wrestling for my pay packet every week. I could get better money waitressing.'

This woman had some nerve. She didn't even have the job and she was already protesting the conditions of employment. Michael was annoyed now and he shifted forward in his chair to pose the obvious.

'So what are you doing here?'

'I want this job, that's what.' As she snapped the words out they seemed to remind her just why she was there. She paused, and when she spoke again her tone was considerably more conciliatory. 'I like working with kids. And besides, the hours suit me. I want to do full-time study this year.'

The answer took him by surprise. 'University?'

'High school. I didn't finish. I want to do year twelve.'

'Why?'

Her lip curled again and he could still see a sparkle in her clear green eyes. 'You know, you should be a cop. I think you'd enjoy it.'

This time she was right: it was none of his business. But now he was genuinely interested, and he was smart enough to come up with a plausible reason to make his question relevant.

'So as soon as you get tired of studying, or you flunk out, or you get through your course, you move on and my son is left without a carer again.'

This time she didn't take the bait. She just stared at him passively with those green eyes. 'You know, Mr Whats-your-face, nothing is forever. You need to teach that to your little boy. Otherwise he's going to get real hurt sooner or later.'

It occurred to Michael Wiltshire that behind all the make-up and the tough talk there was something curiously compassionate about her. He doubted he could trust her with the job, but she interested him.

'Wiltshire.'

'What?'

'Why don't you just call me Michael.'

CHAPTER THREE

'Fred, the party needs someone like Michael Wiltshire in Marrickville.'

Fred Hunter growled. He didn't like what he was hearing, but Sharpey was probably right. No one had his finger on the party pulse quite like Gary Sharpe.

'He's young, articulate, good-looking. A professional bloke. Mate, the sheilas'll love him. You can't overlook that. You want to get good people in the party at branch level these days, you've got to think about these things, I'm telling you. The women are going their own way these days. They're not going to vote with hubby any more.'

Fred Hunter had heard enough of all this fancy, new-age Labor bullshit to last him a lifetime. Maybe Sharpe and his flashy mates up in Sussex Street were all wearing pin-striped suits these days but they'd do well to remember that out here in Petersham and Stanmore navy singlets and stubby shorts were still the go. And you didn't dud your old chinas just to grab the sheilas' vote, or anybody else's.

Michael Wiltshire might be the face of modern Labor, but if last night's performance was anything to go by, he had a lot to learn about staying staunch and toeing the party line.

Two young leftist yahoos had crashed the local party's branch meeting, bleating about branch membership and claiming that Fred and his mates had cooked the books and stacked the membership to shore up their power in the branch. Fred had naturally expected his office-bearers, including Michael Wiltshire, to back him up. So when the two interlopers had started insisting on inspecting the books Fred wasn't worried in the slightest. But things soon got decidedly heated, and if Fred hadn't stepped in the lefties probably would have got their heads punched in right there and then. It was Fred who'd saved their bacon by decreeing that because they hadn't given sufficient notice, they had no right to inspect the books. Then one of them had the nerve to throw to Michael Wiltshire, being the newest branch office-bearer and Sussex Street's golden-haired boy, for his view as to whether the books should be available for inspection. All Wiltshire had to do was back Fred up and they could have turfed those yahoos straight out without further ado. Fred couldn't believe his ears when he heard Wiltshire coming up with a whole load of crap about how he didn't think it was 'appropriate' that the books should be kept secret from the members.

Indignation was still burning in Hunter's eyes as he glared across the table at Gary Sharpe the next morning.

'That's your problem, Sharpey. Not mine. Y'understand? All I know is, the bloke doesn't know his place, and that can be a dangerous mistake in Marrickville.'

Sharpe sighed wearily and smoothed his thinning hair. He understood Fred Hunter well enough. He was speaking a familiar language, one that Sharpey had been born to, one he had spoken all his life. It was the language of the party faithful, the rank and file, the heart and soul of the labour movement that had carried Gary Sharpe to where he was today. Loyalty was everything.

'Mate, I'll talk to him, alright.'

'You do that, Sharpey.'

Fred Hunter was as fired up as Gary Sharpe could remember seeing him. He strode off, leaving half a schooner on the table, which was something you didn't see Fred Hunter do too often. Tensions were obviously running high in Marrickville.

Sharpey raised his glass and sucked up a cooling swallow. What the bloody hell was Wiltshire playing at? There was no value in getting up Fred Hunter's nose. The old bloke had been running the game in Marrickville for as long as anybody could remember, and you weren't going anywhere in the inner city without his support. Whether you wanted to be the lord mayor or just another shit-kicker on the council truck, first you had to get the nod from Fred. The same thing applied to state politics. Marrickville was the safest seat in New South Wales, the jewel in the crown. There were only two types of voters out here: Labor and very bloody Labor. So if you were going to put your hand up for Marrickville, the boys expected you to play the game and pay your dues. And that was fair enough.

Michael Wiltshire hadn't put his hand up to run for a state seat yet, but it was Sharpey's guess he would eventually. And it wouldn't necessarily be a cake-walk to get him pre-selected. He might have a fine old Labor pedigree, but to a lot of these hard-nosed union blokes he had the smell of a silvertail about him. As the son of Charlie Wiltshire, the longest-serving state secretary in the history of the NSW Amalgamated Postal Workers Union, Michael was always destined for a place in Labor politics. Dux of De La Salle, Bankstown, captain of the First Eleven, stand-out performer in the centres in the junior grades at Saints. Everybody loved him then and he dead set looked the goods. But when he got to uni and gave up footy and the old neighbourhood, a lot of the old-timers started wondering where Charlie had gone wrong with his lad. A double major in Business with first-class honours didn't impress anyone in the public bars of Leichhardt, Balmain or Petersham, and all the stories of astute real-estate investments on the north shore and beachfront apartment-block developments in Queensland had a few people in the party wondering whether Charlie's boy had turned his back on the old neighbourhood and wiped his mates. But sure enough he'd returned to the heartland, to the grimy streets of Marrickville. And he hadn't wasted any time in looking up his Labor Party mates.

No one was happier than Gary Sharpe when his old schoolfriend Michael Wiltshire finally expressed some interest in state politics. They'd been thrown together as teenagers in Hurstville, two very different boys allied by their parents' mutual passion for the party and the labour movement. Gary Sharpe, a short plump boy with blemished skin and average grades, had been at first surprised by Michael Wiltshire's easy acceptance of him, and later honoured by the opportunity to bask in his good friend's glory on and off the sporting field. The affable, easygoing Wiltshire had been a stand-out in those days, and all the good things of life seemed somehow naturally his. He excelled at university, married the best-looking bird Sharpey had ever seen before or since, and made a fortune out of beachfront real estate. No wonder he wasn't much interested in Labor politics back then. As Sharpey worked his way up the party ladder he heard news occasionally of his old friend's successes but they didn't see too much of him in Labor circles. In recent years the news had changed. His young wife had died suddenly of an aneurism three years ago and word had it that Michael Wiltshire had done it tough. Very tough. He was in the middle of a major credit squeeze and was struggling to keep his Queensland-based development company afloat while he did his best to hold himself together and get his little boy through it as well. A lesser man would probably have gone under, one way or the other. But Michael Wiltshire had come out on top, as Sharpey had always expected he would. He'd held on through the slump and in the heat of last year's economic surge his company had off-loaded virtually all its Queensland holdings at record prices. Wiltshire had walked out a rich man. And now he was back in Sydney, sniffing around the political mantle that some said had always been rightly his. Even if Mick Wiltshire had become something of a poodle, his pedigree was Labor through and through. And Gary Sharpe, for one, was glad to see him back.

Wiltshire had everything the modern Labor Party needed. He was young, intelligent and astute, a well-educated, articulate man who came complete with a genuine working-class background, an accomplished sporting record and Hollywood good looks to boot. With a bit of work he could go all the way. Every bloke would want to have a beer with him, and the sheilas would take one look and go all gooey. To Sharpey he was the complete man, the perfect Labor politician.

'Don't tell me you've decided to take up working for a living!'

Gary Sharpe was genuinely surprised to find Michael Wiltshire in the front yard of the Old Priory pushing a wheelbarrow filled with turf. He'd heard Wiltshire had bought the once-abandoned stately mansion from the church and started renovating, but he hadn't anticipated that his well-heeled friend would want to roll up his sleeves and get physical himself.

'G'day, Gary.' Wiltshire's broad grin lit up his handsome face as he swiped a grimy forearm across his glistening brow. 'Come on up.'

Sharpey pushed his way through the front gate and scaled the tiled stairs up to the central path.

'Jesus, mate, it's looking good.'

The old sandstone building had long been a landmark, perched on the high end of Shaw Street below the water tower where it presided augustly over the streets and lanes of Petersham below. Though years of neglect had stained the walls and ravaged the grounds, the place had retained a kind of tarnished glory that helped to elevate its humble working-class surrounds. In their youth Wiltshire and Sharpey had passed here more than once, lobbing the occasional stone high onto the roof to listen to it bounce and rattle down across the steep slates, then scurrying down the hill and round the corner to escape. Keeping pace with Mick Wiltshire when he bolted was never easy going, so Sharpey always made sure he gave himself a bit of a head start.

'I've just been over at Marrickville, having a beer with old Fred Hunter.'

'Yeah?'

Good old Sharpey — predictable as ever. Michael Wiltshire had been expecting a visit from his wily little friend over last night's local branch meeting and Gary Sharpe hadn't disappointed him. It had been a fiery affair, largely presided over (as usual) by Hunter and his mates, who generally managed to dictate the agenda and move things along in the direction they wanted. Michael was relatively new to the game of party politics but he knew Marrickville well enough to know that it paid to get along with the likes of Fred Hunter, and so far he always had. Hunter had promptly closed the meeting and the two young gatecrashers proved that discretion is the wiser part of valour, beating a timely retreat before things escalated. The books were bundled out of sight, accompanied by stony stares for Michael from Fred Hunter and several others of his erstwhile supporters.

'So how are things over in Marrickville, Sharpey?'

'Crook, mate. Things are crook in Marrickville. Real crook. Crook as Rookwood.'

Michael Wiltshire couldn't help but smile. His old mate Sharpey was an operator, a consummate performer, always looking for the right angle, the right button to push. There was nothing random in his choice of language. It was meant to remind Michael where he'd come from, where he was. This wasn't some flash northern Sydney suburb, this was Petersham. And just down the road a bit was Marrickville. In these parts, if things weren't good, they weren't bad, they were 'crook', and if they were really crook then they were 'crook as Rookwood', because Rookwood was where the cemetery was, and simple working folk knew well enough that when you got as crook as you could be you ended up in Rookwood. This was Sharpey's Labor heartland language, meant to evoke in Michael all the old Labor Irish loyalties and working-class traditions, and to subtly remind his flash friend of their history together and of long-standing Labor folklore. Their parents' jokes about the legendary Labor mayor whose electoral rolls were populated by more dead voters than live ones were part of their upbringing: *the citizens of Rookwood were Labor's best supporters.* They both had too much Labor heritage in them to become precious now.

'Blokes like Fred Hunter are the heart and soul of the labour movement, Michael.'

'Is that right?'

'Too bloody right it is!'

There was a note of cynicism in Michael Wiltshire's voice that disturbed Gary Sharpe. He had a lot invested in his star recruit and he didn't need him turning into a loose cannon on the deck. Wiltshire had to be convinced.

'Fred Hunter's on first-name terms with every punter in every public bar in the inner west. If any one of them has ever pulled up short, Fred's lent them money. If their kids are on the dole or in strife, he gives them work. He's old-style, mate, salt of the earth. And come election time he rounds up the crew to man the booths and nail the posters up. Who do you think hands out the how-to-vote cards and does the letter drops and all that shit? Not me and not you, that's for sure!'

'Maybe so.'

Michael had no doubt his friend understood the politics implicitly, knew all the risks and all the possible advantages. Whatever game they might be playing he'd already worked out how to win. Gary Sharpe was not necessarily the most intelligent of men but he'd always had more street-smarts than anyone else Michael had ever known. It was the quality he most admired, which had made them good friends back when they had nothing in common but their parents' fervour for the Party. Sharpey couldn't run out of sight on a dark night, he couldn't play footie to save his life, and he was a specialist twelfth man in schoolboy cricket, but he was always ahead of the game. It didn't matter what game it was, Sharpey always had been and always would be one step in front. Michael had no doubt about that.

'Trouble is, I think Fred might be doctoring his books.'

'So what if he is, mate? So he's stacking his books, so what? All he's trying to do is make sure we get the right people in the right jobs, for God's sake.'

'You mean *his* people, don't you?'

'Yeah, that's right, his people. And if you're smart you'll be one of his people too.' Gary Sharpe stepped a little closer. 'Hey mate, that's the inner west, alright.' If there was a tinge of indignation in his voice it was because he wasn't sure how much of his old friend's criticism of Fred Hunter was actually aimed at him. 'Don't think you're going to come in here, slap a new coat of paint on this old joint and somehow create a little piece of Mosman in the western suburbs, 'cause you're not. This is a working-class suburb full of ordinary people. That's why it's the safest seat in town. With these people the old ways die hard.'

'Well maybe so, Gary, but the old way isn't always the right way.'

Sharpe gritted his teeth and shook his head in frustration. What was this bloke playing at?

'Mate, take it from me, if you want to make a go of politics in this town you give the people what they want. Don't go trying to change anything, particularly in Marrickville.'

Michael Wiltshire looked silently into the flushed face of his friend. They had gone their separate ways a long time ago.

'You know, Gary, I didn't decide to get into politics because I need the money.'

'I know that.'

Gary Sharpe didn't believe a word of it. Wiltshire might once have had some notion of fulfilling his father's aspirations to see his son champion the working classes in the inner west, but that was a long time ago, before he discovered how much money could be made bulldozing workers' cottages and replacing them with inner-city residential complexes. The local councils controlled real-estate development in Sydney and party politics controlled the local councils. That's why Michael Wiltshire was back in the inner west and that's why he was back in politics.

'I'm looking to make some sort of difference.'

Michael had no sooner got the words out than he wished he hadn't. They had come spontaneously, but now they lay between the two men heavily, creating an embarrassed silence. Verbalised, it sounded like a corny notion to these two sons of politics, raised in their parents' passionate rhetoric of the labour movement and schooled in the struggles of the working class. It sounded hollow and pretentious, at best naive, irrelevant to the world of modern politics. The old ways weren't always right.

'Make your money first then practise your philanthropy, ay?' Sharpey smiled at the thought of a politician trying to change the world. 'The problem is, old mate, in Marrickville, without Fred Hunter's support, you're not going to be able to do either.'

CHAPTER FOUR

Gary Sharpe was right. No one was going anywhere in Marrickville without the support of Fred Hunter and his cronies, and the more Michael Wiltshire thought about it the more it troubled him.

Barry Dougherty had been secretary of the local branch for as long as anyone could remember, almost as long as he had worked for Hunter Transport. As an invoice clerk in Fred Hunter's office he had seemed a logical choice for the position and no one had any reason to doubt he did a first-class job. But then no one had actually seen the books of the local branch in such a long time that there wasn't much to measure his performance by. Barry lived alone in a dilapidated single-storey worker's cottage just off Stanmore Road, not far from the Newington Hotel, where he spent far too much of his spare time. Most nights, just after closing time, he could be seen carefully picking his way home along the footpath, cradling his after-hours supplies. Mornings were not a particularly good time for Barry, and Saturday mornings were generally the worst, because a good part of his pay packet went across the public bar of the Newington each Friday night. This Saturday morning was no different, and when he opened the front door of his humble abode he looked wearily at Michael Wiltshire through bleary, bloodshot eyes.

'Hello, Barry. Michael Wiltshire.'

'Oh, g'day, mate, how are you?'

Dougherty tried to straighten himself a little, but without much marked improvement. He was a simple man who had lived largely with his own company since his wife had wisely left him years ago, and he was unaccustomed to visits of any sort, particularly from the likes of Michael Wiltshire.

'I didn't recognise you there,' he croaked, opening the door wide enough to reveal more of the squalor that he lived in. 'Come on in.'

Michael did his best to find a vacant spot on the stained and lumpy couch as Barry Dougherty rattled through the kitchen cupboards. 'You mentioned on the phone there was something I might be able to help you with.'

'Yeah.' Dougherty suddenly appeared in the lounge room with an empty cup hanging from each thumb and a jar of instant coffee in one hand. 'Yeah,' he said again, then stood looking at Michael as though he was about to say more, before eventually turning and disappearing back into the kitchen, accompanied by the sound of further rattling.

Michael sat gingerly on the edge of the couch, conscious of the stale smell of empty beer bottles and cigarette ash, his eyes drifting around the cluttered, untidy room. They settled eventually on what seemed the only order in the room: a row of photographs framed in various styles and sizes neatly lined up on the mantelpiece. In pride of place was a black-and-white snapshot of the great Gough Whitlam posing with the party faithful outside the old Balmain Leagues Club, shoulder to shoulder with a black-haired, horn-rimmed-spectacled Bob Hawke, a younger and dapper-looking Fred Hunter and a host of others, including what looked to be a fresh-faced Barry Dougherty smiling broadly and proudly at the edge of the auspicious group.

'Recognise the little bloke in the pork pie hat?' Dougherty was standing alongside him, gazing fondly at the photograph. Michael leaned closer and studied the faces.

'That's my dad.'

'Sure is. He was a good bloke, old Charlie. That was during the "It's Time" campaign in '72.' Barry Dougherty was smiling wistfully, remembering old friends and old times. 'We were really fair dinkum then.'

It was an odd comment and caused Michael to turn quizzically towards the older man. Dougherty handed him a coffee and turned away.

'I've give him the coke and sars.'

'Pardon?'

'Fred Hunter.' Barry pushed a telephone directory off one of the armchairs onto the floor and sat down carefully. 'I give him the arse yesterday. Told him he could stick his job.' He sucked up a noisy slurp of coffee and then mumbled into his cup.

'Thirty years I've been working for Fred Hunter. Thirty years.'

Michael sat down opposite the older man. Barry Dougherty seemed to want to talk about something. 'What happened?'

'Did you know old Tommy Attwell?'

For some reason the name Attwell rang a vague bell in the back of Michael's brain, but he couldn't place it. 'I don't think so.'

'No, well you're not from around here originally, are you.' Barry put the cup to his wrinkled lips again and sucked up another mouthful. 'Salt of the earth he was, old Tommy. Lived in Marrickville just about his whole life.'

There was obviously a point to all this but Barry Dougherty was going to take his time coming to it. Michael sipped at his coffee and sat silently awaiting the next instalment.

'Couple of months ago Fred Hunter sent some joker round to Tommy's place to give the poor old bloke a touch-up.' The thin voice wavered as the older man stared into his coffee cup. 'Don't know what it was all about, but some bloke's given him a fair old clip. Give it to him good and proper, you know what I mean.' He looked at his visitor, his eyes glistening with emotion. 'It was Fred who had him fixed up, sure and certain.'

Michael Wiltshire shifted uncomfortably. He'd been raised a Hurstville boy, the son of a union man, and he'd heard all the stories about the violence and intimidation of the city streets and building sites. But the modest southern suburbs of his youth were a world away from the hard working-class boroughs of the inner west, and his comfortable upbringing, and later the privilege of his successful career, had insulated him from the culture of brutality that ruled these parts. The resigned tone of the older man's voice as he calmly relayed the allegations made them even more disturbing.

'Mate, I was dirty when I heard about it. Old Tommy was in his seventies. Doesn't matter what he done or who he owed, you don't dish up an old bloke in his seventies, fair dinkum. It's a low bloody act if you ask me. When I fronted Fred about it he just told me to mind me own business.'

In his croaky drawl Barry Dougherty was making allegations of the most serious kind against Marrickville's number one party heavyweight, a Labor icon in the inner west, the man whose support could make or break Michael Wiltshire's political aspirations. They were allegations that gave a terrifying face to the unspoken reputation of Fred Hunter, and to the hidden fears of so many in the party that things were badly out of control in the western branches. Should he ask for detail, find out what proof there was, if any? Did he really want to know?

'Tommy moved out of the neighbourhood straight after that. Went into one of them retirement joints at Lidcombe. Poor old bastard.' Barry delved into his shirt pocket and retrieved a half-smoked rollie which he perched on his bottom lip as he delved for matches in his trouser pockets. 'He'd lived here all his life. Fair dinkum, he loved that old place of his.'

Dougherty scratched a match alight and then lit up, squinting painfully as he exhaled a shaft of thick white smoke. 'Anyway, he didn't last no time at all at Lidcombe. Keeled over dead from a heart attack inside a fortnight.' He sat in contemplative silence for a moment. 'I suppose Lidcombe'd do that to you.'

Michael Wiltshire searched for something safe to say, but before he found his voice Dougherty went on, as if speaking to himself.

'I only found out the real story just the other morning.'

He took the cigarette from his mouth and picked absently at the moist end for several seconds. When he raised his head there was new vigour burning in his eyes.

'Then I come into work and told Fred Hunter to stick it up his arse.'

His silent stare said he expected some response. There was danger in it for Michael and he understood that clearly.

'Have you spoken to the police about any of this?'

'Turn it up. It doesn't work that way with blokes like Fred.'

Dougherty dragged himself out of the chair and walked into the narrow hallway where he started rummaging amongst papers stacked a metre deep on top of a painted wooden bookcase. 'I'm pissing off out of Sydney,' he called as he threw books and papers down onto the floor. 'Probably back up north where I come from.' He walked back into Michael's view and added earnestly,

'But I don't want you telling no one about that, okay?'

'Sure.' He wondered why anyone would want to know.

'Fred Hunter's a bad man, you understand me?' Barry Dougherty's voice crackled with genuine fear and he held the younger man's gaze for emphasis. 'In the old days we tied in with him because we thought he stood for the working man, but Fred Hunter doesn't stand for nothing but Fred Hunter.'

Dougherty disappeared again into the hallway and Michael watched as books and papers slid across the wooden floor.

'I'm not sure I understand,' he said eventually.

'You don't have to understand nothing.' Dougherty reappeared and somehow he seemed to have more life in him. In one hand he was holding a white plastic carry bag, and with the other he was delving and leafing through its contents, what looked to be a heavy wad of A4 paper. 'Just take a look at this.'

He pulled out a dog-eared, hard-covered ledger book and pushed it under Michael's nose, leafing through what appeared to be the blank pages of some sort of register.

'You know what that is?' Dougherty's craggy face was contorted into an almost comical sneer. 'I'll tell you. That's the first four pages of the Enmore branch register as at last Thursday. If you're wondering why they're blank it's because that's how we always kept them. So come preselection time we can fill in the names with whoever we need to vote for whatever candidates Fred wants to get up.'

Michael flicked through the book. It was obviously what Dougherty said: the Enmore membership register, drawn up but, for the most part, left blank, ready for whatever creative contribution the branch office-bearers might consider advantageous. It was highly irregular of course, and would undoubtedly add some real fuel to the fire that had been burning about Hunter stacking branches, but it hardly came as a surprise to Michael Wiltshire, born into a union family and raised in the fierce, ambitious world of party politics.

'I got no clout with party headquarters but you have.' Dougherty was hovering over him like an excited schoolboy. 'Believe me, mate, with what's in here you could bring the bastard down.' He was shaking the plastic bag in Michael's face. 'Have him charged under the party rules for doctoring the books.'

Michael Wiltshire looked up at Barry Dougherty. He saw a bitter old man whose eyes were filled with hate and anger, an old man with a score to settle and absolutely nothing to lose. In his hand he was holding a bundle of trouble. Trouble for Hunter, trouble for the party, and trouble for Michael Wiltshire. He wanted to hand that bundle to Michael and ride out of town, watching from afar as Michael Wiltshire led the public charge to destroy one of Labor's favoured sons, the very man he needed to realise his own political ambitions. And on what grounds? On the basis of practices that had been around since

Adam was a lad, followed at one time or another by half the office-bearers of all the major parties in every local branch in every state throughout Australia.

It was true this could bring Fred Hunter down. It could break his hold in Enmore, and possibly in Marrickville itself, maybe even bring about expulsion from the party. But who would thank Michael Wiltshire for stabbing old Fred Hunter in the back? And who would trust him in the party after that? Fred Hunter had a lot of friends in Marrickville.

When all was said and done, Sharpey was right. No one was going anywhere in Marrickville without the support of Fred Hunter and his cronies.

CHAPTER FIVE

The Shield was a workers' pub. More particularly it was a BLF pub. In its time, the Builders Labourers Federation had been the tightest and most militant union in the state of New South Wales and the closest thing it had to a headquarters was the public bar of the Royal Shield Hotel. True, the BLF had been deregistered years ago, but that changed nothing in the Shield.

'What the fook d'y' think ye're doin' in yere?' Byron McPhee, better known around the building sites of Sydney as Little Ronny or Ron the Pom, spoke English with a thick Midlands accent that was almost unfathomable, and yet he always seemed to get his message through. 'This yere's a BLF pub; ye're not welcome yere and y' never will be.'

No one had ever doubted Roger Baston's courage. As an ex-copper who had worked for the developers to break the union picket lines he had a lot of nerve walking into the Shield. But Baston was too crazy and too mean to be afraid of anyone or anything. He was looking for Trevor Ellowe, and the fact that Ellowe was in the public bar of the Royal Shield having a few drinks with his old mates from the BLF didn't worry Roger Baston in the slightest. His thick bull neck and deep-set piggy eyes gave him a demented look that warned he was best given a wide berth. Anyone with any sense could see he just wasn't worth the trouble.

'What are you going to do about it?'

Ronny McPhee was a squat, muscular, coffee-coloured man whose African features had been diluted by generations in the northern collieries. He wasn't much more than half the size of Roger Baston, who now stepped up close to him to emphasise the point, causing several drinkers to pick up their beers and move away. But Little Ronny was every bit as mad as Baston, and twice as mean. He looked up at Roger Baston and bared a row of gold-capped teeth in a humourless sneer.

'Ay'm goin' to finish me beer an' if ye're still yere when I'm done I'll put the empty glass across your face an' give you a permanent smile from one ear t'other.'

The two men were standing toe to toe, eyeing each other unflinchingly. A wall of blue singlets and tattoos collected at the bar alongside Ron the Pom. Trevor Ellowe quickly shouldered between them to establish some neutral space. He knew the Englishman too well to think his words were idle.

'Hang on, Ronny, there's no need for that.'

Baston stood his ground. There was no fear in his eyes, just a cold indifference. 'I'm here to see young Trevor, that's all. No dramas. Just want to have a yak.'

Trevor Ellowe backed up on the ex-policeman, forcing him to retreat several steps.

'It's sweet, Ronny. No probs.'

Ronny McPhee turned back to the bar and took a swig of beer. 'You choose your own friends, Trevor. It's not to do with me. But as far as ay'm concerned, if Roger bloody Baston wants t' talk he can talk out on the footpath, 'e won't be doing it in yere.'

Baston scowled and started to advance again but Trevor Ellowe stood his ground. 'That's fair enough, Ronny, fair enough.'

He took Baston by the elbow and motioned him towards the door. Baston didn't move at first, but under Ellowe's steering hand he eventually turned, peeling his disdainful gaze away from the little man at the bar. He swaggered defiantly across the room and pushed out through the door onto the footpath, followed by his young companion. When they got to the car park Baston turned and spoke for the first time.

'Did you know your ex-missus works for that Wiltshire?'

'Kirsten?'

'Yeah.'

'Is that right?'

'Anyway, he's been playing up again.'

'Want me to make another call?'

'No. It's a bit more serious than that this time.' Baston's voice was a malevolent growl as he squinted into the warm afternoon sun that was settling below the rows of shabby terraces. 'I need you to get round there and shorten him up a bit.'

* * *

Little Simon Wiltshire had his face up against the car window, the brim of his school hat bent almost at a right angle.

'Kirsty, there's a man in the front yard.'

Kirsten Foster had spotted him standing at the bottom of the garden when she first pulled into the driveway. 'No, sweetie, that's not a man. That's just my ex-husband.'

Kirsten had surprised even herself when she somehow convinced Michael Wiltshire to employ her as a nanny to seven-year-old Simon. The interview had got off to such a bad start that she'd abandoned any hope of actually getting the job and their meeting had turned into simply a one-on-one discussion, in which they'd jousted for a while, then chatted, then eventually relaxed and found some common ground. For all his snooty interviewing style Wiltshire had turned out to be an interesting man who actually had a sense of humour buried deep down under all that paranoia. He was pleasant, and polite, and obviously intelligent enough to recognise that Kirsten Foster was just perfect for the position he was trying to fill. So for the past two months, Kirsten had been turning up for work at the Old Priory at two each afternoon, where she would get started on preparing an evening meal and then head off to collect young Simon from the local convent school.

As they cruised past him up the driveway of the mansion, Trevor Ellowe flashed one of those beautiful white smiles that used to make her instantly forget how mad she was at him for staying out all night and spending her money on drugs and alcohol and other women. It was the same broad, boyish smile it had always been, the one that always got him back into her bed and her life, but the teeth were just a little longer and the lines around his eyes a little deeper. Now those once-clear blue eyes were jaded with fatigue and perhaps a hint of desperation.

'G'day, cobber, how was school?'

'Good, thank you.'

The little boy backed cautiously towards the door. Kirsten turned him round and shuffled him into the house. 'Okay, Simon, you go up and get changed out of your uniform and then you can turn the TV on for a while. I'll be up in a minute.'

When she turned back, Trevor's handsome face was there in front of her, his smiling eyes greeting her warmly.

'Wow, you're the picture of domestic bliss these days. How are you, babe?'

He leaned forward and kissed her gently on the cheek. Her skin tingled as she felt his hand lightly touch her elbow and she breathed in the familiar fragrance of his face pressed against hers.

'What are you doing here, Trevor?'

'I came to see you.'

He looked surprised at the question, as only Trevor could. She hadn't seen him in nearly six months. The last time they were living together he had emptied her purse and disappeared without even waking her to say goodbye. He'd showed up a month later with a bunch of roses and a pocketful of cash that he must have won or stolen or got from God-knows-where. And that same surprised expression on his face.

'Who told you I was working here?'

'I just heard.'

'From who?'

'Why? What's the big deal?'

Now he looked so genuinely offended that she folded her arms and eyed him suspiciously.

'What are you doing here, Trevor?'

'Jesus, Kirst, chill out. What's with the Gestapo routine? I just dropped round to see you, that's all.'

'Why?'

'I don't know.' The edge left his voice. 'To talk to you, I guess.' He looked away at the garden and then back into her eyes. 'To say I'm sorry about all that shit that went down last time I saw you.' She remembered that softness in his voice, the tenderness of his gaze. 'I just wanted to see you again, and to tell you that I'm working now, and I'm making alright money and, you know, that I've kind of got my shit together a little bit, you know what I mean?' He was looking straight into her eyes now, the way he had a thousand times before, and she wanted to believe him, just like she had a thousand times before. 'I just thought you might be interested, that's all.'

They had met when Kirsten was sixteen and working for a tyre company in Parramatta. Trevor was seventeen, off-siding to a local truckie. She could still remember the first time she saw him, when he walked in one day to get new tyres on the boss's truck, tall, suntanned and broad-chested, his long sun-bleached brown hair hanging loose around his shoulders. He'd flashed that same broad smile at her and it was so handsome and warm and welcoming that it literally took her breath away. Even now that smile made her heart race just a little. He swept her off her feet. She lost her heart to him across the counter at the tyre company and her virginity in the back seat of his car. And for all the tears and the heartache he had brought her through the years, Kirsten Foster wouldn't trade a single memory of Trevor Ellowe and those times. She had loved him blindly, helplessly, completely. She didn't see the things her parents hated about Trevor; she refused to hear the things her close friends told her.

When they got married she was nineteen and he was barely twenty. He was wild, headstrong and vibrant, the most beautiful person that had ever walked into her life. When he held her in his arms and smiled that smile and whispered in her ear, there was no one in the world but Trevor. Life was perfect. She could put up with the drinking and the late nights away, the gambling, the pot stashed in the ceiling and the used bongs in the laundry cupboard. When he quit his job she understood that too — that was Trevor. But as the years went by and the drugs got heavier, things changed. He spent all the money she had saved and all that she could earn, and then he spent whatever he could steal or scam from wherever he could get it. Gradually her Trevor disappeared, little bit by little bit, until she didn't recognise him any more. He was gone, replaced by a stranger who she didn't know but everybody told her had been there all the time. And when he finally left it didn't hurt at all. She had loved him and she had wasted nearly ten years of her life on him, but she was over Trevor Ellowe. Very over him.

Except for sometimes, when he looked straight into her eyes and he smiled that smile, and she thought for a moment that she recognised the old Trevor and it made her want to believe that this time things just might be different.

'I'm not supposed to have any visitors here.'

'Can't we just sit down for two minutes and talk?'

She was looking into those eyes, past the wrinkles etched by smoke and late nights, at the young man she had once loved.

'Trevor, I haven't seen you in nearly six months. Now you turn up at my work and you want to talk. I can't do this here and now, okay?'

'What time's your boss get home?'

'Why?'

'I just want to know when you knock off, that's all.'

'Usually between about six and seven.'

'And you leave as soon as he gets back?'

'Yeah, usually. I should be home by seven-thirty anyway.'

'And there's just the kid and him at home after that?'

The charm had faded from his eyes and his brow was folded now, like a man processing information. She was puzzled by the changes in his face and looked at him quizzically.

'Yeah, I guess so. Why?'

He could see a familiar mistrust welling in her eyes. It shouldn't have surprised him but it did.

'I'm just asking, that's all. Jesus, settle down, will you. I'm just making small talk, babe.'

She felt bad, but that was to be expected. When Trevor was around, sooner or later she always ended up feeling bad. Either she saw it coming and he punished her for her mistrust, or she didn't see it coming and it devastated her. So much had happened between them that things were always complicated now. There was always heartache one way or another.

'Yeah well, I can't talk now, okay.'

'Okay, babe, that's cool.' His eyes were soft and understanding, his voice gentle. He leaned forward and pressed his lips to her cheek again. 'I'll ring you, okay.'

As she watched him saunter down the driveway to the street, his arms swinging loosely from his broad shoulders, she wished things could be different, even though she knew they never would be.

'Don't be a sap,' she muttered to herself as she turned back to the house. 'He's not going to ring you.'

* * *

Kirsten Foster wasn't accustomed to spacious surroundings. She was the youngest of five children, and though her four older brothers had come and gone from the family home from time to time, there was never any extra room in their parents' humble three-bedroomed cottage. She'd learned to fight hard for her own space, but there was always precious little of it. That was probably why she loved her afternoons in the kitchen of the Old Priory so much. The room was bigger than the unit that she lived in, with stark white walls and glistening tiles, twelve-foot ceilings that seemed to disappear above her and long broad benches topped with shiny stainless steel and granite. When she prepared food she made a point of laying out the ingredients on the benchtops by the fridge, then chopping them on the island bench, so she could walk from one point to the other as the task progressed, savouring the space.

'Is that man gone now?'

Little Simon was making one of his snap raids on the pantry, delving for TV snacks.

'Sure is.' Kirsten caught him by the wrist and held him long enough to extract two of the three biscuits crammed into his hand and slide them back into the barrel. She took him by the other hand and they strolled together back into the television room.

'Listen, sweetie, how about we don't mention to your dad that that man came here today, okay?'

'Why?'

'Well, because your daddy doesn't like me having friends around when he's not here and I don't want to lose my job.'

She dropped into an armchair and pulled him onto her lap.

'Is that man a friend of yours?'

'Yeah. Well, he used to be.'

'Do that man and you have any little kids?'

'No, sweetie.'

Simon swivelled in his seat and smiled sweetly at her. 'Are you in love with him?'

'No.' It was a reflex answer, and she thought about it for a moment. 'I used to be, but I'm not any more. He's still in love with him, but I'm not.'

The little boy giggled playfully, repeated the line to himself several times, then giggled a bit more.

'Do you like my dad?'

'Yeah, he's a nice man.'

'Would you like to marry him?'

'You know, you ask too many questions, just like your old man.' She slid him off her knee onto the floor and headed back into the kitchen. 'You should be a cop one day.'

CHAPTER SIX

'Yaaaayyyy! Whooo-hooo!'

The young man raised his beefy arms to the mock cheers of his drunken mates who were passing round the bourbon in the darkness. As he stepped out of the doorway onto the footpath they encircled him, slapping his shoulders, shoving him around playfully and pushing the bottle into his hand. He led them back to the street, swigging the bourbon, the drone of traffic and the beat of music drawing them back to Darlinghurst Road like moths to a flame.

'What about your friends? Who's next, fellas? I'll do a discount for a job lot.'

The guffaws and raucous jibes floating back down the alley told Lana that she had exhausted this particular profit centre. As the boys disappeared into the night she checked her watch. Three thirty-four. The graveyard shift. There were at least two more good hours to go. The footballers, the sailors, the drunks and the gamblers and all the other punters would have drunk their fill and tried their luck by now, and if they were ever going to become one of Lana's customers it would happen in the next two hours. She hitched her skirt up a little, to show just a tantalising glimpse of what was up for grabs, pulled her bustline down and rearranged her breasts, then stepped into the street and headed back towards the Cross.

She was feeling good. The heroin had lifted her, its warm glow still coursing through her body, making her feel strong and alive. She had barely loaded up when she jagged him, but the young footballer had been an easy trick, the sex polite and gentle, even pleasurable, so now her body felt as it rarely did these days: warm, pain-free and functional. She walked slowly and comfortably through the isolated backstreets of Kings Cross, not seeing the thick grime caked on the walls and windows or the garbage sprawled across the footpath, not smelling the vomit in the gutters or the urine pooled in darkened doorways. She was oblivious, feeling only her own body, knowing no fear, thinking only of herself. Decent folk rarely ventured through these streets even in daylight. But Lana wasn't decent folk. Not any more. She was safe here. She'd worked these streets since she was seventeen years old and she was on first-name terms with anyone who was ever likely to cut a person's throat round here.

By the time she reached the corner she felt a dull ache in her bladder. She focused for the first time on the job ahead. Most of the action would still be around the Bourbon and Beefsteak end. She would head in that direction. She peeled off into a narrow sidestreet and selected the first doorway, pushing her pants down around her knees and squatting in the blackness. As the discomfort drained pleasantly from her bladder she heard the whine of a small car labouring up the rise. Some childhood imperative of modesty made her bow her head chastely as the headlamps flashed onto the wall opposite and the car swung into the narrow lane and sped past. Then the engine throttled back as though the vehicle had stopped. Lana wondered if the driver had seen her squatting there in all her glory, and readied herself to reclaim some dignity and prepare for business. But then she heard the car accelerate again, the engine roaring angrily as it careered off down the street, the reflected glow of headlights disappearing into the night.

A second later the sound of crunching metal and shattering glass exploded in the darkness of the lonely street.

'Shit!' Lana toppled backwards with the shock, her bare buttocks chilled by the cold cement step below, one foot soaked in urine. 'Shit!'

As she reached for a handful of tissues she heard a dislodged hubcap rattle to its rest somewhere down the street, then the bang of a damaged car door pushing open, one door, and the scuffling of footsteps on the road. Lana dabbed her foot and ankle dry and threw the scrunched-up tissues into one black corner of the doorway. As she pulled up her underpants and straightened her dress she heard the car door bang again and then more footsteps echoing off into the night.

When Lana stepped off the footpath in Darlinghust Road and waved at the windscreen, Senior Sergeant Bob Clarke figured she was off her face again. He stabbed one fat finger in the direction of the kerb and the young constable driver compliantly pulled over as directed.

'G'day, Lana. What's happening, sweetheart?'

'Youse'd better get down the road, mate.' Lana's once-pretty face was framed in the window of the police car, looking even paler than usual. 'Some bloke's just wrapped himself around a light pole. I think he might be dead.'

The smart thing was to keep your head down. Bob Clarke knew that. Do your job, don't ask too many questions, and keep your head down. In this job everybody learned that lesson sooner or later, provided they survived long enough. And Bob had survived a long time. He'd been in the police force twenty years and understood instinctively when he should pull his head in.

There was something not quite right about that crash scene from the start. The young bloke in the passenger's seat was dead alright, but he didn't look like any road accident victim Bob had ever seen before. They were usually mangled, twisted things with bits skewed out at weird angles and blood everywhere, deep gashes filled with splintered glass or jammed under jagged metal. This guy was just sitting there, his head against the seat, his eyes rolled back and his big mouth open like he was catching flies. Hanging from the crook of his left arm was a loosened tourniquet which had obviously just helped him pump his veins up for a shot of something, probably heroin. The bonnet of the car was crushed back from the front nearside panel and the windscreen had shattered from the left on impact, but directly in front of the passenger it was mostly clear. He had no seatbelt on but he didn't look to have hit the windscreen and the dashboard seemed to be intact. But the impressive-looking dint from his hairline to the middle of his forehead suggested he had recently faced up to something pretty solid.

The car turned out to be hot, stolen from the car park of the Newington Hotel. The dead bloke had no ID on him. No wallet, driver's licence, nothing. Not even drinking money. By the time Bob had organised the doctor and the scene-of-crime photographers, done all the measurements and arranged things with the morgue, then tracked down the owner of the car and a dozen other things, it was time to clock off so he left it to the next shift to try and pin a name on John Doe.

When he clocked on again at midnight he was surprised to hear that they'd made real progress, even if it was by accident. One of the forensic boys thought the dead guy might be Trevor Ellowe, a small-time hustler and junkie from over in the western suburbs. It had checked out to be dead right. The boys had tracked down his last known address, a flophouse at Petersham. According to his landlady he hadn't been seen there since the early evening of the previous day.

Bob Clarke was putting the finishing touches to

his incident report when the call came through to his desk just after midnight.

'Hello. Sergeant Clarke.'

'Bob. Phil Manning.'

'G'day, Phil.' He didn't mean to sound as cold as he did, but then he didn't care either. It wasn't that he disliked Phil Manning; he just didn't have a lot of time for him as a copper or a bloke. 'How're you going?'

'Not bad. Haven't seen you in a while.'

'No. Whereabouts are you these days?'

'I'm over at Petersham, mate. I'm head of the detectives out here.'

'Is that right, ay?'

It didn't surprise Bob one bit. Phil Manning was always going to end up head of something somewhere sooner or later. He was a brown-noser who wouldn't keep his head down even if he knew how, and Bob Clarke seriously doubted that he did. Manning was always trying to work some sort of angle, sucking up to someone, beating his chest over something. Ever since they were both young constables together Manning had wanted out of uniform, wanted to get in with the big boys in the detectives, so he could ponce around in plain clothes wearing a pistol strapped around his ankle and impressing all the sheilas. He'd got what he wanted pretty early on, and for a while he looked like a star on the rise as one of Roger Baston's boys at the Armed Robbery Squad. Armed Robbery was the glamour crew in those days, and Manning lapped it up, bathing in the fame and glory, doing his best to get his silly head on television or in the papers every time Baston pinched another crim. It was all pretty heady stuff until Baston hit a hurdle and resigned from the job under a cloud. Then the big brass started asking lots of questions about Baston's boys, and when Manning was transferred from the Armed Robbers back to Petersham detectives it looked like his dream run might be over. But obviously he'd persevered and all the brown-nosing had paid off. He was back up on top, in his eyes anyway.

'So, what can I do you for?'

'Mate, it's about that single-car fatality you had out there last night. Looks like we've got a positive ID on the passenger.'

'Yeah.' What did he mean *we*? The Darlinghurst uniformed boys had done all the work so far.

'Yeah, he's a local bloke from out this way.' There was a curious little waver in Phil Manning's voice but that was none of Bob Clarke's business. 'Anyway, mate, the coroner will want a report and I think we may as well handle it from this end. So I might just get you to bundle up whatever you've got and shoot it over to us.'

Road accident fatalities had never been the glamour end of policing and there could be a lot of paperwork involved in putting together a brief for the coroner on a job like this. It wasn't every day you had a detective holding up his hand and asking for a hospital pass like this one, particularly not a silvertail like Phil Manning. There must be something in it that Bob wasn't seeing, maybe a sling from the assessors, or a chance to put some lawyer mate into the gap for some insurance claim. Who knew? Who cared? All Bob Clarke knew was it's smart to keep your head down.

'Yeah, sweet. No worries.'

CHAPTER SEVEN

Gary Sharpe was feeling slightly ill. Since the Petersham police had written off Trevor Ellowe's death as just another road fatality twelve months ago, Sharpey had hoped never to hear Ellowe's name again. So today's news that the New South Wales State Coroner was planning to hold a coronial hearing into the death had put him badly off his breakfast. He dropped onto a chair and raised one shaky finger to summon the waiter.

'So, how's it all looking?'

'Sweet.' Roger Baston was slumped forward on his elbows, the leather jacket folded against his thick neck and shoulders accentuating his muscular bulk. 'She'll go straight through to the keeper.'

They ordered coffees and stared silently at the table until the waiter finally withdrew.

'Who's in the know?' Sharpe's voice crackled with tension and he cleared his throat self-consciously.

Baston fixed him with a look as cold and hard as steel. 'No one. Alright? No one. All anyone knows is the bloke was a junkie and he's run into a pole.

That's it. Right? It's all bedded down. No questions asked, no fuss. The coppers will make sure of it.'

'But Jesus, Roger, I wasn't expecting the coroner to be conducting a public inquest.'

'That's what coroners do, mate.' Baston stretched his lips into a wry smile. 'Don't worry, son, it's sweet. We've been down this track before.'

Gary Sharpe felt a new wave of nausea wash over him. *We've been down this track before.* What the hell was Baston talking about? What had he got himself into? He sucked in a deep breath and tried to settle his nerves.

'I just don't want anybody turning over any rocks, that's all. A public hearing like this, you've got press and bloody lawyers and Christ knows who else sticking their noses in and trying to stir up shit.'

Baston was so far forward in his seat that when he growled his response Sharpey could smell the stale cigarette smoke on his breath. 'Mate, it's going through without a hiccup, okay? Trust me.'

It seemed more threat than reassurance. Sharpey looked into the cold eyes and nodded cautiously.

'I've got the right coppers on the job. They'll word the coroner up, just a simple single-vehicle fatality — it'll be all nicely served up to him on a silver platter surrounded by watercress. He'll listen to some evidence, make the appropriate finding, and then close the file. End of story. And that's it. Sweet.'

The waiter set down two coffees and they sipped silently for a while, Baston's wary gaze taking in his edgy companion's every movement, trying to assess his mood, calculate the risks. Eventually Sharpe rattled the coffee cup onto its saucer and looked at him.

'I just don't want anything going wrong.'

He was on board. Baston could see it in his eyes.

'Mate, nothing can go wrong. She'll be "death by misadventure, person or persons unknown". Trust me.'

'Will the family have a lawyer there?'

'The family are all fly-blown. They're not interested. The only one who's even likely to show up is an ex-wife and all she's interested in is the insurance payout.'

'Has she got a lawyer?'

'Just some hayseed solicitor from up in Queensland. He's not going to cause any trouble.' Baston could see slight relief seeping into Gary Sharpe's face. 'Relax, mate. I'm telling ya. It's a done deal.'

* * *

'Will you be having breakfast, sir?'

The voice was a soft intrusion into his fitful sleep.

'Sir?'

Eddie Moran's uncomprehending eyes flew open as he felt the stewardess's hand lightly touch his shoulder and he pushed his eye-mask up onto his forehead. 'Ugh?' he grunted, quickly swallowing to avert the impending escape of saliva from the corner of his mouth.

The young woman looked into his bloodshot, irritated eyes and her air of confident efficiency suddenly drained away. 'Will you be having breakfast?'

Edwin C Moran had been a practising lawyer long enough to know there were always going to be some good days and some bad ones. This was not going to be one of Eddie's better days. His neck creaked painfully as he pushed his chin down onto his crumpled tie and struggled awkwardly to find room for his long legs. He had been up half the night poring over the police brief to the coroner, and the few hours he had dedicated to sleep had been filled with dull abstracted visions and disconnected words and phrases somehow vaguely linked to the death of Trevor Wayne Ellowe. Long after he had finally crawled off to bed his brain had worked on, trawling incessantly through a confused matrix of jumbled facts, all the time expecting the ring of the alarm to force his tired body out of bed at 5 a.m., into the car and on the road to Coolangatta airport, ready for the early morning flight to Sydney. He had hoped the woman on the counter at the Qantas Club wouldn't notice that his card was out of date, so he could sneak in and get some decent coffee and wake up slowly over the morning papers. She had spotted him immediately, and though he had launched into a lame argument about overdue renewal notices his heart wasn't really in it, and he soon found himself slumped with the other cattle in the public lounge waiting for the flight to be announced. Of course the flight was late, and as usual his fee for the case wouldn't stretch to business class, so it was close to seven when he finally battled and wrestled his way to an economy seat jammed against the rear toilets, rolled up his suit-coat and pushed his briefcase into the overhead locker, and fell exhausted into his seat. The overweight car wholesaler squashed into the seat beside him introduced himself immediately and opened up a conversation that ended promptly when Eddie slipped on the eye-mask, dropped his head back and commenced snoring. He had just a little over one hour to get whatever sleep he could. He hadn't expected anyone to wake him up.

'What?'

The stewardess looked worried. Eddie was almost awake now and he was feeling very cranky. When she spoke again her voice was no more than a feeble whisper.

'I was just wondering if you would like something to eat.'

She pushed the plastic tray in front of him but Eddie scowled at it so venomously that she hurriedly withdrew it.

'Lady, do I look like I want something to eat?' The stewardess shaped a word but Eddie wasn't waiting for an answer. 'See this mask I was just wearing? Do you think I'm trying out for a part in the next Lone Ranger movie?'

'I'll have another one!' The fat car wholesaler reached across and grabbed the food tray, at the same time passing back his own, which looked as if it had been ravaged by a locust plague. An empty plastic juice cup rolled off onto Eddie's crumpled chest. He looked down sadly at the drops of orange juice that stained his new silk shirt. This wasn't going to be his best day at all. He slipped the mask back over his eyes and cursed himself for ever travelling cattle class.

In the blackness, visions of Trevor Ellowe reappeared, frozen in police photographs of a crumpled motor car, his head slumped back against the headrest, his long arms splayed casually alongside him as though reposing peacefully at the centre of an ugly snapshot of suspended violence. The tourniquet still hanging loosely from his left arm was a fitting reminder of the way he'd lived his life and the damage he'd done to himself and those around him. Eddie Moran had known Trevor Ellowe since he wasn't much more than a teenager, still bright-eyed and bushy-tailed, still capable of making something of himself. It was hard to hate anyone you'd known that long. But Eddie had also seen what followed, and the tourniquet brought it back to mind. He wasn't wasting any tears over the passing of Trevor Ellowe.

It was a simple job: Trevor Ellowe was dead and Eddie had to wind up his estate and get whatever he could for the grieving widow. Ellowe had been killed in a motor car collision in Kings Cross and, by the looks of things, he hadn't long finished jacking up a hit of high-grade heroin when the crash occurred. The car was stolen of course, and the driver had taken off, but Trevor Ellowe's widow was still entitled to damages. In such circumstances the government's Nominal Defendant office stepped into the shoes of the missing driver, and since in this case there could be little doubt that the driver had caused the accident, all Eddie had to do was think of a figure and get the Nominal Defendant to agree. They were very close already. No doubt the government insurers would be represented at the coroner's inquest to poke around and see if there was anything that might help them to limit their client's exposure, but no one was better at running interference than Eddie Moran. Hopefully, once the Nominal Defendant's lawyers figured out there was no joy in the inquest for them, Eddie might even be able to crunch a deal while he was down in Sydney.

The estate had been worthless, as Eddie had expected. He was no probate lawyer, but in a moment of weakness years ago he'd done a will for Trevor, on the arm of course, and he couldn't refuse now to administer the estate, even though there were never going to be any fees in it for him. By the time the car was sold, and three or four pieces of crappy furniture, the proceeds had barely covered his outstanding rent, electricity and telephone accounts.

As Eddie teetered on the edge of sleep, the jet engines droning in the background, something niggled at his mind, like a pebble in the bottom of his shoe. It had been there for the past few weeks and he couldn't seem to shake it. The circumstances of Trevor Ellowe's death were not those of the usual garden-variety single-vehicle fatality; they were sordid and messy. But that was what one would expect of any junkie and, considering who the deceased was, they were wholly unremarkable. And yet there was something about Trevor's death that just wouldn't go away. So far Eddie still hadn't worked out what it was. He'd checked out the owner of the stolen car, without really knowing why or what he was looking for; he'd been through the telephone accounts checking all the numbers; he'd even rung the landlord who assailed him with complaints about his late tenant, but nothing he had seen or heard made Eddie understand what it was that was troubling him about the death of Trevor Ellowe. The photographs appeared and disappeared in the blackness he was staring into and telephone accounts and rent bills floated in and out of his consciousness. He slowly drifted back to sleep.

* * *

'Thank you, sir. Have a nice day.'

Eddie grimaced and nodded Grinch-like as he passed the pretty young stewardess smiling at the end of the walkway. He couldn't help it. He'd been up too early, he hadn't had a decent cup of coffee or a smoke, and outside the rain was drizzling against the airport windows. He was crumpled and sore, he had a juice stain on his new silk shirt, and he was back in Sydney. This wasn't going to be his day. He could sense it.

CHAPTER EIGHT

If you were smart you always stayed one step ahead of the plebs. Eddie knew that. He'd stuffed everything he needed into his carry bag to make sure he wasn't queuing with the other cattle for his baggage. That meant he'd be the first one to the taxi rank and he'd be long gone before the Monday morning rush created the usual triumph of demand over supply. By the time he got to the escalators he was puffing hard, quietly congratulating himself and pondering whether he should think about easing up a little on the cigarettes some time soon. He soon forgot all that.

'Fuck!' The cramped line of disheartened commuters stretched away in each direction from the covered taxi stand outside. 'Fuck, fuck, fuckety-fuck!'

Eddie pushed one hand into his coat pocket and pulled out a smoke. Local time was nearly nine-fifteen. With this line-up he'd be lucky to make it into Glebe by ten.

'Hey, hey sport! Where do you think you're going?'

The meticulously dressed gentleman in the navy

pin-striped suit hadn't meant to jump the queue, he'd simply failed to understand the barriers that led the cattle to their trucks. That was obvious enough, but Eddie had now been standing less than patiently in line for more than twenty minutes, inching painfully towards the raincoated attendant directing passengers to cabs, and the thought of anybody denying him what little progress he had made was all too much.

'What's your problem, pal, you need new glasses or something? Can't you see the line here?' The elegant, pin-striped man looked genuinely surprised for a moment, then cast a disapproving look over the top of his spectacles as Eddie emphasised his point. 'What d'you think, pal, we're all just standing here to get a suntan?'

As the compliant line took one step back in unison to allow the chastened interloper to take his rightful place, Eddie sucked hard on his cigarette and nervously checked his watch. Nine thirty-five. Even if he was in a taxi right now, with traffic like this he'd still be pushing it to get to the Coroner's Court on time. He growled malevolently, sucked in another breath of smoke and puffed it out in a cloud of profanities.

'You can't stop there, lady.'

The traffic attendant was waving furiously at the little red hatchback that had slipped into the kerb at the head of the taxi line.

'Yeah, yeah, okay Dirty Harry, keep your shirt on.' The driver's side door flew open and Kirsten Foster waved at Moran. 'Eddie!'

'It's okay, officer, I know her. She's with Qantas.'

The traffic attendant looked unamused as Eddie stepped past him and bundled his bag into the back of the hatchback. As he slammed the hatch down, Kirsten pressed the car keys into his hand.

'Here, Eddie, you know where we're going. You drive.'

He watched her strut towards the passenger door and smiled to himself conceitedly; she obviously still couldn't handle the prospect of him critiquing her atrocious driving. She preferred to be a back-seat driver when Eddie was around and he prepared himself for the usual barrage. Slick loved giving lip, especially to Eddie. He always called her Slick, for reasons that even he couldn't remember any more. She was the little sister of his best mate, Terry Foster, and they had known each other almost all their lives. When Eddie and Terry first started making model aeroplanes in the old man's back-yard shed, Slick was always there, giving cheek and playing up. When they got old enough to hit the town she was always around to tell them just how silly they looked in their trendy clobber, and when they started up their first garage band she was their toughest critic. And of course for his part Eddie treated her like dirt, not because he particularly disliked her, just because that's how he was — Eddie treated everyone like dirt. It hadn't stopped him noticing over the years that she'd grown all the necessary bits, and mostly in exactly the right places.

They hadn't seen each other in over two years, but as she bent to climb into the car, he couldn't help but notice that things were looking good. It came as no surprise to Eddie Moran that Slick was looking a whole lot healthier and a whole lot happier since the demise of her ex-husband. As far as Eddie was concerned, Trevor Ellowe always had been a waste of space. Slick had carried him around like a sackful of rocks for years, even after he'd walked out on her half a dozen times, and every time she looked like getting back on her feet old Trev would turn up again like a bad smell. When Eddie got the call from Slick twelve months ago to tell him Trevor had died in the car crash and asking him to take care of all the legals, he could only feel relief for her. And now she was looking trim, taut and terrific — every inch the merry widow.

'Jesus, Slick, what have you been doing — working out? That's the tightest piece of arse I've seen in a long time.'

She waved her hips playfully at him and climbed into the car. 'Yeah, yeah, yeah. Okay, Harry Hormone, get in and drive.'

Eddie leaned his face into the open doorway. 'Seriously, that's a mean piece of butt. You could crack fleas on those buns, baby.'

Slick puckered up and planted a fulsome ring of ruby red on his lips. 'Yeah well, I wouldn't go cracking anything if I was you, Eddie, 'cause you ain't getting any of it anyway. So don't punish yourself, big boy.'

Eddie chuckled and wiped off the lipstick with the back of his hand. He liked Slick. She was a tough chick and she took shit from absolutely nobody, not even Eddie Moran, and you had to love that. She was looking great, and she was entitled to: she'd just offloaded a heap of dead wood from her life, and she was about to get paid a bonus for doing it.

The fact that Trevor Ellowe had been in a stolen car on the night he died wasn't going to stop his widow claiming compensation from the Nominal Defendant under the compulsory third-party insurance scheme, and that meant Slick was about to cash in on the biggest liability of her life. Eddie had somehow convinced the insurers that there was some prospect of Trevor actually working for a living if he'd stayed alive, and he'd even got them to believe that if the lowlife had earned any money he'd have used it to support his wife, so they were already talking settlement figures of around a hundred grand. Now that'd make anybody smile. But Eddie had convinced Slick to hold off a little, at least until the inquest was over, to see if anything of use came out before trying to finalise a settlement. Still, even though Eddie knew well enough that money had a way of putting a glint in anybody's eye, there was something else about Slick that was making him curious, something he couldn't quite put his finger on. Not yet at least, but he was working on it.

'So what's happening in your life, kiddo? Apart from all this drama, I mean.'

'Heaps.'

'Such as?'

The indignant blast of a car horn behind them momentarily distracted her. Slick glanced over her shoulder briefly then turned back to him with a bemused expression on her face. 'I see you still can't drive your finger up your bum.'

Eddie smirked and settled comfortably in his seat. She was obviously avoiding the question.

'Such as?'

She flipped her handbag open and started rummaging for cigarettes.

'Such as lots of things. I'm still studying . . .'

'Yeah.'

He could tell she was hedging. She slipped a cigarette into her mouth and lit up. 'And I've got a part-time job.'

'Yeah?'

Eddie wasn't going to give up. She blew out a puff of smoke.

'As a nanny to a gorgeous little eight-year-old boy, if you must know. I start every day at two and I'm finished by six, which gives me plenty of time to do my study.'

'Really?' Eddie raised his eyebrows and looked across into her deep green eyes. There was that curious glint again. 'And who's this for — some rich yuppie couple in the eastern suburbs?'

'No, it's at Petersham actually.'

'I don't remember too many young urban professionals living in Petersham.'

'I work for a single father.' She blew out another puff of smoke and looked down her nose at him. There was just the faintest hint of a smile nudging at the corners of her mouth, and if Eddie didn't know her better he'd have sworn that she was blushing. 'He's a widower.'

'Really?' Eddie was starting to enjoy himself. 'Obviously one rich enough to hire a pretty nanny for his gorgeous little boy.'

The green eyes narrowed into killer mode.

'You're the biggest creep, you know that don't you, Eddie.'

Eddie rattled off an irritating little chuckle and shifted gleefully in his seat as he pulled a pack of cigarettes from his pocket.

'Gee, fancy that.' He flipped a cigarette into his mouth. 'A rich single dad and a young grieving widow. That's an awful lot of hormones rolling around in one household, isn't it?'

'Bite your arse, Eddie.'

Eddie laughed again, then lit up and sat back with a smug expression on his face. Bingo. Mystery solved. Got it in one.

* * *

Eddie had checked on the address for Glebe Coroner's Court before he left, and he had a fair idea where it must be, but he'd never actually appeared there before. In fact, if the truth were known, Eddie had never actually appeared in any coroner's court before, anywhere. This was to be his first coronial inquest. He hadn't seen the need to mention any of this to his client, but then why should he? After all, how hard could it be? He had taken the time to acquaint himself with the Act, and as usual he'd read all the relevant cases. The procedure was straightforward. Whenever someone died in unexplained or controversial circumstances the state coroner had the right to hold a public hearing to look into the circumstances of the death, consider issues of culpability or negligence, and make recommendations to avoid similar tragedies. The tribunal was purely inquisitorial, unconstrained by any onus of proof and the strict rules of evidence, so it was all likely to be pretty relaxed. For lawyers practising in the personal injuries jurisdiction it was common fare, and if a personal injuries lawyer could manage it, it held no fears for Edwin C Moran.

Still, Eddie was no personal injuries lawyer. He'd been practising law in the glitzy tourist town of Surfers Paradise for more than ten years now, during which time he'd gained quite a reputation in the sunshine state as a maverick one-man band who liked upsetting police, country magistrates, judges and just about anyone else who happened to get in his way, and wasn't frightened of controversy or the spotlight it attracted. He'd been known to do bits and pieces of all sorts of things, but mostly he'd done criminal law. And of the bits and pieces of other things he'd done, none of it was personal injuries work. Eddie's office was up in Queensland so he didn't get into the courts in New South Wales too often, and when he did it certainly wasn't to appear before the coroner at Glebe.

Kirsten Foster discovered most of this for the first time between about nine fifty-five and ten past ten that morning, after she and Eddie realised they must have missed the Coroner's Court the first time through Glebe and had circled once or twice around the block trying to locate it, all of which focused her mind on the question of why Eddie didn't actually know where the court was.

On their third time around, Eddie spotted the drab brown-brick building on Parramatta Road just where it should be, and tried to ignore his passenger's whining about having been kept in the dark and fed the usual crock of shit as he probed through the sidestreets looking for a park. Considering she wasn't paying for his services, Slick was getting value for her dollar.

* * *

Slick's umbrella was one of those trendy ones that was just big enough to keep her completely dry while redirecting a steady flow of rainwater off its rim onto Eddie's left shoulder and down his back. To further punish him she refused to hold it high enough to accommodate his lanky body, so by the time they rounded the corner onto Parramatta Road, Eddie was stooping and straining to one side like an elongated hunchback trying to get whatever meagre shelter was on offer. He could feel the water soaking through his suit-coat and his cold wet shirt sticking to his skin.

Slick was striding along the footpath at full pace, heading for the glass doors of the Coroner's Court complex. Suddenly she stopped, and Eddie's forehead swiped past the rim of the umbrella as he stumbled into the rain and up onto the front steps of the court. He did his best to shake the water off then he turned back to see Slick frozen at the bottom of the stairs, looking up towards the double doors.

'Michael!'

All the whingeing and the whining had evaporated; suddenly she was wearing a sweet smile on her face and that mysterious glint had reappeared in her eye.

'Kirsty!' A tall, well-built man standing beside Eddie at the top of the steps smiled warmly down at Slick, then suddenly the smile disappeared. 'What are you doing here?'

'I'm just here with a friend. He's a lawyer. Eddie, this is Michael Wiltshire, the man I work for. Michael, this is Eddie Moran, an old friend of mine.'

As they shook wet hands Eddie tried to remember where he had heard the name before. He could see something decidedly uncomfortable in the man's eyes. At first he wondered if Slick's new boss just wasn't buying her assurance that Eddie was nothing more than an old friend. His reaction when he and Slick had first eyeballed each other made it clear to Eddie that he had more than a master–servant interest. But as Wiltshire shifted nervously from one foot to the other Eddie could see that something more was bothering him. He had a look Eddie had seen all too often on faces cornered in the witness box: the look of a fat cat hiding a gobful of feathers.

'Eddie's doing a case down here so I just thought I'd tag along.' As they all pushed through the doors into the building Slick shot a glance at Eddie that warned him this was all the information she wanted published, and she particularly didn't want the subject of Trevor Ellowe raised. 'So what are you here for?'

Wiltshire looked like an errant schoolboy with his hand deep in the cookie jar. 'Ah, well, I, er ...' Eddie half expected to see feathers fluttering out of his mouth. He stumbled and stuttered for several seconds before regaining his composure. 'I had to meet someone just down the road from here and I got caught in the rain.'

If Eddie had tried to sell Slick a lame story like that she'd have given it to him with both barrels, but from this guy she seemed content to buy it without question. In fact she and Wiltshire were being so polite and charming to each other that Eddie was starting to feel a trifle nauseous. Both of them were lying through their back teeth, that much was clear, for what reason Eddie didn't know and wasn't interested. Maybe Slick didn't want Wiltshire to know she was once married to a drop-kick like Trevor Ellowe; maybe Wiltshire didn't want her to know he was checking up on why she wasn't coming into work that day. Whichever way it added up, it was obvious there was a whole lot of hormones mixed up in the equation. And Eddie Moran always did his best to steer clear of hormones. Besides, he was too busy to stand around and watch them play their games. Without a word he turned and strode off to check the court list on the notice board.

The Ellowe inquest was listed in court number two. Slick caught him by the elbow just as he was about to push through the heavy door into the courtroom.

'What did you walk off for?'

'He's your boss, you lie to him. I've got an inquest to get on with.'

CHAPTER NINE

Eddie had never seen a police detective wearing a club jacket. Some barristers wore a club jacket in chambers, or when sipping wine over lunch in their favourite restaurant, but that was understandable since barristers didn't live in the real world. Most detectives Eddie had encountered worked in shirt-sleeves, usually with a tie but sometimes not, and he'd known plenty to wear a jumper or a sports coat, particularly south of the border. A few mug lairs wore leather coats or jackets, and the flashy ones wore a suit, sometimes even with a waistcoat. He'd known the odd one to sport braces and once he even saw one in a bow tie. But never, in all his years of practice, had he ever seen one wearing a club jacket.

Not only was Detective Senior Sergeant Phil Manning wearing a club jacket, he was wearing it with a silk tie and matching handkerchief ballooning from the breast pocket. As Eddie entered the courtroom Manning was perched casually on the bar table, imparting his opinions at full volume to anyone who cared to listen — which included the prosecutor, the coroner's clerk and two younger detectives — and looking every bit as relaxed as if he were sitting in his own lounge room. It made Eddie feel uneasy seeing a prospective witness looking this at home in any courtroom, and it didn't help when Manning bounced off the bar table and introduced himself in a manner that suggested he thought Eddie was somehow interested in who he was, then announced that proceedings wouldn't be getting under way until the barrister who had been briefed by the insurers arrived. Apparently Mr Bowling QC had been delayed on a flight back from Melbourne.

Walter Bowling QC arrived with his instructing solicitor half an hour later, in the same elegant navy pin-striped suit he had been wearing at the airport when Eddie had so indelicately relegated him to the end of the taxi line.

It was clear Bowling recognised Eddie the moment Detective Manning obligingly made the introductions, and as the two men shook hands he cast the same disapproving look over the top of his spectacles as he had previously.

'Yes, I think we've already met once this morning.'

Eddie couldn't help himself. 'Hopefully you'll find your right place at the bar table.'

'Who's that snooty prick?' Slick whispered into Eddie's ear as they all rose and waited for the coroner to enter the courtroom.

'It's a long story.'

Mr Roly Roberts LCM had been the New South Wales state coroner for over fifteen years, and it was clear from the moment he appeared that he was perfectly suited to a jurisdiction in which the main player was already dead and nothing was at risk of happening quickly. He lumbered slowly to his chair, settled gradually into position, shuffled through a pile of papers and mumbled to his clerk, then rustled through his papers some more before finally looking at the bar table through his snow-white eyebrows with a polite 'Yes?'

The police prosecutor rose to announce his appearance as counsel assisting the coroner. Eddie bounced one foot nervously below the bar table and checked his watch. It was already nearly eleven o'clock. He was hoping to be on the 4:10 flight back to Coolangatta that afternoon, which meant he'd have to wrap this up by three at the latest. Detective Manning had assured them all earlier that this was a pretty straightforward one and wouldn't take long, but Eddie wasn't quite so sure. There were some things about the death of Trevor Ellowe that he couldn't quite work out. And Eddie didn't like unanswered questions.

* * *

'It was apparent from all our investigations that the accused had, in fact, injected himself with heroin whilst he was seated in the passenger compartment of the vehicle, and that this more than likely occurred very shortly before impact.' Detective Manning was looking even more at home in the witness box as he laid down his holy writ. 'We would speculate that the driver similarly injected himself with heroin at some time prior to the accident and that this occurrence contributed to his having lost control of the vehicle.'

The police version was simple. Trevor Ellowe and one of his junkie mates had stolen a car from the car park of the Newington Hotel and gone for a joyride down to Kings Cross, where they probably picked up the smack that Ellowe had stuck in his arm shortly before the big bang. The driver had probably done likewise and then went 'on the nod', causing him to crash the car. Wearing no seatbelt, Ellowe was thrown forward and struck his head heavily on the dashboard or elsewhere in the car and died as a result. Exhaustive investigations had failed to disclose who the driver may have been and no person had been identified as a subject of prosecution in connection with the death.

Walter Bowling embarked on an unspectacular line of questioning designed to probe whether it was possible that Ellowe had been the driver of the vehicle at the time of the accident; if he was, the collision that led to his death would have resulted from his own negligent driving and therefore his widow would have no claim on the insurer. But Phil Manning summarily and confidently dismissed any such suggestion. He disposed of the issue by reference to the fact that not only was Ellowe found in the passenger's compartment, he had a tourniquet hanging loosely from his arm and the syringe he had used to inject himself with was lying at his feet in the passenger well of the car. People and objects can be thrown about wildly in a motor-car collision but undoubtedly Manning's answers were good enough to satisfy a civil court on the balance of probabilities that Ellowe was a passenger and not the driver at the time of the crash. That meant someone else was responsible for the car crash that took Trevor Ellowe's life, which meant the insurer was going to have to pay up.

It was pretty much all that Eddie needed. He didn't have to cross-examine Manning, but he couldn't help himself. There were still those niggling unanswered questions.

'Detective Manning, I note from the police incident report that when Senior Sergeant Clarke and his offsider first arrived at the scene they recorded some of the deceased's vital signs.'

'That's right.'

'He wasn't breathing, they found no pulse and they also noted that his pupils were fixed and fully dilated.'

'Yes.'

'Each of those facts was confirmed by the paramedics who arrived at the scene shortly thereafter.'

'Yes.'

'By the looks of things he was stone dead when the police first arrived.'

'Looks like it.'

'Fair enough.' Eddie was still trying to get his mind around precisely what it was about this set of facts that was causing him such aggravation. 'And so far as we can work out, it looks as though the police must have been on the scene within three or four minutes of the collision.'

'About that.'

'So the deceased must have died almost instantaneously.'

'He had a massive head injury, sir. It's our understanding that he sustained a severe concussion of the brain stem in the collision and died as a result — virtually on impact.'

'Is that right?'

Still grappling with some of the observations in the pathology report, Eddie looked up from the page distractedly. His eyes were met by the steely gaze of Detective Manning, who was glaring at him. It took Eddie by surprise. The witness's countenance had changed. Manning was still sprawled casually across the witness box but he was no longer relaxed; he was now alert, on edge, listening, anticipating the next question. It was a subtle change, but one that Eddie recognised immediately. Where had it come from? Eddie skimmed through the pathology report again as the court waited silently. What was it about all this that made no sense?

'So you think the deceased ingested heroin shortly before his death?'

'Yes.'

'Did you find the packaging the heroin came in?'

'No, sir, we believe the driver took that with him. It's our guess he originally had the heroin, injected some of it himself, then handed a shot to the deceased, retaining the packet and taking it with him when he decamped the scene.'

'Was there a second syringe found?'

'No, sir. We believe they either shared the same syringe or the driver took his with him.'

'Find any spoon or other receptacle used to prepare the injection?'

'No, sir. Once again, the driver has obviously taken that with him.'

'So you're currently on the lookout for an extremely tidy junkie, are you?'

'I'm not sure I follow you, sir.' Manning clearly did not appreciate the lawyer's flippancy. He was staring at Eddie, his gaze cold and steady. There was something about all this that was obviously troubling the detective at least as much as it was troubling Eddie, but he still couldn't put his finger on it.

'Did you test the potency of the heroin the deceased injected?'

'There was none left in the syringe.'

'None?'

'No.'

Manning looked uncomfortable. The blank expression on his face was stretched tight at the edges as though he was battling to look Eddie in the eye. They both knew his answer wasn't good enough.

'Surely there'd be enough for testing purposes.'

'There was no point in testing the contents of the syringe.'

'Why not?'

'We didn't consider it relevant.'

When a witness did an about-turn like Manning had just done, it wasn't hard to see that he knew something that he wasn't keen to share. But what was it?

'Where is the syringe now?'

'I believe it was disposed of.'

Eddie stared at Manning for several long seconds. The detective was impassive, his gaze challenging Moran to probe further, to give it his best shot. It was a contest now, and they both knew it. Eddie was happy to join in — just as soon as he could work out what game they were playing.

'Have you canvassed the deceased's known associates, to ascertain his movements earlier that night?'

'What known associates are these, Mr Moran?'

Manning's jaw was thrust forward defensively and he looked like a witness who was ready for a fight. But what did he want to fight about? So far Eddie was in no position to shape up to him.

'I don't know. You tell me.'

Manning looked conscious that he'd become a little too defensive. When he spoke again his tone was more subdued.

'We don't know anything about the deceased's earlier movements.'

'Well, the car was stolen from the car park of the Newington Hotel shortly after 3 a.m., is that right?'

'Yes, sir. The Newington had a 3 a.m. licence at that time and one of the security staff reported seeing the vehicle in the car park just after he knocked off work.'

'He says "at about three-fifteen", doesn't he?'

'That's right.'

'Well, the trip from the Newington into the Cross would take a good twenty minutes wouldn't it, even at that hour?'

'I'd say so.'

'And we know the collision occurred around 3:35 a.m.?'

'Yes.'

'That doesn't leave much time for the deceased and his friend to have found a dealer, bought the heroin, and then prepared two shots and injected them, does it?'

Manning fired his answer straight back at the lawyer. 'It's not impossible.'

Eddie Moran was still moving all the facts around in his mind. 'No, it's not impossible.'

Manning was keen to elaborate. 'It appeared to us, from the positioning of the tourniquet on the deceased's arm, that he was virtually still in the act of injecting when the collision occurred.'

Eddie thought about that for a moment in the context of the various post-mortem observations. Trevor Ellowe was supposed to have just finished injecting himself when the car crashed and he received a head wound that killed him almost instantly. It didn't fit. Eddie opened the post-mortem report and ran his finger down the page.

'Detective Manning, the deceased showed signs consistent with a heroin overdose, didn't he?'

'I wouldn't know, sir. I believe the pathology report shows quite high levels of opiates in the blood, but whether that indicates an overdose is something you'll have to ask the doctors, I would think.'

The reports that you obtained refer to biochemical changes indicative of deep respiratory depression?'

'Yes.'

'And that's something we see in drug overdose cases, isn't it? The victim becomes so deeply intoxicated by the drug that his respiration becomes depressed and he takes increasingly shallow and irregular breaths.'

'I'm no doctor, sir, but I believe that's right.'

'And if it's acute enough and goes on long enough, there's insufficient oxygenation in the blood to sustain life and the victim dies of hypoxyia, doesn't he? In other words, he suffocates.'

'Yes, sir.'

'And those biochemical changes mentioned in the pathology report take time to manifest themselves during this period of depressed respiration, don't they?'

'I told you, sir, I'm no doctor. I wouldn't know.'

Manning was clearly in defensive mode. Whether it was because he was just determined to protect his original hypothesis as to how events unfurled that night and didn't want some half-smart lawyer discrediting his good detective work, or whether there was something more to it than that, Eddie couldn't tell. But he now knew in his own mind that the theory was askew, and he moved to dismantle it as carefully as he could, trying to put all the pieces in their right places.

'Detective Manning, the autopsy report noted that the body showed signs of severe acidic burning associated with gastric contents in the trachea and bronchi, consistent with aspiration pneumonia. That suggests that at some stage the deceased inhaled some of his own vomit, doesn't it.'

'I believe so.'

'Again, a not uncommon feature of heroin overdose.'

'No.'

'And, of course, to be inhaling vomit you've got to be alive at the time, haven't you?'

'I expect so.'

'It looks very much as though the deceased suffered a heroin overdose, doesn't it?'

'That's possible.'

'And that, having suffered that overdose he remained alive, although perhaps unconscious, for some time thereafter, battling the effects of that the overdose. Isn't that so?'

'It's possible.'

'It's more than possible, isn't it?'

Manning hesitated as if he was carefully processing the information that they had traversed so far, perhaps assessing why the lawyer had taken him on the journey, and where it might be leading. 'Well, yes, sir, it is.' He started slowly, as if still digesting what had been said, then nodded sagely and launched into a confident discourse. 'In fact, now that you point all that out, I think you may be right. We may well have misinterpreted the sequence of the events. It may be more likely that the deceased suffered an overdose at some point earlier in the night and was later placed in the car, perhaps with a view to being taken somewhere for treatment.'

There was an audible shuffle further down the bar table as Walter Bowling's instructing solicitor sat back in his chair, a wash of smug satisfaction lighting up his face. He knew that if Trevor Ellowe died of injuries sustained in a motor-vehicle collision, the Nominal Defendant was liable for damages to his widow; but, if he had already died of an overdose before the accident occurred, the insurers were in the clear.

'It may be he was already dead of an overdose before he sustained the head injury in the accident,' Bowling boomed from the bar table.

Roly Roberts smiled pleasantly. 'I see it's almost one o'clock. We'll adjourn now until 2.30.'

When His Worship had finally retired to his chambers, Bowling plucked up his brief and swept past Eddie Moran towards the courtroom door.

'Moran, you're on notice — all previous offers are now withdrawn. Liability's back in issue.'

Slick was no lawyer but this did not sound good. Eddie had told her the insurers had been talking about admitting liability, which would only leave an amount to be sorted out. In other words, there was no question she was going to get a payout, it was only a matter of how much she was going to get. Suddenly that all seemed to have changed. Suddenly the insurers were withdrawing offers instead of making them and as far as Slick could see, that couldn't be a good thing.

As Slick backed her way into the interview room, easing the door open with her buttocks and juggling two cups of coffee, Eddie Moran was hunched over the table, running his fingers through his unruly hair and squinting at a dog-eared colour photograph. At first she stopped, thinking the photographs spread out across the table might be of the accident scene. She began to turn away — she couldn't look at those images — but then she turned back. It wasn't a police photograph Eddie was looking at. He had the bundle of old snapshots she'd collected at his request and was now staring quizzically at one of them, an old wedding picture of the young newly wed Mr and Mrs Trevor Ellowe.

As she set the coffees down, Eddie dropped the photograph, searched through his file and extracted a stack of papers. He propped both feet on the edge of the table and leaned back precariously, the papers pressed against the notepad balanced on his knees, as he leafed through them studiously with one hand, scribbling notes with the other.

He looked a mess as usual, his trousers pulled half-way up his skinny calves, showing off his ludicrous red iridescent socks and chunky black suede shoes. As he chewed voraciously on his gum, blowing little pink bubbles that popped and quickly disappeared into his mouth, Slick wondered how she'd ever ended up with Eddie as her lawyer.

She rounded the table towards him but was then distracted. The photograph was lying face-up where he had dropped it on the table. She gently picked it up, holding it delicately in both hands for a moment and remembering the scene it showed. There they were, two young newlyweds signing the wedding register, arm-in-arm, healthy, happy and very much in love. Trevor was smiling that beautiful smile of his, the pen held confidently in his hand ready to sign on the dotted line, attesting his life-long commitment to his bride.

Slick tossed the picture aside. She was back to business.

'Okay smartarse, so what's happening here?'

Moran was doing his best to ignore her.

'Michael Wiltshire — is that what you said your boss's name was?'

'Yeah. Why?'

He ran his finger down the page in front of him until it came to rest in the centre page

'You reckon you finish work at his place by six o'clock. You haven't been having any little sleepovers there by any chance, have you?'

'Get fucked, Eddie.'

There was more than a little venom in the answer and Eddie paused, looking up at her with an insolent smirk. 'I'd say that's a "no".' He scratched a note onto his pad as if he was filling out a questionnaire. 'You ever still at work at 10.30 p.m.?'

'Never.' Slick had one hand propped against her hip and a lethal look in her eyes. 'And what's all this got to do with the price of fish, anyway?'

'Did Trevor ever ring you at work?'

'Never,' she growled. She'd had enough. 'Why? What's all this, Eddie? What's going on?'

Moran slipped his feet off the table and his chair dropped forward to the floor.

'They're feeding us a crock of shit, that's what's going on.'

'What are you talking about?'

'I don't think Trevor died in that car crash at all.'

She rolled her eyes and let out a deep sigh.

'Eddie, you know what? I don't give a shit. What the fuck are you doing to me here? Before all this started this morning I was being offered a hundred thousand dollars or something, and now suddenly Shit-face in there is saying all bets are off. And excuse me if I get the feeling it's because of all these those half-smart questions you've been asking.'

Eddie gave Slick one of those self-righteous, sanctimonious looks he pulled out every now and then when he had convinced himself that she was behaving atrociously.

'Do you want to know the truth about how Trevor died or don't you?'

'No.' Having spat the answer angrily at him she paused for a moment to consider it, and then continued. 'No, I don't. I don't want to know the truth, alright. I can't remember the last time I knew the truth about anything to do with Trevor, so why would I want to start now?'

Eddie Moran wasn't listening.

'What was Wiltshire doing down here today?'

'Bite your arse, Eddie.' She flung the door open and then turned back to face him, pointing one long painted fingernail in his direction. 'Listen, I don't need you to start playing Sherlock Homes around here, okay. You're my lawyer. You're here to get me money. So start getting me some friggin' money, Eddie.'

* * *

'I'm a legally qualified medical practitioner currently employed at the Royal North Shore Hospital. At the time this matter arose I was a registrar at the New South Wales Institute of Forensic Medicine at Glebe.'

Dr Andrew Thornton was a pleasant-looking young man with delicate pink skin and a fine Scottish brogue that enunciated every precious syllable carefully and precisely. He had arrived at the courthouse earlier than expected, just as Eddie was beginning his cross-examination of Detective Manning. Eddie agreed to have this interrupted so that the good doctor's evidence could be interposed, allowing him to get his contribution to proceedings over and done with promptly and return to the care of the sick and needy. It was nice to be credited with a spirit of cooperation and gentility, but the truth was that it suited Eddie perfectly to have the doctor clear a few things up before he went much further with Phil Manning.

'The inadequate oxygenation that results from the depressed breathing pattern will normally manifest itself in disproportionately high levels of lactic acid and carbon dioxide build-up in the blood,' Dr Thornton explained.

The police prosecutor was questioning the young doctor closely on the indicia of aspiration pneumonia and respiratory depression, and he was doing his best to sound as learned as he could. He was only halfway through the third year of his five-year course in anatomical pathology, and had been at the tail end of a three-month stint doing autopsies at the city morgue when he'd cut up Trevor Ellowe, so perhaps he wasn't quite as learned as he might have been, but he knew enough to answer confidently the questions being put to him by the prosecutor. And whether the answers he was giving were right or wrong, it was clear the prosecutor knew precisely what to ask and what answers to expect. Obviously someone had made a point of getting the doctor down from Royal North Shore and into conference with the prosecutor in sufficient time to canvass pretty carefully the territory that Eddie had covered in his cross-examination before lunch, and now the prosecutor was taking the time and care to traverse it all fully and make it part of the theory that was to be served up to the coroner.

'Tests revealed quite massive levels of opioids in the blood of the deceased.'

The heroin overdose had suddenly become an integral component of the factual matrix of the case. Trevor Ellowe had suffered a drug overdose that night; Dr Thornton could be confident of that. The bio-chemical changes in the blood, the evidence of aspiration pneumonia, various other features, all led him firmly to the view that the deceased had suffered a serious narcotic overdose prior to his involvement in the collision.

'Can you tell us, Dr Thornton ...' Walter Bowling QC was barely ten minutes into his questioning of the doctor, but now he paused dramatically, allowing the silent seconds to draw the attention of every ear in the spacious courtroom before he wound up his killer punch. 'Can you tell His Worship the coroner and the rest of us here in this courtroom whether that overdose was in fact so serious that it caused the death of the deceased even before the collision in which he was involved that night?'

The doctor looked startled, as though finally he had been asked a question that he had not rehearsed. He fumbled briefly with his notes then looked back at the barrister with a slightly pained expression on his face. Every eye in the courtroom was fixed on him.

'Well, no, sir, no. I don't think I could say that categorically.'

Kirsten Foster breathed out a silent sigh and eased the tight grip of her fingers around the armrest of her chair. When she looked across at her lawyer she could see one foot bouncing nervously below the bar table, but the eyes behind his slim-line glasses were narrowed like those of an eagle circling a fieldmouse.

'Certainly it is possible, is it not, that this man died as a result of that narcotics overdose before he sustained any injury in the collision?'

'I don't think one could rule out that possibility.'

'Possible' wasn't good enough. The civil standard of proof was on the balance of probabilities, and if Bowling wanted to make anything of the evidence of overdose he would have to prove that it was more probable than not that the drugs and not the car accident had killed Trevor Ellowe.

'And, doctor, given all of the indicia that you observed, is it not fair to say, particularly in view of the massively high levels of opioids which you discovered in this man's bloodstream, and the various other indicia, that it is in fact probable that this was a fatal overdose?'

Dr Thornton squinted hard to readjust the glasses on his nose and looked thoughtfully at Walter Bowling, as all the lawyers in the courtroom held their breath.

'Well, yes, I suppose that would be fair to say, yes.'

* * *

'It's bullshit. You and I both know it.' Eddie was talking fast, probably a little too fast. 'You might have got Dr Dolittle in there to say it, but we can stack a civil trial full of specialists who'll testify there's no way anyone could tell whether the drugs killed him. And you won't find a medico anywhere to contradict them.'

Eddie Moran was no personal injuries lawyer, but Walter Bowling QC was. He knew that if the concession he had just wrung out of Dr Thornton was correct, if it was more probable than not that Trevor Ellowe had died of a heroin overdose, then Kirsten Foster's claim was somewhere down the toilet. He also knew that the doctor was probably incorrect, and that under cross-examination by

Moran there was every chance he would abandon his position. But right now, as the evidence stood, midway through the doctor's cross-examination, things would be looking very bleak to Kirsten Foster, and Bowling knew that too. He had asked for a fifteen-minute adjournment before Moran commenced his cross-examination, made a point of inviting Eddie's client into the conference room with them, then proceeded to paint the bleakest picture he could. Kirsten Foster's worried countenance was darkening by the second.

'On this evidence your client has no claim whatsoever. She walks away without a cent and she's up for all my client's costs to date. At the moment I'd say they stand at about five thousand, but they're rising rapidly.' He paused to let that sink in, but when he saw the rabid snarl forming on Eddie's lips jumped in quickly to present his panacea. 'Nevertheless, as a once only offer we're willing to give her fifteen thousand all up to walk away right now.'

He slid a fully completed settlement deed for the sum of fifteen thousand dollars across the conference table, and gently rolled a ballpoint pen across the top of it.

'Are you serious?' Eddie Moran was standing now, both hands on his hips, leering churlishly at his opponent. 'Have you got any idea at all?'

Bowling peered disdainfully over the top of his glasses; it irked him to be spoken to in such a manner, but he could tell by the look on the plaintiff's face that Eddie's insolence was worth enduring.

'If we have to go back into court today and my client is forced to incur further costs, then this offer will be withdrawn and we'll proceed to trial. Your client will end up with nothing but a debt for costs.'

Moran was already bundling up his papers. 'You're hallucinating, pal. You want to peg back on whatever it is you've been shoving up your nose lately.'

'Eddie, could I please speak to you for a moment?'

When Eddie looked at Slick he was grateful she wasn't armed, except with a lethal stare that demanded his attention and immediate compliance. As she led him from the room into the foyer of the court, Walter Bowling shot a confidential wink in the direction of his instructing solicitor. Once Slick had put a respectable distance between them and the conference room she turned on him.

'Eddie, what are you doing to me here?'

Her eyes were narrowed and her teeth were clenched as though she was about to bite him.

'Listen, it's all hogshit, alright.'

'Take the fifteen, Eddie.'

'You can't take the fifteen.'

'I'm taking the fifteen.'

'Slick, this clown is full of it, alright. That doctor's talking horseshit. I'll turn him round.'

'Eddie, we're dying in there.'

'We're not dying.'

'We're dying.'

'We're not.'

'Trust me. We are. We are dying. In fact, you're killing us.'

Slick snapped out the last few words in a voice loud enough to fill the entire foyer and looked around self-consciously. Then she re-set a deadly gaze on Eddie.

'Slick, handle it, alright. I know what I'm doing.'

'Eddie, get me some money. They're offering me fifteen — take the fifteen.'

'Slick, listen. You've got to trust me, alright?'

She was staring into his face, her eyes charged with the panicked look of someone who knew she was about to make a very stupid choice.

Eddie Moran had been sticking grasshoppers down her shirt since she was ten years old and as she looked at him now, with his bird's-nest haircut and his stupid glasses, his sixties' retro tie skewed untidily to one side, she couldn't think of a single reason why she would trust him. Except he was still the smartest person she had ever met and, for some unknown reason, in his own obnoxious way Eddie always seemed to get it right.

'You fuck this up, Eddie, and I'm going to have to kill you.'

He breathed out a small sigh of relief.

'I don't want you to say anything when we go back in there, right. I'm the lawyer. When you've got a dog it makes no sense to bark yourself.'

When they filed back into the room, Walter Bowling and his instructing solicitor were both sprawled comfortably in their chairs wearing looks of smug self-congratulation. Eddie slapped his folder onto the table so loudly that Bowling jumped.

'You've got one chance and one chance only to settle this thing, pal, so you'd better sharpen your pencil.' Eddie thrust one foot up onto the table edge in front of Bowling, exposing a red iridescent sock and a length of skinny, hairy leg, and propped forward on his knee. 'We'll take ninety and not a cent less, provided it gets settled here and now. Otherwise we take you to the cleaners.'

The two lawyers scoffed in unison and Bowling shook his big head vigorously. 'You can't even establish liability. This man died of an overdose.'

'Think again, sport. The bloke's got a head injury that would kill a bull elephant. And you know and I know that there's not a judge in Australia who's going to want to deny a poor bereaved widow her bag of lollies. If we can put up any sort of a case he'll find liability alright. So how about you get your hand off it and we start talking business.'

Bowling sat back silently and pursed his lips; Eddie had him thinking.

'We might stretch to thirty.'

Bowling had just doubled the ante without so much as deferring to his instructing solicitor. They had obviously discussed figures already and had authorisation from their client to negotiate a settlement within an agreed range. Eddie had played enough poker in his life to know that Bowling had more in him yet.

'You're dreaming, pal. My client and the deceased were in the process of reconciling when he died. She could have expected him to fully maintain her throughout the rest of her life. If that's not worth at least ten grand a year then God didn't make small strawberries. And this bloke was barely in his thirties. That leaves him another thirty years of wage-earning. Work it out for yourself, buddy. Thirty years by ten Gs — discount it how you like, that's starting to look like very serious money and you know it.'

'Ellowe wasn't even working. He was drawing the dole.'

'Maybe he was, but he was also drawing a wage.' Eddie flipped open the Coroner's Court brief and dropped it on the table in front of the barrister. 'Didn't you read your brief, buddy? It's right there, annexed to the landlord's statement.'

Bowling peered down through his glasses at the open page. It was a copy of a reference letter purporting to be from the deceased's employer; he had presented it when applying to the landlord for tenancy. It was signed 'Frederick A Hunter, managing director of Hunter Transport'. Walter Bowling sat back, looking sceptical, as Moran continued.

'Now I don't know the truth of it, but I know one thing: Fred Hunter will back it up. You boys might not know of old Fred but he's pretty well-known round Petersham way for having all sorts of people on his books. They all draw a wage on paper and they all get Fred a nice deduction on his tax. And if push comes to shove, all I have to do is subpoena Hunter Transport's wage records and sure as there's shit in a cat they'll show Mr Ellowe pulling down a fair old weekly wage.'

Bowling folded his glasses and slipped them into his pocket. 'I've never heard of this fellow Hunter.' He shot an inquiring glance to his instructing solicitor who curled his lips and shook his head. Eddie knew he had them worried.

'I suggest you go and ask the police about him.'

Bowling and his solicitor formed a scrum out in the foyer with the prosecutor, and then with Manning and one of his boy detectives who joined them and proceeded to make animated contributions about something or other that, try as he might, Eddie couldn't overhear. At one point Manning looked up from the scrum and spotted Eddie in the doorway to the conference room. He held his gaze for a moment with a look that seemed curiously threatening. Manning was taking all this very personally, as if the money was going to come out of his own pocket.

When Bowling strode back into the room he cut straight to the chase. 'We'll give you seventy all up.'

'Make it eighty plus costs and you've got a deal.'

'Seventy plus costs and that's our final offer.'

Slick jumped forward and shouldered her lanky lawyer to one side. 'Done. Where do I sign?'

Eddie Moran scowled at his client as Walter Bowling QC handwrote the appropriate amendments onto the deed of settlement.

CHAPTER TEN

Slick was grinning like a Cheshire cat as she stuffed her copy of the settlement deed into her handbag. The solicitor had signed it on behalf of the Nominal Defendant with a bright assurance that she should have his client's cheque within a week. She was already working out how she would spend the money. Eddie struggled out of the conference room with his papers bundled under one arm and his briefcase in the other. He walked past her without a word.

'Where are you going?'

His pace slowed as he turned to face her, momentarily walking backwards. 'Back into court.'

'What for?'

'To cross-examine Thornton.'

She scurried to catch up with him. 'I thought you had a four-ten flight to catch.'

'There's another one tomorrow.'

As he reached the courtroom door she caught him by the sleeve of his suit-coat. He propped and turned to face her, this time with a genuinely bewildered look splashed across his face. Slick looked at him, equally uncomprehending.

'We just settled, didn't we?'

'Yeah.'

'They can't take it back, can they?'

'No.'

Eddie's eyes had a familiar, unfathomable look. She had seen it many times before. It appeared whenever he came up with some brainstorm which made him think he had everything worked out, or just about worked out, and he naturally assumed that it was as plain as day to the whole world, and everyone should know exactly what it was he thought he knew and where it was he thought he was going with it. But of course it wasn't clear to anyone but Eddie, because Eddie was a freak and his brain was somehow living on another planet and always had been, ever since he was a kid, and trying to keep up with Eddie when he got in one of these brainstorm moods of his was a nightmare. It was partly why he'd been in trouble all his life, at home, at school, around town. Eddie marched to the beat of his own drum and he didn't understand that other people couldn't hear it. Plus, he really didn't care if they couldn't; he just knew that they were wrong and he was right. And most of the time he was. That was what made Eddie Moran such an unbearable, obnoxious creep. That was why she loved him.

As she looked into his eyes now she knew there was no point in asking for explanations; he was incapable of providing them. His mind was spinning around somewhere, and he knew where he was going but if anyone needed to find out they were just going to have to follow him. All Slick knew was that as far as Eddie was concerned, the inquest wasn't over yet. There were some questions he had to know the answers to. Her compensation claim was settled, they didn't need to prove anything or find out anything. All that needed to be done was done; she would get her money now whatever happened at the inquest. But Eddie had some questions in his mind. The money didn't matter any more, the flight home didn't matter, he just had to know the answers. If she wanted explanations she was going to have to sit back in the passenger seat and watch what happened.

'Okay. So let's go back into court.'

Detective Phil Manning was discussing with the prosecutor and the other police how the evidence might be tailored somewhat now, in view of the fact that the only outstanding civil claim arising from the death had been settled by the lawyers, and therefore it looked likely that none of the witnesses or next of kin would be separately legally represented, when Moran dropped his briefcase and papers in an untidy heap on the bar table, and proceeded to arrange himself in preparation for the next session. When the clerk inquired politely whether all parties were ready to proceed, he announced they were, without reference to the police. The prosecutor dutifully took his place at the end of the bar table while Manning and the other police left the courtroom, scowling mistrustfully at the lawyer as they went.

Dr Thornton resumed his seat in the witness box, smiled politely at the coroner and cupped his fine white fingers neatly on the bench in front of him. Moran rose calmly to his feet.

'Doctor, the body of the deceased was received at the city morgue within hours of the car crash, is that right?'

'I believe so, yes.'

'But it wasn't until a day or more later that you conducted your examination?'

'That's right.'

'There were no ambient temperature readings or rectal temperature readings taken, so it's not possible to try and estimate an approximate time of death by reference to body temperature.'

'That's true.'

'All you can say is that he died at some stage between when he was last seen alive on the Tuesday afternoon and when his body was discovered at the crash scene in the early hours of that Wednesday morning.'

'That's right, somewhere within that roughly twelve to fourteen-hour period.'

'And you know he suffered a serious head injury and a narcotic overdose, but you can't tell us which one of those events led to his death.'

The doctor hesitated slightly, his lips stretching into a courteous smile.

'Well, they may both have been contributing factors, of course.'

Eddie held his gaze until the smile faded.

'What we do know is that he was stone cold dead when the paramedics arrived at the scene shortly after the collision.'

'Yes.' There was a slight tremor in the doctor's voice. 'They found him with pupils fixed and dilated.'

'Nevertheless they did endeavour to initiate revival procedures.'

'Yes, that would be standard procedure I would think.'

Eddie flicked through the coroner's brief until he found the page he wanted and pinned it to the lectern with one long, spindly finger.

'Well, I appreciate you probably haven't seen their statements, but if you'll accept from me for the time being that as part of those revival procedures they tried to insert a drip into the deceased's arm but had difficulty straightening the arm, and then had difficulty actually getting the line into the arm.'

'Yes.'

'In fact, according to their statements, they were ultimately unsuccessful in inserting the drip, and they proceeded directly to the hospital where the medical staff performed what is referred to as a cut-down.'

'Yes, that's an emergency procedure where the vein is accessed by actually cutting through the skin.'

'Thank you. And when the vein was located by that method, the doctor who performed the procedure discovered that the drip could not be initiated because the blood was clotting in the veins.'

'Yes, well, post-mortem clotting of the blood occurs within the vessels.'

'And the difficulties that the paramedics experienced would suggest that post-mortem clotting had commenced even as early as their arrival, isn't that so?'

'That's possible.'

'Indeed the difficulty in straightening the arm could suggest the onset of rigor mortis, couldn't it?'

'It could.'

Eddie kept his place in the brief with one finger as he flicked through and settled on another page.

'Likewise, both the paramedics at the scene and the doctors at the casualty ward checked the eyes for signs of any papilloedema which might signal raised intra-cranial pressure consequential to the head injury, and both found the fundi — that's the area at the back of the eye — quite white and drained of any blood in the vessels.'

'Right.'

'The doctor at the hospital noted,' Eddie ran his finger through the text as he read from it, 'that "the blood had drained to the back of the head and was pooled and clotted in that region."' Eddie leaned one elbow on the lectern and posed his question in a careful, measured way that suggested he was working hard to fit the pieces into place. 'Now, doctor, that suggests, doesn't it, that this deceased was lying somewhere face up for a period of time such that the blood naturally drained away from the eyes towards the back of the head, and he was in that position long enough after he died for post-mortem clotting to have commenced while he was still in that position.'

Dr Thornton gave the proposition several seconds of silent contemplation before he finally answered.

'Yes, that seems to be the case.'

'You wouldn't expect to see signs of post-mortem clotting and rigor mortis for at least an hour after death, would you?'

'Not normally, no.'

Moran nodded contemplatively.

'So given the observations the paramedics noted at the scene, it's most likely, isn't it, that this man was already dead for an hour or more before they even arrived on the scene?'

'I would think that's likely, yes.'

As Kirsten Foster looked at her lawyer she could almost hear the cogs whirring noisily and feverishly in his brain. Eddie had answered one question for himself and she had no doubt from what she saw that the answer somehow fitted neatly into the theory he had floating in his head.

'You found only the one external abrasion associated with the head injury, is that so?'

'Yes.'

'And associated with that evidence of external trauma, you found upon internal examination the presence of a fairly significant intra-cerebral haemorrhage.'

'Yes.'

'That's a bleeding into the brain tissue itself.'

'That's right.'

'And of course for that bleeding to occur the person must be still alive, because with death the heart stops pumping blood through the veins.'

'Well, there can be some draining of blood from the vessels after death, but certainly one wouldn't expect to see this level of bleeding after death.'

'Obviously this man received a severe blow to the head and then remained alive for a considerable period of time, possibly several hours.'

'Yes.'

'Of course you can't say whether he was unconscious or not.'

'I would think it very likely that the injury would have caused rapid loss of consciousness, at least for some period.'

Eddie paused again, this time leaning forward with both elbows on the lectern before continuing in an almost confidential tone.

'Is it possible that he was knocked unconscious and then subsequently injected with heroin?'

'Yes, it's possible.'

Moran straightened up quickly, as though he had the answer he'd expected all along, closed up his copy of the coroner's brief, dropped it on the bar table, then rifled through the other papers lumped untidily in front of him as he continued robustly with his questioning.

'The fact is, isn't it, doctor, that you found scarring on the deceased consistent with previous intravenous drug use?'

'Yes.'

'That scarring was all on his right arm, wasn't it?'

'Yes.'

Eddie pulled a photograph from the bundle of papers.

'I want you to have a look at this photograph of the deceased. It shows him holding a pen in his left hand, poised to sign a wedding register. Now I appreciate you know nothing of his habits in life, but I want to suggest to you that the deceased was left-handed.'

Dr Thornton squinted through his glasses at the colour photograph.

'Yes. Well, that's consistent with the scarring that I saw.'

'You found only one puncture mark on the deceased's body recent enough to be associated with the overdose he suffered on the night he died, didn't you?'

'Yes.'

'That was in the crook of his left arm.'

'Yes.'

'What does that tell you, doctor?'

The doctor sat upright in his chair and looked nervously at Mr Roly Roberts LCM, who peered back at him over his half-glasses. Then he looked over at the prosecutor, whose face was buried firmly in his brief, and finally he returned to the questioner, who was patiently awaiting his response.

'Well, it perhaps makes it somewhat less likely that the drug was self-administered.'

'It would be cumbersome and somewhat unusual for a left-handed drug user to inject into his left arm, wouldn't it?'

'I would think so, yes.'

Eddie Moran gripped the lectern with both hands and looked the doctor firmly in the eye.

'Dr Thornton, all of your observations of the deceased are consistent with this man having been severely assaulted and then subsequently administered with a lethal injection of heroin and left lying on his back until he died, perhaps an hour or more before his body was found in the wreck of that car in Kings Cross. Isn't that the case?'

'I certainly couldn't rule that out.'

Moran sat down and had started scribbling notes even before he got out the words confirming that he had no further questions.

CHAPTER ELEVEN

The young detective sent to fetch Phil Manning was absent from the courtroom for an inordinately long time. When he finally returned with Manning, the senior officer had a steel-hard edge to his countenance and looked like a man prepared to tough it out. Slick had no idea where Eddie Moran was heading with all this but there was something in Manning's scowl that suggested he did. Eddie showed no interest in him whatsoever, busily scratching notes while Manning passed behind him and stepped back into the witness box. While the coroner reminded Manning he was bound by his former oath Eddie kept on writing, and when the coroner invited further cross-examination he rose clumsily to his feet still finishing off his notes. He didn't even look up as he launched into his first question.

'Witness, we've just been told by Dr Thornton that it's possible this deceased was murdered by a lethal injection of narcotics.'

Now Eddie did look at the witness, his voice dripping with incredulity. 'What conceivable reason could you have had for disposing of the used syringe that was found alongside his dead body?'

It was a question clearly designed to unsettle Manning, but he looked equal to the challenge. He answered without hesitation, his voice strong and unfaltering as he glared at his interrogator.

'I didn't dispose of anything, Mr Moran.'

They were locked eyeball to eyeball and Manning's tone said he was beyond any criticism.

'The Darlinghurst police took possession of the exhibits. I wasn't called in until nearly forty-eight hours after the event. I never saw any syringe.'

Moran quickly flicked over several pages until he found what he was looking for.

'The exhibit room register from Darlinghurst shows a syringe was booked in with the other exhibits and was checked out when they went over to Petersham police station.'

'Well, the syringe wasn't booked in at Petersham.'

'I can see that, detective. But why?'

'I wouldn't have a clue. Overlooked by the uniformed police maybe. I don't know. But I can tell you I never got it.'

'But surely when you took the matter over, you checked what items were located at the scene.'

'No.'

'Why not?'

Moran was firing questions quickly now, each one jammed in behind the answer that preceded it. His tone was brash and the timing bullying, and with each exchange the resentment showed more patently on Manning's face.

'That was a matter for the police who attended the scene.'

'But the matter was handed over to you as an experienced investigator.'

'Yes.'

'Well, surely your first step was to find out what was located at the scene.'

'No.'

'Why not?'

'Didn't really occur to me, I suppose.'

'What?'

'I assumed the exhibits that were lodged at Petersham were all that were found.'

'Are you serious, detective?'

It was classic Eddie. Leaning awkwardly with one hand propped on its fingertips against the bar table, the other firmly on his hip holding back his crumpled coat, he squinted insolently at the witness, his top lip curled in mock derision. Slick still had no idea where he was heading, but she could see clearly that step one in Eddie's game plan was to get right up Manning's nose.

'You can't be, surely?'

The scowl on Manning's face turned into a snarl.

'Yes, I am.'

'You can't be.'

'I am.'

'You can't be, surely.'

'I am.'

Manning's face was flushed, his jaw set angrily.

'You've been a detective fifteen years, haven't you? A probationary constable in his first week out of the academy would know enough to question the uniformed police about what was found at the scene, wouldn't he?'

'I don't know, you'd have to ask one, wouldn't you.'

'Well, never mind a probationary constable; a kindergarten kid would work that one out, wouldn't he?'

'I don't know. Go ask one.'

'No, I'm asking you, detective.'

'And I've answered you.'

'No, you haven't.'

'Yes, I have.'

'You must have been told about that syringe.'

'Heard nothing about it.'

'You're not serious?'

'Course I am.'

'You can't be.'

'I am.'

'You couldn't possibly be.'

The prosecutor, who had been hovering nervously in his seat, waiting to finally convince himself that Moran had overstepped the mark, broke in at last, albeit somewhat hesitantly. 'Well, Your Worship . . .'

'Yes, Mr Moran.' Roly Roberts was looking down from the bench like a kindly grandfather speaking to a small child. 'I think you've probably covered that point, don't you?'

Eddie didn't even look up; he moved seamlessly onto a new point, leaving Manning still grappling angrily with the issue just abandoned. For half an hour he pressed on with his cross-examination relentlessly and disrespectfully, closely questioning the witness about procedures involved in collating and recording exhibits at crime scenes and fatal incidents, the records of the police personnel attending the scene, what the documents revealed about how and where exhibits had been located, handled, transported and recorded, what the guidelines were, what procedures had been put in place, which had been followed and which ones ignored. The questions were posed in what was undoubtedly Eddie's most obnoxious manner, which by any lofty standard was objectionable, and as the cross-examination proceeded Manning grew increasingly frustrated and belligerent, his answers becoming ill-considered reflex swipes at his examiner.

Eddie could see that Manning had stopped thinking. He wasn't being careful any more; he was angry and insulted and he was looking for whatever cheap shot he could find to put one on Eddie's chin. Now was the time to up the ante.

'Detective Manning, you're an associate of Mr Fred Hunter, aren't you?'

The question clearly took the witness by complete surprise. He stopped dead, gasping for an answer.

'So?'

It was a particularly dumb answer and Eddie loved it. When you'd seen the inside of as many courtrooms as Edwin C Moran, you knew that it paid to come prepared, know your facts and never ask a witness any question that you don't already know the answer to. But sometimes you don't already know, and you've got to find out, so you go with your gut feeling and you take a punt. Eddie had no idea what, if anything, Fred Hunter had to do with Trevor Ellowe's death or whether he was mixed up with Manning and, if so, how or why. But he knew enough to want to ask the question. He also knew that if Phil Manning denied knowing Hunter, or couldn't recollect ever making his acquaintance, Eddie was stuck with the answer, whether it was true or false, because he hadn't a single document or shred of evidence to prove otherwise. That meant he had to get the truth first up, and work from there. And Eddie knew you didn't necessarily always get the truth from a cautious man like Detective Manning, particularly when he was lounging in the security of his comfort zone. You had to get him out, pushing and shoving, stir him up a bit. That's when he was likely to do something stupid — as Phil Manning had just proved.

'So ...' Eddie leafed through several pages of the brief until he came to one that had nothing whatsoever to do with anything, then pretended to read it carefully while Manning waited and wondered what intelligence the document might hold regarding his relationship with Fred Hunter. 'So what say you explain to His Worship the circumstances of your association?'

It was a game of blind man's bluff. Manning couldn't know how much, if anything, the lawyer knew. All he knew was that Moran had somehow found out he knew Hunter, and he had in front of him a document that could potentially prove him wrong if he told any lies about his dealings with Hunter.

'I've worked for him a couple times, years ago, that's all.'

Moran looked up from the page. His raised eyebrows said he had information that could trap Manning on his answer.

'You're not suggesting you haven't seen him since you worked for him?'

'No, I still have a beer with him occasionally. We're friends.'

'When did you last see him?'

'Can't remember.'

'Did you see him around the time of Trevor Ellowe's death?'

'Wouldn't have a clue.'

Manning was starting to slip back into his comfort zone: questions about casual meetings months ago could be answered non-committally without danger of serious criticism if the answers were proved to be wrong. Eddie needed to get back to more specific information before Manning realised he had nothing.

'Alright. Explain to His Worship the work you did for Mr Hunter.'

'Just a bit of part-time labouring as an offsider on one of his trucks. In those days police were allowed to do extra work.'

'How did you come to get that work?'

Manning shifted uncomfortably in his seat. Eddie could see the witness was considering lying, so he held his gaze with a confidence that said he had the answer written on the page in front of him.

'I was introduced to him by a mutual friend.'

It wasn't the fact of the introduction that was causing Detective Manning such apparent discomfort, so it had to be the identity of the mutual friend.

'Who was that?'

Manning swallowed hard then spat the answer out.

'Roger Baston.'

The name was familiar to everyone in the courtroom. At the mention of it the coroner aimed a casual glance over his glasses at the witness, while the prosecutor kept his head down and his eyes fixed firmly on the brief in front of him. Eddie Moran hadn't lived in Sydney since his teens but even he knew of the infamous Roger Baston. Baston's name had featured in New South Wales news stories and court cases for more than a decade and in recent years had been linked to allegations of suspected police corruption and extortion. The controversial Sydney detective had resigned from the police force some years earlier in the wake of sensational allegations about him in a ransom-kidnap trial, and the well-publicised but ultimately fruitless investigation which followed had done nothing but heighten public indignation over the hefty superannuation payout he received when he left the job. The spotlight had followed him into civilian life when his high-profile inquiry and collection agency was contracted by several major real-estate developers to stand up to militant building unions in Sydney's inner west, and later when his name was connected to largely uncorroborated stories of extortion and corrupt dealings with members of the New South Wales Police Force. It was a name synonymous with controversy, particularly in this town, and Manning's obvious reluctance to mention it, although no doubt understandable, somehow made it even more significant, and clearly sparked new interest by the coroner in Eddie's line of questioning.

'You mean Roger Baston, the disgraced ex-New South Wales police detective?'

'I object, Your Worship.' It was a reflex reaction to Moran's inflammatory language and the prosecutor surprised even himself with the vehemence in his voice.

'I withdraw the word "disgraced". Are we talking about ex-detective Roger Baston?'

Eddie had made his point. If there was anyone who hadn't known who Manning was talking about before, they certainly did now. As the prosecutor sat back, privately congratulating himself on his new-found vigour and the victory of his objection, Moran pressed on, exploring in detail the relationship between Manning and the controversial Mr Baston.

The witness started shakily, like a man with something to hide and everything to lose, stumbling over his answers about how he had first met Baston when he was a young detective in the Armed Robbery Squad and how they had become friends, how as a young police officer with a young family he could always use a few extra dollars to pay the bills, how in those days the

Commissioner had no objection to police taking on casual employment in their spare time, how Baston had introduced him to Fred Hunter and how he had done a few isolated jobs labouring for Hunter Transport. But as the evidence proceeded Manning became more confident. He had nothing to be ashamed of and nothing to hide in having befriended his workmate and superior officer. Nothing had ever been proved against Roger Baston, so why shouldn't he have continued the association after Baston left the force? Yes, he was still friendly with ex-detective Baston, he still had a beer with him from time to time, just as he did with lots of people, even lawyers. Manning was starting to relax, his arm once more draped comfortably across the wooden partition of the witness box, a renewed authority returning to his voice and colouring his answers. Still Eddie pressed on, filling in the detail, carefully charting the history of the relationship, until finally the prosecutor applied his rediscovered self-confidence.

'Your Worship, I can't see what the witness's friendship with Roger Baston has to do with anything.'

It was clear from the lazy way Mr Roberts LCM peered down at Eddie from the bench that he was starting to lose interest.

'I won't pursue it, Your Worship.'

A self-congratulatory smirk lit the prosecutor's face. He was starting to pin back this half-smart lawyer: this was the third objection he had raised and the third that had been successful. This fellow was raising a lot of smoke-screens and carrying on with a whole lot of irrelevant nonsense, but he wasn't going to get away with it any more.

Eddie Moran paused briefly to clean his glasses and slid them back onto his face as he resumed.

'The point is, it was ex-detective Baston who introduced you to your erstwhile part-time employer Fred Hunter.'

'That's right.'

'A man that you still have a friendly association with to this day.'

The prosecutor jumped to his feet again. 'What's his friendship with Fred Hunter got to do with anything?'

This time Eddie didn't look at Roly Roberts. He didn't look at the prosecutor either. He kept his eyes fixed firmly on Detective Phillip Manning and boomed his next question at the witness in a loud, accusatory voice that filled the courtroom and jolted the coroner to attention.

'You can answer that question for him, can't you, witness? You can tell us the relevance of your friendship with Mr Fred Hunter, can't you?'

The witness looked back at him sourly, his eyes laced with distrust.

'I don't know what you're talking about, Mr Moran.'

'I'm talking about the fact that your friend Mr Hunter was the last recorded person to speak to Trevor Ellowe prior to his death.'

'Was he?'

Eddie Moran met his gaze and held it silently before continuing in a quieter tone.

'Well, you tell me, Mr Manning. You got copies of the deceased's mobile phone records, didn't you?'

'Yes.'

'And they showed that his last recorded call was made at 1:12 a.m., a little more than two hours before his body was found.'

'Yes.'

'And the number shown in the records as the recipient of the call is a mobile phone service registered to Fred Hunter.'

Manning tugged uncomfortably at his collar.

'Is it?'

For some unfathomable reason he hadn't anticipated that Eddie would have checked the telephone records, and now his brain was scrambling frantically to keep up with events.

'You know it is, Detective Manning.'

Moran's voice was quiet and self-assured, intended to convey that there was no way out. He paused briefly, long enough to give the witness time to think about that proposition, but not long enough for him to make the wrong decision. 'We both know it would be ludicrous to suggest that you police didn't check that number out.'

'Yes ...' Manning shifted nervously in the witness box, like a man sitting on a nest of ants. 'I think we probably did. I can't really remember.'

'And when you did you'd have discovered it was Hunter's mobile phone, I suggest.'

'We might have, yes.'

'Might have?' The lawyer's voice was laden with disdain. 'Well, assuming you did check, detective, and assuming you did discover it was your friend Fred Hunter's phone, did you go and see him to find out what it was that he and Ellowe were talking about at one o'clock in the morning, about two hours before Ellowe mysteriously wound up dead?'

'No.'

'Why not?'

'I didn't consider it relevant.'

'Didn't consider it relevant?' Eddie was leaned over the bar table again, squinting contemptuously at the witness. 'The records suggest that they spoke together for four and a half minutes. Weren't you interested in what they were talking about for four and a half minutes at that hour of the morning?'

'No.'

Moran shook his head incredulously as he rifled through the file beside him and pulled out a copy of the telephone accounts.

'Of course this wasn't the first time Mr Hunter's number showed up in the telephone records, was it?'

'No.'

'No, it's a number that features quite regularly in the accounts throughout the three-month period preceding Mr Ellowe's death, isn't it?'

'Yes.'

'Did you ever ask Mr Hunter about any of those calls?'

'No.'

'Why not?'

'I couldn't really see any need to, Mr Moran.'

'Do you have those phone records available to you now? I want to ask you about three entries in particular.'

Manning froze for a moment, then nodded tentatively and reached down for the slim leather briefcase at his side. Flipping it open he slipped out several sheets of paper and placed them on the bench in front of him.

'On the Wednesday night preceding his death, Ellowe telephoned your friend Hunter at approximately 10:35 p.m. Is that correct?'

'Yes.'

'That's pretty late to be ringing someone.'

'Could be. Some people stay up later than others.'

'Did you ask Hunter what that call was all about?'

'No.'

'On the Thursday before that Ellowe made another call to Hunter, this time at close to midnight.'

'Yes.'

'Ask him about that call?'

'I didn't speak to Hunter about any calls.'

'What about the one on the Monday before that? At 11:16 p.m. Did you ask him about that one?'

'I told you, I didn't talk to him about any calls.'

Moran pulled the lectern to him and leaned forward on it on his folded arms, his voice confidential once again.

'What are these late-night calls between the deceased and your friend Mr Hunter all about, Detective Manning?'

'Wouldn't have a clue.'

'Then why not ask him? He's a friend of yours — why not ring him up and ask him?'

'Why should I?'

'Why should you?' Eddie stood bolt upright again, waving his arms theatrically. 'Because here you found a peculiar pattern of late-night telephone conversations between these two men, ending with Ellowe's call to Hunter on the night of his death — apparently the last call that he ever made. Surely it was worth a phone call to your mate Fred Hunter to find out what it was all about?'

'Well, you call it peculiar, but as I said, some people stay up later than others and if Ellowe's in the habit of making late-night calls, so what?'

'But Ellowe wasn't in the habit of making late-night calls.' Eddie snatched the telephone accounts from the bar table and waved them in the direction of the witness. 'In fact, the accounts suggest he rarely used his telephone after about 6 p.m. If you look at them you'll notice that on the three occasions I've mentioned to you today, he made only two calls after 5 p.m. on each occasion, isn't that so?'

'Yes.'

'And it was to the same two numbers on each occasion, wasn't it?'

'Yes.'

'On each occasion the last call of the night was to Fred Hunter.'

'Yes.'

'And it always immediately followed a call

made by Ellowe to another number listed to the land line of a residence at Petersham.'

Manning's anger and defiance had drained away, leaving him open-mouthed and vulnerable.

'I'm not sure we had that information.'

'The subscriber to that number is a man by the name of Michael Wiltshire.'

Manning closed his mouth and swallowed.

'That could be right. I'm not sure.'

Kirsten Foster was on her feet, making her way to the bar table half-crouched like a soldier crossing 'no man's land'. Eddie anticipated her arrival and dropped the telephone accounts onto the table in front of her, pointing one long finger to a number that she recognised instantly. Trevor Ellowe had called the Old Priory mansion at precisely 10:33 p.m. on the Wednesday before he died. The call was recorded as lasting just under a minute. Almost immediately following that call, Ellowe had called another number. When Kirsten flicked to the photocopy of the subscriber records she saw instantly that Eddie had highlighted the number and the name of the subscriber: Frederick Hunter. She flicked back to the telephone accounts: there on the previous Thursday was the second call. Trevor had called Michael Wiltshire at 11:53, spoken to him for about thirty seconds, and then immediately telephoned Fred Hunter. On the Monday before that the call had lasted just a little longer, followed once again by an immediate call to Hunter. What did it all mean? What was going on between Trevor and Michael Wiltshire? What did Fred Hunter have to do with it? Was any of this related to Trevor's death? Kirsten had no idea that Trevor knew Michael Wiltshire; she'd never heard him mention her employer's name and she'd never told Michael anything about her ex-husband. She'd heard stories about Fred Hunter, but she didn't know him, and she'd never heard either her boss or her ex-husband mention him. Her confused thoughts were permeated by Eddie Moran's irreverent voice still barking in the background.

'In any view, this was a peculiar pattern of phone calls, wasn't it? You must have checked this out?'

'No, we didn't.'

'You must have.'

'We didn't.'

'Well, why didn't you?'

'It didn't occur to me as relevant.'

Eddie groaned and huffed and threw documents around the bar table, complaining to the coroner that these issues were clearly relevant to any proper coronial investigation and that the inquest could not hope to effectively explore the circumstances of the death of Trevor Ellowe without hearing from both Hunter and Wiltshire at the very least, and probably Roger Baston, who undoubtedly could shed some light on the nature of the relationship between Hunter and the investigating police officer. The prosecutor leapt to his feet, complaining bitterly about suggestions that there had been any impropriety on the part of Detective Manning, and Eddie returned fire, while the soothing voice of Roly Roberts broke in from time to time exhorting everyone to settle down. The witness looked on expressionless, his eyes glazed over as though he had just taken a particularly heavy knock.

It was all a blur to Kirsten. She heard Eddie ask the coroner to issue summonses to Hunter, Wiltshire and Baston to appear the following day to give evidence of what they knew about Trevor Ellowe and the circumstances of his death, then the prosecutor responding that this was all a beat-up by Mr Moran and the witnesses had absolutely no relevance whatsoever, and in any event there was insufficient time available to have subpoenas served on them and provide them with the notice required by legislation.

Then there was silence.

Mr Roberts LCM looked troubled. A copy of the telephone accounts had been handed up to him and he was leafing through the document, closely studying its contents. Finally he laid it flat on the bench in front of him and addressed the bar table.

'I won't make an order now. I want to give the matter some consideration overnight. In the meantime I'll stand Detective Manning down.'

The coroner had hardly got the words out before Manning was on his feet and out of the witness box. Kirsten Foster was still recovering from the shock, doing her best to process the information that had just been thrust upon her, unprepared for what was to come next. Roly Roberts leaned over the bench, peering down at the prosecutor.

'Sergeant, are there any further witnesses available this afternoon?'

The prosecutor had already started shaking his head when Manning reached him at the bar table and bent to whisper instructions. After a brief muffled confabulation, he struggled to his feet. 'Apparently there is one further available witness who should be quite brief, Your Worship. A Ms Bagley — she was a girlfriend of the deceased at the time of his death.'

Eddie detected audible rustling from where his client was sitting in the gallery behind him as Ms Bagley sauntered in confidently several minutes later and sashayed down the stairs bordering the public gallery. He turned and couldn't help but notice the intensity with which Slick was following the woman's every move. They weren't bad moves either. Ms Bagley clearly knew what her best assets were and fully understood the power of advertising. Her low-cut knit top and tight skirt showed off a body that jiggled and swayed magnificently, the focus of every male eye in the room. As she stepped into the witness box, Roly Roberts LCM nodded and smiled like an old pervert with a pocketful of boiled lollies.

Up close, with her shapely hips hidden by the witness box and the rest of her still and less distracting, Wendy Bagley looked a little older than at first sight. Eddie put her in her mid to late thirties, older than her dear and recently departed. Her hair was too blonde to be natural and the thick black eyelashes and long painted nails gave her a distinctly dangerous aura. She had a kind of hungry, demented look in her once-pretty green eyes which Eddie had seen before in desperate women who were usually well past their prime. They wore it like a sign that cautioned the young and foolish: DANGER — DO NOT ENTER. It didn't surprise Eddie that Trevor Ellowe had been too thick to heed the warning.

She gave her evidence dramatically, as Eddie had expected she would from the moment he first saw her, sighing and pausing to contain her grief at all appropriate opportunities. She was a barmaid by profession, and had worked at several inner-city hotels during the past decade or more. She had met the deceased when she was working at the Newington, where he had been a regular, and they first became intimate about five years ago when he was still living with his wife. He often came to her flat in Stanmore when she wasn't working or stayed the night with her after she had finished at the pub. When he split with his wife he moved into her flat for about two weeks, but then moved out again, and after that they had been 'on and off' from time to time.

She had run into him by chance on Crystal Street in Petersham the afternoon two days before his death, and they had spent the next few hours in the saloon bar of the Oxford before going back to her flat where they spent the night together. The next morning Trevor was up late and left her flat shortly before midday, saying he'd made arrangements to meet a couple of mates for a counter lunch at the Royal Shield. They had talked about maybe doing something later on that evening and he said he'd call her. Just before three that afternoon he rang to say it looked like he'd be jammed that night but he would drop back round to her place in the morning. She never heard from him again.

It was uncontentious evidence from the last known person to have seen the deceased alive. There was nothing much to ask her, but as Eddie scribbled a note to remind himself to find out if Manning had made any investigations at the Royal Shield Hotel, he was wondering what effect all this was having on his client. The revelation about Ellowe ringing her beefcake boss was one thing, but Eddie knew the evidence from Wendy Bagley about her fling with Trevor would be really hurting Slick. She was normally a smart girl, just about as switched on as they came, but not when the subject turned to Trevor Ellowe. The day she met the bloke she had seemed to take her head right off and put a pumpkin on instead, and it had been that way ever since. Eddie could understand it in a way, particularly in the early days when Trevor was young and fit and had the movie-star good looks. But it didn't make it any easier to see a smart cookie like Slick made a fool of by a pork chop like Trevor.

'Ms Bagley, did the deceased mention the name Fred Hunter to you?'

The young prosecutor obviously intended it as a masterstroke that would defuse the earlier controversy, but it backfired on him.

'Yeah, he'd been working for Fred, he reckoned.'

The questioner paused, somewhat deflated, before he tried again.

'Did he ever mention the name Michael Wiltshire?'

'Don't think so.'

A look of relief washed over the prosecutor's face and he moved ahead more confidently now to make his point.

'That name Wiltshire doesn't mean anything to you?'

'No.'

'You never heard the deceased talk about ringing up a Mr Wiltshire, or having any dealings with a Mr Wiltshire?'

'No.'

The prosecutor looked up at the coroner and then over at Eddie, who ignored him, then sat down with a satisfied look as though he had achieved at least a minor victory.

Without waiting for an invitation from the coroner, Eddie jumped to his feet and rattled off his cross-examination in a manner that suggested the answers were both elementary and inevitable.

'According to your evidence, Ms Bagley, you hadn't seen the deceased for several months prior to your meeting on Crystal Street, is that right?'

'Yeah, that's right.'

'So you weren't with him on the night he died, or on the previous Wednesday, or the Thursday before that, or the Monday before that?'

The witness screwed up her face comically, as if totally bewildered.

'No.'

'So you wouldn't have a clue whether he rang Michael Wiltshire, or Fred Hunter, or anybody else for that matter, on any of those nights?'

'No.'

'Thank you.'

Moran sat down and waited while the prosecutor conferred *sotto voce* with Detective Manning then announced to the coroner that there were no more witnesses that afternoon.

Roly Roberts LCM sat silently for several long seconds, apparently deep in thought, before he finally stirred.

'Adjourn the court.'

As everyone rose to their feet and shuffled their papers together, waiting for the coroner to rise, he obviously had an afterthought. 'Oh, Sergeant ...' He looked at the prosecutor thoughtfully and momentarily fell silent once again. 'You might like to have inquiries made as to the availability of at least Mr Hunter and Mr Wiltshire to give evidence in this matter before me tomorrow afternoon.'

CHAPTER TWELVE

Slick was nothing if not direct. Always had been, always would be. She couldn't help herself. It was all very well for Eddie to swear her to secrecy and make her promise not to speak to her employer about what had happened in court that day, but now that she had heard what she had heard, now that she had so many unanswered questions spinning around in her head, how could she just sit back and mildly wait and see what happened the next day? She had to deal with things head on: people or problems. Her mum used to say to 'call a spade a spade, and not a bloody shovel' and that was pretty much what Kirsten Foster did, so even as she dropped Eddie off at his hotel and listened to him repeat the warning that it was important to retain the element of surprise, she had little doubt that she wouldn't be waiting for some coroner to make up his mind before she got the answers that she needed. Besides, if Eddie wanted to lie in ambush for Michael Wiltshire, he'd have to lie alone.

As the big door opened little Simon Wiltshire's smiling face popped out from behind it.

'Hello, little big man.'

'Hello.'

Michael Wiltshire appeared in the hallway, his relaxed attire of T-shirt and jeans offset by an unfamiliar tension in his face.

'Hi, Kirsty, come on in.'

He attempted a smile but it was flat and humourless and as their eyes met he looked away self-consciously. Simon had her by one hand and was pulling her with all his weight towards the family room.

'I thought you weren't supposed to come today.'

'I wasn't. I'm just here to see your dad.'

'What for?'

'I just have to talk to him.'

'What about?'

Michael Wiltshire scooped his son up under one arm and carried him off towards the family room. 'Never you mind, champ. You just finish that homework. Kirsty and I'll be in the kitchen.'

As Kirsten walked alone into the spacious kitchen it felt cold and stark to her for the first time. There was a pile of diced vegetables on the chopping board and a half-empty glass of ice and spirits sitting alongside a whisky bottle on the corner of the bench. Michael Wiltshire was no drinker. She gathered up the peelings in her hand and flipped the waste bin open. She was remembering how Michael and Simon had unexpectedly moved out of the house for several days around the time of Trevor's death. He had telephoned her to say that something had come up and he was taking Simon to the beach house up at Palm Beach for a few days; he would pay her usual wages for the time they were away and they would both see her next week. His voice had sounded strangely distant and distracted and she had hoped there was nothing wrong. The next day the police rang to tell her about Trevor's death.

As she brushed the peelings off her hand into the bin she felt a nervous flutter in her stomach and asked herself what she was going to say to him. Where would she start? Would she just tell him what had happened in the court? How much did he already know? Or was there anything to know? Was it all some sort of ludicrous coincidence with a perfectly simple explanation and she was about to deeply insult her boss by implying he was somehow connected to the murder of her husband? Not that she'd ever been afraid to insult any boss who deserved to be insulted. But Michael Wiltshire wasn't just her boss. There was something more developing between them: friendship, at least. He had been kind to her; she had come to know him as a courteous, generous employer, a loving father to his son, a truly gentle man. They had certainly become friends, and she realised now that she had hoped, at least subconsciously, that someday there might be something more. Sometimes, when they were all together in the house, it was almost as though they were a family, living a normal life, just as she had once thought she and Trevor would. What now? How could she start to tell a friend that she had heard things about him that disturbed her, that posed questions she couldn't answer, that made her suspicious of him? And what exactly had she heard? What did she suspect — that Michael Wiltshire had killed Trevor, or that he had conspired with Hunter or someone else to do it, or perhaps that all three of them were mixed up together in some sort of sinister dealing that ended up costing Trevor his life? It made no sense at all. The more she tried to pin it down, the sillier it seemed. But it was there nonetheless, and she had to deal with it.

Hearing his footsteps in the hallway, she snatched up the glass of whisky and drained it in several bitter swallows. The fumes swam around her head as Michael faced her in the kitchen, his eyebrows raised at the sight of the empty glass cupped in her hands.

'Michael, I've got to tell you what happened to me in court today, and I need you to tell me what you know and what the hell's going on.'

She blurted it out breathlessly, a long soliloquy about the day's proceedings, how she had once been married to Trevor Ellowe, how he had died in a car crash in the Cross, how when Michael had seen her that morning she was actually going to court with her lawyer for the coroner's inquest, how the evidence had fallen out, how the police had thought Trevor was killed in the crash but now it looked like someone might have murdered him, and how Eddie had discovered from the telephone accounts that Trevor had been ringing Michael's number late at night for weeks before his death.

As she spoke Michael listened silently, pensively, propped against the kitchen bench, his eyes trained on a spot somewhere in the middle of the floor and his brow knit deeply in concentration, carefully processing all the information as it flowed. As she spat the story out she watched for his reaction, but he stood motionless, seemingly unchallenged by anything she had to say. When she was finished he crossed the kitchen, pulled a new glass from the cupboard and offered up the whisky bottle. She held out the glass she had emptied and he poured in several swallows.

'So you know what, Michael?' Kirsten gulped back a mouthful of the whisky. 'I've just got to know what's going down here with you and Trevor and this other Mr Hunter guy, 'cause this whole thing is driving me insane, y'know?'

Michael lifted the glass to his lips and took a long, careful sip. His eyes were on her now, thoughtful, wary, intense. They were burning with a cruel strength she hadn't seen before.

'He was obviously the one.'

She waited for an explanation, searching his expressionless face as he took another deep swig of the whisky and swallowed it down. She could feel that sad, hollow feeling in her stomach that came only when the news was going to be bad and sensed the beginning of a tiny tremble tickling her chin. She pursed her lips to steady it. She wasn't going to cry; she was going to muscle up, tough it out, get the answer one way or another. Michael Wiltshire took another sip of whisky before he finally spoke.

'I'd been getting late-night phone calls. Some guy kept ringing, threatening to break my legs. I didn't know who it was. I didn't really take it all that seriously. I guess now it must have been this guy, your ex-husband.'

'Why would Trevor want to do that?'

'I don't know. You tell me.'

'Didn't he say?'

'No.'

'Didn't you ask?'

It was an obvious question and it demanded an answer. She was looking deep into his eyes, searching for the truth. His gaze fell away and he shook his head disconsolately.

'Look, there were some things happening at that time.'

'What things?'

Her tone was demanding; he was avoiding answering questions she deserved to have answered — *had* to have answered. When he looked at her again his face was stamped with cold resolve. 'Just things, Kirsty — I can't tell you.'

'You weren't at the court by accident today.' There was a faint waver in her voice and her eyes were glistening with tears.

'No. But I had no idea he was your ex-husband.'

A tear broke free and rolled down her soft white cheek. She sniffed, rummaged through her handbag and then daintily dabbed a tissue at one eye.

'How did you connect him with the man who'd called you?'

'That I can't tell you.'

The teary eyes narrowed, but she still looked more hurt than dangerous and her voice wavered perilously.

'Michael, I need to know the truth about how Trevor died.'

'I'm sorry, Kirsty. I can't help you.'

'Why not?' It was little more than a whisper.

'I can't, that's all. I'm sorry, I just can't.'

Slick lifted the whisky glass to her lips, drained its contents and then indelicately spat the ice cube back into the empty vessel. Placing it firmly on the bench beside her, she flicked a mock salute at Michael Wiltshire, sniffed in a reviving breath and strode out of the kitchen. She blinked away the moisture in her eyes as she walked to the front door, determined not to hesitate, not to look back. She swung the door open and felt the cool refreshing night air on her face.

'Kirsty. Are you going home now?'

She looked back into the dimly lit hallway where little Simon was wandering after her. 'Yes, sweetie.'

'Can you read me a story before you go?'

She crouched down to his eye level and gently brushed his soft blond hair to one side with her fingertips. 'Not tonight, little man.'

There was a sadness in his innocent eyes that made her wonder if they both knew she would not be back. As she leaned forward to kiss his cheek he wrapped his arms around her and held her tightly. She felt a painful emptiness in her chest as she buried her face in the nape of his neck and breathed in his familiar fragrance. He was the baby she had never had, perhaps never would. Bitter tears welled in her eyes, blurring her vision and spilling onto her face as she pressed her lips against his little ear and whispered, 'I love you, darling.'

As Michael Wiltshire walked towards them down the hallway Kirsten took the little boy's face in her hands, kissed him firmly on the cheek, then hurried out the door and down the front steps. Wiltshire squatted down behind his son, wrapping his strong arms around the little boy, and they watched together as she wrestled open the front gate, clambered into her compact car and noisily sped off, into the darkness and out of their lives.

They stayed there for a long time, looking out into the night, Simon asking questions about why Kirsty seemed so sad and his father doing his best to give reassuring answers, ultimately diverting his son's attention to more pleasant subject matter, such as the beauty of the night sky and a discussion of the constellations and the cycles of the moon. When finally the boy nodded wearily and laid his head against his father's broad chest, Michael carried him inside to the warmth and safety of the home that they still shared.

Simon was already taking long, deep slumberous breaths when Michael tiptoed from his room, flicking off the light and easing the door closed. He walked directly to the lounge room, scooped up the telephone receiver and punched in a familiar number. When he heard the answer he spoke softly in the silence of the empty room.

'Sharpey, it's me, Michael. I need to speak to you urgently.'

* * *

Roly Roberts opened his front door to the smiling face of Gary Sharpe. It was not an unexpected visit. They shook hands warmly and exchanged pleasantries about how long it had been since they had caught up with each other and how busy life was for them both these days and how it was a shame the old crew didn't get together for a good lunch on a Friday any more. By the time he had greeted Mrs Roberts in the lounge room and charmed her with his usual witty repartee, and Roly had led him off into the study and closed up the double cedar doors, Sharpey had his older friend chuckling heartily with the latest gossip about who was misbehaving down in Sussex Street and with whom, and what the security cameras had caught an unwitting member of parliament doing in the Parliament House dining room. Life on the bench could be a solitary existence and Roly Roberts missed the camaraderie of his mates. He loved to catch up on all the news and scandal, and Sharpey knew it.

They shared a glass of Glenfiddich while Sharpe filled the lawyer in on what the Labor Party's polling was telling them about their prospects in the federal election, and where he thought the on-going ructions over the national leadership were likely to end up before the federal poll. Some of it was highly sensitive stuff, but they were old mates and Roly Roberts was one of the party's trusted friends. It was a friendship some said had served him well, taking him from a lowly suburban solicitor, carving a modest living out of wills and cottage conveyancing, to Local Court magistrate then state coroner. It was a highly esteemed position but Roly had remained ever-true to his humble working-class upbringing and his old Labor Party pals.

'I wanted to talk to you about my little mate Fred Hunter.'

When Gary Sharpe finally got to the point of why he had paid this visit to his old friend it came as no surprise to Roly Roberts. He had never met Fred Hunter but he had heard his name many times before and he knew he had a lot of friends in Sussex Street. He also knew that Michael Wiltshire was the son of his old friend Charlie Wiltshire, who had been a lifelong stalwart of the labour movement. Involving men like these in this inquest would cause a lot of people heartache and maybe even damage, probably unjustly. That was why he had delayed his decision till the morning; it was one of the issues he had wanted to consider carefully. And he wasn't surprised to have Gary Sharpe turn up offering him some friendly advice on the subject.

It wouldn't be the first time Roly Roberts had been asked to spare one of the party faithful the inconvenience of a taxi ride to Glebe, but Roly took his oath of office seriously and it was well-known that if the job needed someone there they got there, no matter who their friends might be.

But this was different: this was a drug death, one that even had a little sniff of possible foul play about it. In the Coroner's Court you couldn't mention drugs and politics in the same breath without stirring up a storm, and Fred Hunter's appearance at an inquest into an unexplained drug-related death in Kings Cross was sure to raise a flock of eyebrows in the press and add a very high-profile political dimension to the case. Roly had to be sure that he didn't go dragging a lot of good people into the headlines for no good reason but to sell newspapers and win votes for the conservatives.

'It's just a complete bloody beat-up, mate.'

Gary Sharpe had come prepared to argue his case. He took Roly Roberts through several photocopied pages that showed Ellowe had been employed by Fred Hunter until several weeks prior to his death, and went on to explain that he was laid off for absenteeism, no doubt associated with his drug-use, which of course his employer knew nothing about. Ellowe had complained bitterly about his dismissal but Fred Hunter, being a good old-style working man who expected an honest day's work for an honest day's pay, refused to reconsider. Ellowe didn't seem able to take no for an answer and started ringing Hunter at all hours of the day and night, protesting his sacking and claiming that he was still owed money by way of back pay and sick-leave entitlements.

'Of course it was all bullshit, but whenever he got on the juice this bloke'd jump straight on the blower and give poor old Fred an earful.' Sharpey was watching carefully for his friend's reaction as he threw in a quick burst of his trademark staccato chuckle. 'How'd you be, two o'clock in the morning you've got some spaced-out druggie in your ear whingeing about his holiday loading?'

Roly wasn't laughing, so Gary Sharpe got straight back to the facts.

'It turns out Fred wasn't the only one getting late-night calls.'

Sharpe flipped to the next photocopy, showing Michael Wiltshire's cheque butts for Kirsten Foster's babysitting wages on the three days when the telephone accounts had shown calls by Ellowe to the house at Petersham. Roly Roberts recognised the babysitter's name immediately as the deceased's widow.

'See, this bloody lawyer's trying to make out there's something sinister in Ellowe making calls to Michael Wiltshire's house, but he doesn't mention that Wiltshire wasn't even there. Ellowe was just all juiced up, ringing his ex-missus, probably giving her an earful just like he was Fred Hunter.'

Sharpe folded the photocopies and slid them back inside his coat as he continued his animated discourse on how the facts had been shamefully distorted. He spoke quickly and with unfailing conviction, inviting neither question nor comment from his older friend. He spoke about the fact that good men had to build a reputation over the course of a lifetime of honest deeds, how, when all was said and done, one's reputation was perhaps the most valuable and cherished of all one's assets, and how cruelly and quickly it could be destroyed by conniving or unthinking persons. He threw in for good measure mention of young Wiltshire's aspirations for a state seat, and how Labor had a fine tradition of supporting those who had been loyal, and the Wiltshire family's dedication to the cause of the working man would no doubt be rewarded with Michael's pre-selection for a safe seat. Of course he made no mention of the fact that it was that same fine tradition that had helped Roly Roberts to get where he was today, but they both understood that and there was no point in ventilating the obvious.

'I'm told this Moran bloke has a Tory background, might even have political aspirations himself.'

Roly Roberts looked at Gary Sharpe, his troubled brow deeply furrowed. The last thing he would want was to have his inquest manipulated to serve some grubby political agenda, and Sharpey knew it.

'All this joker's trying to do is turn the whole thing into a media circus and drag the Labor Party down into the dunny for no good reason whatsoever.'

* * *

As soon as Eddie saw the blotched eyeliner and the red eyes he knew Slick had dropped the ball on him. She'd been gone about two hours and he wasn't expecting to see her again that night. But now she was back and he knew why. She sailed through the piano bar, pushed her bottom up onto the stool beside him, snatched a cigarette from his packet and lit up.

'Shit. You did it, didn't you?'

'Well, what did you expect me to do?'

He had no answer. The truth was, if he'd stopped to think what Slick might do when she dropped him off he would have realised then she'd do just what she had: take matters into her own hands and try to find out the answers for herself.

'So what did he say?'

'He said some guy was ringing him and threatening to break his legs, but he never said why and he never said who he was.'

'Sounds like hogshit to me.'

'Well, thank you, Mr Sherlock bloody Holmes. You're a friggin' genius you are.'

Eddie took a swig of bourbon and watched the ice cubes swirl around as he gently jiggled the glass in both hands. Things would be tough tomorrow. Now Wiltshire knew where they were coming from and he was obviously pretty worried, or at least enough to have started telling lies already. That probably meant he'd be on the telephone to Hunter and they'd both be up all night, or as long as it took to get the story right. That was going to make this one a harder nut to crack. But then any nut will break, provided you can find a big enough brick to drop on it.

'Why, Eddie?' Slick plucked the whisky from the barman's hand as Eddie pushed a note across the bar. 'Why would Michael want to have anything to do with Trevor's death?'

'Husbands and lovers don't always get on that well together.'

'Fuck off, Eddie.' She shot a sour look in his direction and took another swig. 'The guy's never even made a pass at me.'

Eddie flipped his eyebrows. That answered one question he'd been dying to ask her. Maybe that was the real reason she was so steamed up. He watched as she gulped down several more swallows. She was doing it pretty tough, he could see that. But then it had been a big day for her, raking over Trevor's death, crunching compensation deals for more money than she'd ever seen in one place in her life before, and then the big bombshell about the boss and maybe boyfriend. Eddie moved closer and slid a comforting arm around her slender shoulders and she leaned her soft hair gently against his cheek.

'There are only two things'll get you killed in this town, kiddo. Sex and money. If this bloke hasn't tried to lay a tread on you, my guess is you can rule out sex. But it sounds like money's something he's got plenty of and you can bet he didn't earn it digging ditches.'

Slick sat up and delved into her handbag for a tissue, then dabbed her eyes and loudly blew her nose as Eddie pushed a cigarette into his mouth and clicked it alight.

'I rang a bloke before and got a bit of lowdown. Wiltshire's got a development approval in for a major townhouse complex at Marrickville, and according to everyone who knows anything Fred Hunter's got the council out there on a string. He and Wiltshire are both office-bearers on the local state branch of the Labor Party. My guess is they were cooking something up together and Fred was getting his man Trevor to do the legwork. Whether it's got anything to do with Trevor's death, who knows? Maybe we'll find out tomorrow.'

Slick pushed the tissue back into her bag and sniffed efficiently. 'I won't be there tomorrow.' She pushed out her chin and tried to blink away the lingering tears. 'I'm sick of all this, Eddie.' The tears welled again and the defiant chin began to tremble as she dived back into her handbag for the tissue. 'I'm sick of the shit Trevor's been dragging into my life for the past ten years. Sleeping around with the likes of Ms Wendy frigging Wonderbra or whatever her name is. Even now he's dead he manages to stuff things up for me. I don't want to hear any more about his dirty deals or his crooked friends. I just don't want to know any more.'

Eddie wrapped his arms around her and she pushed her face into his chest, sobbing quiet, private tears into his lapel. It seemed strange; he had never seen her cry before. He had seen her teary, dabbing moisture neatly and efficiently from her eyes as she had done at Trevor's funeral and one or two of her brothers' weddings, but it was always carefully contained. She was too tough a chick to ever lose the plot in front of anybody. When she was just a kid, try as Eddie and her brothers might they could do no better than reduce her to a seething, dangerous rage. No one could make Kirsty cry; it was a well-known fact. She was just too tough.

He held her for what seemed a long time as the pianist tinkled serenely in the background. As her breathing settled she leaned her body comfortably against his and they swayed gently to the rhythm of the soft piano music. He was thinking bemusedly about their first and only date, the disastrous evening they had spent stepping on each other's toes on the dance floor at her high-school graduation ball.

'You still dance as bad as you always did?'

She looked up at him with smiling, glistening eyes that were remembering the same terrible evening.

'Worse than ever.'

The pianist seemed to take encouragement as they walked together onto the compact dance floor. He buried his head in the keyboard, swaying his shoulders to the beauty of his music as Eddie Moran and his best mate's kid sister danced together to the gentle rhythm.

'Michael lied to me, Eddie.' She lifted her face from Eddie's shoulder and looked up into her old friend's eyes. 'I can't believe it. I thought he was such a decent guy.'

Eddie's smile was flat and philosophical.

'Sydney's a low joint, baby, you know that. Everyone's lying to someone about something in this town. Everybody's got an angle. That's life. The Rum Corps never left New South Wales. That's why we all love the place so much.'

'Yeah well, screw him.'

She looked almost angry again. The tears in her eyes weren't quite the seething, dangerous ones he remembered from her childhood, but there was more determination there than self-pity.

'You don't need him any more, kid. You're a woman of independent means now.'

'Yeah, screw him. I don't need his job.'

They danced on in silence for a while, her head resting comfortably against his shoulder. When she finally spoke it was a private murmur that barely rose above the hushed tones of the music.

'Sydney's a pit. I'm getting out of Sydney.'

It seemed to take a minute to sink in, before she looked up at Eddie with brighter eyes.

'You'd give me a job if I went up to live in Queensland, wouldn't you, Eddie?'

'Sure. You can come to the Gold Coast and be my nanny if you want to. So long as you don't mind wearing those skimpy black leotards with the little fluffy tail and the cute bunny ears.'

She dropped her head back on his shoulder. 'You're an arsehole, Eddie.'

'That's true. But you know I'll never lie to you.'

She looked up at him again, a sweet smile softening her face. 'That's why I love you.'

She stretched up and kissed him gently on the cheek.

'Yeah well, if you're thinking about trying to get me in the sack you're going to have to wait in line. Everybody loves me, kiddo, you know that.'

'That's because you're such an arsehole.'

'I know. It's great, isn't it.'

* * *

When the inquest into the death of Trevor Wayne Ellowe resumed the next morning before Mr Roly

Roberts LCM in the Coroner's Court at Glebe, Edwin C Moran appeared without his client.

The coroner opened proceedings by delivering his decision on the application made the previous afternoon by the legal representative of the deceased's widow, Ms Kirsten Foster. He noted for the record that it had been submitted on behalf of Ms Foster that answers given by the investigating police officer, Detective Manning, had revealed that there had been telephone contact between the deceased and one Mr Fred Hunter on the morning of the deceased's death and also during the weeks preceding his death and that Mr Hunter should therefore be called at these proceedings. He further noted that it had been also submitted that because telephone calls had been made by the deceased to a Mr Michael Wiltshire from time to time, Mr Wiltshire should also be called. He pointed out that police assisting the coroner had conducted extensive investigations into the circumstances of the death and there was nothing revealed by those investigations that in any way suggested that either Mr Hunter or Mr Wiltshire would be likely to be of any assistance to the coroner in arriving at a finding in relation to any of the matters of the subject of inquiry within the terms of the legislation. To require witnesses to attend and be examined at proceedings such as these merely on the grounds that they had had some telephone or other contact with the deceased in circumstances apparently unrelated to his death would not only be unnecessarily onerous upon those individuals concerned but would undoubtedly increase the court's time and costs without any likely benefit to the proceedings or the parties. Accordingly the application for orders requiring the attendance of Mr Hunter and Mr Wiltshire was denied.

The proceedings limped on somewhat uneventfully from there. Of course Eddie Moran made a nuisance of himself as best he could throughout the morning, but by the afternoon he too seemed to have run out of steam. When the inquest was adjourned indefinitely that same afternoon there was a familiar air of inevitability permeating the proceedings.

Ultimately the coroner returned an open finding. Trevor Ellowe had died as the result of a closed head injury most likely sustained in a single-motor-vehicle collision. A secondary cause of death was narcotics overdose. There was no evidence to justify a finding of wrongdoing by any party and no basis upon which to recommend criminal proceedings against any person. The investigation into the curious circumstances of the death of Trevor Wayne Ellowe was closed forever.

CHAPTER THIRTEEN

The ringing of Fred Hunter's mobile phone stirred him from a momentary slumber. As his eyelids bobbed open he glanced into the disapproving glare of his wife sitting alongside him in her best frock. He nodded, climbed out of his seat and made his way politely for the exit, secretly relieved to have been rescued. It wasn't that he hadn't been enjoying the occasion; it was just that speeches were harder to sit through the older he got, and academic speeches had never been easy, not for a humble working man who had left school in the eighth grade to pack crates and lift boxes. His father had worked the waterfront all his life, hauling freight up and down the wharves from Balmain to Woolloomooloo, until he keeled over dead one day and got no thanks for it, leaving a widow and nine hungry kids to make a go of it.

Fred Hunter had done just that: he'd made a go of it, and not a bad one by his estimation. He had a thriving business, more real estate than he knew what to do with, and three of the most beautiful kids that God had ever put breath into. He'd done alright for a wharfie's son. But formal education and academic speeches had played no part in it.

That was what made this one of the proudest moments of his life. Seeing his youngest daughter up there, all decked out in her academic clobber, sitting with the other kids waiting to graduate, lining up to be called on one by one to go up and shake hands with the head sharang and be handed their ticket while all these well-heeled, educated people looked on and applauded, made him realise just how far he'd come. It put everything into perspective, made it all worthwhile. It took the salt out of the tears he'd cried to see his mother working sixteen hours a day, cleaning floors and ironing other people's clothes; it took the sting out of the memories of icy mornings as a fourteen-year-old kid lifting boxes till his eyes were popping in his head and his hands were worn red-raw with cuts and blisters. It erased the bitterness of all those years struggling to survive and clawing his way out of the abject poverty that had been his only birthright.

It had also helped him to forget for a few hours the drama and controversy that had been turning his life upside down and driving him insane for the past few weeks. He'd seen enough mug journos and lairy newspaper headlines lately to last him a lifetime. Ever since one of his trailers got pulled up on the border with a load of dope strapped to the undercarriage the press had been buzzing around like blowflies round the bishop. They wanted to know how it got there, and who was the driver who'd bolted from the scene, and how come Fred didn't have his details if was he driving a Hunter Transport truck? How the hell was Fred supposed to keep tabs on every driver in his fleet? Half of them worked under bodgy names to dodge the tax, and anyway, who was to say it was the driver who strapped the dope to the trailer undercarriage? Anybody could have done it. There'd been lots of cases of drug-runners using long-haul trailers to do their dirty work for them. The press was bad enough, but now he had those bloody lawyers from the Royal Commission knocking on his door and wanting to interview him.

It was the worst possible timing. The Royal Commission into the Transport Industry had been conducting public hearings for just over a month, and was showing signs of winding up to a pretty uneventful close when Fred's truck got pulled up at the border. The former Labor lawyer and now currently serving Supreme Court judge Walter Bowling had been appointed to head up the inquiry, and it came as no surprise to Fred or anybody in the labour movement that Mr Justice Bowling hadn't showed too much interest in dragging the show out any longer than was absolutely necessary. The Royal Commission had been forced on the Labor government by public pressure mounted through the Tory-controlled newspapers, and if the party hadn't done something to quell the newspaper talk about the rorts and shonky practices that were said to be endemic in the industry, it could have done Labor some real damage at the next election. What was needed was a short, sharp public inquiry that flushed out a few bad eggs, put a little expendable blood on the floor and the public's mind at rest, and got things back on the track for business as usual, and His Honour Mr Justice Walter Bowling was the right man to deliver it. So far he was showing every sign of going through the motions: calling drivers, union reps and a few operators to talk about overloading and doctoring logbooks and some of the scams with the coppers and inspectors and suchlike, but nothing that was going to change the world — hardly enough to make the morning papers. Unfortunately that all changed when Hunter Transport, one of the state's biggest transport companies, was linked to a major heroin haul and suddenly questions were being asked about the involvement of its owner and well-known Labor Party stalwart Fred Hunter.

Fred didn't like drugs any more than the next bloke. But they were part of the scene nowadays. That was just the way the world was. You couldn't stick your head in the sand and pretend they didn't exist. You had to make a quid the best way you could. Fred didn't like cigarettes either, but that didn't mean he wouldn't haul them if there was a dollar in it.

So now he had those poofter lawyers from the Commission knocking on his door and telling him it was in his interests to provide them with whatever information he could. What crap! They ought to know better than to think Fred Hunter was ever going to talk to them. Any son of the waterfront knew well enough that what you don't say can't come back and bite you on the bum.

'You're heading for a fall, you bastard.'

It was a slow drunken drawl, growled into the telephone with a pathetic fading slur.

'Is that right?' Hunter knew the answer but he asked the question anyway: 'Who's this?'

'You know who it is.'

'Fuckin' wake up to yourself will you, Barry, y'idiot.'

'You killed my mate Tommy Attwell.'

A sudden bitter rage flooded Hunter's mouth and chest. He was sick of getting drunken late-night calls from Barry Dougherty. It had been nearly five years since Tommy Attwell had copped his flogging; since Dougherty had first accused Hunter of it and he'd told the silly old bugger to get his nose out of it and mind his own business. Five years since Dougherty had walked out on Hunter Transport with photocopies of all the books, and did his best to make as much trouble for Fred as he could. It was a pretty ordinary way of repaying thirty years of Fred carrying him, and if Hunter knew where to find him he'd have put one on Barry's chin a long time ago. He spat his answer back into the telephone.

'I've told you before, Tommy Attwell had a heart attack. Now you get off my phone and don't ring me again or I'll have the fuckin' coppers onto you.'

Barry Dougherty's voice droned on with a new hint of relish.

'Don't worry about that, I'll be talking to the coppers soon enough. I might not be able to prove what you done to Tommy, but I still got plenty on you, mate. Them Royal Commission blokes'll be real interested. You're heading for a big fall, don't you worry.'

'Yeah well, you want to be a bit careful you don't fall over yourself, Barry. You could get badly hurt.'

Hunter punched the 'no' button so hard he almost put his finger through the telephone. His surging blood pressure was poking needles through his prickling scalp and palms, and he could feel the powerful muscles in his jaw grinding his back teeth mercilessly. He wished he had that useless Barry Dougherty in the room now: he'd crush his ugly head down to a fine powder. How many times did he have to tell the bloke? When would he get it into his thick skull? What happened to Tommy Attwell was ancient history. It was none of his business and there was nothing anyone could do about it anyway.

* * *

'Sorry, Barry, that'll have to be your last.'

Barry Dougherty looked up from the cracked glass lying empty on the carpet between his feet. As the barman came into focus Barry's look of mild confusion firmed into abject disgust.

'What?'

'I think that'll have to do you for tonight, old mate.'

'What are you fuckin' talking about?' He steadied himself with one hand on the bar as the young man wiped it clean of the spots of beer and spittle he had sprayed with his response. 'I only just got here.'

Old Barry Dougherty was harmless enough. He always got in early and spent most of the afternoon on the pokies, drinking steadily and smoking cigarettes, sticking to the ten-cent machines and keeping his own company. He was never any trouble. When his mates came in, usually between four and five, they'd all sit together at the far end of the public bar, drinking quietly and yarning and causing no one any strife. Once he'd had a few, Barry always had plenty to say, big-noting himself about what a big wheel he used to be in the old days back in Sydney and all the flash, important people he supposedly knew down there. But he was no trouble. If you listened to Barry you'd think he was on first-name terms with every bigwig in the Labor Party from Gough Whitlam down, and personal mates with every gangster, copper, Flash Jack and politician in the town. But no one in Mackay was silly enough to listen much to Barry Dougherty. He was just another old bloke propping up the bar.

'Come on, Barry, I'll get you a cab.' It was the third glass Barry had spilled that night and Blind Freddy could see he'd had enough. 'You come back tomorrow and I'll shout you one.'

The old man was mumbling incoherently as the barman walked him to the door, one strong arm wrapped around his shoulder to support his unsteady gait and direct him out onto the footpath. He muttered something about the liquor laws and discrimination, and how the party would soon be cracking down on all these licensed clubs, but offered no resistance as the barman eased him onto the back seat of the taxi. The last he saw of him, Barry was sitting upright in the cab, his head hanging forward slightly, talking to himself.

When the taxi pulled up outside his house, Barry paid the fare with a twenty-dollar note and breathed beery fumes into the driver's face as he waited for his change. Then he wrestled the handful of coins into the side pocket of his baggy trousers and staggered off into the night. When the cab-driver left him, he was negotiating an unsteady course along the narrow cement path leading to the front door of the humble fibro house where he had lived for the past five years.

What happened after that no one could really say. It had been a cold, clear night with little or no moon to speak about. A light breeze blew in from the south until the early hours and then settled gently into a cool, breathless dawn. None of the neighbours remembered hearing anything abnormal through the evening or night; certainly nothing that could possibly explain the gruesome sight that confronted Mavis Winter when she went out for the papers the next morning.

Mavis had known Barry Dougherty most of her life. He was the older brother of the Dougherty girls she had gone to school with and Mavis remembered Barry working at the hardware store in town as a teenager. He'd left Mackay when he was still quite young, and although she had seen him once or twice over the years on the rare occasions when he came back to visit his family, and had spoken briefly with him at his mother's funeral, she knew little of the man until he came back to rent the house next door some five years ago. The Doughertys had never been particularly well regarded in the humble mid-north Queensland town of Mackay, and as a neighbour Barry soon lived down to the family name. He kept his doors closed and his curtains drawn, never gave much more than a cursory nod of greeting on his way back and forth along the crumbling cement path that led to his letterbox, and allowed the grass in his front yard to grow to atrocious lengths without the slightest thought of mowing it.

Still, for all his faults, Mavis would never have wished Barry Dougherty, or any other living soul, the fate that obviously had befallen him that night.

'I'd say that whoever he was running from finally caught up, ay.'

Sasha Kelly looked at the skinny, sun-dried little man leaning on the rickety front fence, shading his dark-circled eyes from the morning sun with a rolled-up copy of the Mackay *Post*.

'You knew him, did you?'

'Bit.'

The craggy-faced little man looked suddenly tentative, as if he might be getting into something he should best stay out of. Kelly held his gaze and nodded gently as she watched him work through it. He had something he wanted to say, she could see it in his eyes.

'Loved a beer on a hot day old Barry did, ay.'

Senior Sergeant Sasha Kelly had been on the scene for more than an hour now, watching and directing as the uniformed police and crime scene investigators picked carefully over the front yard and through the house. When the radio room first got the frantic call from the neighbour, Mavis Winter, and despatched the nearest mobile patrol crew to the scene, it didn't sound like too much. The sight of Barry Dougherty's twisted, dew-soaked body curled up amongst the weeds in the garden bed below his front verandah had shaken Mavis, but she hadn't touched him and she couldn't say what sort of shape he might be in. Even the narrow pool of coagulated, black-red blood caked around his head didn't necessarily mean they had a serious incident on their hands. It wouldn't be the first time since she came north that Sasha Kelly had known one of these old pensioners on his way home from the pub with a bellyful of beer and Bundy to not quite make it through the front door before deciding to sign off for the night. And sometimes when they went down, they went down hard. It was amazing the punishment they could absorb with a few under the belt.

But it didn't take the uniformed police too long to realise they had a problem. As they walked up the narrow cement path they could see the back of Barry's head, his thin hair covered with a shiny film of crusted blood. The body was pressed hard against the earth, legs bent and arms painfully askew. It had a peculiarly still and ugly quality that they recognised instantly. The first touch confirmed it. The constable felt the stiff chill of rigor mortis as he rolled one shoulder carefully back until he was looking into Barry William Dougherty's vacant eyes.

'He always reckoned they was after him, ay.'

Even at this early hour, and with both doors of the patrol car splayed open to catch what little breeze there was, the cruel north Queensland sun already had some bite. Kelly clicked the ignition on and the air conditioning whirred into operation.

'Who's they?'

'Nah, never said who.' Dougherty's old drinking companion stared absently into the air vent as cool air blew back in his face. 'But it was always like it was someone from down south, ay. Someone from his old Sydney days. Reckoned he come back up here to give them the swerve like.'

Crime operations had been working through the morning to get what they could on Dougherty's background but so far the information was all too sketchy. He was born and bred in Mackay but left in the late fifties, when he was about twenty-two. He married in Sydney in 1962, at which time his occupation was noted as 'clerk', and the same occupation appeared on his divorce papers in '83. He came back to mid-north Queensland about five years ago and settled in Mackay. So far they had nothing on his employment or known associates. They'd turned up a couple of minor gaming convictions back in the late sixties, and three drink-driving entries over a period of nearly fifteen years, two old ones in New South Wales and the latest a little over eighteen months ago in Bowen. So far they hadn't found any bad debts, jealous wives or unsettled arguments, nothing to give anyone a motive to give poor old Barry Dougherty a good crack on the scone. In fact, at this stage Sasha Kelly couldn't even be sure anyone had cracked him on the scone. He may just have had a nasty accident. It didn't look that way, though. He had a very ugly injury to his head: some blunt instrument had caved in his forehead and fractured his skull, opening up a deep tear in the skin from the hairline down, dissecting the eyebrows to the bridge of his nose. Something, an iron bar maybe, had hit him pretty hard and right where it was going to do most damage. But there was no weapon in sight, and so far no motive, just an interesting comment from a little man leaning on a fence.

'Excuse me, Senior Sergeant.'

Gerry Copeland was slouched over the car door looking straight down at her partially exposed breasts. Kelly stepped out of the car grappling with the top button of her blouse and wondering how it was that the male of the species could be investigating a violent death under the hot Queensland sun and still be thinking about breasts. What was it with these people? Even Copeland, who hated her with a vengeance and couldn't even find it in himself to use her Christian name; he always addressed her in that same resentful, condescending tone. She knew why. He'd made sergeant when she was still just a struggling senior connie and had considered himself a shoo-in for the job of OC of the Mackay Investigation Branch, until Sasha Kelly had been transferred north that previous summer. As far as Copeland was concerned, the Labor government's affirmative action policy was the only reason Sasha Kelly had come out of nowhere to pip him at the post, and it told in his voice.

'You might want to have a look at this.' The leather of the thin brown wallet in Copeland's broad hand was worn smooth and cracked with years of handling. 'Looks like his wallet. One of the uniformed boys found it on the footpath.'

Kelly carefully pinched one corner of the wallet and plucked it from Copeland's grasp. 'Anyone think about preserving prints maybe?' she snapped curtly as she dropped it into a plastic exhibit bag.

Copeland curled his lip disdainfully.

'Uniforms picked it up when they first got here. Went through about ten sets of hands before we even heard about it.'

Kelly wasn't interested in Copeland's explanations of his incompetence. She had already prised the wallet open through the plastic.

'No cash in it.'

'And no credit cards.'

'Did he own any credit cards?'

'Don't know.'

'Find out.'

Kelly hadn't intended to be quite so blunt, but then discretion and diplomacy were not her strongest suits. She'd fought too hard and put up with too much shit to worry about pandering to the sensitivities of the likes of Gerry Copeland and his mates from the old boys club. Making excuses and turning a blind eye for these clowns brought the whole force down; she'd realised that way back when she was still in uniform. She was just a kid still wet behind the ears when she went forward with her complaint about corruption in the CI Branch in Surfers Paradise, and back in those days the Gerry Copeland types had made her pay. In their eyes she had breached the unwritten code, breaking rank, speaking out against her workmates, so the old network made her life a living hell. If the Fitzgerald Inquiry into Police Corruption hadn't come along she may never have lasted in the force. But it did, and she was vindicated, and she'd thrived in the new post-Fitzgerald police service, and now at just thirty-two years old she was a senior sergeant and OC of the Mackay Investigation Branch. So she didn't care if the likes of Gerry Copeland thought she was a little blunt.

Besides, right now she had no time for please and thank you. She had a possible robbery motive. That meant she had to find out quick smart whether this old bloke had any credit cards, and if so she had to get an alert out on them as soon as possible. If some blow-through or drug addict turned up somewhere trying to pull cash out on one of the old bloke's cards she wanted to make sure the coppers were right there to meet him.

So where did Dougherty's claim of being on the run from someone down south fit in? Probably nowhere. Probably just the ramblings of an insignificant man trying desperately to make himself seem important to his drunken mates. Or maybe it was all a myth; maybe Dougherty never said it at all. Maybe the man leaning on the fence was the one who wanted someone to listen to him. Still, he hadn't looked that way when he thought Sasha Kelly wanted to know more. He'd looked like a man who had seen enough of life to know it wasn't always healthy to get mixed up in other people's business, particularly when that other person wound up murdered, and when he told his story about Dougherty in his cups, whimpering about some evil bogey man lurking in every shadow, he was describing a man whose fears were terrifyingly real, at least to him. And that raised another possibility. Maybe this was more than just another robbery gone wrong; maybe it was something far more sinister. Maybe the bogey man was real.

'This is all we found in it.'

Copeland slipped several dog-eared business cards and scraps of faded paper from his shirt pocket. Kelly silently held out the exhibit bag and he resentfully dropped them in. There was little or no chance any assailant had touched them but Kelly was more than happy to underscore her point. As Copeland strode back in the direction of the house, Kelly lightly shook the bag to see what she had. Nothing much, by the looks of things. Some old receipts from retail outlets in Mackay, all for small amounts and all for cash. They might help to reconstruct his recent movements. Business cards from two taxi companies and a 'you-drink, we drive' service — Dougherty obviously liked to be prepared. An old colour photograph of a woman and two children — probably his wife and kids — and half a used toothpick. And a folded piece of torn white paper.

Kelly reached into the bag and delicately peeled the paper open. An eight-digit number was scrawled across it in smeared blue ink. A telephone number. The first two digits were both five, which meant it was probably a listing on the Gold Coast, where Kelly had been stationed for more than a decade.

'Wait a minute!'

The words jumped out of her mouth before she realised they were coming, so loudly that the young constable combing the fenceline several metres away looked up inquisitively.

'I know this damn number.'

CHAPTER FOURTEEN

The guy with the flat nose and the stickers on his face was definitely a potential problem. The teardrop tattooed under one eye and the dotted line marked 'cut here' on his throat suggested he didn't have a lot to lose, and as Frank Vagianni sized him up from the safe distance of his table in the corner of the bar he asked himself again what the hell he was doing here.

Of course he already knew the answer. Three hundred bucks. It wasn't a sum to be sniffed at. The Frank Vagianni Private Investigation Agency wasn't exactly setting the world on fire at the moment and Frank had to take whatever job came along. He needed to pay his rent and alimony somehow, and he also liked to eat occasionally. In skinny times like these the small-firm solicitors were doing most of their own process-serving and all the traffic accident investigation stuff was spec work, which meant it had been a long time between drinks for Frank Vagianni. He still did a bit of missing persons work but it was really only rats-and-mice stuff; he was never going to get rich looking for wayward spouses and runaway kids. And there wasn't too much else on offer.

Francesco Vagianni, better known to his old copper mates as Frankie Box, had been doing this kind of stuff for longer than he wanted to remember, firstly in the police service for about a decade, and then for about the same time out of it. It was all he knew. A balding ex-copper in his forties carrying a little bit more weight than he ought to be didn't have a lot of options. No corporate head-hunters had rung him lately offering him high-powered, highly paid executive positions. And the truth was, Frank looked lousy in a neck-tie and he'd never been too good with that nine-to-five thing. So he had to take what came along. And after all, it wasn't every day someone offered three spot for a simple process-serving job. Then again, this had never sounded much like a simple job.

Bobby Lees had sold enough shonky deals and blue sky in his time to have a lot of enemies around town. The Gold Coast was too small a place for a guy who'd made an estimated twenty million bucks in the past three years by selling dog-box units to the great unwashed at grossly inflated prices propped up by shonky valuations and rental guarantees. As the rent ran out and harsh reality struck home the natives had become very restless and Bobby's two-tier marketing empire had been under siege. Everyone from the ACCC to Channel Nine had been camped outside his flashy office headquarters in Surfers Paradise and neither Bobby nor his red Ferrari had been spotted there in weeks.

Frank Vagianni's brief was simple. His lawyer client had issued a Supreme Court writ claiming damages for deceptive and misleading conduct against Lees on behalf of several of his purchasers and he needed it to be served on Bobby personally. The problem was, Bobby was not at all keen on collecting any paper at the moment, and his minders had become very particular about who got within cooee of their boss. All attempts to serve the writ on Lees had run up against his wall of goons, who were making sure no one got close enough to hear him singing in the shower, so a job that would normally pay fifty bucks was suddenly worth three hundred. Provided, of course, Frank could get close enough to Bobby Lees to shove the bluey up his jumper.

Finding him was easy. For a guy intent on keeping a low profile, Lees was everywhere. On the glitzy Gold Coast tourist strip they didn't award points for hiding your light under any bushels and no one liked to walk the walk with the beautiful people like Bobby Lees. Frank knew he wouldn't miss Friday night drinks at Boris Levsky's bar/restaurant at Marina Mirage. Levsky's ritzy waterfront joint at Main Beach had become the trendy place for all the Gold Coast glitterati to parade their silicone tits, gold chains and hairy chests at the end of a long week in the solarium, and Lees had been a permanent fixture for the past three months. All Frank had to do was pick the moment.

'Give us another Corona will you, love.'

At the obscene prices Levsky was charging for his grog, Frank would have his fee spent long before he got the job done unless he moved pretty soon. As the waitress left his table and headed back towards the bar he counted out the minders. There was the gorilla with the tattoos on his face standing on the left of Lees and his select group of admirers and spongers at the bar. There was the big Islander in the black sports coat on the other side of them, and Jimmy who used to work the door at Melba's. Behind them were the two Croatian boys from Chevron Island, who had obviously picked up a part-time gig to shadow Bobby and keep him out of trouble. That made five in all. Bobby was obviously feeling vulnerable.

One thing Frank had learned over the years was that life was all about timing, and he knew the time to move on Bobby Lees was when he eventually headed for the dunny. Not even Bobby would take five blokes to the trough with him, and it was only a matter of time before all that imported beer was going to get the better of him.

There it was. As Lees nodded to the tattooed gorilla and peeled off from the bar, following his bodyguard towards the toilet door, Frank took a last swig of beer and sucked in a fortifying breath. His heart was beating firmly in his chest as he moved quickly through the crowded bar, keeping his eyes fixed on the target and his gargantuan companion. Now it was down to two, which looked about as good as it was going to get. What he was going to do from here he wasn't certain; he'd just have to play the game by ear.

Lees reached the door and the big man pushed through, followed closely by his boss. Frank slipped one hand into his pocket and felt the writ folded against his thigh, ready for production. He sucked in another breath and pushed through after them.

It was one of those pokey little dunnies with three porcelain urinals and a single cubicle. When Frank came through the door the gorilla was right in front of him and locked an evil eye on him as Frank nodded politely and filed past, making his way down to the action stations at the other end. He could feel the gorilla's narrow eyes burning two holes through the back of his neck as he walked steadily to one of the urinals. Lees was nowhere in sight and Frank could see from the closed cubicle door that his target was being uncustomarily discreet. He unzipped and took position, straining to keep the big hulk by the door within his peripheral vision.

Suddenly the cubicle door swung open with a thud and Lees strode out. He hadn't flushed — just what Frank would expect of a grubby lowlife hood.

'Bobby!'

Frank was struggling to pull his zip up with one hand and the writ out with the other as Lees turned, uncomprehending.

'Do I know you?'

'No, but I've got a little present for you.'

Lees couldn't have looked more horrified if it was a pistol instead of a piece of paper that Frank pulled out of his pocket. He backed away with both hands in the air like a cowboy in a cheap western.

'I'm not accepting that.'

'Too bad, pal.' Frank dropped the writ onto the tiles between his feet. 'You've been fuckin' served.'

Now came the tricky bit — dealing with King Kong. As Frank pushed past Bobby Lees, who was protesting loudly and indignantly in his ear, the big man squared off at him, baring his yellow teeth as though preparing to take a bite of something.

'Who the fuck are you?'

It was Frank's experience that mongrel dogs and large men baring their teeth and threatening to take a bite of you were best dealt with in a loud, assertive fashion. He flicked a business card from his breast pocket and pushed it in front of his antagonist's face.

'That's who I am, pal. Frank Vagianni, private investigator. You can tell your boss he's got twenty-eight days to appear in the Supreme Court.'

The mention of the word 'court' seemed to have the desired effect, as the gorilla stared back at Frank with a vacant, confused expression on his face. But Frank could see there was going to be a limited window of opportunity to extract himself from this somewhat unhealthy situation. As he reached for the door, doing his best to squeeze ever so delicately closer to the opening, he saw the big man's countenance clouding over. Suddenly one big hand slapped against the door, slamming it shut, and the other grabbed a hungry handful of Frank's shirt and chest-hairs. The man was growling like a rabid dog as his other hand closed around Frank's neck and jammed him back against the wall behind him. His eyes bulging and the breath wheezing desperately and painfully in his throat, Frank felt himself being shaken like a rag doll and slammed repeatedly against the wall.

Life was all about timing. The big ape would get sick of playing with him in a minute and as soon as he slowed down long enough Frank would get a shot on him. Provided he was still conscious.

It only took one good swing. Frank's knee hit his assailant's groin so hard a loud thud echoed off the tiles. The big man grunted and crumbled to the floor, moaning pathetically and grasping at his crotch. As soon as Frank's feet touched the floor again he stepped up onto one of the gorilla's huge arms and grabbed for the door. He wasn't wasting any time: once the big boy caught his breath Frank was in a lot of trouble. He had to put a healthy distance between them as soon as possible. The only problem was the big lug was doubled up across the doorway and as Frank pulled frantically at the door all he was succeeding in doing was to bang it repeatedly and violently against the head and shoulders of the immovable object he was now standing on, which undoubtedly was not improving the man's mood. This situation did not look good.

'Get out of my way.'

Frank pushed Bobby Lees aside as he stepped into the cubicle and locked the door behind him. Propping his back against the door and jamming one foot firmly against the opposite wall, he punched Levsky's number into his mobile phone.

'Yeah.'

'Levsky, it's me, Box. I'm locked in the bog in your gents' dunnies. I've just served a bluey on Bobby Lees and one of his rock-apes is outside trying to monster me. You get your bouncers in here in the next fifteen seconds or my next call's to the coppers.'

The last thing Boris Levsky needed was police charging into his bar and scaring all the beautiful people, and Frank knew it. All he had to do was hold the fort until Levsky's cavalry arrived to deal with Stumbo the Giant and his sidekick. As it turned out, it took less than fifteen seconds. The gruntings and rumblings of people forcing their way into the dunnies were quickly followed by lots of shouting, loud complaints and arguments back and forth. It would soon settle down, Frank knew. Bobby Lees wasn't going to get himself involved in any escalated public incident, and besides, no one, not even Bobby Lees, was dumb enough to take on Levsky's boys.

Frank slid off the wall and sat down on the pedestal, waiting as the boys outside let off a little bit of steam arguing the toss. He was feeling good. He was three hundred dollars richer. That was nice. He leaned back and smiled to himself, listening as Bobby Lees assured the management that he and his boys were just there for a good time and there would be no trouble. Frank broke into a quiet chuckle. It wasn't just the money that was making him feel so good. It was the thought that a balding, overweight ex-copper could still shorten up a sleazy grub like Bobby Lees, goons or no goons. Frank had never met a grub yet he couldn't get the better of. It was like that when he was a cop and it was like that now. Nothing had changed. That's what had made him such a good cop, and that's why when no one could get near a half-smart, jumped-up shonky Saturday-afternoon gangster like Bobby Lees, they came to Frank Vagianni.

Frank missed the old days in the CIB, sniffing out the bad guys and the dodgies like Lees, busting druggies, pinching crims, dishing it up to all the half-baked hoons and standover merchants poncing around the town. He loved it, and he'd been good at it. It was all he'd ever wanted to do since he was a little kid kicking around the cane fields in North Queensland. And he'd done it well. He'd never forget the pride in his father's eyes the first time he saw his only son in uniform. Who would've thought the son of a wog cane-cutter would ever make it?

The ring of Frank's mobile telephone almost startled him.

'Hello.'

'Is that Frank Vagianni?'

Frank thought he recognised the voice, and it wasn't every day he had young women ringing him, but a guy with as many unpaid bills as Frank Vagianni couldn't afford to be too careful.

'Who's looking for him?'

'I know it's you, Frank. I recognise your voice.'

'Kelly?'

'You've got a good memory.'

He hadn't seen or heard from Sasha Kelly in years but he could tell from the razor edge in her voice that the old scores remained unsettled. Not that she had any reason to square up. She was the one who'd tipped the bucket of prawn-heads all over his career in the police force in the first place. It was Kelly who'd got it into her head that Frank and a few of the boys at the Surfers Paradise CIB had borrowed seventy grand out of the proceeds of the Waterworld armed robbery to punt it on a sure thing at the Surfers races. And so what if they did? It was all black money anyway, and the nag came home and the boys all made a motza. They even put the money back before the exhibit officer realised it was gone. But that didn't satisfy little Miss Serpico Sasha Kelly. She had to stir up a whole lot of shit that ended up with Frank and several others being charged. By the time the jury finally acquitted them his police career was well and truly down the dunny. And he could thank Sasha Kelly for it. So what she had to be snakey about he didn't understand, but he could tell from her voice she still had a big chip on her shoulder.

'How could I ever forget anyone with cans like yours, Kelly?'

'Bite your arse, Frank.'

Frank smiled despite himself. He wasn't kidding. Kelly had a body that was hard not to notice and a lot harder to forget. Too bad she was such a bitch.

'Yeah, you know what, Kelly? It's nice you rang to abuse me and everything, but I'm actually a bit busy at the moment. Is there something specific I can do for you?'

'Yeah. You can tell me all about Barry Dougherty.'

It took Frank a second or two to place the name. By the time he answered it was a dead giveaway.

'Who?'

'Careful, Frank. You go obstructing a police investigation and it could mean your licence.'

She'd never get an obstruction charge to stick just on the strength of his telling porkies to the coppers. But then again, Kelly was enough of a bitch to try it on. The last thing Frank needed right now was a charge on his plate.

'What's the interest in Dougherty?'

'My interest is the fact that he was murdered last night.' Frank's stunned silence probably told her that this was the first he'd heard of it. 'What's your interest?'

Frank needed a little thinking time before this conversation went much further.

'I guess that depends on who he is.'

'You telling me you don't know Barry Dougherty?'

'I'm not telling you nothing, Kelly.' Frank stabbed the 'no' button on his phone. She might make out obstruction if he told her lies, but she couldn't pin a man for saying nothing. Like the old crims used to say: *what you don't say can't hurt you*. 'Have a nice life, sweetheart.'

By the time Frank got back to his car he had dredged up all the information about Dougherty that was stored in the dusty warehouse section of his brain. Kelly's news that the old bloke had been murdered came as a shock, and it worried him in the same way the whole Dougherty job had worried him from the start. It was like reaching down a deep, dark hole: he knew he had something by the tail, but until he pulled it out he wasn't going to know if it was a little pussy cat or man-eating tiger. He was sure of one thing though: Kelly was right; he was interested in Barry Dougherty. Holding his address book open awkwardly in one hand he thumbed a set of numbers into the phone.

'Hello.'

'Slick.'

'Hey, Frankie, how're y'doing?'

'Good, baby, good. Listen, what're y'up to?'

'Just meeting a few friends for dinner at the Attic. Why, what's up?'

* * *

The Attic was a little joint above the old laundromat on Chevron Island. Like half the sleazy dives around Surfers Paradise Levsky had owned it for years, but tonight Frank could see a big change in the place. Ever since Levsky had opened up his bar/restaurant at the Mirage all his rough-head mates had started drinking over there, in the hope of chatting up one of the steady stream of dolled-up talent that got through the place, instead of hanging out in the shady corners at the Attic, smoking cigarettes and talking in riddles through the corners of their mouths, scaring off any decent folk who happened to venture in. Frank noticed the difference the moment he dragged himself to the top of the stairs. For a start Morrie, the maitre d', was wearing what looked like a clean shirt and none of the women at the cocktail bar looked like harlots. As he shook hands with Morrie he even suspected he detected a faint whiff of aftershave.

Frank was only half-listening to Morrie's customary repartee as he headed for the bar. He had too much on his mind to get involved in the usual light-hearted mutual sledging session with the portly maitre d'. He was still trying to process the information he'd picked up so far about Barry Dougherty's death. Fortunately his old mate Gerry Copeland from Mackay CIB had been working the four to midnight shift and Frank had rung him on the way over to Chevron Island. Gerry knew plenty about the case, although Kelly obviously hadn't mentioned anything to him about Frank's number being in the old bloke's wallet.

What he did know filled in the picture a little. Dougherty had landed in the Mackay area about five years back, and he'd kept pretty much to himself. Yesterday he was found dead in his front yard with his head caved in. Something had fractured his skull, maybe an iron bar. None of the neighbours had seen or heard anything out of the ordinary, although one of his old chinas claimed he'd been talking about being on the run from someone from down south. But so far there was no weapon and no motive, and until the forensics came back with something positive they couldn't even be sure whether it was a homicide or just a nasty accident.

Hopefully it was all a false alarm, but Frank had an ugly feeling in his gut about this one.

'Hello, big boy.'

Slick was sitting cross-legged at the bar, a cigarette held elegantly in one hand, a drink in the other, and a big cheesy grin splashed across her face.

'G'day, spunky.'

Frank wasn't kidding: Slick was looking good. Even in his currently distracted state he couldn't help but notice the obvious attractions straining to pop out of her low-cut top and the way her shapely hips looked like they'd been sewn into her skin-tight jeans. If she wasn't such a good mate he'd give her one for sure. But then, come to think of it, the way Frank had been travelling lately, there probably weren't too many sheilas under fifty that he wouldn't give one to.

He'd known Kirsten Foster for about four years, ever since she'd come to the Gold Coast to work as a receptionist/girl Friday in Eddie Moran's office, and she and Frank had hit it off right from the jump. She was a straight-talking, no-nonsense girl. What you saw with Slick was what you got. And it wasn't bad viewing either.

'What's Boy Wonder up to tonight?'

'Who knows? Probably out signing autographs somewhere.'

Slick enjoyed putting shit on Eddie Moran, Frank knew that. She saw it as her solemn duty to drag her arrogant, egotistical boss back down to earth as often as she could, even when he wasn't around. He deserved it. Eddie had to be without doubt the world's most irritating man to work for. He treated her like crap. But then he treated everyone like crap. It wasn't his fault, it was just the way he was. He was a natural-born arsehole and Slick considered it part of her role to remind him of the fact as often as she could, just to keep his runaway ego in some kind of check. Right now she was having to work overtime at it. Over the past few years Eddie had become quite a celebrity. Following his success in the high-profile Kelliher case last year and then the McCabe kidnapping inquiry he had been on the front page of every newspaper in the country, and lately one of the glossy magazines had even done a four-page feature on him entitled 'The Talented Mr Moran'. His flash office overlooking Surfers Paradise beach was suddenly full of blonde Gold Coast socialites wanting to sue their rich husbands. It was enough to make a bloke sick to the stomach.

'I think he's hoping to get his own game-show gig.'

It occurred to Frank that Slick was enjoying the added opportunities that Eddie's current celebrity status was offering her to come up with her best one-liners. She loved the sport, and Frank also knew that deep down she was proud of her exasperating boss. Frank was kind of proud of him as well. He knew what an arsehole Eddie could be — he'd learned all about that way back when he was a cop and he'd had to put up with the Eddie Moran Show every time they came head to head in court. But he'd also learned years later, when Sasha Kelly and the Fitzgerald Inquiry boys came after him over the Waterworld job, that Eddie Moran was a good man to have in your corner. He'd hired Eddie to defend him, and Eddie had pulled him through. He had more smarts and more mongrel in him than anybody Frank had ever known. And when Frank's money finally ran out he even found that Eddie could be a loyal friend, and that came as a real surprise. Frank Vagianni would never forget it.

Levsky's barmen never seemed to be in much of a hurry to do anything and by the time the big Maori bloke had taken Frank's order and finally delivered their drinks, Slick had filled him in on most of what had been happening during the past fortnight. She could tell he wasn't interested.

'Okay, so what's this big secret you need to talk to me about?'

Frank's knitted brow suggested it wasn't necessarily good news. He sucked back a draught of beer.

'You know an old guy called Barry Dougherty?'

'Barry Dougherty. Don't think so. Where's he from?'

'Mackay originally, but he was in Sydney for a long time.'

'Dougherty.' Slick shook her head. There was something about the look on Frank's face that was starting to make her feel nervous. 'No, I don't think so. Why, who is he?'

'Just an old barfly.' Frank took another swig of beer and wiped his mouth with the back of his hand. 'About three weeks back a bloke hired me to track him down. Didn't give no reason. Just "find him, expense is no object" sort of thing.' He paused briefly as though trying to decide whether to go on. 'So I started looking, but it became pretty obvious that this old bloke was keeping his head down for some reason. I traced him up north to Proserpine, found a couple of people who knew of him and that, but I just couldn't seem to pin him down. I spun the old bullshit line about wanting to talk to him about an unclaimed legacy under an estate and left my number with a few shopkeepers and publicans. But I never heard from him until one night he rang me out of the blue.'

Frank paused again, looking straight into her eyes. 'He was dead set toey, ay, he was running scared, you could tell it in his voice.' He took another swallow of beer. 'He tried to suss me out and then he just hung up and I never heard from him again. Anyway I eventually tracked him to an address in Mackay and I passed the info back to the client.' He set his beer carefully on the bar. 'Two days later the old bloke was found dead in his front yard.'

'You think your client had something to do with his death?'

'I don't know, but that's where you come in.'

'Me?'

'Yeah.'

Slick could feel that nervous flutter in the pit of her stomach again.

'Do you know a guy called Michael Wiltshire?'

'Sure.' She hadn't spoken to Michael Wiltshire since that confusing, agonising night four years ago when she had walked out of the Old Priory for the last time. The sound of his name made her stomach jump a little and suddenly a flood of painful emotions and unanswered questions was swirling in her head. She lifted the glass to her lips and took a deep swallow, hoping Frank wasn't reading too much in her face. 'I used to work for him in Sydney.'

'He's the client. He's the one who hired me to find Dougherty.'

Michael Wiltshire had contacted Frank a little over three weeks earlier, wanting to retain a private investigator to locate a couple of people. He wasn't saying what his interest was or what he intended doing when he found them, he just wanted someone to start looking for them both immediately and he was happy to pay whatever the freight was plus expenses in advance. At the time it was all Frank Vagianni needed to hear. But a dead body had a way of changing things.

'He also hired me to find you.'

'And?'

'I'm still looking.'

Frank had been drip-feeding him for the past three weeks with reports about the costly inquiries he'd been making looking for the girl, all to no avail. He figured Wiltshire was chasing her for some old debt, maybe unpaid rent she'd left behind in Sydney. Slick was a mate and naturally he wasn't about to give her up if she didn't want to know the bloke, but that hadn't stopped him stringing out the job a little and milking it for all he could get out of his newest and richest client.

'What do you know about this bloke Wiltshire?'

Slick batted her eyelids and looked away, praying she would hold it all together. What did she know about Michael Wiltshire? She'd asked herself the same question plenty of times over the past four years. Once, for the shortest time, she thought she knew a lot about him but everything that had happened since told her she was wrong. She'd seen enough at the inquest to know Wiltshire wasn't the man she'd thought he was. So what did she know about him? Nothing, except that he was obviously another handsome, charming, devious scam-merchant like Trevor Ellowe had been all his life, only he had more money, presumably because he was a better scammer. Ten years with Trevor had taught her that you never really get to know a guy like that. She took another swig from her drink, looked Frank straight in the eye and answered his question the only way she could.

'Pass.'

CHAPTER FIFTEEN

The infamous Christopher Skase was either one of Australia's biggest white-collar crooks or just a poor misunderstood slob who had too much money and stuck his head up once too often. As Frank Vagianni climbed the hill into one of Brisbane's oldest and most palatial suburbs, the car air-conditioning whirring loudly as it struggled with the steamy midday heat, he looked over at the stately Skase mansion perched high on Hamilton Hill, overlooking the sprawling manicured lawns of Newstead House and the broad, cool expanse of the meandering Brisbane River leading back up to the city, and wondered what shady stories the big house could tell. It had become a part of Brisbane folklore, the magnificent Taj Mahal built by the flashy eighties' corporate swashbuckler Christopher Skase right in the middle of the city's oldest money. When things were going well and greed was good the banks had lined up to throw their money at him, but when things eventually went bad everyone was lining up to take a shot, including the Australian Securities Commission who did their best to lock him up. As it turned out, Skase hadn't hung around to tell his side of the story; he preferred to spend his days in the sunny south of Spain, working on his tan and dodging extradition. Frank didn't blame him. Life was way too short. But now all that remained of the Skase story was the big house on the hill: either a proud monument to hard work and entrepreneurial initiative, or just part of the filthy lucre. Who knew? Sometimes it wasn't much more than a fine line.

Michael Wiltshire's house was not more than a stone's throw from the Skase mansion, right there in the middle of all that old money, and maybe a little bit of filthy lucre too. Could be this house had a few stories of its own to tell. Could be there was more to Michael Wiltshire, high-flying property developer, than what Frank Vagianni had been reading in the papers.

Certainly what Slick had told him last night about the inquest into the death of her ex-husband, Trevor Ellowe, had got Frank thinking. It sounded like Wiltshire's name was all over Ellowe's unfortunate demise, and the various references to late-night calls to Fred Hunter did absolutely nothing to alleviate suspicion. There wasn't a cop or an ex-cop on the east coast who hadn't heard of Fred Hunter, and the mention of his name only served to confirm that Wiltshire might have a few dodgy skeletons hiding in his closet. That morning Frank had done a bit of checking. Ellowe had been on the Hunter Transport books while Barry Dougherty was working as Fred Hunter's clerk. Exactly what that meant Frank couldn't start to say, but it was making the ugly feeling in the pit of his stomach even uglier.

His call to Wiltshire earlier that morning had been simple: he wanted to talk to him about Barry Dougherty as soon as possible. Wiltshire was anticipating his arrival and the impressive wrought-iron gates opened automatically as the labouring Falcon swung into the driveway. As Frank steered up to the house his well-heeled host was already walking out to greet him, juggling a football in one hand, the other resting on the shoulder of his young son, Simon.

'G'day, pal.' Frank winked at the young boy as he climbed out of the car.

Michael Wiltshire smiled and held out a welcoming hand. 'Frank.'

As they shook hands Frank did his best to size him up. They had met once before, briefly, at a coffee shop at Main Beach a few weeks earlier when Wiltshire had handed over a cheque to get things started. Right now he looked mildly concerned, just as he had at their first meeting. In the current circumstances it was probably the least to be expected. Frank couldn't see too much of anything else in his eyes. Maybe it was a good sign, maybe not.

'Come on through.' Wiltshire tossed the football to the little boy, who promptly punt-kicked it into a corner of the huge front yard and sprinted off to chase it down. 'Can I get you a cold drink?'

As Frank Vagianni sank into the soft comfort of a leather armchair in the air-conditioned lounge room, a frosted glass of cold beer and a bowl of peanuts lined up invitingly in front of him, he couldn't help but wonder whether he was about to get the whole truth or not. Experience told him that the truth usually came from desperate guys with sweat running down their face and tears in their eyes, not cool, comfortable customers like the man sitting opposite, idly shaking the ice cubes in his glass of bitters. Maybe it was time for Frank to do a bit of shaking up himself.

'I don't like being set up as an accessory to murder.'

The word hit home. Wiltshire squinted across the coffee table as the blood drained from his face.

'What are you talking about?'

Suddenly Wiltshire was looking a whole lot more like those guys with the sweaty brows and teary eyes, and Frank knew he had to keep the hot light on him.

'You hired me to find Dougherty for you and I did. And then my guess is you had him knocked.'

Frank didn't have anywhere near enough information to bring him to that conclusion, but it was a nice opening gambit, good enough to turn the pressure up on a rich developer and hopefully get him to start talking straight. So far Wiltshire had done precious little of that.

The two men held each other's gaze for several seconds. Then Wiltshire leaned forward in his chair and carefully set his glass down on the coffee table.

'Look, I invited you up here today so you could tell me what if anything you've learned about Barry Dougherty's death, not to accuse me of murdering him.'

'Yeah well, if the shoe fits, pal.'

Wiltshire obviously thought this was going to be a one-way information-sharing session. He was right, but it wasn't going to be Frank doing the sharing.

'All I know is, three weeks ago you're throwing sheep stations at me to find this old guy, and when I go looking I find he's running scared. Then I hand you his address and two days later I find out why he's running scared, 'cause he winds up dead in his front yard.'

'You said the police thought it might be an accident.'

'I said they're working on it.'

When Frank had telephoned that morning he was doing his best to play the whole thing down, keep Wiltshire relaxed enough to ensure he got a meeting with him. Now the agenda was different.

'But from what I hear it doesn't look too good. He's got a dint in his skull the size of the Great Australian Bight.' Frank was sitting forward in his seat now too, so they were facing off across the coffee table. 'They know I was looking for him right before he died, and my guess is they're going to be knocking on my door any minute. Now I don't know why you were chasing him, but I want to know, and if I don't get some satisfactory answers I figure I might just give your name to the police and they can work it out.'

Michael Wiltshire was looking straight into his eyes now and, for the first time, Frank thought he recognised a glimmer of something familiar. It was a tired, vacant look that he had seen in the eyes of a lot of guilty men. There came a time when the burden of some secrets just got too heavy.

Wiltshire picked up his glass and took a quick swallow. 'It's a long story.'

They generally were. Frank scooped up a handful of peanuts and settled back into the soft leather, ready to be entertained.

'Great. I love stories.'

He didn't mind good fiction, and who could tell — it might even be the truth. Frank tipped his head back, dumped a load of peanuts in and chomped noisily. Wiltshire's eyes tracked the course of the peanut crumbs siphoning through the detective's stubby fingers onto the imported Italian leather and disappearing into the luxuriant pure wool carpet.

'Before I left Sydney I was pretty tied up with state Labor politics.' A mild wash of irritation settled momentarily on Wiltshire's face. 'I got myself involved in a bit of a disagreement with a local Labor Party heavy by the name of Hunter.'

'Fred Hunter, the transport bloke?'

'That's him.'

He filled in the details of the local political geography at the time while Frank crunched peanuts on the couch opposite, studying his client's expression closely, trying to assess what he was being told, and how much he wasn't.

Wiltshire's voice was measured, each word carefully selected.

'There were certain allegations circulating at the time. A lot of people in the local branch were contending that Hunter was somehow cooking the branch books. Because I was an office-bearer I somehow got dragged into it.' Wiltshire cupped his glass in two hands and shook it gently, watching the ice cubes as they glided in a circular motion around the surface of his drink. 'It all got a bit ugly. Hunter's people were making all kinds of threats against me.'

It was obviously still a pretty touchy subject. As Wiltshire paused, the detective could see real anger burning somewhere deep within him. Whatever might be true or false about what he had just been told, one thing was certain: as far Michael Wiltshire was concerned, there were still some scores unsettled between him and Fred Hunter. But that still left the most important question.

'So where does Dougherty fit into all this?'

'Barry Dougherty had information on Fred Hunter that I wanted. He'd been Fred's branch secretary for years but they had a huge falling out. When he quit five years ago he took a copy of all Fred's books with him, apparently enough to prove serious electoral fraud.'

It was a story. It didn't cover everything Frank had been told by Slick the night before, but it did fill in a couple of gaps. At least it was a start, and Frank knew from experience that you had to be patient, that sometimes the truth had a way of dribbling out in drips and splotches. He shovelled another handful of peanuts into his mouth and munched robustly as he posed the obvious.

'Your blue with Hunter was five years ago. Why the sudden renewed interest in him now?'

Wiltshire silently contemplated the glass in his hands for several long seconds, then drained its contents and placed it firmly on the table in front of him, his expression stiffened with a new resolve.

'That's my business. All you have to know is I had nothing whatsoever to do with Dougherty's death.'

Maybe it was true, maybe not. Wiltshire didn't look much like a hit-man, but you never could tell. He seemed the mild-mannered Clark Kent type, but maybe underneath the Country Road wool sweater he was wearing a Superman suit with a big M for murderer on the chest. Frank had seen enough trembling housewives with their husband's crusted blood still lining their fingernails, and blubbering wimps crying about how they'd just stuffed their lover's body parts into the insinkerator, to know that murder doesn't always come in readily recognisable packaging. In any event, Frank could tell he already had about all the information he was going to get from Michael Wiltshire in this particular instalment.

It was a good start. The fact that Barry Dougherty had helped himself to copies of Fred Hunter's shonky books was likely to have made plenty of people more than a little cranky with him, and from what Frank knew of Fred Hunter, it didn't pay to get on his wrong side. It was all a little long in the tooth now, but people like Hunter seemed to have particularly long memories. Besides, if Michael Wiltshire was scratching around trying to dig up old skeletons, the old scores were likely to have regained their currency.

'Frank, I need to know whether Dougherty's death was an accident or not, and whether Fred Hunter had anything to do with it. I'm willing to pay whatever it costs.'

Normally it would have been music to Frank's ears, but this one was way too close to home. He needed a lot more information before he was going to feel comfortable taking any more money from Michael Wiltshire.

'Why would Hunter have had anything to do with it?'

Frank had his own answers to the question, but he couldn't help suspecting that Wiltshire might have one or two he hadn't thought of yet. If he did, the look on his face suggested he wasn't about to tell Frank Vagianni.

'I don't know.'

For a moment Wiltshire looked like he was going to continue, but instead he stood up and walked out of the room. He returned seconds later with his chequebook and a fountain pen.

'I can give you a cheque now for your time and expenses to get back up to Mackay and find out what you can.'

Frank hated it when people did this to him. He'd got so used to eating three meals a day it was hard to turn his back and walk away when someone started waving money underneath his nose, even when he knew he should. As he watched Wiltshire filling out the cheque he was reminded of a question he'd been wanting to ask his rich client since the first day he'd spoken to him.

'What about the girl?'

'What girl?'

'Kirsten Foster.'

'Did you find her?'

There was a slight lift in Wiltshire's intonation that Frank was anxious to discourage, so he lied as quickly as he could.

'No. What's all this got to do with her?'

'Nothing.'

It takes a thief to catch a thief and Frank could see Wiltshire was lying through his teeth.

'Then why were you looking for her?'

Wiltshire squinted self-consciously and told another pathetically transparent lie. 'She owes me money, that's all.'

When Frank left the house that day he had a cheque in his top pocket and a load of unanswered questions in his head. After five years, why was everyone suddenly so interested in an old drunk propping up the public bar of the Mackay Hotel? Why was Michael Wiltshire suddenly so keen to get the goods on Fred Hunter? And even if Barry Dougherty did have a five-year-old set of bodgy books, would anyone really care enough to send old Barry off for it? Or was there something else? Did Barry Dougherty have more than just a collection of dusty photocopies evidencing some dodgy record-keeping in the local branch? Did he have something valuable enough, or maybe dangerous enough, to make it worth someone's while to kill him?

Frank had no doubt Wiltshire had told him a few porkies, but he'd also levelled on a few things. Knowing where the truth began and ended was always the hardest thing, but for now Frank felt okay. He told himself that if his client was responsible for Dougherty's death, he wouldn't have that cheque in his top pocket. If you wanted to bury a crime it made no sense at all to pay a private eye to go scratching around hunting for whatever information he could dig up on the case. Only a fool would do that, and whatever Michael Wiltshire was, he didn't look to Frank to be a fool.

As Frank swung the door open on the Falcon and climbed inside, young Simon Wiltshire grubber-kicked his football across the yard and in behind the imaginary tryline of his imaginary opposition, regathered skilfully and put the ball down for a winning try.

'Nice move, pal.'

Frank winked at the boy, closed the door and kicked the engine over.

As Michael Wiltshire watched the iron gates slide shut behind the detective's car his thoughts were shrouded in a dark, uneasy melancholy. He knew what Frank Vagianni would find when he went digging. And he knew what he'd have to do next, and that it could land him in gaol.

'Dad, catch.'

Simon Wiltshire kicked the ball high into the air and his father instinctively stepped forward, positioning himself beneath where it spiralled above and hung for a moment before falling. As it dropped neatly and comfortably into his arms it made a solid, compact sound that was somehow consoling. The shape and familiar texture of the leather in his hands felt good, and he spontaneously shaped up, dropped the ball onto his right foot and deftly speared it back towards the little boy. He watched as Simon positioned himself quickly behind the ball's trajectory and cradled both arms perfectly, waiting to take a comfortable catch. His father had taught him that: work hard to get yourself into the right position, then keep your nerve and calmly swallow up the spoils.

'You're kicking the ball well, mate.'

'Yeah.' Simon dummied to pass, sidestepped an imaginary opponent, and then chip-kicked the ball back to his father. 'I reckon I'll probably make the As this year.'

Michael couldn't count the number of times the two of them had played out here together, passing the ball to one another, flicking it and kicking it, talking about it, how to hold it in both hands, how to get a pass straight and flat, how make a ball roll end-on-end or sit up perfectly.

'You'd probably be a better chance if you were boarding, don't you think? More time to train.'

'Yeah, maybe.'

Michael fired a long pass back to his son, who rushed himself into position and then took it calmly and safely in two hands.

'Reckon you'd like to board for a little while?'

'Not really.'

Simon threw himself into an ambitious attempt to duplicate his father's long pass, sending the ball at an angle towards the side fence. Michael jogged after it, scooped it up in one hand and then slowed to an amble as he walked back to his son. He'd picked out the boy's school carefully — one of Brisbane's best. Simon was a day student, but Michael had made sure to choose a school that had boarding facilities so, when the time came, he could board if he wanted to. When it stopped being just the two of them, as it inevitably would, and Simon's friends eventually became the centre of his life, the boy would be able to get whatever space he needed. It gave them both a safety net. And if Michael couldn't be there, for whatever reason, his son would be cared for by familiar faces. As they came together he popped the ball up and Simon plucked it out of the air.

'What about if I had to go away for a little while later this year, for work?'

Simon looked up at his dad, a faint hint of uncertainty in his clear young eyes. 'I'd come with you.'

He'd been through a lot for a little bloke. Michael could only hope he remembered little of losing his mother when he was barely three years old. They'd moved around a bit since then, probably too much, and Simon had seen a lot of changes in his short life. He'd got very close to Kirsten, and even though he toughed it out when she left, Michael could tell at the time it knocked the little bloke around. But sometimes changes came whether you welcomed them or not.

Michael ruffled the boy's hair and gave him a reassuring smile. 'Yeah, mate, sure.'

CHAPTER SIXTEEN

Gary Sharpe's normally placid stomach was dancing a jig. He knew how to play the game as well as anyone in politics, and normally he'd have been content to order another bottle of the best wine in the house, tell a few more dirty jokes and let his gracious hosts try out their best lines on him. But today he just couldn't do it. He was thinking about the call he'd got from Michael Wiltshire the day before. He hated loose ends and this sounded like the mother of all loose ends. This one could really come back and bite them on the bum.

The smooth-talking young man opposite him knew his business. The US company he represented had gone into large-scale manufacture of gaming machines relatively recently and on all accounts it had established a reasonably strong foothold in Queensland over the past twelve months. Now they were looking to come in through the back door and get a piece of the real action south of the border. Taking the big boys in Sydney head-on from a standing start would have been well nigh impossible, so they'd gone about it cleverly, establishing some market share in the Queensland clubs and pubs, checking out the general lay of the land, paying their dues, making influential friends in the right places. It wasn't hard to tell from the way the wine was flowing and the back-slapping that was going on that those friends included Sharpey's Queensland Labor Party mates around the table, but he knew they weren't the reason for the lunch today. There was only one guest of honour at this banquet, and that was Gary Sharpe. When he got the call from his Queensland counterpart in the Brisbane ALP state headquarters saying that the American newcomers were keen to talk to him about their plans to expand their operations into the New South Wales leagues clubs, Sharpe was more than pleased to accept the invitation to fly up to Brisbane for a boozy lunch. It was the sort of opportunity he never let slip by. It was what made him the best fundraiser in the game.

As the effusive young American traded cues with his associates, and they collectively waxed lyrically about the company's great achievements and even greater plans, Sharpey looked out through the glass wall to the green waters of the Brisbane River bathed gloriously in the warm Queensland winter sunlight below the steel grey arches of the Storey Bridge. You couldn't afford to have loose ends. Sooner or later they'd always come back to bite you on the bum. You had to cut them off.

'Listen, fellas, much as I'd love to sit around here and get on the piss with you, it turns out I've got another meeting to get to this afternoon, so why don't I cut straight to the chase.'

The broad, sparkling smiles on the faces of the young man and his colleagues faded quickly into stunned silence.

'You blokes make poker machines and that means to make money you've got to sell as many of them as you can.' The scowl wasn't meant for them particularly; it was just that it was a simple enough equation and the churning feeling in his stomach made him irritable and impatient to get to the point. 'New South Wales has about ten per cent of all the poker machines currently operating throughout the world. And it's an expanding market. Next to New South Wales the whole Queensland market, the whole rest of Australia for that matter, isn't even a piss in the bucket. And right now we control New South Wales. That means we dictate what happens with all those pokies you blokes are trying to flog — who gets them, how many they get and what they look like. That's why you're here right now, filling us full of fancy tucker and expensive piss.' He stretched his face into a cynical smile. 'That's nice, but it doesn't put us in power and it doesn't keep us in power.'

Gary Sharpe delicately wiped the corners of his mouth and folded the crisp white serviette flat on the table in front of him. 'Now, where I come from there's the friends of the party and there's the also-rans. It's not hard for me to recognise my friends because, as we all know, a friend in need is a friend indeed. And the Labor Party's always in need. Mainly because election campaigns are bloody expensive things to run. You work it out, boys. If you want to be mates I'll be more than pleased to have you.'

Sharpe pushed up out of his chair and cheerily said his farewells. It felt good to see the look of awed admiration in the eyes of his Queensland colleagues. They were all good operators but none of them knew how to ask the question quite like Gary Sharpe. For years the Queensland Nationals had been past masters at wringing campaign dollars out of the big end of town, but these young Labor blokes were relatively new to the game and in this league they were mere novices. They needed an expert like Gary Sharpe to show them how it was done. If there was a feed on, Sharpey never got up from the table without a nice big juicy bone in his bowl. It was simple enough: all you had to do was ask the question.

As he shook the last hand and slapped the last back he slipped some business cards from his shirt pocket. 'There you go, fellas.' He slid the cards across the table. 'Give us a ring sometime. Labor doesn't forget its mates.'

By the time Sharpey got onto the broad footpath outside the Riverside Centre the warm glow of self-congratulation had already given way to that gnawing, unsettling feeling in the pit of his stomach. He wrestled the mobile phone from his side pocket and punched in the number.

'Hello.'

'Yeah, mate, it's Sharpey. I'll see you there in five minutes.'

'Okay.'

He hadn't seen Michael Wiltshire in over four years but the cool edge to his old friend's voice suggested there were still a few unsettled issues between them. Even if there hadn't been, loose ends like this one were guaranteed to open old wounds. The Trevor Ellowe business had been awfully messy, and no one regretted that more than Gary Sharpe. But then life was messy, and political life was the messiest of all. If Ellowe had had half a brain he'd be still walking around today, doing grubby drug deals and generally wasting space. Simple as that. What was done was done, and no amount of hand-wringing or breast-beating was going to change a thing. All you could do was clean up the mess and make sure there were no loose ends.

Michael Wiltshire was propped against one end of the deserted lobby bar. Sharpey was surprised again by the impression that always seemed to strike him when he laid eyes on his old schoolfriend after periods apart. Wiltshire was an impressive-looking man; even now that flecks of grey had begun to colour his dark hair, his broad shoulders and handsome face made him stand out in a crowd. He was leaning casually against the bar on one elbow, his other hand pushed deep into the pocket of his light wool slacks, looking chic and debonair in his dark jacket and open-neck silk shirt, like some fancy model in a fashion magazine. As Sharpey made his way towards him his stomach almost turned. It was so typical of Wiltshire, the man who had everything, the one to whom it all came easily, the man whose hands were always clean, pockets always full. It had been that way all their lives. Wiltshire was always there to take the final pass, put the ball down across the line, take the bows. But he didn't have the ticker to do the hard yards up the middle. He'd come back to Sydney thinking he was going to saunter straight into politics and walk away with a safe Labor seat, without ever having to kiss a single baby or shake any grubby hands along the way. Well, politics didn't work that way, not in Sydney or anywhere else. You had to be willing to take the tough decisions, do what needed to be done.

Michael Wiltshire could have been anything in Labor politics. He could have been another Neville Wran, maybe more. He had the brains, the looks, the charm, the pedigree. But when push came to shove, he didn't have what it would take.

He had left Sydney not long after the coroner published his findings in the Ellowe inquest, sold up everything and slunk back to Queensland with his tail between his legs and his not-so-clean hands in the air. He had proved he didn't have the mongrel that it took to survive in politics. Even then he had fallen on his feet: the Old Priory had fetched over two million — at that time it was the biggest price ever achieved for a residential property in Petersham. In the past few years the tales of his real-estate conquests in the sunshine state had come thick and fast. It made Gary Sharpe sick to the stomach to think how easily things came to Michael Wiltshire.

'I think Fred Hunter had Barry Dougherty murdered.'

'What?'

Sharpe had been worried it would be something out of left field like this ever since Wiltshire had rung him earlier in the week. The conversation had been ominously brief. All he'd said was that he wanted to talk about Barry Dougherty, but the cloak-and-dagger tone in his voice had spelt trouble with a capital T.

'Don't be so bloody silly.'

The uneasy feeling that had been troubling Gary Sharpe's stomach all day turned into a dull pain and he could suddenly feel his heart pumping stiffly in his chest. These were serious allegations with the potential to drag them all into a very ugly controversy. As he pushed his head back and drained the Scotch into his mouth his mind was racing feverishly, searching for the angles. This thing had to be managed carefully: he had to take control, and quickly. Michael Wiltshire had the dangerous look of a man who was suffering a bad case of the Hail Marys, and if Sharpey didn't bring him into line quick smart, put a little bit of lead into his pencil, he might end up doing something silly, something they would all regret. He rattled the ice cubes gently in his glass and placed it carefully on the bar, shuffling ideas into order in his head, then looked into his old friend's eyes with perfect timing.

'Dougherty got rolled on his way home from the pub. According to the papers he was mugged for his wallet.'

The Mackay news didn't normally make its way into the Sydney papers. Gary Sharpe had obviously made it his business to find out about Barry Dougherty's death. Undoubtedly the explanation that the press was peddling suited him just fine, but Michael Wiltshire knew it wasn't true.

'Dougherty was threatening to expose Fred Hunter.'

'How do you know that?'

'I spoke to him two days before he died.'

Wiltshire blurted out the words like a man who hadn't been intending to, looking almost surprised to hear them coming from his own mouth. Then he paused, meeting the intense stare of his companion. The tension in Gary Sharpe's stomach suddenly leaped into his mouth and he erupted involuntarily into an abrasive cackle of nervous laughter. Michael Wiltshire wasn't laughing. His eyes had a hollow, wearied look. Gary Sharpe felt the tension settling back into his gut as he looked deep into Wiltshire's anxious glare.

'What did he say?'

Wiltshire's voice suddenly took on a razor edge, strung so tightly that the words spat out in short, breathless grunts.

'He was drunk, raving on about how he was going to put Hunter behind bars. He said he'd already rung Hunter and told him he was going to the police.'

He dropped his head and searched for courage amongst the ice and cola swirling in the glass he was jiggling absent-mindedly in both hands. The guilt was painted thickly on his face. Gary Sharpe felt nothing but revulsion for him now: the self-righteous philanthropist who had been so quick to take the moral high ground and spout sanctimonious rhetoric when there was nothing much at stake. Now things were different. Now everything was on the line.

Wiltshire looked back at him as he found a feeble voice. 'Anyway, I suspect Fred Hunter got to him before he went to the police.'

He poured some of the contents of his glass into his mouth before he looked at Sharpe again, his eyes set with new resolve.

'I'm going to ring the police, Gary, tell them what I know.'

'Is that right?'

Sharpe's pockmarked chin was stretched into an involuntary scowl as his mind darted desperately in all directions, searching for the right approach. He had to turn this thing around right now. He had to get the lid back on. Michael Wiltshire was talking crazy talk that could destroy them all and Sharpey had to pull him up right now and for good. He had to hit exactly the right chord, touch the right nerve.

He leaned forward and whispered into his old friend's face, 'Well, since you're in the mood for telling, Michael, are you going to tell them what you know about what happened to Trevor Ellowe?'

'I don't know anything about what happened to Trevor Ellowe. Do you?'

'You know enough.'

'I know enough to know Fred Hunter is a dangerous man.'

'You might know enough to put yourself behind bars for a long time.'

He was right. Some mistakes never go away. You just keep paying for them all your life.

'I don't know what I'm going to tell them, Gary. All I know is two men are dead. I can't sit back and say nothing.'

The beating in Sharpey's chest picked up a notch or two. Wiltshire was talking nonsense, dangerous nonsense. The Royal Commission and the media were already working themselves into a frenzy about Fred Hunter. Any mention of his name in connection with a suspected homicide was going to open up the whole ugly can of worms.

'Michael, don't be bloody stupid.' He checked himself, glancing over his shoulder self-consciously, then continued in a hoarse whisper. 'Dougherty was a drunk and a no-hoper. Some junkie's rolled him for his pension cheque, that's all. It's got nothing to do with Fred Hunter, and all you're going to achieve is to risk opening up that whole Ellowe business again.' The two men were standing toe to toe, looking deep into each other's eyes. 'Don't do it, Michael. You don't know these people the way I do.'

They had a lifetime of friendship between them, but now all Gary Sharpe could recognise in Michael Wiltshire's face was an obstinate resolve.

'I'm sorry, Gary. I've made up my mind.'

By the time Sharpe dropped onto the soft leather rear seat of the limousine half an hour later the dull pain in his gut had disappeared. He was over it. Now was the time for planning, not for worrying. And no one planned like Gary Sharpe.

He had to get this right, just right. He had put all the logical arguments to Wiltshire as to why it was preposterous to suggest that Fred Hunter would have Dougherty murdered, and how sticking his nose into it was only going to start people asking a whole lot of questions which it was in nobody's interests to have asked and nobody's interests to have answered. He had tried to explain that if people started pointing the finger at a bloke like Fred Hunter he was certain to come out swinging, and if he did someone would get badly hurt. Wiltshire was no fool, he understood all that, he knew the risks, but he just wasn't listening to reason. He wanted to do things his own way; he was sick of living with the guilt, waiting for the axe to fall.

Guilt was an emotion Sharpey didn't trust, because he didn't understand it. You made a decision and you lived with the consequences. There was no point in feeling guilty; feeling guilty didn't change a thing. It made no sense at all and, like most things that made no sense, it was dangerous. Very, very dangerous.

* * *

As soon as he got back to his office Michael Wiltshire checked his list of messages. Vagianni still hadn't returned his call. It was probably a bit early to expect anything concrete but he was keen to keep abreast of whatever the detective might have been able to find out. If anything, his first conversation with Gary Sharpe in several years had only served to increase his unease. The anxiety that had been driving him ever since he heard of Dougherty's death now seemed to intrude on all his thoughts.

He shuffled through the papers on his desk, looking at the printed words without reading them, asking himself why he had arranged the meeting. At one level he had wanted to float his theory about Dougherty's death with Gary just to gauge his reaction. After all, Gary knew Fred Hunter far better than Michael ever had. His view of whether it was likely that Hunter was connected with the old man's death would surely count for something. But the truth was, Michael didn't need Gary Sharpe's opinion. They both knew what Fred Hunter was capable of if the stakes were high enough.

It was more than that. He had wanted to confront his old friend with the ugliness he had brought into both their lives. Gary Sharpe had been riding the fast-track to where he was going for so long he'd lost sight of where it was taking him. All his life he'd had a fascination with clever short cuts and the easy way of doing things. It had set him apart. It was what had made him the most dynamic, innovative and successful operator in the New South Wales Labor Party. But it was also the reason his progress through the party had caused disquiet in some circles. Many of his colleagues had expressed misgivings as to whether the often impressive ends achieved by Gary Sharpe justified his means, which seemed dangerously at odds with the proud, deep-seated ideals of the party and the labour movement. Increasingly they had questioned the wisdom of Sharpe's obsession with controlling grass-roots power at any cost, and in particular his cosy relationships at local branch level with some people who seemed to be little more than thugs and gangsters. People like Fred Hunter.

Gary Sharpe's response was that everyone was entitled to a vote, and the likes of Fred Hunter's vote was worth as much as anyone else's. He had it all worked out. He had it all under control. You tied in with whoever you needed to get the job done. If you wanted the punters' support you had to talk their talk and walk their walk. You had to get into their boardrooms and their pubs, down there on the street with them or wherever they were, and give them what they wanted. When Sharpey told the tale it had a way of sounding absolutely logical. Even Michael Wiltshire, raised in his parents' ideology of working-class socialism, had been seduced by the confident pragmatism of Gary Sharpe's cynical version of modern party politics. It all seemed to make so much sense and to make life so easy. There was a fix for every problem, a contact for every deal. So long as you kept your own hands clean, what did it matter if the hands you were shaking had a little dirt on them? That was their business not yours. It was that simple. The only problem was, dirt had a way of sticking.

The buzz of Michael's private line startled him slightly. Vagianni had the number; hopefully he was ringing to report.

'Hello.'

'What money do I owe you?'

Michael struggled to place the female voice snapping angrily at him.

'I beg your pardon?'

'I owe you nothing, you big jerk.'

It was a familiar voice, feisty but fragile, and it felt good to hear it again.

'Kirsten?'

'How dare you go around telling people I owe you money!' She was fired up, angry and hurt at the same time; he could hear it as she spat the words into the telephone. 'I owe you nothing, you creep. I owe nothing to anyone. I pay my debts.'

'I know that. I just said that —'

'Yeah, right.' In his mind's eye he could see the venom in her green eyes and the red lips resolutely pursed. 'You just lied, you shithead, you liar, you big dickhead.'

'I just needed to find you.'

'So you lied.'

It was true, he had lied, just as he had lied to her about Trevor Ellowe on the night he had last seen her.

'Kirsten, I had to talk to you.'

There was silence for a moment, and when she spoke again her voice was sad and paper-thin.

'Yeah, right. Well, you know what? I don't want to talk to you.'

'Listen, Kirsten, when I last saw you ...' Michael found himself faltering for words like a nervous teenager. Where should he begin? 'I didn't tell you the truth about Trevor. I want you to know the truth.'

'Yeah, hello — did I mention?' The resilient Kirsten Foster was back on the line, her voice still wavering but now stiffened with a tough brassy edge. 'I don't give a shit. Get it? I don't want to know. I don't want to know about you, I don't want to know about Trevor, I don't want to know what the two of you were talking about with all your late-night phone calls together. I'm not interested in your lies or your shonky deals or any of your crap.' Michael heard her choke slightly on the words; when she spoke again she sounded firm and fortified. 'I'm getting on fine all on my own.'

He wanted to say something in the brief, bitter silence that followed, something that would explain all that had happened, something that might make some sort of difference. But before the words came to him she had found her strength again.

'I don't need it, okay? So as far as I'm concerned, you can all just go and stick your heads up a dead bear's bum.'

The loud click on the other end was followed by a dull continuous tone that buzzed sadly in his ear. Michael Wiltshire slipped the receiver quietly back onto the telephone.

CHAPTER SEVENTEEN

For the first time in his life Michael was looking forward to seeing Darryl Beane. It wasn't that he'd ever had anything against Darryl; they were just very different people, and always had been. Michael had known the clever lawyer since their university days, when they shared a common view of student politics and not much else. Darryl had been president of the student union for a brief period and after graduation had unsuccessfully run for pre-selection for the ALP. Their paths had crossed regularly during that period and later, when Beane became a trusted confidant and legal adviser in Labor circles, a close associate of many of Michael's old friends, including Gary Sharpe. But Michael had never really liked him much. Darryl was a born lawyer. Highly intelligent, shrewd and meticulous, he had built a peerless reputation as a clever and influential advocate and lobbyist with impeccable contacts. But his self-absorbed and calculating personal style had always irritated Michael, and their relationship had been cordial but never warm. Michael invariably found conversations with Darryl Beane to be all about giving Darryl something that he needed rather than getting much of anything in return.

Today was different. Darryl Beane had some information that Michael desperately wanted to hear about. The lawyer had telephoned him from Sydney a few days earlier. They hadn't spoken in years, but Darryl had called as a friend to pass on that one of his contacts in the Major Crimes Squad North had told him confidentially that new information had been received in relation to the death of Trevor Ellowe, and that police were considering going to Queensland to interview Michael in relation to the matter.

As soon as the plane came to a halt Michael Wiltshire got to his feet and pulled his briefcase from the overhead locker. He was keen to get going. Beane would be waiting for his call the moment he got into the terminal so they could arrange a time as early as possible to meet at his office and discuss the matter further. The lawyer had been understandably reluctant to go into any detail over the phone, but he'd assured Michael the information was spot on. They would go through it all thoroughly when they met and then work up a strategy as to how they should respond.

Michael nodded and smiled absently at the pretty young hostess standing by the cabin door as he stepped into the hallway leading towards the terminal. His mind was raking over what he'd learned so far about the death of Barry Dougherty and how it might be connected with Trevor Ellowe.

He hadn't heard from Frank Vagianni in more than a week, except to note from his bank records that the detective had cashed the expenses cheque he had given him when they last met. But Michael had to believe that this new development in the Ellowe case had everything to do with Dougherty's death, which confirmed in his mind that the old man had been murdered and that Fred Hunter was behind it. Maybe Vagianni had even passed on details of their conversation to the New South Wales police; it was clear enough he'd been less than discreet with Kirsten Foster, so why wouldn't he have been just as talkative to the police? A part of Michael felt sick at the thought that he was about to be drawn into what could turn into a very ugly and controversial police investigation, but at the same time he had an oddly consoling sense of anticipation at the prospect of finally unburdening himself of the details of what he knew.

'Have a good day, sir.'

Michael again nodded politely as he stepped out into the terminal and strode towards the broad aisle leading to the escalators. He pushed his hand into his pocket and pulled out his mobile phone, pressing his thumb onto the button until the battery beeped on. At this hour the trip into the city should take no more than twenty minutes.

'Excuse me. Michael Wiltshire, isn't it?'

The words jolted him from his distracted state. He didn't recognise the two men standing directly in front of him.

'Yes.'

One of them slipped a police identification

from the inside pocket of his jacket and discreetly flipped it open.

'I'm Detective Senior Sergeant Nick Phelps from Major Crime. This is Detective Senior Sergeant Phil Manning. We were wondering if we could have a quick word with you.'

Michael felt his whole body seize up slightly. The thoughts that had been flowing through his brain in such an orderly fashion seemed suddenly clogged in a kind of mental log jam as he groped clumsily for his voice.

'Is this about Barry Dougherty?'

The taller man standing alongside Phelps stretched his face into a sarcastic smirk.

'You must be psychic, Michael.'

Michael looked at Detective Phil Manning uncomprehendingly, trying to process in his mind exactly what was happening.

'Have you been in touch with Darryl Beane?'

'No.' Phelps's face was expressionless. 'Should we have?'

'He's my lawyer. I was just going to call him.'

'Well, we just wanted to have a yarn with you first if you don't mind, Michael.' Manning still had the same sardonic smile on his thin lips. 'Is there some reason why you think you might need a lawyer?'

'No.' Michael couldn't help thinking he sounded like a guilty man as the answer leapt out of his mouth.

'Fair enough.' Nick Phelps didn't look as if he was interested in getting into any arguments. 'Have you got a couple of minutes to talk to us?'

'Well, I'm due in the city in about half an hour.'

'Perfect.' Phelps turned slightly and motioned towards the exits. 'We're going that way. We'll give you a lift in.'

By the time they got to the car Phelps had asked him all about the weather up in Queensland and the flight down from Brisbane, and had filled him in on the traffic problems getting to and from the airport these days, and how lucky he was to be living up in Queensland because Sydney traffic was atrocious and they'd been getting a lot more rain than was usual for this time of year. Michael chimed in mechanically as and when the conversation required, but his brain was somewhere else. He was struggling to assess exactly where all this was coming from and how he should be dealing with it. The policeman's idle conversation wasn't helping him to collect his thoughts. When Phil Manning swung the rear door of the police car open, waiting for him to slip into the back seat, the smug expression on his face made Michael feel even more unsettled, and suddenly he had a sick feeling deep in his stomach. The look was unmistakable. Not only did this police officer suspect him of something, he was obviously very confident he had the goods on him. What was it? How much did they know? What could they prove? As Manning shut the door firmly behind him and climbed into the front passenger seat Phelps kicked the engine over.

'Where've you got to go to in the city, Michael?'

Michael rummaged slightly for the answer before it came to him. 'King Street.'

Phelps looked genuinely enlightened. 'Oh well, that's just up the road from headquarters. We might just slip in there first for a few minutes and have a yak about this thing if that suits you. Alright?'

The conversation felt like it had lurched forward quickly and Michael was struggling to keep up.

'Sure.'

The two police silently watched the road ahead as they glided up the ramp and slotted into the lanes of traffic jockeying for position on the eastern distributor heading for the city. The casual chatter was finished, at least for the time being, and Michael couldn't avoid the uncomfortable notion that his companions had got the answer they were working for. They were now all on their way to police headquarters together to discuss some new information about Barry Dougherty, something they wanted Michael to hear about, something they clearly preferred to discuss behind closed doors. No doubt it was the information he had given Frank Vagianni, who had obviously breached confidence and spoken to police. But then that didn't quite explain the sardonic smirk and smug expression Michael had seen on the face of Detective Phil Manning. He seemed to believe they had something more, something that implicated Michael Wiltshire. The sick feeling in Michael's stomach flared again as he leaned forward in his seat.

'Should I have a lawyer with me for this?'

Phelps looked at him over his left shoulder with a slightly shocked expression.

'I don't think so, but that's up to you really.'

Michael wished he hadn't asked the question; it made it look as though he had something to hide.

'You can if you want to. We've just got some information about Dougherty's death, that's all. We were going to take you through it, see if you could comment at all.'

The smirk was back on Manning's face as he swivelled in his seat.

'Only guilty people need lawyers, Michael.'

He was right, and Michael was angry with himself. All they wanted to do at this stage was tell him what information they had about the Dougherty case and get whatever comment he wanted to give. Michael had been in business long enough to know it never hurt to listen. The more information they laid on the table the better. He was under no obligation to say a single word. He slid back on the seat, took a deep breath and told himself to get a grip. He would take whatever information they were willing to give him and relay it back to Darryl Beane. He and Darryl would then factor it into their strategy as to the best way forward. This was a process of discussion and negotiation, just like any business dealing. Collect the information first, then set your strategy and go after a result.

By the time they turned into the car park beneath the Sydney Police Centre in Goulburn Street Michael was feeling almost as relaxed and self-assured as he would be going into any business meeting. The feeling was short-lived. As the police car left daylight behind and swung into the fluorescent-lit cement greyness of the basement the sickly feeling seeped back into his stomach. The clang of the heavy cell doors and the barking busy voices echoing through the concrete corridors of the adjoining watch house sent a cold lonely chill through him, and he was relieved to finally step into the lift and watch the doors glide closed. When they opened again Phelps led the way through the police offices as Michael fell in behind him and Manning brought up the rear. There was something slightly unsettling about being the middleman in this impromptu parade.

'Take a seat, Michael. I'll just grab the file.'

Phelps disappeared almost before Michael had even stepped into the interview room. It was small and bland, nothing on the walls except a clock and a calendar. The only furniture was three chairs and a narrow desk with a computer and a keyboard. Michael ventured tentatively towards the desk and selected a chair. Phil Manning slouched casually in the doorway, leaning on the doorjamb, his impeccably tailored light-wool jacket rumpled slightly by the arms folded resolutely across his chest. It occurred to Michael that he had the look of a man who was standing guard.

'So how long had you known Barry Dougherty, Michael?'

'Oh, a while.'

Manning nodded silently, his eyes fixed on Michael Wiltshire.

'Long while or a short while?'

'Well ...' Michael was fumbling slightly for his words. 'Actually he was more a friend of my father's.'

'Oh right.' Manning nodded again. 'Didn't you know him yourself?'

'Well no, not really.'

'I thought you said you'd known him for a while.'

He was staring straight into Michael's eyes, his expression cold and unflinching.

'No. Not really.'

Nick Phelps appeared suddenly in the doorway, cradling an untidy file in one arm and a large briefcase in the other, and pushed his way through into the room. As he dropped the file onto the desk and the briefcase onto the floor and pulled up a chair, Manning followed him in, closed the door and took up a position behind Michael's shoulder. Dragging the third chair towards him, he propped a foot on it and leaned forward casually on one elbow to listen to the conversation. Phelps opened matter-of-factly.

'So, before we get started, Michael, is there anything you can tell us about what happened to Barry Dougherty?'

It was a question Michael hadn't expected and it took him by surprise.

'Well, no.'

'Nothing?'

'No, of course not.'

'But you knew him, did you?'

'Well no, not really.'

Phelps glanced up at Manning who took the opportunity to chime in.

'Had you spoken to him at all lately?'

'Not that springs to mind.'

'Not that springs to mind?' Manning's face was screwed into a derisive grimace and there was venom in his voice. 'I thought you told me just a minute ago you didn't know him at all?'

'Well, I'd met him.'

'That means you know him, doesn't it?'

'Well, I suppose I knew him in the sense I'd met him a couple of times.'

Phelps cut in again, his voice softer and more conversational.

'Yeah, in what circumstances, in what context sort of thing, would that be, Michael?'

'Well, he was very involved in the Labor Party at one stage. So was I.'

'That'd be what, going back to when you were living here in Sydney, would it?'

'That's right.'

'You haven't had anything to do with him since then?'

He was leaning forward, eyebrows arched, peering straight into Michael's eyes.

'Not that I recall, no.'

Phelps flipped the file open on the desk in front of him and slipped a biro from his top pocket.

'Okay, mate, that's fine, we might just get some of this down.'

He scratched a few notes on the inside cover of his file then reached down into the briefcase on the floor beside him.

'Actually I might just whack it down on tape if you don't mind. Saves me trying to keep notes.'

He laid a small black tape recorder on the desk between them and carefully clicked it on. The glow of a tiny red 'record' light burrowed into Michael's consciousness.

'Right, we're just talking about Barry Dougherty,' Phelps resumed pleasantly. 'So, Michael, have you ever done business of any kind with Barry.'

'No.'

'He's never worked for you?'

'No.'

'Ever bought anything from him?'

'No.'

'Never had cause to pay him any money?'

Michael Wiltshire felt an unexpected palpitation in his chest.

'Pardon?'

Phelps paused, looking slightly nonplussed at the interruption.

'Did you ever pay him any money?'

The breath was temporarily suspended in Michael's throat. Did the police know Dougherty had asked him for money? Should he tell them that?

'No.' The answer leaped out in a breathless, unconvincing whisper.

'Has he ever asked you for any?'

Should he be going into any of this now? Or should he be waiting to discuss it with Darryl Beane first? If he mentioned Dougherty's approaches to him, the police would want him to go through the whole story and he wasn't ready to deal with any of that now. Perhaps he should simply refuse to say anything more, or perhaps he should ask permission to ring Darryl Beane for advice before he answered any further questions?

No, that would look as though he had something to hide. Phelps was staring at him expectantly, waiting for his answer.

'No.'

'Okay, fair enough.' The questioner seemed content with the answer. For now the crisis was over. 'Well, you hardly knew him, I suppose.'

'That's right.'

'Do you know a female by the name of Wendy Bagley?'

Manning barked the question so gruffly from behind Michael's shoulder that Michael swivelled in his chair to look up at him.

'No.'

The detective snorted contemptuously as Phelps quietly resumed his questioning.

'What about a bloke by the name of Trevor Ellowe, do you know him?'

The mention of the name sparked another minor flutter in his chest but Michael did his best to mask any apprehension.

'I know of him.'

'In what capacity?'

'I can't recall right now.' He paused briefly, searching for a sensible response. 'I think he may have been an employee of one of our local branch officials.'

'Did Trevor ever work for you at all?'

'Never.'

The reply came back so promptly and positively that Phelps hesitated a moment, evaluating it carefully before he resumed with apparent detachment.

'Did you ever have occasion to speak to him on the telephone?'

'I'm not sure now.' Michael was suddenly awkward again, stumbling across his words. 'I may have.'

Manning leaned forward, curling his lip derisively.

'So what might you have been talking about if you did talk to him?'

Michael Wiltshire looked into Phil Manning's sneering face and recognised the same certain conviction he had seen back at the airport. He could see that whatever he said now wasn't going to change Manning's obviously unwavering view that he was a guilty man.

'Look, I think I'd prefer not to take this any further for now. I think it's best if I get back to you guys later on some of this stuff.'

Nick Phelps's geniality faded quickly from his face. He reached forward and clicked the tape recorder off.

'Why's that, Michael?'

'Well, I was actually planning on seeing my lawyer, Darryl Beane, about all this today.'

Manning leaned so far forward Michael could feel the puff of his growled whisper against his cheek.

'And why would you need to be seeing your lawyer about it?'

Michael turned his head to face the policeman, holding his contemptuous stare defiantly.

'Well, I'd say that's between my lawyer and me, isn't it.'

Manning's scornful face was just inches away, his teeth bared and his chin threatening.

'I don't think so, sport.'

The nervous feeling in the pit of Michael's stomach dissolved instantly and completely. Now, as he looked into the policeman's eyes, he felt nothing but anger and contempt for Manning's insolence.

'I'm leaving.'

He pushed to his feet but before he could turn towards the door Phelps was standing in front of him. He wasn't a tall man but his broad muscular shoulders and thick balding head blocked any vision to the door.

'I'm afraid it's not quite that simple.' It was clear from the look in his eyes that he had something he intended to say whether Michael Wiltshire wanted to hear it or not. 'Why don't you take a seat.'

The anger drained from Michael's face and he folded slowly back onto the chair. Phelps sat back down opposite him.

'I told you earlier we have some new information on the Dougherty matter. That information directly implicates you in the murder of Trevor Ellowe.'

'What?' Michael Wiltshire recoiled. 'That's nonsense.'

Bang. Manning's hand slammed flat on the desk so suddenly and violently that Michael jumped involuntarily in his seat.

'Cut the fucking bullshit, Wiltshire.' Now Manning laid both hands flat on the desktop and leaned forward on them, glaring into Michael's face. 'I'm sick to shit of your bullshit, you hear me?'

The blood was rushing in Michael's ears and his heart was pumping painfully in his chest as he stared back at Manning. Nick Phelps's quiet voice was almost soothing as it broke into the confrontation.

'We know all about it, Michael.' His brow folded into an almost sympathetic countenance as he counted off the stubby fingers of one hand. 'We've got the phone records. We know about him threatening you. We know you arranged to have him bashed. We know all about the set-up with the car crash in the Cross.'

Michael stared back at him incredulously, struggling to decipher the confusion of information that was congesting his brain.

'What the hell are you talking about?'

'Let me summarise it for you, smartarse.' Phil Manning was still leaning forward on both hands, his snarling face hanging over Michael threateningly. 'You were getting around Marrickville big-noting about how you were going to expose branch-stacking in the Enmore branch of the Labor Party, putting a whole lot of noses out of joint, including Trevor Ellowe's.' Manning flipped his eyebrows comically, searching Wiltshire's face for any sign of a reaction. 'Next thing Ellowe starts putting the weights on you to back off and pull your head in. But you weren't going to cop that so you cracked the shits and called in the heavies.'

He straightened up off the table and paced a tight semicircle as he continued. 'And they did a real good job, maybe a bit too good, because old mate Trevor winds up very dead. So you and your boys decide to fix it all up nice and tidy so it looks just like an accident. In fact, you did such a good job you even fooled us silly coppers.' The palms of Manning's hands fell back onto the table as he leaned forward again to emphasise his point. 'For a little while, smartarse, but not any more. Now your bullshit's caught up with you.'

Michael wasn't looking at him, but he could feel the tiny flecks of spittle landing lightly on his forehead and cheeks. Across the desk Phelps sat absolutely motionless, his eyes fixed on his suspect. When he spoke again his voice was as hushed and confidential as that of a priest whispering forgiveness in the sanctity of the confessional.

'We know he was threatening you, Michael.'

It was true, and it felt good to know that Phelps believed it.

'No doubt you were just trying to protect yourself. You probably didn't intend them to do anything more than just give the bloke a bit of a touch-up. No one's saying you intended to kill him. We just want to know the story.'

Manning dragged his hands off the desk and stepped out another compact semicircle in the little room. 'Yeah, and we don't want any more of your fucking bullshit.'

He turned his sneering face back to Michael and waited impatiently with both hands propped against his hips. A mixture of anger and desperation was coursing through Michael's brain. A compelling urge to physically assault the jeering policeman standing in front of him was barely tempered by the painful pumping in his chest and the sickly churning in his stomach. One part of him wanted to get up and walk out, leave Manning to think whatever he wanted, do whatever he thought he was entitled to do. Nothing Michael could say to him would make any difference, that much was clear. His mind was closed. All he was looking for was Michael's confession that he had arranged to have Trevor Ellowe murdered. He didn't care about the real story, didn't want to know what had happened, or why, or who was involved. But Phelps was a different kettle of fish. He at least seemed willing to listen. He seemed genuinely interested in investigating the facts, finding out the truth.

'Okay look, I'll tell you what I know —'

Phelps held up one hand, signalling him to stop, as he reached forward with the other hand and clicked the tape recorder on. Michael nervously eyed the minute red light as the policeman's flat voice resumed its questioning.

'Michael, is there something you would now like to tell us about the death of Trevor Ellowe?'

'It's true.' The answer jumped out of Michael Wiltshire's mouth as though he was gasping for air. 'He was ringing me up, threatening me, just before he died.'

'Did you report that to the police?'

'No.'

'Did you report it to anyone?'

'Only Gary Sharpe.'

'Gary Sharpe, the Labor Party bloke?'

'Yes.'

'When was this?'

'At the time it was all happening.'

Manning's voice, now restrained and unemotional, broke into the questioning.

'So I take it you were lying to us a few minutes ago when you said weren't sure whether you'd ever spoken to him on the phone.'

A flood of resentment washed into Michael's mouth as he looked up at Manning standing against the opposite wall. It quickly ebbed away.

'Yes, I was.'

'Why did you lie to us about that, Michael?'

'I'm not sure really.'

'Were you trying to hide something from us?'

'No.' He spat the answer angrily at Manning, but then hesitated, reconsidering. 'Well, yes, I suppose I was.'

'What were you trying to hide?'

'Well, I —'

'Was it the fact that you arranged to have him bashed?'

'No.' Now there was more desperation than anger in his voice. 'No, I didn't arrange anything.' Michael switched his gaze plaintively to Nick Phelps. 'Look, I don't know what happened to Trevor Ellowe.'

As Manning paced the room again, shaking his head theatrically, Phelps inched a little closer on the desk, his brow still knitted in apparent concern. He stared silently into Michael's eyes for several seconds then resumed as solemnly as if he were delivering a eulogy.

'Wendy Bagley's given us a full statement, Michael.' He slipped a dog-eared photocopy of an A4 document from the file and laid it on the desk in front of him. 'She's currently in police protective custody under a witness protection program. She rang the Darlinghurst station a week ago and told them the whole story.'

Michael Wiltshire looked quizzically at the statement lying on the desk between them. 'What whole story?'

Phelps was staring back at him gravely, as if silently urging him to face the truth. Michael held his gaze unflinchingly until eventually the policeman took the statement in both hands and folded over the top page. He resumed his questioning in a formal monotone.

'If you like I'll read part of her statement to you and you can comment or not as you see fit. You're not obliged to make any comment, but if you do make any comment it'll be recorded here on the tape recorder and it can be used in evidence. Do you understand that?'

Michael hesitated, startled and confused, wondering what statement Phelps was talking about and what danger there could be in hearing part of it read.

'Yes.'

'Do you want me to read the statement to you?'

He looked at the document suspended between the policeman's stubby fingers.

'Sure.'

Phelps leafed through the document, scanning

the contents and summarising in a dull, almost uninterested tone as he turned the pages over.

'Wendy Bagley is the former de facto of Trevor Ellowe. Ellowe had told her about a disagreement he'd had with you concerning allegations of branch-stacking in the Enmore branch. She relates a number of incidents shortly prior to his death in which she overheard Ellowe making telephone calls to you on his mobile phone. Most of them were concerned with branch-stacking and other political issues but the calls became gradually more heated and Ellowe eventually became openly threatening and abusive towards you over the phone.' Phelps stopped leafing and folded back the pages already scanned. 'Then, in reference to the night of Ellowe's death, Bagley says this.' He flattened out the statement and commenced reading from it:

'Trevor had been drinking heavily and he was in a very aggressive mood. He started on about Michael Wiltshire as he often did, calling him a silvertail and saying he would like to belt him. He said he was going to ring him. I didn't want any part of it but Trevor was wild and I couldn't stop him when he got in that kind of mood. He dialled a number on his mobile and he got into an argument with someone over the phone. He was abusing the person on the line, calling him "Wiltshire". Then I heard him say, "I'm sick of you, Wiltshire, I'm coming over there right now to give it to you." Then he hung

up and demanded I drive him to Petersham. He was raving on saying Michael Wiltshire had "put some muscle on him" which I understood meant Wiltshire had hired someone to bash Trevor. He was furious and said he was going to teach Wiltshire a lesson. I had been drinking too and I didn't want to drive but Trevor was very insistent. He directed me to a house somewhere up near the water tower at Petersham. It was very dark but I could see it was a big house with steps up to the front door. Trevor went up to the house and I stayed in the car. I saw him go to the front door and he knocked very loudly. Someone came to the front door and I could hear what sounded like an argument just inside the front door of the house. I could see that there was more than just the two of them. I'm not sure how many men there were but it looked like at least three apart from Trevor. Next thing they all seemed to go inside and they closed the door. After about ten minutes a man came out the front door and walked down to my car. At first I thought it was Trevor coming back but then I realised it was someone else. He walked around and knocked on the driver's window. I had not seen this man before but I now know him to be Michael Wiltshire. He said to me words to the effect of "Trevor's going to hang around for a while. We'll drop him home later." I remember quite clearly that he used the word "we" and I assumed he was referring to the men I had seen at the front door with Trevor. I then drove home to my flat in Stanmore. I did not see Trevor Ellowe again after I left the house.'

Phelps laid the document flat on the desk between them.

'What have you got to say about that, Michael?'

Now the anger and resentment were completely gone, supplanted by an overwhelming sense of panic. Suddenly Michael Wiltshire could feel his whole existence falling away beneath his feet like sand sliding into a bottomless abyss.

'It's untrue.' The words leapt out frantically. 'The whole thing — it's a total lie.'

'All of it?'

'Of course.'

Manning stepped forward again, breaking into the conversation with renewed vigour.

'But you told us just before that Ellowe had been calling you.'

'Well, yes, that part of it's true.'

'You also told us he'd been threatening you.'

'Yes, that's right, he had.'

'So that part's not a lie?'

'No.'

'Well, make up your mind — is it a total lie or not?'

'Part of it's true, part of it's not.'

Manning rolled his eyes and threw his head back.

'Well, what part of it's not true?'

'He didn't come to my house that night.'

'But you did tell him you'd put some muscle on him.'

'No, of course I didn't.'

'Oh, that part of it's a total lie as well is it?'

'Yes.' Michael turned back to Phelps, desperation welling in his eyes. 'Look, I didn't even see Trevor Ellowe that night. I've got no idea what happened to him.'

All trace of sympathy had faded from Phelps's countenance.

'Michael, it may interest you to know that during the course of our investigation into this matter we had Queensland police obtain an interception warrant to authorise monitoring of your telephones. As a result, extensive recordings were made of a number of your telephone conversations which we believe directly implicate you in the death of Trevor Ellowe.'

'What?' The question was not much more than a bewildered whisper. 'You bugged my phones?'

'That's correct.' Phelps's voice was cold and clinical. 'I propose to play back a brief excerpt of one of those conversations. Should you wish to comment on the contents of that conversation you may. You're not obliged to make any comment, and any comment that you do make will be recorded and may later be used in evidence against you. Do you clearly understand that?'

'Yes.'

'I'll play that excerpt now.'

Phelps reached into his briefcase and produced a second, larger portable tape recorder which he placed at the opposite end of the desk to the small handheld machine with the threatening red light. Then he pulled out a bundle of four C–90 cassette tapes bound together with a rubber band. He selected one, slipped the tape from its cover and placed it in the tape machine. It had been pre-set at the desired point of a hushed conversation between a man and a woman. Michael heard his own pained voice trying to penetrate the barrier of mistrust and anguish he had raised between him and a cherished friend.

'Kirsten, I had to talk to you ... when I last saw you ... I didn't tell you the truth about Trevor ... I want you to know the truth.'

Phelps pressed one finger on the pause button and resumed his questioning in a lifeless monotone.

'Michael, on that tape we have just heard a male person speaking to a female caller. Firstly, is that male person you?'

'Yes, it is.'

'You're heard to say to the female caller, "I didn't tell you the truth about Trevor. I want you to know the truth." Were you there referring to Trevor Ellowe?'

'Yes.'

'When you spoke about "the truth about Trevor" to what were you referring?'

Michael Wiltshire's trembling lips began to form a word, but no sound came out. He had no idea what he had intended to say, what he wanted to say, what he could or should say. The question was already gone, his brain numb from the battering of the garbled, incoherent snippets of information swirling in his head.

'Would you like to take a break, Michael?'

Michael nodded absently as Nick Phelps reached forward and clicked the tape recorder off. Cupping his hands in front of him the detective settled into a contemplative pose, peering up at Michael through his eyebrows for several long, silent seconds.

'Look, Michael, we've got more than enough to pin you with this.' Nick Phelps was looking straight into his eyes now, urging him to confide. 'So either you tell us what happened that night and who else was involved, or you're going to end up wearing the whole thing yourself.' He paused just long enough to let the proposition sink in. 'If someone's gone a bit overboard, got a bit more heavy-handed than you intended, you have to tell us now, otherwise the court's going to figure you've just lined the bloke up for a hit. Mate, it's in your own interests to get the full story out.'

Michael Wiltshire buried his face in both hands, searching for a strategy in the blackness where his fingertips pressed into his eyes. Slowly, wearily, he dropped his hands and focused on Phelps's unrelenting stare.

'Look, I've got absolutely no idea what happened to Trevor Ellowe. That's the full story, if you want to know the full story.'

Nick Phelps sighed and sat back in his chair. Manning spat out a string of muttered expletives.

'Well, to be fair, Wendy Bagley says you said something similar to her.' Phelps flattened out the statement once again and turned over several pages. 'I'll just read that part of her statement to you.' He stabbed one stubby finger at the page and began to read verbatim:

> 'One afternoon Michael Wiltshire rang me at home. He said there was going to be a public inquest and the police would probably want me to give evidence. He said he didn't want me to say anything about Trevor going to his house that night because if the newspapers got hold of it it would be politically damaging for him. He offered me money to keep quiet about it. He said Trevor had left his house not long after I left, claiming he was going into Kings Cross to score some heroin. Wiltshire said that if it came out that Trevor was at his house and then later died of an overdose it could be very damaging to him politically. He offered me two thousand dollars to keep quiet about it. At the time I had been told that Trevor had crashed a stolen car down in the Cross so I believed what Wiltshire told me. I agreed to say nothing to anyone about Trevor going to Wiltshire's house that night. The next day Michael Wiltshire came to my house and gave me two thousand dollars in cash.'

'Michael, did you have that conversation with Wendy Bagley?'

'Absolutely not.' The vigour had returned to Wiltshire's voice. 'I've never spoken to the woman.'

'Absolutely not, ay?' Phil Manning scooped up the statement, leafing roughly through the pages. 'What about this one, Michael, did you have this conversation with her?' Finding his place he folded the pages over. 'Have a little listen to this:

> 'After the inquest I realised that Michael Wiltshire had been lying to me about what had happened to Trevor. I rang him up and accused him of being involved in Trevor's death. He became very angry and threatening towards me. I recall clearly that during this conversation Michael Wiltshire admitted to me that he had arranged Trevor's death. He said, "That's right, I had him knocked. And if you so much as breathe a word of any of this to anyone you're next."'

Manning slapped the statement onto the table. 'What about that conversation, Michael? Does that sound familiar to you?'

'No, it doesn't. It's garbage.'

Manning was leaning on the table again, spitting venom at his suspect.

'So why do you reckon Wendy Bagley would be telling all these porkies about you, Michael?'

'How would I know?' Michael Wiltshire snapped the answer back at his tormentor. 'I don't even know the woman.'

'Just like you don't know Barry Dougherty, is that it?'

Michael turned back to face Phelps who was still staring blankly at him across the narrow table.

'Look, I knew Barry Dougherty in the sense I'd met him once or twice.'

Manning pushed his face forward, barking into Wiltshire's ear. 'According to Wendy Bagley you knew him alright. You knew Barry Dougherty because he was the only person she ever told about Trevor Ellowe coming round to your house that night, and poor old Barry was silly enough to try and make a dollar out of it, wasn't he?'

Michael Wiltshire looked straight into Phil Manning's accusing eyes.

'What are you talking about?'

'Barry Dougherty threatened to go to the police, so you had to pay him to keep his mouth shut too.'

Nick Phelps's unemotive voice broke in quietly. 'Bagley says you had Dougherty killed because he was blackmailing you.'

'No.'

There was a shrill panic in Michael Wiltshire's voice that sounded like the protestation of a guilty man. It faded into the silence as Phelps stared relentlessly into his eyes.

'Have a look at these bank statements, Michael.' Phelps slipped three photocopied pages from the file in front of him and pushed them across the desk. They were copies of statements from Michael's account, with three entries, months apart, highlighted in yellow marker pen. 'See these withdrawals? Cash, two thousand. Cash, three thousand. Cash, seven thousand. Do you know what they relate to?'

Michael Wiltshire's heart was beating painfully in his chest.

'That's nearly four years ago. How would I remember back that far?'

Phil Manning's sneering face was inches from his ear.

'That's twelve grand, Michael. That's a lot of money.'

Wiltshire was looking straight ahead, struggling to ignore Manning's interjection.

'So?'

Nick Phelps quietly resumed his questioning.

'So each of those withdrawals from your account corresponds to a deposit by Barry Dougherty into his account. How do you explain that, Michael?'

'He was down on his luck.' Wiltshire's voice was strained and breathless. 'He asked me if I could help him out.'

'But you hardly knew him.'

His mouth opened but no sound came out.

'Dougherty was blackmailing you, wasn't he?'

'No.'

The answer fell out feebly and unconvincingly.

'Didn't you tell us earlier on that you'd never paid any money to Dougherty?'

'Yes.'

'You were lying when you told us that, weren't you?'

'Yes.' Michael Wiltshire's head was bowed like a sinner asking for forgiveness. 'I guess I was.'

'Why'd you lie to us about that, Michael?'

He looked up into Nick Phelps's eyes, struggling to think what the true answer was. As his brain wrestled with the question Manning's jeering tone burst into his consciousness.

'It's because these were blackmail payments, weren't they, Michael? Barry Dougherty was blackmailing you.'

'No.'

'And you were willing to cop it at first, so long as it was relatively small beans, but then about a month ago old Barry Dougherty upped the ante, didn't he? He decided to go for the big pay-off.'

There was a long silence while the two policemen waited for an answer.

'I don't know what you're talking about.'

Michael Wiltshire was looking into the face of Nick Phelps. In his plaintive eyes the policeman could see something familiar, the wretched weariness of a man who was tired of lying, ready to give up.

'Yes, you do, Michael.' He came a little closer. 'See, we already know the whole story. Barry sent you another blackmail letter and this time you'd finally had enough. So you rang Wendy Bagley looking for him, didn't you?'

As Wiltshire's eyes narrowed into an uncomprehending squint Manning burst back into the dialogue.

'Bad blue involving Bagley, Michael. All you did was create another witness against you. She didn't know anything about it until you rang her, until you told her you were looking for the old bloke and when you found him you were going to shut him up permanently.'

The brash interruption seemed to focus Michael's brain. He looked up at Manning.

'Shut him up for what?'

'Two million bucks, that's what. He was demanding two big ones from you, wasn't he, Michael? And that ain't small beans, even for a bloke like you.'

Wiltshire regarded Manning's sneering visage with absolute contempt. Then he turned back to Phelps.

'Barry Dougherty was threatening to expose Fred Hunter.'

'Fred Hunter? What for?'

'I don't know, all that branch-stacking business from years ago, I suppose. He told me he had evidence Hunter was rigging the books.'

Phil Manning snorted incredulously.

'Are you saying Fred Hunter had Dougherty killed?'

'No.' The answer leapt out automatically. 'Maybe. I don't know.'

'Did you ever tell Hunter that Dougherty claimed to have evidence on him?'

'No.'

'Then how would Hunter even know about it?'

Michael was still groping hopelessly for the answer as Phelps clicked the tape back on and resumed his questioning.

'Did you ever make any payments to Barry Dougherty to buy his silence?'

'Not really, no.'

'Not really? What do you mean by not really?'

'No. I mean no. I never did.'

The look on Phelps's face said he didn't believe a word of it.

'Did Dougherty ever send you a blackmail letter?'

'No.'

The questioning stopped. For several long seconds Nick Phelps sat silently, looking straight into Michael Wiltshire's eyes until he blinked and looked away self-consciously at the clock up on the wall. When he looked back Phelps was still sitting motionless, staring at him. The look on his face was unmistakable: he didn't believe what Michael was telling him and he wanted the truth. He was waiting for another answer, a retraction, a qualifying comment, something. As Michael looked back at him his thoughts were frozen by the panic surging in his chest. The police knew he was lying, they knew why he had come to Sydney, knew all about the letter. They had been listening to his phone calls. What had they heard? Whom had he spoken to about all this? What had he said? Incomplete and frantic thoughts darted in and out of his brain as he looked back into the detective's vacant stare. Should he say anything more? What could he say? He blinked awkwardly into the detective's face again and finally looked down at the desk.

Phelps turned to Manning and nodded. A cynical smirk spread slowly across Phil Manning's face as he looked down at Wiltshire. He straightened up momentarily, shook his head, then bent to scoop up a briefcase from the floor, placing it flat on the table between Nick Phelps and the suspect.

'Is this your briefcase?'

'Yes.'

'Would you mind opening it up for us, please?'

Now any doubt was gone. They knew everything. Michael stared nervously at the closed briefcase.

'All that's in there are papers for my lawyer.'

When Nick Phelps spoke his voice was subdued but resolute. 'Open it up, please, Michael.'

Michael rolled the combination on each side with his thumb and flipped the catches open. He was still lifting the lid as Manning reached in and pulled out a slender pile of freshly photocopied documents. The detective flicked through several pages before he settled on what he was obviously looking for.

'Well, well, well, what do you know.'

He slipped two photocopied pages from the bundle and dropped them onto the desk in front of Phelps, leaning over his partner's shoulder as together they digested the contents of the document. When Phelps had finished reading he looked up at Michael Wiltshire.

'What do you know about this letter?'

Lying between them on the desk was a poorly typewritten letter. Michael didn't have to look at it. He had read it a hundred times. Phelps rotated the document with his stubby fingers as he slid it across the desk towards his suspect.

'I believe this is the blackmail letter Barry Dougherty sent you threatening to expose you for your involvement in the death of Trevor Ellowe. What do you say about that?'

Michael looked down at the letter and then back at Phelps.

'I don't think I should say anything more until I speak to my lawyer.'

Nick Phelps rose purposefully to his feet.

'Michael Wiltshire, you're under arrest for the murder of Trevor Wayne Ellowe.'

CHAPTER EIGHTEEN

Darryl Beane looked ludicrously out of place. When the young policeman yanked the door open and pointed to the vinyl-covered chair tucked in under the interview bench, the first thing Michael saw was Darryl's crisp white cuffs and his carefully manicured fingers fiddling with a diamond-studded silver cufflink. The clean white collar, subtly and tastefully contrasted against his sky-blue silk shirt, the pale yellow satin tie that blended perfectly with his immaculately tailored light-weave woollen suit, clashed comically and painfully with the dirty grey wall behind him. As Michael stepped into the watch-house interview room Darryl Beane smiled sympathetically through the glass partition.

'Hello, Michael. Got here as quickly as I could.'

Michael wondered just how long he had been lying on the hard, flat bench in the holding cell. He remembered sitting propped up against the cold wall for a long time, troubled by the urgent churning in his stomach and the cacophony of frantic, angry pleas and other harsh noises that rolled through the cement corridors connecting the honeycomb of cells. Eventually he had lowered himself onto the bench as the fatigue of his ordeal numbed his apprehension and pulled him down into a deep, shrouded slumber. How long he had slept he couldn't say but the stiff ache in his neck and the chill in his shoulder and back suggested it had been several hours at least.

'They gave me a copy of the note.'

Beane pressed the photocopied pages flat against the glass partition separating them. Michael nodded silently and bowed his head. He didn't need to look; he had seen the document recently enough in the stubby grasp of Detective Nick Phelps. Besides, the contents were printed indelibly in his consciousness. They had arrived in his post office box not more than a month ago. Even as he slipped them out and flattened them against his palm he had felt a strange, fragile sense of impending doom fluttering in his stomach. With the pages pinned between his fingers he had nervously skimmed the contents and realised it was a poorly typed letter, probably belted out on an old electric typewriter, almost entirely in upper case with exceptions randomly interspersed in a manner that suggested inadvertence or incompetence rather than design, and signed 'A Concerned Citizen'. It was obviously a photocopy of a photocopy, but despite the poorly reproduced type the message was crystal clear.

It's time to pay the piper, Wiltshire. You and your mate Fred Hunter murdered my friend

Trevor and now you're gonna pay. You might have fooled the coroner but just because he didn't commit you for trial doesn't mean you're not gonna end up in the dock. The DPP will soon present an ex officio indictment when they get a look at the evidence I've got for them.

You thought there were no witnesses but there were. They know all about your dirty little deal and why Trevor was on his way that night and who you called to get him sorted out. They know the so-called fatal accident in the Cross was just a set-up. You were a party to everything that happened: you procured the offence and that means you're as guilty as the blokes who bashed him and you're gonna pay for it. I have written it all down in lurid detail in a letter, the whole ugly story, including the names of the witnesses and where they can be contacted. One copy will go to Homicide, one to the Attorney-General, and one to all the papers.

The only way out of this for you is to do exactly as I tell you. Otherwise you'll go for murder and even if by some fluke your lawyers get it down to manslaughter you're still gonna be in gaol for a bloody long time, and that kid of yours is gonna grow up in a foster home. Think about it carefully, Wiltshire, because you're only going to get one chance.

I want $2 million. In return you get my silence, along with the destruction of the *letter and all details. You will never hear from me or any of the witnesses again.*

Otherwise I send the letter and you go to gaol and young Simon goes into a home. Your choice. If you don't want that to happen here's what you do.

First, you make whatever arrangements you have to make to get two million into an account ready to be transferred according to my instructions. Then, you put an ad in the personal column of the Sydney Telegraph *to appear on 16 October. The ad should read 'Mark Wallace has lift-off'. That's it, nothing more. When I see that I'll know you've got the money ready and you're ready to take this to the next level. I will contact you and tell you what you do next. If the ad doesn't appear it's all over for you, Wiltshire. No excuses, no haggling, no second chances, nothing. Be sure to understand that. This is not an auction, and it's not a game. You didn't give my mate Trevor any second chances and I won't be giving you any. One chance, that's all there is. Two million to buy your freedom or rot in gaol where you belong. I don't care which way you choose. Either one will make me happy.*

Beane's eyes were probing to make contact with his client's.

'Where did it come from?'

'It turned up in the post office box, just like that, about a month ago.'

There was a long silence before Beane continued, a bemused lilt colouring his cultured voice. 'And you think Barry Dougherty's behind it?'

The lawyer arched his eyebrows incredulously as Michael met his gaze for the first time. He could understand Darryl Beane's scepticism; after all, there was something mildly pathetic in the notion of poor old Barry Dougherty, Hunter Transport's alcoholic invoice clerk for over thirty years, the long-serving secretary of the Marrickville ALP branch, being the mastermind behind a two-million-dollar blackmail bid.

Michael nodded sullenly.

'Dougherty had it in his head that I was somehow responsible for Trevor Ellowe's death.'

'How do you know that?'

He looked up at the lawyer with weary eyes.

'I know.'

Beane was staring back at him through the glass, waiting for more. It didn't come. Wiltshire fidgeted idly with his fingernails then changed the subject.

'I hadn't seen or heard from him in nearly two years. That letter just came out of the blue. My guess is he probably read something about the Chiberta deal.'

Beane folded the pages on the narrow bench in front of him and nodded silently. Michael Wiltshire was a very astute man. He had hit the nail right on the head. Everybody in Australia had heard about the Chiberta deal. The newspapers had been full of stories about Queensland's so-called real-estate whiz kid Michael Wiltshire and how he had managed to tie up a stretch of long-forgotten beachfront mining land south of the Tweed River and turn it into the Chiberta Beach Estate, a major up-market secure residential development site that he had off-loaded to the Arabs at a profit of just over fourteen million dollars. It was an obscene amount of money for any man to make, and it shouldn't be a surprise to hear someone else wanted a piece of it. If Wiltshire was hiding any skeletons in his closet, he had to realise that kind of money made him a prime candidate for blackmail.

When Darryl Beane spoke again his voice was so hushed Michael strained to hear him through the glass.

'So what did you do when you got it? Did you report it to anyone?'

Michael felt a surge of bitter anguish somewhere in the back of his throat. He lowered his eyes to the desk and shook his head. Suddenly Beane's voice was more insistent.

'Did you respond to his demand?'

He slowly raised his eyes to meet his lawyer's gaze.

'I'd cancelled that PO box months ago.' Michael Wiltshire had a sad, ironic smile painted on his face. 'Didn't clear it out until the twentieth. By then the ultimatum date had come and gone.'

He buried his face in both hands and rubbed wearily, as if trying to wash away the frustration of his memory. When his fingers trailed across the stubble on his chin his bloodshot eyes held a new resignation.

'I had no address for Dougherty, no phone number, nothing. So I got someone to make some inquiries and eventually they came up with a contact number, somewhere up in north Queensland. I rang him one night, just a couple of days before he died.' Wiltshire paused, staring blankly at the glass in front of him, as if marshalling his recollection of the conversation. 'He was drunk. I couldn't get any sense out of him. I asked him if he'd sent me a letter about Trevor Ellowe. He denied it, but then he went into a long tirade about Fred Hunter and how he was going to bring him down.'

'For what?'

'Everything and anything. He claimed he'd already contacted Hunter and told him he was going to the police.'

Darryl Beane was leaning forward, the tip of his sharp nose almost touching the glass as he peered deep into Michael's eyes.

'Did he try to get more money out of you?'

Michael Wiltshire shook his head wearily.

'But he had been blackmailing you?'

Michael paused, thinking carefully about the question. Could he really say Barry Dougherty had ever tried to blackmail him? It was a strong word, and Barry had always been a bit more subtle than to threaten or demand anything. Until the letter, of course.

'You'd made payments to him.'

The insistent tone in Darryl Beane's voice made Michael focus on his fine features. The lawyer's eyes were opened wide, fixed cruelly on his client, demanding an answer. His thin lips were pursed in a humourless arch and the muscles in his jaw and neck were stretched tightly into a grim mask that underscored the seriousness of Michael's circumstances.

'Sure.' As Michael whispered his response, Beane nodded pensively, looking almost relieved. 'But it was always sort of on the basis that he was down on his luck. You know, he'd claim he needed cash for one reason or another and could I spare him a couple of dollars to see him through. Always "for old time's sake" more or less, and he'd promise to pay me back as soon as he could. There was never any suggestion of any kind of threat.'

'So why did you pay him?'

The question was an obvious one, but it came at Michael so quickly that it took him by surprise. It was one he still wasn't quite prepared to answer.

'For old time's sake, I guess.'

Darryl Beane curled the corners of his mouth, weighing up the answer. By his own admission Michael Wiltshire had been paying money to Barry Dougherty, a man who had accused him of involvement in the death of Trevor Ellowe. When he received the anonymous letter he was convinced Dougherty had penned it, and shortly thereafter Dougherty had wound up dead. It wasn't looking good.

'The police claim you denied ever paying Dougherty any money.'

'I did. I just thought if they got any sniff of blackmail I'd be their prime suspect.'

A dry, almost involuntary chuckle rattled in Darryl Beane's throat. He wasn't about to argue with his client's assessment of the situation. Any sniff of blackmail undoubtedly would make Wiltshire the prime suspect. The problem for Wiltshire was that the payments into Dougherty's account and now the blackmail letter in his briefcase raised a very healthy whiff of blackmail, and Wiltshire's denials only made his behaviour all the more suspicious.

'Ever think of simply exercising your right to silence?'

Michael Wiltshire stared coldly back at Darryl Beane, remembering all too clearly what it was about the haughty, self-opinionated lawyer that had always irritated him. Beane's eyebrows were arched superciliously, as though he was expecting a response.

'How soon can you get me out of here?'

Beane breathed out a long, exasperated sigh as he sat back in his chair and eyed his client. Now the muscles in his face seemed to relax, his tanned skin sagging gently into his jowls.

'Let me tell you what sort of trouble you're in here, Michael.'

As Beane went through it step by step and Michael listened to each piece of the jigsaw clicking into place, a sickly, hollow feeling built in his stomach. The case against him was a strong one. He was facing a great deal more than an uncorroborated claim by Wendy Bagley that he had confessed murder to her. Bagley's account was supported in almost every detail by reliable independent evidence. Michael had admitted to the police on tape during his interview that Ellowe had been threatening him over the telephone, just as Bagley had claimed. That gave him a motive to want retribution or at least protection from Ellowe. The telephone records showed that several calls were made to Michael's house by Ellowe in the weeks leading to his death. His last call was on the night he died, again consistent with Bagley's statement. She claimed she last saw Ellowe in the company of Michael Wiltshire and at least one other man at the house, and despite the car-crash scenario in the Cross the forensic evidence confirmed Trevor had been seriously, probably fatally assaulted much earlier in the night, closer to the time when Bagley saw him last at Michael's house. While the exact circumstances of Trevor Ellowe's death remained a mystery, Michael Wiltshire seemed to be telling Kirsten Foster in their tape-recorded telephone conversation that he knew 'the truth about Trevor'. According to Bagley, so did Barry Dougherty, and he had tried to use that knowledge as a means to extort money. Despite Michael's denials, her claim that Dougherty was trying to blackmail him was true, and the police could prove it with the bank records and the blackmail letter they'd turned up in Michael's briefcase.

'Getting bail isn't exactly going to be a walk in the park,' Beane said.

It wasn't until he climbed the creaking wooden stairs that led from the cells into Number One Central Local Court that Michael realised what an understatement that had been. As he stepped into the dock he caught a glimpse of a short, balding man shuffling papers on the bench that presided loftily above the courtroom. Warren Hyatt LCM had the irritated air of a busy administrator whose stamp pad was running short of ink. Michael heard the police prosecutor drawl his name, the inauspicious announcement closely followed by a gruff, uninterested grunt emanating from the bench.

'I have an application for bail, Your Worship.'

'What?'

Darryl Beane's announcement sounded almost apologetic, and in response Warren Hyatt sounded positively affronted.

'He's charged with murder, isn't he?'

'Yes, Your Worship, but this court does have jurisdiction to grant bail.'

'Yeah, alright.'

As the magistrate begrudgingly leaned back in his chair with a deep sigh, at least pretending to be listening to the prosecutor reading out the alleged facts, a mild panic washed over Michael. He felt a sickly flutter in his chest and stomach and the blood was rushing in his ears. He heard little of what was being said, his mind numbed by the sudden realisation that Darryl Beane may have been exactly right about the prospects of him getting bail. Michael had objected to the lawyer's negativity, protesting that he was not guilty of the charge. He would demonstrate his innocence when the time came, but in the meantime he had to get out of custody and back to Queensland, back to his home. He had a twelve-year-old boy to look after and a business to run. He needed time to think, time to collect himself, time to sit down and sort out just how he'd got himself into this mess.

'The defendant is remanded in custody until the sixteenth of next month, bail refused.'

Mr Hyatt LCM was already onto the next case as a heavy hand dragged Michael to his feet, his bewildered brain still struggling to process exactly what had happened. As he was shuffled in the direction of the wooden stairs, he was vaguely aware of Darryl Beane's perfumed presence close by, whispering frantically into his face, something about seeing him shortly back in the cells, and about bail in the Supreme Court. Images and voices swirled around him in a confused, nauseating blur.

'Come on, hurry up.'

The painful pressure of the officer's powerful hand locked like a vice around his upper arm focused Michael's mind. As Mr Hyatt LCM barked impatiently at someone in the courtroom behind him, Michael looked down the steep, dark stairway that led back to the cells. Cautiously, he started his descent.

CHAPTER NINETEEN

'What're y'in for?'

The young man opposite Michael in the back of the prison van was at least 190 centimetres; his long beefy legs jutted out from the low bench seat he was perched on, taking up what little space there was. His big hands lay flat on his knees, the chain of the handcuffs swinging rhythmically between eight tattooed fingers that spelled out the words 'hate' on his right hand and 'love' on his left. His cropped hair and rough unshaven face were no doubt designed to toughen up his boyish features, but even the scars on his broad jaw couldn't hide the fact that he was barely in his twenties.

'Murder.'

Michael hadn't been asked the question before and hadn't had to say the word, but as he heard it come from his own mouth in a callous grunt it shocked him.

'Whoa!' The young man held his hands up in feigned horror and began to giggle. 'Whoa! A murderer! Jesus, don't hurt me, man, I'm just a fuckin' harmless crook, ay. I'm no fuckin' murderer!'

He threw his head back and roared with laughter so hearty that it made Michael self-consciously. 'Hey, what's the fuckin' go here, man?' He was calling futilely to the van driver. 'What're you doing locking me up with a vicious murderer like this? I'm just a fuckin' harmless kid!'

He obviously thought this last line was particularly hilarious as it set him off into renewed peals of raucous laughter. Michael looked down at the steel handcuffs bordering his shirt sleeves. The thick hot air in the van had turned stale and Michael sucked hard to get a refreshing breath into his lungs. His cotton shirt was wringing wet with perspiration and stuck in clammy patches to his skin; he could feel rivulets of sweat spilling from behind his knees and rolling down his legs.

'I didn't murder anyone.'

The young man caught his breath and wiped his eyes. 'I know, man, I know. You're innocent like the rest of us.' He resumed his giggling at this latest clever quip, then added, 'So who didn't you murder? Your missus?'

Michael dropped his head and soaked up the agony of this young fool questioning his innocence on no more evidence than the fact that they were cast together, prisoners in the same mould, accused and manacled. He wondered what his family had concluded, his friends, his business associates. What had his sister told young Simon? He had finally convinced the watch-house keeper to allow him one pressured call, but time and circumstances had not permitted more than a frantic, hurried explanation that he had been charged with a serious offence in Sydney, that it was all a big mistake, that he would explain it to her as soon as he got back up to Queensland, but in the meantime could she take Simon to her house and keep him there until he got things sorted out. What had she told Simon? What did she believe? His thoughts jumped to Kirsten Foster. He was now charged with murdering her ex-husband.

'I didn't murder anyone.'

It came out feebly, but even in the noisy van it somehow hung in the air between the little group of men travelling together to the same uncertain future. Michael's young tormentor obviously felt it too. He chortled awkwardly, then coughed, and settled down.

'Fair enough, man,' he said thoughtfully. 'That's cool.'

* * *

If there were a million bumps on the road from the Central Courts to Silverwater, so far the van had not missed one of them. Each jerk and thud drove up through the metal bench into Michael's spine, shaking his brain and rattling his teeth, dislodging heavy blobs of sweat that plopped onto his manacled hands or splashed onto the floor below. The silent faces of the men around him were flushed and shiny in the stifling heat and with each bang and jolt they groaned more loudly and the air seemed to become more hostile and more dangerous. The young man opposite fidgeted and mumbled inanely to himself, occasionally breaking into what might loosely be called song, followed by wild falsetto guitar riffs and the drumming of his heavy hands against the metal bench. The longer the journey continued the more he rocked back and forth on the bench. Occasionally the squat, muscular little man sitting alone at the front end of the van looked up at him through one hairless eyebrow then dropped back into his own thoughts, cradling a crumpled suit-coat in his cuffed hands in front of him. His shirt-sleeves were rolled back over powerful forearms decorated with long-faded blue tattoos, and his thin black tie had been pulled well clear of his solid neck. He was an odd-looking man with fine coffee-coloured skin, deep brown scars across his eyebrows and cheeks and a flattened nose that attested to a troubled life. The close-cropped tufts of his dark curly hair gave him a vaguely African appearance.

'What about you, coconut? What're you in for?'

'Who, me?' The little brown man raised his head, his scarred eyebrows arched politely. 'Ay'm in for gross cruelty to doom fookun animals, ay am.' It was almost unrecognisable English, spoken in a Midlands brogue so thick you couldn't cut it with a power-saw. 'Ay cut the 'ead off a big doom Aussie bastard, not unlike y'self mate.' He smiled gleefully at the young man, revealing a mouth full of gold-capped teeth. 'Joost t' shut 'is big fookun gob.'

The two men sat in silence, eyeball to eyeball, one twice the size of the other but facing a chilling unflinching grin that was oddly pleasant and at the same time deeply menacing. Michael sensed a lethal tension gathering in the air and felt his heartrate quicken. The young man's face had hardened. It was suddenly vicious and intimidating. His self-esteem was on the line; he was being belittled, challenged. The only question was whether he was proud enough, and brave enough, to do something about it. His eyes narrowed cautiously.

'Is that right?'

'True as I sit yere, stand by me.' The coffee-coloured man still had him gripped in an unrelenting stare. 'But y' know that fookun 'ead still wouldn't shut oop, joost went on bletherin' a whole lot of fookun shite.'

The anger in the young man's eyes now had a tinge of uncertainty. His voice crackled.

'Yeah?'

'God as m'witness, mate, stand by me. So y'know what ay done then?' There was a long silent pause. Michael's arms and legs tensed painfully, waiting for a sudden eruption. 'Ay stoock it in a pail o' water. An' th' fookun thing went an' drowned on me, would you believe it!'

A thickset, flat-faced man squashed on the bench beside the young prisoner snorted and then chuckled huskily. Two others sitting opposite the back doors joined in.

'So yere I am today, just like the rest of yez, an innocent victim of cruel fookin' circumstance!'

The men around him erupted in laughter and the young prisoner glanced at them in bewilderment, not quite sure what or who the joke was meant to be. When his eyes shot back to the Englishman the untroubled stare greeted him courteously and the scarred eyebrows flipped once as if to say 'Now isn't that a curious thing?'. The young man looked away, shaking his confused head.

'Sounds like a load of fuckin' bullshit to me.'

The chuckling subsided into easy conversation at the far end of the van but the little coffee-coloured Englishman lowered his head and retreated to his private thoughts. Michael could feel the eyes of the young man opposite trained on him. He looked up to see his big head bobbing idly up and down with the rhythm of the road.

'Y'ever been to Silverwater, man?'

Michael shook his head.

'I have.' The young man sat silently for a moment, a sad hollow look in his boyish eyes. 'It's a zoo, man. It's a fuckin' zoo.'

* * *

A grey corridor stretched ahead like some terrifying reminder of a long-forgotten nightmare. Above the cement-block half-walls was perspex, double-plated and bullet-proof, right up to the ceiling. If there was a fire in here the fumes from the melting perspex would kill them long before they ever smelled the smoke. Who cared? It was cheap, it was secure. No one who counted was ever going to walk this walk. No one with the power to change anything would feel like Michael Wiltshire felt today. Utterly alone, worthless, terrified. As he paced he clung pathetically to his only remaining possessions, one spare pair of underpants and one spare pair of socks, green, just like the ones he was wearing, the same colour as his tracksuit and his T-shirt, just like those covering the body that sat on the cement floor at the end of the corridor, propped awkwardly against the heavy iron door.

'May as well get comfortable, man. We could be here for hours.'

'Do they know we're here?'

'Course they do.' The prisoner lifted one finger and pointed towards the surveillance camera in the corner of the ceiling. 'They just don't give a fuck.'

He lowered his head again and shuffled his feet closer, signalling that the conversation was over. Michael looked back up the corridor: it was blank and empty, a steel door at one end and a steel door at the other, and in between cement and perspex and two men waiting forlornly to be noticed by a fish-eyed camera in a faraway corner. What time was it? He looked at his bare wrist and was reminded that the guards at reception had taken everything from him. Was it day or night? The sun was still strong when they had driven in through the main gates, but they had sat for what had seemed like an eternity in the van, waiting for someone to open up the doors, listening to prison officers barking orders and cracking jokes outside and moving around freely, apparently oblivious to their existence. When the van doors had finally swung open they were led to the main reception desk where they began the soul-destroying process of being stripped, kitted and photographed, questioned and fingerprinted, each man allocated a prison number. In here he was no longer Michael Wiltshire, he was prisoner number 2874, just another green-clad statistic in the motley line of human misery that shuffled its way down blank corridors, waited endlessly in cement and grey-brick spaces and was gruffly barked at by bored and irritable warders in blue military-style uniforms.

How long had the whole stultifying and demeaning process taken thus far? What time was it now? The stark corridor with its flat fluorescent lighting told him nothing. Michael dropped the socks and underpants onto the floor and slid down the wall until he felt the cold cement hard beneath his buttocks. And he waited.

The darkness behind his eyelids was warm and soft. He could hear the comfortable sounds of home, the punt of Simon kicking his football in the front yard, the patter of his feet on the driveway and his playful, animated voice calling his personal commentary of every kick, dart, dummy, swerve and try. It was a sweet sound and Michael listened contentedly, feeling on his face the gentle puff of the pre-summer breeze washing up from the river, rustling the leaves of the big jacaranda and wafting the familiar smell of jasmine from the hedges. As he drifted down into a deep slumber Simon's face was pressed against his cheek, excitedly whispering happy words that meant nothing. His soft skin pressed gently against his father's, the sweet smell of his perspiration flavoured Michael's every breath.

'Righto.' The click of the metal door and loud buzz of the intercom jolted him awake. 'Through yez come.'

The prisoner opposite Michael groaned to his feet and lumbered automaton-like through the sliding door. Michael followed, still struggling to surface from the sleep that had enveloped him. As the realisation of his circumstances flooded quickly back into his consciousness the pleasant oblivion he had been wrenched from was replaced by a painful awareness of hard cement beneath his feet and angry echoes bouncing off the perspex, steel and block-work all around him.

'Who are you?'

The square-jawed officer behind the central desk in Goldsmith Wing was at least a decade Michael's junior, but he snapped at him like a headmaster scolding an errant schoolboy.

'My name's Wiltshire.'

'I don't give a fuck what your name is!' The look of apparent anger in the young man's eyes startled Michael. 'You don't have a fucking name in here, dickhead! What's your number?'

'2874.'

The words stumbled clumsily out of Michael's mouth, but seemed to appease the officer behind the desk. He scowled disdainfully at his prisoner then scribbled the number down.

'2874. That's your cell over there.' He flicked his head towards two storeys of grey steel doors. 'Number twenty-seven, bottom row.'

As Michael turned tentatively to walk towards the cell the officer barked again without lifting his head. 'Stay there.'

Michael waited while the young man struggled to fill out whatever details he was carefully recording on the form in front of him. It was clear from the way he held his pen and the arduous labour of his writing that it was a task that didn't come easily to him. As he waited obediently on the other side of the counter Michael glanced cautiously over his shoulder at his new home. An open area roughly twenty metres long, perhaps fifteen metres wide, stretched out before him, dotted with stainless-steel mesh tables and surrounding chairs, all bolted securely to the cement grey floor, and flanked on three sides by two imposing levels of steel-barred cells. At the end closest to the counter that separated the warders' observation post from the cell unit were two long steel mesh tables with attached bench seating, where several heavily tattooed, green-clad prisoners sat huddled forward on their elbows, deep in conversation. One of them looked up at him and sneered a gap-toothed smile that seemed intended to deride more than to greet or welcome. A desperate, hollow feeling settled in Michael's stomach and a string of confusing words filtered back into his head.

'You know it doesn't have to be like this, don't you, Michael.'

He wondered what those words had really meant, why they had been spoken.

''done?'

Michael looked uncomprehendingly at the prison officer, trying to fathom what he was asking. 'Pardon?'

The warder sighed loudly with an air of weary irritation. 'Methadone — you want methadone?' Before Michael could process the question he snapped cantankerously. 'You on the 'done? You got a habit?'

The confused look on the face of prisoner 2874 said it all.

'Obviously not.'

He scrawled another entry on the form, his mouth arched as though he had just been deeply insulted.

'You been fed?'

Michael hadn't thought of food all day. 'No.'

The warder reached to one end of the counter and dragged into sight a plastic plate of cold meat and salad, pressed flat by a tight covering of plastic wrap, followed by a plastic knife and fork, and a plastic cup from the rim of which dangled a solitary tea bag. The sight of the food only served to deepen Michael's nausea.

'Thanks, I'm not really hungry.'

'Suit yourself.'

Without looking up from the form the warder pushed the plate of food back out of sight. A string of questions followed and Michael answered meekly, adopting what was clearly his allocated position of subservience. Eventually the young man stopped writing, looked the form up and down once or twice, took it in both hands to review it again, then set it down looking marginally less irritated.

'Righto. Through you go.'

Michael walked to cell number twenty-seven of the Goldsmith Wing in a daze, oblivious to all but the narrow doorway drawing steadily closer.

'You know it doesn't have to be like this, don't you, Michael.'

As he stepped into the cell the hollow feeling that had been aching in his chest instantly deepened. The little block-and-iron room looked to be about three metres square, with a neat bench desk on one wall and a built-in twin bunk on the other. At the far end was a half-wall divider partitioning off a stainless-steel toilet bowl and the opening to a shower recess, both fully reflected in the large convex mirror bolted in one corner of the ceiling, allowing vision of every aspect to the warders from the cell door. The cell looked clean, almost sterile, its walls covered with thick, glossy blue-grey paint to resist all marking; only the most ineffectual scratches here and there recorded the presence of its former occupants. A high window crossed with thick steel bars allowed in light but no vision of the outside world.

'You know it doesn't have to be like this, don't you, Michael.'

Michael sat down on the bottom bunk, his belongings cradled in his lap, and stared at the blue-grey wall as the words repeated over and over in his head. What did they really mean? He knew he had to work it out. He started carefully stepping through the circumstances of his last meeting with Detective Phil Manning of the Major Crimes Squad.

After Phelps and Manning had left Michael alone in the interview room, another officer had appeared within several minutes, an older man whose introduction and instructive words Michael hardly heard. He vaguely understood that this man had to ask some questions to ensure that Michael had no complaint to make about the officers who had interviewed him. It was standard procedure required by law, and tedious as it might seem the police were obliged to go through the motions. When he had finished his spiel he mechanically reeled off a brief series of formal questions. Michael shook his head on cue and then the officer disappeared, leaving him alone to ponder his position. It seemed like a long time before the door swung open once again.

'Bad luck, Michael.' Manning had a comic look of sympathy painted on his face as he stepped into the room. 'Phelpsy wants you charged with attempting to pervert the course of justice as well. Over all them payments you made to old Barry Dougherty.' He shook his head. 'That makes it awful messy, mate. Soon as the jury see that ransom letter and hear about how old Bazza copped it, I'd say you might just be a dead set gone coon, son.'

A dry chuckle rattled in his throat as he took Michael by the arm and ushered him into the day room. As soon as they stepped out of the interview room Manning adopted a formal tone.

'I'll take you down to the cells now where we'll prefer the second charge and get you processed.'

He slipped a finger firmly through the belt loop at the rear of Michael's trousers and guided him through the maze of desks, across a cluttered corridor, through a door and into the fire escape. Now there were just the two of them, stepping down the cement stairs slowly and methodically, keeping a restrained pace set by the detective, their footsteps echoing above and below. Michael could hear that they were quite alone in the stairwell.

Desperate thoughts darted into his head. Once they got where they were going he would be charged with murder and locked up. His future would be unknown, and he wouldn't have any opportunity to speak to Simon and offer some sort of explanation. Now there were only the two of them, he and Manning, alone together in the stairwell. If ever there would be a chance, this was it. Should he try to break away, run for freedom, snatch enough time to at least put his house in order, speak to his son, make arrangements for the boy's care?

They were almost shoulder to shoulder, their bodies bumping gently together with the rhythm of their progress down the stairs, step by step. Manning's only hold on him was the finger curled through the belt-loop of his trousers at the back, the grip now less constraining than it had been, as if the policeman had relaxed slightly. Perhaps he was off guard now, convinced the job was almost done. He was strolling down those stairs like a man who had clocked off for the day, a man who was already on his way home. Michael's heart began beating harder. If there was to be a time, it was now. A full-blooded backhand strike with his elbow should at least knock the policeman off balance, dislodge his flimsy hold. Then what? Each landing had a fire-escape door, but where did they lead? Were they unlocked, or did they only open one way, into the stairwell? And what was on the other side if he did make it through the doorway? Michael braced the muscles in his right arm. All he had to do was wrench his arm up and swing his elbow back into Manning, quickly enough to catch him off guard. Then it would be a sprint to the nearest door, praying it wasn't locked. Now the blood was pumping loudly in his ears, every fibre of his body tingling with dreadful anticipation.

'You know it doesn't have to be like this, don't you, Michael.'

'What?'

Manning's voice was soft and mellow as he stepped slowly, methodically down the stairs, measuring each step, looking straight ahead.

'Two million bucks can buy a lot of favours.'

Michael was struggling with the confused jumble of thoughts and emotions cluttering his brain. He turned to Manning, squinting at the policeman's blank profile, trying to assess what was being said.

'What's that supposed to mean?'

Michael felt the tug of Manning's hand on his waistband as the policeman stopped and turned to face him. His face was deadpan as he looked directly into Michael's eyes.

'What do you reckon, Michael?'

Michael stared at Manning's blank expression. So many things had been said that day, so much had happened so quickly, he was struggling to collate them all, to make some sense of them. He no longer had confidence in his capacity to accurately interpret what was being said, what he now thought was being put to him. Anxiously, awkwardly, he fumbled for the words.

'Are you asking me for a bribe?'

The question seemed to unsettle the detective and his eyes narrowed instantly. He stared into Michael's face for several long seconds then growled viciously.

'What did you say to me, you fuckin' grub?'

Startled, Michael was again fumbling for words. Before he could get them out Manning had an iron grip on his right wrist, twisting it violently and spinning him around until he was folded awkwardly across the metal railing. His right hand was jammed excruciatingly between his shoulder blades. Manning caught his left hand and pulled that behind him too.

'I've never taken a sling in my life, arsehole. I didn't ask you for fuckin' nothing.'

Michael felt cold steel against his wrists and then the stabbing pain of the handcuffs being jammed tightly closed. A wave of nausea descended on him as he stood pressed hard up against the metal railing, the air squeezing from his diaphragm. Manning was grappling with his clothing, grabbing at him, pulling and ripping. With a heavy hand he slapped at Michael's chest and thighs, grasped the inside of his upper legs and groin, then pushed deeply into each of his trouser pockets, dragging them inside out and spilling the contents onto the stairs. With his left hand jammed painfully into the small of Michael's back, pinning his handcuffed wrists against his body, Manning dipped quickly down and scooped up the keys, wallet and papers that had fallen from the trouser pockets. He was breathing heavily, the full weight of his body now pushing against Michael's back as he sifted through them. Eventually his breathing slowed. He grunted satisfaction and pushed the various items back into the side pocket of Michael's trousers.

'Arsehole.'

He stepped back, gripped Michael's forearms and pulled him back off the railing, then with a handful of his prisoner's shirt in one hand and his cuffed wrists in the other, he pushed him towards the landing below. As they descended his chin was on Michael's shoulder, his voice a hoarse whisper in his ear.

'You say anything about bribes to anybody and you won't make it to prison — you understand that, shithead?'

It had troubled Michael ever since, lying in the pit of his stomach like something rotten he had eaten. He had eventually mentioned it cautiously to his lawyer, almost as an afterthought, during their anxious conversation through the glass panel in the cells. Darryl Beane had pressed one index finger to his lips and leaned forward till his face was almost touching the glass.

'He might have been worried you were taping him.' His whisper faded into the silence of the little room as he looked deep into Michael's eyes. 'You didn't get him on tape, did you?'

'Don't be bloody stupid.'

The silence hung between them briefly before the lawyer continued. 'It might be on.' His eyes peered intently over the silver frame of his glasses, holding Michael's gaze, delving deeply as if searching for something hidden in his client's brain. 'Do you want me to see what I can find out?'

There was something Michael found profoundly offensive in the proposition. He felt the blood rushing into his face as he spat out his reply.

'All I want you to do is get me bloody bail!'

But now, as prisoner 2874 sat on his bunk in cell twenty-seven of Goldsmith Wing, the anger was gone, replaced by a grim realisation of his circumstances. He stood accused of murder, a vicious criminal in the eyes of anyone that mattered. He had been refused bail and now he was to be locked up with the tattooed, unshaven human flotsam around him, his only lifeline the hope that his lawyer would bring another application for bail soon, this time to the Supreme Court, where hopefully someone would realise that he didn't deserve to be in gaol. Or did he? A heavy shroud of depression settled on him as he stared blankly at the wall.

'Whoa, looks like I'm in with the murderer, ay.'

The loud-mouthed young man from the prison van dropped a plate of food onto the desk then slapped his possessions down on the top bunk.

'I guess I'm up top.'

He had already dragged the chair from under the bench and was perched on it, unwrapping his meal. 'No worries, mate, I'm sweet with that. So far as I'm concerned you can sleep wherever you want, so long as you don't try to sleep with me.'

Tickled by his witticism, the man guffawed loudly as he began shovelling food into his mouth with the plastic fork. After several seconds he turned his big head and glanced over his shoulder at Michael.

'Looks like we're gonna be roommates for a while, ay.' He held out his hand. 'I'm Jason.'

Michael Wiltshire reached out and shook the hand. 'Michael.'

'Sweet.'

Jason nodded once, as if to mentally register the name, then swung back to his meal. When he'd finished eating he stood up, stepped to the cell door and grasping the doorjamb with both hands called in the direction of the observation post.

'Hey, boss, when do I get me 'done?'

CHAPTER TWENTY

Michael Wiltshire opened his eyes slowly, staring without focus at the wall in front of him. The buzzer would sound soon and the cell doors would open, beginning a new day in Goldsmith Wing — his thirty-seventh.

He rarely awoke early. At night he lay in bed exhausted and aching with the emptiness of his circumstances, his nerves tingling and his thoughts racing through the dark foreboding prospect of his future. Days were for dealing with the present, walking the razor's edge, treading a careful line between the hair-trigger sensibilities of the warders and the explosive violence of his fellow inmates, each word, each action, carefully moderated to acknowledge and reflect his base position in the prison pecking order. But each night brought the future back, dark, desperate and terrifying. It would roll around in his brain, stabbing at his heart, until his chest was pounding painfully and his body was swathed in perspiration. He tossed and turned and struggled until finally, mercifully, weariness eventually prevailed, dragging him down into a deep slumber.

Normally he was awakened by the buzzer, but this morning the unfamiliar noises in the pod outside his cell had crept into his sleep, prising his eyes open. He could hear the warders grunting, struggling with something outside.

'Shit, he's heavier than he looks, that's for sure.'

It was Phallon's voice, the brash young warder who had admitted Michael. He could hear Stiles with him.

'Just whack him down here while we get something to carry him on.'

When Michael got to his cell door and peered out he saw Stiles spreading a thin prison blanket over the body of the curly-haired young man who had been occupying cell five for the past week. Phallon was strolling back towards the warders' observation post. From a cell upstairs someone whooped and shouted 'Swinger!' and a few uneasy chuckles echoed through the pod.

Today would be a bad day. Suicides were all too common, especially amongst young men like the one now lying crumpled on the cement floor, one of his long-fingered hands protruding lifelessly from the blanket. They came in strung out, howling for methadone, suddenly without heroin or hope. No one was surprised when they didn't last, and no one seemed to care. But deaths of any kind made the warders edgy: there was paperwork to do, reports to be filed, explanations to be given. Michael knew this wasn't going to be a good day.

Wilkinson, the bull-necked older warder who came from time to time to restock the condom-vending machines in all the pods, was opening up the machine on the far wall.

'You wouldn't think they'd be so keen to neck themselves with all the romance they seem to get around here. This is the third time in a week I've had to stock this bloody thing.'

Stiles chuckled as he lifted one corner of the blanket and kicked the dead man's hand out of sight. 'It's a dead-set bloody Love Boat around here, mate.'

Michael dropped onto the chair by his desk, a deep sadness seeping into his consciousness. He hadn't known the young man in number five. He hadn't wanted to. But he'd seen that, like so many of the others, he was young and wild and somehow lost. Michael's thoughts turned to Jason Archer, the loud-mouthed, heavy-limbed young man he had shared with on his first few nights. At twenty-one years of age Jason had already served two terms as an adult and was now back in remand on heroin supply charges. He had no family to speak of, no job and seemingly no prospects. He measured his life in terms of prison spells and his next fix.

'Nothing like the feel of cold steel in your arm, Micko,' he had regularly quipped, obviously aware that the notion of drug-use was even more unsettling to his cell-mate than the nickname. 'That's what I live for, brother, that's what I live for.'

Whatever he had lived for, Archer was dead now. He had died a week ago, beaten, bloodied and mutilated. As Michael buried his face in his hands he could see the young man's bloodstained body in the darkness behind his weary eyelids.

It had happened on the grassy oval at the centre of the prison compound, where for an hour each day the men from several different pods would be released together to exercise, take in the sunlight, play sport or, as most did, simply stroll in the artificial freedom of the simulated outdoors. Michael was standing in the line of men from Goldsmith Wing who had queued at the prison store to collect toiletries and other goods purchased on their 'buy-up' accounts. Archer, big enough and strong enough to intimidate some of the younger inmates, had shuffled himself well towards the head of the queue where he stood noisily espousing his views on prison etiquette.

From his position near the end of the line Michael had seen two young Asian men walking purposefully from the oval in the direction of the store. They stopped in front of Archer, yelling and gesticulating at him. The lumbering Australian guffawed dismissively and Michael heard him protest 'Bullshit!' once or twice. Other Asian men started wandering towards the scene. The protestations of the two who had confronted Archer became more frantic as the seconds passed, and suddenly they both attacked, throwing punches wildly at the much bigger man, who stepped back, shaped up and started swinging in retaliation. At first he seemed to be enjoying the mêlée, knocking the two assailants off their feet before starting on a third and then a fourth as yet more Asian men flooded from the oval.

Now the men in the buy-up line were dispersing, walking with thinly disguised urgency towards the crowded oval. As the ring of Asian men grew deeper, Archer looked around him, still swinging wildly but now desperately casting for support. Two men caught him from behind around his waist and legs, and others struggled to restrain his huge arms, holding him as still others rained seemingly ineffectual blows on his face and chest. Eventually he was pinned and as he staggered under the weight of bodies his eyes met Michael's, pleading silently for help. He stumbled, toppled and fell to the ground as his attackers punched and kicked at him. Others snatched up whatever small stones they could to use as weapons and rushed in one after the other, smacking the stones down against the big man's eyes and face and tearing at his hair and ears.

Michael could see flecks of blood spattering onto the hands and faces of the frenzied group. Instinctively he clenched both fists and moved forward, the blood rushing loudly in his ears. But his progress was abruptly halted by a vice-like grip on his elbow.

'Don't be fookin' daft. Walk away.'

He turned to see Ronny McPhee, the squat, coffee-coloured Englishman whom the older and more experienced inmates referred to simply as Ron the Pom. McPhee wasn't a big man, and in the pod and the yard he spoke softly and kept largely to himself, but both the warders and the inmates treated him with a kind of deference normally reserved for the strongest and most pugnacious. Michael angrily snatched at the fingers wrapped around his elbow, determined to rip them away. But the little man's hand held like a band of immovable stone grafted permanently to his arm. As Michael wrestled futilely McPhee looked into his eyes with a steely stare, stepping him backwards gradually and murmuring to him in a soft, emotionless monotone.

'I said walk away.'

The whole throng had descended upon Archer now, kicking, stabbing and clawing at him frantically. Michael felt tears of horror welling in his eyes.

'They'll kill him.'

'This is not our business. Walk away.'

'They're going to kill him!'

'Look at the guards, man, look at the guards.'

The guards. In his panic Michael hadn't even thought to call the guards for help. He reeled around, searching for the two warders who should be monitoring the men on the oval. Then he saw them. There, on the other side of the wire, they were walking away from the scene, radios held up to their ears.

McPhee was still muttering calmly in Michael's ear. 'Everyone chooses 'is own business. That there's droog business, and the lad chose it for 'imself.'

The siren was howling now as the Asian men turned from the bloodied carcass outside the prison store and stepped quickly back onto the oval, wiping their hands as they dispersed into the crowd.

'That's the way it is in yere. The Lebs and the fookin' gooks run the droogs. I suggest you stay out of their fookin' way.'

With that McPhee released his hold and kept walking, straight ahead into the shuffling throng of prisoners.

As Michael watched Stiles and Phallon lug the body of the man from cell five onto a canvas stretcher and hoist him up, his mind flashed again on the sight of Archer's pulped body lying face-up on the oval, and on the sad and desperate eyes of all the other hopeless young men he had seen filing in and out of Goldsmith Wing for the past thirty-seven days.

'Righto, out you come. You've got a legal visit.'

Michael was pleased, if for no other reason than it meant he would be out of the pod, at least for the morning. The death in cell five meant the warders would almost certainly conduct random cell searches through the day, and he would be glad to avoid that. To Michael, the process of being stripped, searched and then made to stand naked in full view of the whole pod while every item in his cell, down to the mattress on his bed and the photos pinned to his chalk board, were cast onto the floor and ignominiously rifled through, was both harrowing and degrading. It was true he might be strip-searched for his legal visit, depending on the whim of the officer on duty, but this was a relatively brief encounter compared to the hour or more spent standing naked in the pod during a cell search.

'Right, strip down.'

It wasn't surprising that today they were being extra cautious. But Michael happily stripped his clothes off in the visits holding area, thankful that he would soon have news from Darryl Beane about his Supreme Court bail application. So far things had been progressing at a painfully slow pace. On that first day in the Central Courts Darryl had assured him they would get a bail application before the Supreme Court quickly, but things had bogged down since then. Darryl had briefed the eminent Sydney barrister Lyle Phillips QC to advise on the application. Phillips, an ex-senior Crown prosecutor who was said to have an impeccable reputation with the judiciary, had expressed the view that a Supreme Court judge would want to know more about the allegations before granting bail. Phillips had recommended that Beane get a copy of the prosecution brief as soon as possible, and Darryl assured Michael he was making every effort to do that, but the police had been dragging the chain, promising that the brief would be delivered shortly but continuously coming up with some new excuse as to why it wasn't quite ready yet. In the meantime Phillips had advised that they should have another stab at bail before the magistrate while they were waiting for the prosecution brief, as he believed they had a strong argument for bail. Darryl Beane was sure the presence of an eminent silk in the Local Court would prompt Warren Hyatt LCM to behave himself. Michael hadn't shared his confidence, particularly given that in Goldsmith Wing the old-timers universally referred to the Local Court chief magistrate as 'Hang-em Hyatt'. Still, a further application to Hyatt was better than no application at all to the Supreme Court, so Michael had reluctantly agreed.

'Up with the orchestras.'

Michael dutifully lifted his scrotum to show nothing was concealed there.

'Okay, squat.'

He dropped to his haunches, spreading his bare buttocks.

'Up you come. Hands out.'

Michael knew the drill too well. He faced the guard, arms outstretched in crucifix position so as to reveal his armpits, fingers spread to prevent anything being lodged between them.

'Let's see your hair.'

Leaning his head forward Michael dug his fingers deep into his hair and ruffled it vigorously.

'Ears.'

With the tips of his fingers he bent both ears forward.

'Mouth.'

He opened his mouth and rolled his tongue back until the warder's grunt confirmed he had seen enough.

'Righto.'

As Michael pulled his shorts back on he wondered what course his artful lawyer would be suggesting today. It certainly wouldn't be another application to the magistrate — the last one hadn't gone too well. Michael could still hear Warren Hyatt LCM barking down from the bench at Lyle Phillips.

'What are the changed circumstances?'

Lyle Phillips QC, undoubtedly an urbane gentleman, had a way of speaking in a measured and controlled fashion. 'Well ...' he had commenced, apparently intent on selecting his words carefully, as if Hyatt were actually interested in the reply to his question.

The magistrate had been quick to dispel any such impression. 'I've got a full list here this morning, Mr Phillips. I'll be here till after lunch just getting through the mentions without listening to any submissions on bail. So unless you can tell me in five words or less what the changed circumstances are, don't bother wasting your breath.'

At the bar table Lyle Phillips had looked slightly stunned.

'Well, Your Worship, as I said, I have instructions to renew my client's application for bail ...'

Once again Warren Hyatt's interjection was crusty and ill-mannered.

'I sat here for nearly an hour on the last mention listening to Mr Beane on that subject, and I'm not interested in wasting any more time on it unless you can tell me something's changed since last time.' With that he had swivelled forward and glared down at Phillips. 'Now are there changed circumstances or not?'

Lyle Phillips QC was a courteous man by nature. Clearly, it had been a long time since he had ventured down into the Local Court and he had quite forgotten the feeling of being cross-examined by an abrasive, ignorant man like Warren Hyatt. A mild look of distaste tugged at the corners of his mouth but he'd continued, quietly and unemotionally.

'Well, Your Worship, my client is the principal of a substantial business undertaking and his absence from the business during the past fortnight —'

'I know all about your client's business interests, Mr Phillips. Mr Beane went on about all that last time. If you're going to try and tell me I should grant bail just because your client's losing money by being in gaol then save your breath. I'm not interested. Every defendant who comes before this court is going to lose money being locked up, it's just too bad they don't think of that before they go out and break the law.'

Phillips had waited for the briefest moment before he parried. 'Well, Your Worship, my client hasn't been convicted of anything as yet.'

'No, but he's charged with murder, Mr Phillips. Murder! I've already refused him bail and that's it. So unless you can tell me something pretty astounding by way of changed circumstances, such as that the charge has been dropped or the main prosecution witness has died or something like that, then we're just wasting our time discussing it, aren't we.'

Phillips regarded Hyatt briefly in silence, clearly dumbfounded by the inanity of the magistrate's last comment, then he closed his brief.

'Very well, Your Worship.'

There followed a short, relatively courteous exchange regarding further mention dates, which Michael's numbed brain struggled to take in, and then Hyatt gruffly called the next matter on. That was it. Case dealt with.

So much for the Local Court. Now they had to concentrate on preparing a bail case for the Supreme Court, and according to Phillips that still meant getting a copy of the prosecution brief. By the time it finally arrived, an urgent hearing date was set for the committal hearing less than a month away. It was the considered opinion of Lyle Phillips QC, with whom Darryl Beane wholeheartedly concurred, that if a committal hearing date was just around the corner by the time the application came before the Supreme Court, any judge would be inclined to refuse bail and await the outcome of the committal hearing. So Darryl Beane's job had been to convince the Supreme Court registry to give him an urgent date for a bail hearing, and Michael was eager to hear how successful he had been.

Darryl Beane, resplendent in an elegant navy club jacket, was leaning against the doorjamb of the closest interview room in the legal visits area, his arms folded casually against his chest and a patronising smile stretching the delicate features of his face. As Michael walked towards him along the wooden pathway from the holding bay he could tell that the news was not going to be what he had hoped.

'Hello, mate,' Darryl said sympathetically as he shook Michael by the hand. 'Come on in.'

When Michael stepped into the big wooden room he was surprised to see an unfamiliar face staring back at him. A heavy-set man with deep hooded eyes, a thick neck and cropped, grey-flecked hair was sprawled in one of the three chairs surrounding the narrow table in the middle of the room. His intimidating physiognomy belied the gentility of his expensive lightweight suit and the gold and diamonds that adorned his hands. He looked up at Michael with a cold glare as Darryl Beane made the introductions.

'Michael, this is Roger Baston. He's a private investigator. I've retained him to do some investigative work on your case.'

'Hello, Michael.' Baston spoke in a slow, menacing drawl and as he held out his hand his ice-blue eyes held Michael's gaze with a piercing intensity. He gripped his hand so firmly Michael felt the bones in his fingers grinding painfully together. 'Nice to make your acquaintance.'

Darryl seemed unusually agitated as he ushered Michael into a seat and proceeded to get down to business.

The news was not good. The Supreme Court list was chockers for the next few weeks and the earliest date Darryl could even hope for was less than a week before the committal hearing was due to start. No judge would grant bail that soon before the hearing; they would just bat it through to see what came out of the hearing. The problem was that given Wendy Bagley's evidence, the committal was pretty much just a formality. Assuming she stuck to her story the magistrate would at least find a case to answer, enough to go before a jury, which was all he had to do at this preliminary level, and the matter would be listed for trial in the Supreme Court. If Bagley repeated in the witness box what was written in her statement, even if the magistrate wasn't inclined to believe her, it became a factual issue for the jury to determine, and that meant the magistrate had to commit Michael for trial. In the meantime any bail application to the Supreme Court pending the trial would be a bit light on unless they were able to refer the judge to the evidence adduced at the committal hearing, and the transcript of the committal hearing was unlikely to be available for at least another four weeks.

'Unfortunately, Michael, that means it's likely you'll be in here for at least another eight weeks or so before we can get any sort of a decent bail application before the Supreme Court.'

Darryl Beane's brow was deeply furrowed in profound sympathy and he sat with his hands cupped, a compact package of concern. By contrast the man beside him remained splayed nonchalantly across his chair and when he spoke it was with an air of callous indifference.

'Even then you're going to be pushing shit uphill with a stick to get bail.' When Michael looked at him Baston glared back with unflinching eyes. 'Let's face it, they've got a pretty bloody shit-hot case against you.'

Michael felt a hollow ache gnawing at the pit of his stomach, the ugly prospect of at least another two months in custody poisoning his consciousness. 'What are you talking about?'

A cynical smirk spread across Baston's face. 'Bagley puts you right there in it, mate.'

'I don't even know Bagley.'

'Yeah?' The investigator arched his eyebrows

and moved in his chair for the first time, leaning his thick forearms on the little desk. 'Well, everything she says is corroborated a thousand per cent. The phone records, the extortion letter, the blackmail payments you made to Dougherty.'

'They weren't blackmail payments.'

The words jumped out of Michael's mouth and hung in the silence as Baston evaluated them.

'Is that right? Well, what were they then?'

It was a good question, one Michael Wiltshire couldn't answer, even to himself. For now, it seemed Baston didn't need an answer. 'I'd suggest you work on that one, Michael, because from what I hear you're now also wanted for questioning by the Queensland coppers in relation to Barry Dougherty's murder. And I'd say they're going to want to know all about them payments.'

It was a prospect Michael had been expecting, but the news still came like a crushing blow cruelly underscoring the depth of his predicament. Darryl Beane's caring tone did nothing to allay his anxiety.

'Unfortunately too, Michael, the fact that you're wanted in relation to another murder in Queensland will become relevant on any future bail hearings.'

Both men watched Michael Wiltshire process this latest instalment of bad news, the lawyer perched forward on the desk attentively, the investigator exuding indifference, rocking back recklessly on two legs of his chair. There was a long silence before Beane spoke again, this time in a confidential whisper.

'All that means we really should consider revisiting what admittedly is a pretty distasteful alternative.'

He was looking straight at his client as he spoke, but when Michael looked up the lawyer seemed unable to meet his gaze. He blinked nervously then looked away, firstly at Baston, whose deadpan expression remained unmoved, then down at his finely manicured fingers. He stroked them gently before continuing.

'Roger here still has some pretty good police contacts. He's picked up some very interesting intelligence.'

Beane picked delicately at his fingernails, searching for his voice as Baston looked on impatiently. Eventually the big man dropped forward onto the front legs of his chair, leaned in on his forearms and growled a hoarse whisper across the narrow desk.

'The deal's on if you want it.'

'Deal?'

'For the right price the coppers will make the whole thing go away.'

He peered up at Michael through his eyebrows, carefully assessing his reaction. Michael was looking back at him but he saw nothing. His mind was a blur of wild disjointed thoughts and emotions. How dare they try this on? How could they do it anyway? Could it possibly be that simple? Could he just pay money to make the nightmare of the past five weeks, the past five years, magically disappear? Would it ever disappear?

'What coppers?'

'Couldn't tell you even if I knew.'

'So how much is the right price?'

'Don't know yet. My guess is they'll want at least what Dougherty was asking.'

'What — two million? That's insane.'

'I don't think you're in much of a bargaining position, Michael.'

He was right. Michael Wiltshire was in no position to negotiate a price. Baston's eyes were unflinching, delving, searching relentlessly as though to burn a hole deep into his brain. The decision was not about price. It was about something far more fundamental, far more dangerous.

'Even if I did pay, what's the guarantee that they'd deliver?'

'They're like everyone else in business. If they don't deliver they're not in business any more.'

As the words slammed into Michael's brain the terrifying realisation hit him: this process was not new to the man sitting opposite. He had been through it all before. To Baston this was just business as usual.

'How would they make it go away?'

'Who fuckin' cares, mate, provided they do.'

'But this woman says I confessed the murder to her.'

'She won't say it if she's not around.'

'What's that supposed to mean?'

Baston gave a disdainful grunt and straightened up slightly. For a moment he looked angry, dangerous, but eventually it passed. He replied in a low murmur that rumbled like the growl of a wild beast. 'Like I said, mate, who fuckin' cares?'

* * *

Michael strode back to the holding area, his brain numb from the jumble of thoughts and emotions still spinning in his head. He could feel his heart pounding in his chest as his mind danced around the proposition he had just heard. How wonderful it would be to turn the clock back these past five weeks, to return home to Simon, to forget the nightmare he had fallen into, lay down his head every night without this terrifying shadow hanging over his future. Maybe this was his opportunity. He was an innocent man, after all. The woman's story was nothing but a vicious lie. He deserved to be released from this horror. The end would justify the means.

The end always justified the means: that was Gary Sharpe's philosophy. There was a smart way of doing things and a tough way, and only a mug would choose the tough way. Only a dope would turn his nose up at a rails run if it was on offer. That's what Gary Sharpe would be telling him right now if he was here. And even at two million this was a rails run. Michael could almost hear his old friend saying it, cackling derisively at the very thought that anyone would consider even for a moment passing up such a red-hot opportunity.

There was something about that thought that made Michael's heart beat even harder. The last time he had followed the advice of Gary Sharpe it had changed his life forever.

'Oi, Money Bags.'

Ronny McPhee was sitting bolt upright on the narrow bench in the holding area. He had both hands cupped and resting tidily on his knees like a schoolboy posing for the class photograph and as he spoke he kept his eyes trained on the vinyl floor between his feet.

'Y'know what they call y'man Darryl Beane there, don't you?'

Michael Wiltshire looked warily at the little Englishman. The reference to money in McPhee's mouth unnerved him. He knew the news had filtered out amongst his fellow prisoners that he was a wealthy man, and he knew that made him a prime target for extortion or just mindless violence. So far he had avoided any confrontation. But all his instincts told him that McPhee was a man to be treated with extreme caution and he grappled nervously for whatever response the Englishman might be expecting. But the little man wasn't waiting for an answer.

'Three-D-Darryl, that's what they call 'im.' McPhee looked up at him with a cold, humourless smile that exposed his gold-capped teeth. 'D'y'know what Three-D stands for?'

This time he did wait for an answer, his head tilted to one side, his eyebrows arched quizzically and the menacing smile fading from his lips. Michael held his gaze for several long seconds before he responded breathlessly.

'No.'

'Double-Dealing Dog, that's what it stands for.'

The warder at the desk barked McPhee's number. He rose slowly and walked towards the exit, pausing briefly as he drew alongside Michael.

'And that's what he is, stand by me.' His voice was no more than a whisper. 'Darryl Beane's nothin' but a double-dealin' fookin' dog.'

CHAPTER TWENTY-ONE

Frank Vagianni couldn't believe his luck. He was starting to think that at long last he might be about to finally kick some sort of a goal. In the past three days he'd taken fifteen hundred dollars through the door. That was more money than he'd seen out of the Vagianni Private Investigation Agency in the past four weeks.

He was still waiting for that dodgy solicitor to pay him for slapping that writ on Bobby Lees and there'd been precious little else come in since then. Frank was just grateful the New South Wales coppers had fallen on his erstwhile client Michael Wiltshire when they did and charged him with the big M. Otherwise Wiltshire would be wanting to know what happened to the big fat cheque he'd handed Frank for his expenses to get back up to Mackay and suss out the Dougherty investigation. Frank never did get on the plane, but then as things panned out he didn't need to, since it turned out Mr Wiltshire was just doing the old soft-shoe shuffle, trying to cover up his tracks. Now he was in the slammer facing life on a murder blue, so it was a cinch that he wasn't going to be along too soon to rattle Frankie's cage about the dollars that he'd forked out for the expenses. It was just as well: that cheque had lasted about three days, what with the back rent and maintenance payments he was up for, and one disastrous night of mayhem on the craps table down at Jupiters Casino.

But all that was behind him. There were better days ahead. It had been a tough few years for Frankie Box, but now the future was starting to look rosy.

The Gold Coast Aboriginal Artifacts Museum had changed everything. When the old wallpaper shop on Ferry Road went broke and the floor space came up for grabs Frank had managed to talk Levsky into giving him a three-month rent holiday on the premises, and that gave him the opportunity to break into the Aboriginal artifacts business. Frank had the place painted up just right, with a big sign out the front: 'Gold Coast Aboriginal Artifacts Museum — Genuine Artifacts at Genuine Prices'. He found some hippy out in the Currumbin Valley to churn out boomerangs and nulla-nullas and what-not for practically next to nothing, and it turned out Rick Puluwai, the big Maori bouncer from the Liars Bar, was a deft hand at all that Aboriginal-type artwork. By the time Frank got Big Rick to paint his boomerangs up with some traditional Aboriginal spots, they looked a whole lot better than the real thing. The Jap tourists couldn't get enough of them.

Of course he could never have got it off the ground without the help of little Kenny Takahashi.

Kenny ran a business collecting Japanese tourists from Coolangatta Airport and giving them the cook's tour of the Gold Coast, taking in all the essential sights. Like any tourists the Japs liked to take away a souvenir or two, so Frank and Kenny worked it out together. It was such a sweet deal Frank could kick himself he hadn't jagged it sooner. Kenny would run the bus around the kangaroos and emus down at Fleay's Reserve, set up the mandatory koala photo opportunity, walk the troops across a couple of beaches and such-like, and then ensure the last stop on the tour was always Frankie's boomerang shop. And didn't those Jap tourists gobble up the artifacts. Frank couldn't find enough pockets to stuff all his cash into.

Kenny Takahashi was a bright young bloke. Frank had first met him several years ago when Kenny was the star half-back with the under-19 Tigers side. He was a courageous little footballer in those days, and the boys nicknamed him Kenny Kamikaze for his fearless front-on tackling. But he had more than just a big heart. Kenny was a gifted sportsman and he could have played the game professionally, except that he had too many brains. It didn't take the kid too long to work out there was no future butting heads on the rugby field, and as soon as he had enough money together he enrolled himself in a law course down at the Bond Uni. Not that Frank would know too much, but rumour had it Kenny was a star at the university as well, topping all his classes. Of course good grades don't pay the rent, and Kenny had to turn a dollar somehow in whatever spare time he had available between classes. And he was good at it. Kenny Takahashi was an operator. In fact, he came from a long line of operators. His father was a realtor who came to the Gold Coast from Tokyo in the early eighties, back when Kenny was just a little sprog. Old Man Takahashi made a fortune selling Gold Coast real estate to the Japanese, who in those days were obscenely cashed up and happy to swallow up any sites at whatever the asking price. But all good things eventually come to an end, and unfortunately when the Gold Coast property bubble burst in the late eighties the old bloke was left holding enough heavily geared prime real estate to send him bankrupt pretty quickly, along with a good few of his old clients. Since then he'd been scratching out a living on the Coast as best he could. So Kenny had to make his own way, and right now Frankie Box was very pleased he had.

'Good morning, Mr Vagianni.'

'Good morning, Takahashi-san.'

They bowed respectfully to each other, all according to the script, as Kenny's latest batch of souvenir-seekers looked on warmly, obviously impressed to be accorded the rare opportunity to receive individual attention from the curator himself. While Kenny rattled off the usual spiel in Japanese, Frank tried to look as dignified as possible, one hand resting regally on the cash register and the other strategically positioned to conceal the spot where the tomato sauce had dropped from his Egg McMuffin over breakfast that morning. He loved watching Kenny at work. The kid was so polished he had those slopes lining up to eat right out of the palm of his hand. As they bowed back and forth at each other and the eager, hungry shoppers dispersed through the shop, Frank was already starting to count the money. All he had to do was punch the numbers in. No fighting off angry Alsatians trying to stick a bluey up the jumper of some grub, no tedious electoral roll searches and police reports, no more trying to screw dough out of shifty lawyers. Just take the money and whack it in the till.

'Mr Vagianni?'

Frank didn't recognise either of the two pipsqueaks staring at him from the other side of the counter, but he knew instantly he didn't like the look of them. For a start neither looked too Japanese to him, and they didn't look like they were there to grab a boomerang either, but more to the point they both had 'public servant' painted all over them, and that spelt trouble.

'I'm Jeremy Lyons from the Office of Fair Trading, and this is Michael Mayne. We were hoping to ask you a few questions.'

Frank was momentarily paralysed as a sharp, debilitating pain emanating from his hip pocket instantly rushed through his body numbing every limb and organ. Slowly, carefully, he closed his mouth and slid the cash-register drawer shut.

'What about?'

'Why don't we start with misleading and deceptive advertising, Frank?'

Frank recognised the voice immediately, and as Sasha Kelly stepped into view he grimaced at her painfully.

'Argh, fuck.'

Kelly's lips folded into a wry smile. 'Hello, Frank.'

They stared silently at each other across the counter as the perplexed public servants looked on from the wings.

'What's this, Kelly? The coppers finally had the sense to give you the bum's rush did they? You joined the shiny-bums brigade now?'

Stony-faced, Kelly slid an official document across the counter.

'Just assisting with the execution of the warrant, Frank.'

'Yeah?' Frank squinted at the warrant's contents. The more he read, the more the stabbing pain shooting up from his hip pocket radiated through his body.

'"Breaches of the Fair Trading Act ..." Turn it up ... "Deceptive advertising"? What fuckin' deceptive advertising?'

Kelly was leaning casually on the counter now, obviously relishing the experience.

'Well, let's see ...'

She did a little pirouette, casting her eyes across the shop. Kenny Takahashi, hunched inconspicuously at the rear of his little flock of bargain-hunters, herded them hurriedly out through the front door, revealing for the first time the sight of Big Rick Puluwai, paintbrush in one hand and a boomerang in the other, looking somewhat sheepish in a red loincloth and sitting cross-legged on the floor beneath a sign that read 'Authentic Indigenous Art'.

'Isn't that Big Rick from the Liars Bar?'

Frank took a couple of moments to make doubly sure of his identification.

'So?'

Kelly didn't look too anxious to reply.

'Ricky's indigenous, if that's what you're on about.'

She stepped up and placed both elbows on the counter, leaning into Frank's face.

'Indigenous to where? Auckland?'

'Yeah, as a matter of fact.'

She was leaning so far forward Frank just couldn't help himself. It had been so long since he'd had a decent perv on Kelly's knockers that he had to take the shot. His eyes bounced quickly down and back again, but the look on Kelly's face said she hadn't missed it. She straightened up and tugged lightly at her blouse.

'We'd like to start with your financial records if we may.' Jeremy Lyons was opening his briefcase on the counter. 'Are the books on site?'

An hour later Frank was sitting hunched over a cup of instant coffee in the back room, trying to assess the damage, while the OFT investigators rifled through his bank records on the front counter and photographed his merchandise. When Sasha Kelly wandered in he looked up and sneered, then went back to his coffee as she slipped a chipped cup from the shelf and dropped a teabag into it.

'They hand out some pretty hefty fines under this consumer legislation nowadays, Frank. Did you know that?'

She filled her cup with steaming water from the jug and then dragged a chair out from the table.

'Go your hardest, Kelly.' Frank wasn't even looking at her. 'You've got Buckley's chance of pinning me on any of that shit. That gear's all fair dinkum one hundred per cent on the up and up.'

'Maybe.' Kelly sat down beside him and sipped thoughtfully at her tea. 'Anyway, I suppose we could help you out a little bit with OFT if you were seen to be doing the right thing.'

Frank looked up from his coffee.

'I'm listening.'

She took another sip of tea then looked him in the eye.

'I'm still waiting to hear from you about Barry Dougherty.'

Frank looked at her, genuinely confused.

'What are you talking about? They've already pinched a bloke for it.'

'Yeah, I know. Your client.'

Frank didn't know if Kelly was trying to suggest that the fact that Wiltshire might have knocked old Barry Dougherty was somehow meant to implicate him in the blue, but he didn't like the tone of her voice and he wasn't fussed with where the conversation seemed to be heading.

'So if you want the story, go ask whoever pinched him.'

Kelly sat silently looking at him until eventually Frank met her eyes. When she spoke again her voice had lost its edge.

'I don't want some story. I want the truth.'

'What's that supposed to mean?'

She looked back at her cup, hesitating as if she was trying to work out what to say. Then she took a swig, swallowed, and looked Frank straight in the eye.

'Phil Manning's running the investigation.'

The name crackled a little in her throat, and Frank knew why. Phil Manning had a smell about him that dated back to his old days in the Armed Robbery Squad when Roger Baston was directing the show and the Sydney boys were running red hot. Things had settled down since Baston left the force but a corruption watchdog like Kelly would always find it hard to put the old stories in the past.

'He picked up the file from us about three weeks ago. He reckons Wiltshire arranged to have Dougherty murdered.'

Frank breathed out a weary sigh. Suddenly Kelly was getting all skittish just because Phil Manning wanted to pull a murder investigation out from under her. Frank had had enough of all that interstate inter-department copper crap to last him a lifetime.

'Yeah, I know. So what?'

'Manning's in an awfully big rush to wrap a brief around this guy.'

Frank chuckled quietly to himself. 'You're not playing Serpico again are you, Kelly?'

Kelly wasn't laughing. She sat silently for several seconds, as if she was carefully preparing what she had to say.

'When Manning called to say the New South Wales police were taking over the investigation, I told him we were still waiting on the cause of death report, but he didn't seem to care.' She pondered that for a moment then continued. 'He just said Wiltshire was as round as a hoop for it and they wanted to get whatever they could on Dougherty to wrap into their murder charge against Wiltshire.'

Murder was the sexy side of police work. The Barry Dougherty investigation was a red-hot murder brief and Frank could see how any copper, particularly one as ambitious as Sasha Kelly, stuck up there in sleepy old north Queensland, would get a little excited at the prospect of charging someone with the big one. But now that Wiltshire had been pinched in New South Wales and the Sydney blokes were going to have a lash at him, any Queensland murder prosecution was going to be on the back-burner for a long time.

'Sounds to me like you're just dirty because they get first chop at him down there.'

Frank was trying to stir her up, but if Kelly was taking his bait she didn't show it.

'That's just the point.' Her eyes were resolute. 'On what we've got from our forensic people we don't need to take a chop at him at all.'

Frank looked up from his coffee. Was Kelly saying what he thought she was? When she could see she'd made her point, Kelly continued matter-of-factly.

'The report came through on Monday. The post-mortem turned up cement fragments in Dougherty's head wound that matched the surface on his front verandah, and the crack in his skull turned out to be a perfect match to the edge of the landing.'

Frank set his cup down on the table. She was

saying what he thought she was. To remove any doubt Kelly summed it up for him.

'According to our people no one hit Barry Dougherty on the head, Frank. He just fell down and sconed himself.'

Frank screwed his face up. 'Did you tell all this to Manning?'

She nodded. 'He says our reports are wrong.'

'Wouldn't be the first time.'

'I've got a bad feeling about this, Frank.' She slipped her hand into her pocket and drew out a folded wad of paper. Straightening it out she proffered it to Frank. 'Have you seen this?'

Frank quickly scanned two photocopied pages of a typed letter signed 'A Concerned Citizen'. 'What is it?'

'According to Manning it's supposed to be a ransom letter written by Barry Dougherty.'

Frank re-read the contents. He could see immediately why she had a bad feeling. Kelly was a painful bitch but she had always been a first-class investigator and anyone with half a nose could smell a rotten egg in this one. As he read the text again he had a rising feeling of anticipation in his gut. Something pretty murky was on foot and Frank knew well enough that diving into holes like this one could be downright dangerous. He folded the two pages carefully and slipped them into his top pocket.

'I'll talk to Wiltshire. Find out what I can.'

'Great. I'll see what I can do with OFT.'

Her lips formed a soft smile as Frank nodded his appreciation. Their eyes settled on each other for a moment in the closest thing to friendship they had ever known, until she looked away self-consciously, suddenly intent on the contents of her cup again. Frank could see an unfamiliar expression in her profile, a vulnerable look of quiet satisfaction, perhaps almost relief. He watched her silently as she took another sip of tea, both hands wrapped around the cup. It was a tough job for Kelly, Frank knew that: she was such a conscientious Dudley Do-Right type she had always put way too much pressure on herself, and everyone around her. He could see now why she was relieved. The charges against Wiltshire had obviously worried her. She couldn't stand the thought that she might be on the edge of a cook-up and she had to get it off her chest. Frank studied her fine long fingers wrapped around the cup and traced them down across her wrists and forearms. His eyes gradually drifted to the full curve of her bosom.

Kelly looked up suddenly and Frank snapped his eyes away. He could feel her concentrated gaze on him as he frantically poured the last remnants of his coffee into his mouth.

'Were you looking at my tits just then, Frank?' The diminutive detective had a look of lethal inquisition in her eyes. 'Were you?'

'Argh shit, Kelly, give me a break will you.'

Frank screwed his face into a guilty grimace and again tipped the cup against his face, sucking out the last drop of coffee as Kelly pushed her chair back noisily and stomped out of the room.

'Jesus, Frank!'

CHAPTER TWENTY-TWO

When Michael Wiltshire stepped into the contact visitors area Frank Vagianni hardly recognised him. His face was drawn and lined, the once impeccably groomed hair now long and lank and brushed back from his forehead, his eyes hollow and uncertain. It shouldn't have come as a surprise to an ex-copper with Frank's years on the force. He'd seen it a thousand times before. Prison had a way of turning young men into old ones overnight.

'Hello, Frank.'

As Wiltshire shook his hand Frank felt almost embarrassed. The dimensions of the man's fall from grace since Frank had last spoken to him in the comfortable lounge room of his mansion overlooking the Brisbane River were so immense and devastating that an awkward, unexpected silence settled on them momentarily as Frank struggled for his words. Eventually he motioned in the direction of the fixed metal seating and mumbled, 'Pull up a pew.'

As soon as they were seated Frank screwed the top off his soft-drink bottle, took a quick swig and got straight down to business. He hadn't been to Mackay as promised at their last meeting; given the charges he'd thought it better to make more inquiries with other sources before he got under the noses of the investigating police. He'd spent the advance-on-expenses cheque tracking down a few leads and he thought he might have come up with some useful stuff, but to be sure he had to ask Wilshire a few more questions about Barry Dougherty.

When Frank had finished his little introductory spiel Michael Wiltshire dropped his head and studied his hands, as though dredging up some information in response. It was a good sign. It meant that he was buying Frank's lame story about the dissipation of his fat expenses cheque, or at least he was so desperate to find a helping hand that he wasn't going to make an issue out of it. Either way Frank was in the clear.

'Dougherty was trying to blackmail me.'

This guy was desperate for help. Blackmail was about as good a motive as there was for murder, so for a guy in Wiltshire's position to open with a line like that meant he was plenty desperate. He was looking for a friend and, for the right price, Frank was more than willing to be friendly.

'Why?'

'Because he was convinced I was involved in Ellowe's death.'

'Yeah?' Frank paused for a moment, glugging down some more of his soft drink to give himself time to think. He hadn't expected to come quite so far so soon and now he was already getting into dangerous waters where the wrong answer had the potential to wipe out a golden goose. 'And why would that be?'

Things were obviously starting to warm up a little bit for Michael Wiltshire; Frank could almost see the tiny beads of sweat starting to form on his brow as he wrung the fingers of both hands.

'It all came out of that business with Fred Hunter being accused of branch-stacking. At the time a lot of people thought I was going to pull him into line. I started getting late-night phone calls warning me to drop off.'

The next question was an obvious one. Frank hesitated for a moment then asked it.

'From Trevor Ellowe?'

Wiltshire looked up from his hands and nodded gravely. Frank was well and truly in those dangerous waters now. Wiltshire had just corroborated the Crown case that he had a good strong motive to do harm to Trevor Ellowe.

'So how did Dougherty come into it?'

'When Dougherty fell out with Fred Hunter he lifted some documents from Hunter's office. The day before Ellowe's death Barry tried to hand the Enmore branch enrolment register over to me.'

'Did you take it?'

Wiltshire shook his head. 'I didn't want any part of it. But apparently Trevor Ellowe fronted Dougherty the next day to get the books back, and Barry told him he'd already handed them over to me, just to fob him off. Ellowe told him he was going to get them off me, so Dougherty was convinced Ellowe was looking for me the night he died. I guess he put two and two together and decided I'd taken things into my own hands.'

It sounded like a fair sort of mathematical calculation to Frank. It was one that demanded the next question. A lot depended on the answer to that question, but Frank was in too deep now to turn back.

'And did you?'

'Of course not.' Wiltshire spat the answer back so quickly and vehemently he seemed to surprise even himself. Frank could see he was starting to fray at the edges. 'I've got no idea what happened to him. So far as I know he could've died in the car crash.'

It was a good answer and one that suited Frank just fine for the moment, but that brought him back to Barry Dougherty.

'Obviously Dougherty didn't think so.'

'No.' Wiltshire looked worn out but he continued the story. 'A couple of years ago he rang me out of the blue, said he was coming to Brisbane and he wanted to meet with me to talk about Ellowe.'

'Did you agree?'

'I did, yeah.' Frank Vagianni tried hard to conceal the scepticism in his eyes as Wiltshire stumbled to explain himself. 'I guess I was just curious to hear what he had to say.'

Michael Wiltshire didn't look to Frank like the sort of bloke who customarily took time out of his busy working day to chew the cud with visiting barflies just to indulge his curiosity, but if his story was to be believed it was just as well he did. According to Wiltshire, when he met up with Dougherty in one of the city pubs the old bloke announced that he'd picked up some mail to the effect that Ellowe had been bashed and then murdered with a lethal overdose of heroin before his body was dumped in the wrecked car in the Cross to make the whole thing look like an accident. And the story went that Wiltshire had organised the whole thing because Ellowe was threatening to break his legs on behalf of his boss Fred Hunter.

'Of course I told him it was rubbish but he wouldn't hear of it. He just said Ellowe had got what was coming to him and he didn't blame me one bit.'

Frank had spent enough time around police stations, jails and watch houses to fill in the next instalment of the story.

'And then he put the bite on you.'

'More or less, yeah.'

'How much more and how much less?'

'He said he was sick and needed money for an operation. I lent him bits and pieces here and there. I guess I gave him around twelve grand all up.'

That accounted for the cash withdrawals from Wiltshire's account that the police had turned up. Twelve grand was relatively small peanuts, but it sounded to Frank like it was intended to be a pretty permanent loan. And if it was just a bit of charity to an old bloke down on his luck, why were they all cash transactions? It was a question

Wiltshire would have to answer sooner or later, but right now Frank didn't need to know.

'You said that was a couple of years ago. What made you start looking for him when you rang me?'

'He sent me a blackmail letter.'

Frank slipped the two photocopied pages from his shirt pocket and laid them flat on the table between them. 'You mean this one?'

Wiltshire made no move to touch the document. He sat motionless, silently staring at the pages lying on the metal table, his two hands linked together in front of him like a sinner praying for repentance. As Frank waited, studying him closely, he wondered if Wiltshire had done all the soul-baring he was going to do today. After what seemed a long time, the prisoner reached out one hand and pulled the letter across the table towards him. His eyes skimmed the contents then he looked up with a weary sigh.

'I was sick to bloody shit of it. I wanted to get in touch with him, tell him if he didn't drop off I'd report him to the police. That's why I called you.'

Frank Vagianni nodded pensively. So far it sounded logical enough.

'When I gave you his contact details, what did you do?'

'I rang him.'

'And?'

'I asked him if he'd sent me a letter.'

Frank nodded again. The pieces were slotting into place.

'And he told you he hadn't, right?'

Wiltshire looked mildly surprised. 'Yeah.' He nodded absently. 'Yeah, that's exactly right.'

Frank Vagianni had spent a lifetime searching for answers in the faces of practised liars. Sometimes they were easier to find than others, but one thing was clear to him now. Michael Wiltshire was telling him the truth, at least about this part of the story; he genuinely believed Barry Dougherty had sent him that extortion letter.

'I think he was telling you the truth.'

'What do you mean?'

'Barry Dougherty didn't write this letter.'

The quizzical look on Michael Wiltshire's face slowly faded into uncertainty and concern as Frank dropped one of his stubby hands onto the letter flattened on the table between them and rotated it forty-five degrees so they could both look at the contents simultaneously.

'Read it.' Frank poked a finger at the first paragraph as he read aloud. '*You might have fooled the coroner but just because he didn't commit you for trial doesn't mean you're not gonna end up in the dock*. That's talking about the fact that if a coroner thinks the evidence at an inquest amounts to a prima facie case of someone having committed a crime then he can commit them straight to trial for it. Did you know that?' Frank gave no impression of expecting an answer. 'I can tell you there's not too many people around that would.' He looked back to the page. '*The DPP will soon present an ex officio indictment when they get a look at the evidence ...* That's referring to the DPP's power to bypass the magistrates' court and go straight to a judge with what's called an ex officio indictment. Who knows jack-shit about any of that stuff? No bastard, that's who.' He ran his finger down the page. 'See here — *You were a party ... you procured the offence* ... They're legal terms, mate. That's the sort of crap that lawyers spruik, not blokes like Barry Dougherty. The whole thing's full of that sort of shit.' He looked up into Michael Wiltshire's bewildered face. 'I'm telling you, that letter wasn't written by some old pisshead transport company invoice clerk. It was written by someone who knows the criminal prosecution process like the back of his hand.'

'Such as?'

Frank Vagianni was looking straight into Wiltshire's eyes. He'd been on Civvy Street for a long time now, but what he had to say still didn't come too easily to him.

'Such as a copper I'd say.'

They sat opposite each other silently soaking up the significance of that possibility. Eventually Frank threw his head back, gulped down several more mouthfuls of his soft drink and burped, before adding, 'Maybe an ex-copper, or even a dodgy lawyer.'

Michael Wiltshire pulled the letter back in front of him and started reading. He had read the document so many times he could have recited its contents verbatim in his sleep. But now it was as though he was reading it for the first time, as though he had broken a code that had revealed its hidden meaning. Every time he re-read the words it became more obvious to him.

'I think I need to tell you about something that happened here the other day.'

He was huddled forward, whispering, his hands gripping the metal surface of the table as though he was dangling over the edge of a precipice. There was a kind of desperate urgency in his face that made Frank hunch towards him like a dark conspirator.

Michael started with the incident at police headquarters on the day he was arrested, when Manning had told him, 'It doesn't have to be like this', and Darryl Beane's reaction to those words later in the cells beneath the Central Courts. When he came to his meeting with Roger Baston in the prison, he could see from the detective's pursed lips and raised eyebrows that they shared a common view of Baston. But Vagianni made no comment, merely nodding and grunting from time to time as Michael recounted his conversation with the investigator and his lawyer in the interview room. Eventually he got to the point of his story.

'Do you know a man by the name of Ronny McPhee?'

'Byron Winston Churchill McPhee. Yeah, sure I know him. Ron the Pom they call him. He used to be some sort of jumped-up heavy for the unions.'

Michael Wiltshire nodded grimly; they were obviously talking about the same man. 'He fronted me on Tuesday morning.'

It had happened shortly before the midday muster. Along with the rest of Goldsmith Wing,

Michael was strolling idly on the oval, listening to the enthusiastic ramblings of Kurtz, a defrocked accountant who was on remand awaiting trial on a multi-million-dollar investment scheme fraud. For a pathological liar Kurtz was largely inoffensive and relatively civilised, but having already served two terms for fraud offences he knew the system as well as any of the old-time crims and his innate deceitfulness and guile made him a useful font of knowledge as to the art of surviving incarceration. That day he was expounding on another subject, namely what he claimed to be the many virtues of a real-estate investment opportunity that had recently presented itself to him and was certain to make a lot of money for anyone who became involved. As Michael listened sceptically, he suddenly felt himself being bumped to one side as Ronny McPhee stepped between them from behind, shouldering the two men apart.

'Fook off, Bean Counter. I want to talk to Money Bags.'

Kurtz understood enough of prison politics to disappear quickly and without a word of protest, leaving Michael ambling shoulder to shoulder with the little Englishman. They walked on in silence for several seconds before McPhee glanced firstly over one shoulder then the other, then leaned in, muttering from the corner of his mouth.

'We've a couple o'differences between us, me and you, Money Bags.'

Michael continued steadily on his way without looking at the Englishman, an uneasy feeling rising in his stomach.

'D'y' know what they are then?'

Michael turned grimly to the little man beside him. 'What?'

'Well, for starters, yer've got a stack o'money and ay've got fookin' none.' McPhee was looking up at him earnestly. 'It's a fookin' cryin' shame, don't y'think?' A smile lit up his face, flashing his gold-capped teeth. 'Joost a poor dumb fookin' Pom me, with nowt but a sharp wit and a cheery smile.'

He chuckled to himself as Michael turned back to look straight ahead, the muscles in his stomach contracting nervously. Money was a dangerous subject in this world, and as he walked on in silence he was tensely anticipating the point of their so-far cryptic conversation. McPhee's shoulder pressed in closer to him.

'But I know how to deal with fookin' sharks like Roger bloody Baston and his slimy fookin' lawyer mate without losing all me fookin' toes and fingers, stand by me, and that's another difference between us.'

Puzzled, Michael turned to look at the Englishman. His expression was deadly serious now as he leaned in at Michael again.

'There's been talk on't streets about Baston and his copper mates cooking up a scam on yer over that business with Ellowe ever since yer left Sydney. That letter yer got come from Baston.'

Michael stopped dead in his tracks.

'Ye're swimmin' with the sharks right now, lad, so yer'd do well to watch out for yer fingers and yer toes.' He touched one finger lightly on his

333

nose, snapped off a sly wink, then peeled off at an angle and wandered back into the throng of convicts drifting around the oval. 'Toodle-pip, old boy.'

It was a one-sided conversation that had troubled Michael ever since. The demand he had expected from McPhee had not eventuated, nor had there been any offer of help for remuneration or any other proposition that could be interpreted as adding motive or design to what the Englishman had said. It seemed his intention was to do no more than offer a warning about Roger Baston and Darryl Beane. Was the talk of a scam true? And if it was, why would McPhee, a man who seemed largely intent on keeping to himself, communicate it to Michael now? More importantly, if there were such rumours circulating, was there any substance to them or was this merely baseless speculation floating around in the criminal underworld?

They were questions Wiltshire posed now to Frank Vagianni as the two men sat huddled together in the contact visits area. Frank's brow was deeply knit in concentration as he tried to fit the pieces into place.

'There'd be no love lost between Baston and Pommy Ron, that's for sure. Baston kicked a lot of union freckle for the big developers back in the old green-ban days. McPhee and his BLF mates wouldn't forget that sort of thing too quick.'

Michael Wiltshire buried his face in his hands, rubbing his eyes and forehead as he tried to understand what he was being told. 'Alright, supposing it's true.' He blew out a deep sigh and clasped his hands together tightly on the table between them. 'Suppose Baston is up to something. What sort of scam do you think they're talking about?'

'That bit's simple, mate: blackmail.' Frank was looking directly into Michael's eyes and paused momentarily to let the word sink in. 'It's the oldest game there is for a bent copper. Pick someone who's vulnerable, someone who's got plenty to hide and plenty to lose, preferably someone with a heap of brass. Someone like yourself.'

It was intended to be provocative, and Michael Wiltshire knew it, but he was too weary and too confused to take the bait. He listened compliantly as the detective continued.

'Then you wrap a brief around him and offer him an aspirin to make it go away. "We can make the charges disappear so long as you cough up the bugsy." The bigger the headache the bigger the aspirin required to make it disappear. And let's face it: you've got the biggest headache of them all.'

Frank kept his eyes trained on Wiltshire's face, looking for the tiniest reaction. For him it was all by force of habit. He'd spent a lifetime insulting guilty men and waiting for the reaction. But Wiltshire just looked puzzled.

'So where does Barry Dougherty fit in?'

'My guess is he doesn't.' Frank moved in closer, leaning on his elbows. 'Let me spell it out for you. After that business with Ellowe, everyone in Marrickville reckons you got away with murder, and Baston and his mates figure that a rich man like you should have to pay something to their benevolent fund for the privilege. With the papers full of stories about you selling half of Queensland to the Arabs, they see you as a nice big juicy plum, just ripe for the picking. So they dummy up a blackmail letter and slip it into your PO box. But you don't clean out your box, so it looks like you're calling their bluff. And that ramps things up a notch. Now they've got to show you just how messy things can get. And when old Barry Dougherty falls over pissed one night and scones himself it plays right into their hands. So they get Wendy Whatever-her-name-is to make a bodgy statement to the Homicide boys.'

'That means she's in on the scam.'

'Maybe.' Frank kept his eyes trained on Wiltshire's as he delivered his next line. 'Or maybe she's just mightily pissed off that you killed her boyfriend.'

'I didn't kill anyone.'

If he was lying he was good at it.

'Yeah well, we'll come to that some other time. For now the point is the sheila's story puts you well and truly in the shit, and that means the deal has got to be that when you fork out the dough they take her out of the equation.'

'What's that mean?'

'Depends. If she's in the loop, she takes off or just recants her story and they sling her a share of the whack. If she's not, either they pay her a sweetener to disappear or they scare the fuck right out of her, or maybe even worse.'

Wiltshire's face looked haggard. 'What do you mean "maybe even worse"?'

'I don't have to tell you, two million bucks is a shitload of money in this town.'

Michael Wiltshire dropped his head into both hands, running his fingers through his greasy hair. He wondered how things could possibly have got so crazy. He flashed on Gary Sharpe, his slick, conniving friend who had the answer to every problem, and on the frantic telephone conversation they'd shared the night that Trevor Ellowe died. He knew what Sharpe's solution would have been: pay the money, solve the problem. There was a fix for every problem, a contact for every deal. What did it matter if the hands you were shaking had a little dirt on them?

Michael lifted his head and looked straight into Frank Vagianni's eyes with a steely resolve.

'Frank, can you find me a new lawyer?'

The detective sat back in his seat and nodded thoughtfully.

'Yeah.'

He threw his head back, drained the last of his soft drink, burped loudly and nodded again. 'Yeah, I think I know a bloke who might fit the bill alright.'

CHAPTER TWENTY-THREE

Eddie Moran could be a very irritating person, even when you had his full attention. But trying to explain the Wiltshire case to Eddie while he sat tilted back at a precarious angle in his leather swivel with his trouser legs pulled halfway up around his knees and his long skinny feet propped against the edge of his desk was driving Frank Vagianni to distraction. To make matters worse Eddie was wearing the silliest looking purple socks Frank had ever seen. His sharp-toed silver-buckled boots were sitting on a pile of papers in the middle of his desk, and talking to the soles of Eddie's purple feet while he twanged absently on his Gibson hollow-bodied guitar and peered out of his window at the bikini girls on Surfers Paradise beach was making Frank feel a little like an Eskimo ice salesman.

'Hey. Are you listening to me?'

Moran looked over his purple toes at Frank.

'Yeah, I'm listening.'

'So what'd I say then?'

Eddie could see from the knitted brow and turned-down mouth that Frank had his nose a little out of joint. He had burst into the office that morning with what he assured Eddie would be a red-hot paying brief that was guaranteed to be a sure-fire winner and now his delicate Italian sensibilities were offended by the fact that Eddie wasn't sharing his enthusiasm. Moran set the guitar down, slipped his feet off the edge of his desk and dropped forward on his elbows.

'You said that Roger Baston and his mates are trying to extort money out of Wiltshire over the Ellowe murder. And you said Wiltshire didn't kill Dougherty, he just died by accident. The problem is, Wiltshire isn't charged with Dougherty's murder, is he, pal? He's charged with Trevor Ellowe's murder, and whether or not Baston's trying to snip him doesn't change the fact that Michael Wiltshire murdered Trevor Ellowe.'

'How?'

Kirsten Foster had obviously been listening in. Eddie and Frank turned in unison to see her leaning on the doorjamb and sucking on a cigarette. It was a sure sign she was all worked up about something. Slick had been off the smokes for months now, but they both knew she kept a reserve pack in the bottom drawer in case of an emergency. Eddie had hoped to keep her out of this discussion but it was obvious now that wasn't going to happen.

'What do you mean "how"?'

Slick lobbed the cigarette packet onto Eddie's desk as she dropped into one of the leather client chairs, hooking a shapely leg up over one of the arms. As the packet slid towards Eddie, Frank intercepted it and pulled two cigarettes out, slipping one behind his ear and lighting up the other. As he tossed the packet on to Eddie, Slick took another drag and puffed out her answer.

'Wiltshire was alone at home with a seven-year-old kid that night. So how the fuck did he kill Trevor, then go steal a car, somehow get Trev in the car and drive the car all the way to the Cross and crash the car, and then get himself out of there and back home to his kid?'

Eddie lit up one of her cigarettes and lobbed the packet back to her. 'I said he murdered Trevor. I didn't say he did it on his own.'

'Okay, so you're saying someone else was in on it? So who?'

'Who cares?'

Slick sat up and took a deep draw on her cigarette. She was looking Eddie straight in the eye. 'I care.'

Eddie sized her up as she sat there puffing on her cigarette, staring him down. He knew her well enough to see this meant a lot to her. She'd been through more than she deserved, but she was a tough cookie, all attitude, the same little Angry Ant she'd been when she was just his best mate's kid sister playing cricket in the back yard with the boys. Now she wanted answers and she was determined to get them, Eddie could see that. She'd been hurt and she'd survived and now she wanted answers. He could understand that perfectly. He hated unanswered questions more than anyone. But what questions did Slick want answers to? Were they questions about Trevor, how he died, and why? The truth was the truth, and whatever the truth was about Trevor Ellowe, it couldn't harm Slick any more. But were her questions really about Michael Wiltshire? Was she still hanging on to some deluded hope that Wiltshire was going to turn out to be her knight in shining armour after all? If she was, she was lining herself up for another fall and that was one thing Eddie didn't want to see.

'Listen, Slick, why don't you just go out and whip us up some coffee?'

Her eyes narrowed into two ferocious slits as she uncrossed her legs, took a drag on her cigarette and crossed her legs again.

'Fuck you, Eddie. What do I look like, the hired help?'

She was a cheeky bitch, always had been. He should have fired her years ago. 'Yeah, as a matter of fact you do. In fact, as I recall it, that's exactly why I hired you — to help around here.'

As the two of them faced off across the desk, Frank groaned a deep sigh and climbed out of his chair. 'Don't be such an arsehole, Eddie. I'll get the fuckin' coffee.'

'Sit down, Frank.' Eddie grabbed at his desk phone and punched in a number. 'Kenny.'

At the front reception desk Kenny Takahashi pressed the pause button on his Gameboy and snatched up the phone.

'Yeah, boss?'

Eddie winced. Kenny was working out just fine, apart from the 'boss' thing. It was a requirement of his uni course that he do some work experience at a legal office, and Eddie could always use an extra pair of hands to lick stamps and go for coffee, so he was giving the kid one day a week. Not that Kenny was getting too much legal training sitting on reception playing computer games all day, but work experience with a hot-shot celebrity lawyer like Eddie would look good on his CV. It wasn't costing Eddie a cent, so the price was right, and all in all the kid had shown that he was pretty on the ball. Except for that 'boss' thing.

'Get us three cappuccinos in here, will you? You better make Slick's a double shot. I think she's having her caffeine withdrawals again.'

'No worries, boss.'

Eddie winced again as he put down the phone and sucked hard on his cigarette. Slick was still staring at him, her eyes a little softer now. Eddie blew a stream of smoke into the room.

'Trust me, Slick, Wiltshire's in this thing up to his neck.'

He was looking straight into her deep green eyes, now glistening with emotion. The anger was all gone. Slick knew this was a dream job for Eddie; it wasn't every day he got offered a brief to defend a cashed-up millionaire facing a murder prosecution. He wasn't turning his nose up at this job for no reason. She knew why he was dancing all around it, and she loved him for it. Eddie was an arsehole, but she always knew that he was on her side.

'So what?' Slick blinked her eyes and drew back on the cigarette, composing herself. 'What do you care whether he's guilty or not? You act for every lowlife scumbag there is.'

Eddie threw up both hands defensively. 'Hey, go easy on that "lowlife scumbag" shit, sugar. As you know, Mr Vagianni here happens to be one of my very esteemed former clients himself.'

Frank chortled. But when he looked across to share the quip with Slick he saw she was still looking earnestly at Eddie. When she spoke again her voice was quiet and without emotion.

'The guy's loaded. You'll get paid whether he goes to gaol or not. So who cares whether he's guilty or innocent?'

Eddie eyed her cautiously then shook one long finger in her direction. 'See, now you're starting to think like a lawyer, Slick, and that scares me.'

'Yeah well, someone's got to around here.'

'Really? So does this mean you want to start wearing the pin-striped suits from now on, and I've got to wear that cute little black leotard of yours with the bunny ears?'

'Get fucked, Eddie.'

Eddie chuckled gleefully. He loved it when she came out swinging.

'Yeah, I love you too, baby.'

'I'm serious, Eddie.' She was undiverted, still staring intensely across the desk at him. 'This is the best job you've had through the door all year.'

Eddie put the cigarette to his lips and sucked hard on it. He wished this conversation hadn't started, but it had. It was true, this was the best job he'd had through the door all year, and with the way he'd been swanning around lately, taking bows and spending cash, he could do with all the money he could get. But this one was more than just a job.

'Are you sure you're not getting your hormones a little bit mixed up in all this, Slick?' He could see her eyes begin to narrow again, but he had no thought of backing off. Slick wasn't going to give this up without a fight. 'Let's see now, your ex-husband gets himself knocked by your ex-boyfriend. And the main witness is your ex-husband's ex-girlfriend, who he was bonking on the side. Don't you think you're maybe just a tad close to this one?'

He half expected her to come across the desk at him and plant a bone-rattler flash on his chin. But she didn't. She sat motionless, staring at him through the smoke wafting from her cigarette while Frank squirmed uncomfortably in the armchair next to her. Eddie didn't look away. He held her gaze relentlessly. Slick had to be told. She had to confront the reality of what she was proposing. This one was going to hurt her, and the closer she got to it, the more she was going to get hurt. He could see in her face that she understood that now, and as the realisation deepened her green eyes filled with tears.

'Listen, Slick —'
'Get fucked, Eddie.'

She leaped out of her chair and stomped out through the door, causing Kenny Kamikaze and his tray of cappuccinos to put on the best sidestep Frank had seen since Kenny's days as half-back with the Tigers under-19s. Eddie looked accusingly at Frank, who looked away, fumbling sheepishly with his cigarette.

Kenny staggered to the desk juggling his tray. 'What's up, boss?'

Eddie winced.

'Put 'em on the desk, pal.'

Eddie climbed out of his chair, grabbed two of the cups and ambled towards the door, slowing his gait to give her just a little extra time. He found Slick exactly where he thought she'd be, propped against the benchtop in the tea room, sniffing and dabbing her eyes daintily with a rolled-up tissue.

'Coffee time?'

She looked up with a sad little half-smile and shook her head. Eddie set the coffees down and wrapped his lanky arms around her.

'You okay, kid?'

He could feel her face tucked against his chest as she nodded. He held her tightly and they stood silently together in the tea room for what seemed a long time.

Eventually he heard her whisper, 'I have to know, Eddie.'

'I understand.'

Slick was a smart girl. She'd thought about it, weighed it up and worked it out. She knew the dangers in it for her, but she'd decided that whatever pain there was in asking the hard questions, it was outweighed by the agony of never knowing the answers. Eddie understood that perfectly. He wasn't happy about it, but he understood.

'What do you want me to do?

'I want you to go and find out what he has to say.'

* * *

It hadn't been a good day for Gary Sharpe.

It had been his experience that, generally speaking, wives didn't take too kindly to reading in the national headlines that their husbands had been having it off with a little bit of something on the side and, specifically speaking, Sharpey's missus Lainie was certain to go totally ballistic if that young bloke from the *Age* published the breaking story that the newly appointed Foreign Affairs Minister Gary Sharpe had been bunning the ex-Victorian National Party leader Frances Hutton. That silly Hutton bitch had included a whole chapter in her recently released tell-all biography about her steamy fling with a certain unnamed 'Labor Party power-broker' (including all the gory details of their forward roll across the Prime Minister's leather-inlaid desk after the Christmas party, when she left her knickers in the ashtray as a souvenir for the PM) and of course it hadn't taken five minutes for the rats to break their ranks, with every disenchanted Labor lackey on the back bench whispering poisoned darts into the shell-like ear of any grubby journo they could find about how the mystery Labor Party Romeo was none other than good old Sharpey. But Lainie was the least of his problems: she was all too used to his less-than-discreet dalliances with young backroom groupies to care about much more than the public humiliation, and she'd get over that. The real problem was the damage it could do to the party if the story broke. Extramarital affairs were bad enough in the Labor heartland, but porking a conservative was unforgivable.

That was why Sharpey had been working overtime all day to hose the whole thing down. He'd whispered in the right ears, knocked on the right doors, tried to talk a little reason, told plenty of lies, threatened, cajoled and called in every favour he could think of. In the end he'd had to remind a few people why they were where they were today, and how different things could have been — it was just lucky Labor still had a few staunch mates where and when it counted.

So the Hutton scandal was back under the carpet, at least for the time being. But that wasn't the end of Gary Sharpe's bad day. Something a lot more troublesome than sex and politics was churning up his gut.

As Sharpey watched the floor numbers illuminate above the elevator door he was rehearsing the verbal rogering he was going to give that sleazy two-faced conniving little weasel Darryl Beane. As soon as he burst through the cedar doors to Darryl's stately office Sharpey let the lawyer have it with both barrels.

'What the fuck's going on, Darryl?'

He strode to Darryl Beane's desk and slapped the folded letter down so hard the noise made Darryl start, the gold nib of his fountain pen jumping erratically on the page. Beane's eyes dropped to the document and recognised it immediately as a copy of the extortion letter that had been placed in Michael Wiltshire's PO box months earlier. He looked disdainfully over his half-glasses and motioned his startled secretary towards the door. As she left she closed the double doors behind her.

'Ever think of knocking, Gary?'

'What the fuck's going on?'

The lawyer laid his pen down on the desktop. His usual unflappable composure was a thin veneer, his mouth was pursed into a tense colourless slit and his thin face was drawn and pallid. He folded his delicate hands neatly underneath his chin and looked past Gary Sharpe to where a relaxed Roger Baston was sitting in a corner, splayed casually across the leather lounge chair. As Sharpey turned to follow Beane's gaze his surprise was so apparent it was comical. Baston broke into a throaty chuckle at the sight of it.

'Hello, Sharpey.'

Gary Sharpe was momentarily speechless. He wasn't expecting to see Roger Baston. He'd arranged to meet with Darryl Beane alone, hoping to present him with a few home truths and wring some sort of a confession out of him. Darryl was as cunning as a shithouse rat but he didn't handle confrontation well and Sharpey knew a little robust badgering would be likely to make him spill the story pretty quickly. But he hadn't counted on Darryl bringing in Roger Baston. Roger was a whole different proposition. He was sitting back with a broad smile spread across his face, glaring at Sharpey with an intimidating air of self-assurance. But Gary Sharpe had been in politics too long to let the likes of Baston turn the tables on him. He looked the investigator directly in the eye.

'What the fuck are you two up to with this Michael Wiltshire thing?'

The smile faded on Baston's face.

'What are you talking about, mate? We're giving you exactly what you asked for.' He sat forward in the chair, his thick forearms resting on his knees. 'Have you forgotten already?' His sombre gaze was trained intensely on Gary Sharpe. 'Your mate Wiltshire was about to tip a big bucket of prawn-heads all over your political career, remember? And you wanted him discredited — "taken out of the equation" I think you said. Well, old son, he's out of the equation, just like you wanted.'

Sharpey struggled for his comeback as Baston held his gaze. When the words came they sounded weak and clumsy in his mouth.

'You said that as soon as he was charged the girl would change her story and the whole thing would go away.'

Now Baston's expression was deadly serious. 'It will go away. When I decide the time is right.'

A sudden flush of panic flooded Sharpey. This thing was starting to get out of control, just as things always seemed to get out of control when Roger Baston came into the mix. When Michael Wiltshire had told Sharpey he was going to the police about Barry Dougherty's death, Sharpey knew it would involve Wiltshire telling them everything he knew about the death of Trevor Ellowe, including his call to Gary Sharpe that night, and that meant Sharpey had no alternative but to take some drastic measures. Wiltshire simply wouldn't be deterred from a course that was certain to re-open the investigation into Ellowe's death, and turn the spotlight onto Gary Sharpe's involvement. Whatever the outcome of that, it was certain to completely derail Sharpe's political career. He could permanently forget any aspirations he'd ever had for the PM's job, and even his position on the front bench would be under fire in no time flat. Everything was at stake. So Sharpey had no alternative. He had to shift the pressure back onto Michael Wiltshire, make him understand how much was at stake, that none of them could afford the luxury of an overactive conscience. He needed to put Wiltshire under a cloud of suspicion, have him charged, put him in a position where no one would believe a word he said, hopefully make him understand that the less he said about anything to do with the death of Trevor Ellowe the better it would be for all of them.

Baston had promised it would be a piece of cake. He knew Ellowe's girlfriend, Wendy Bagley; she'd hit a few hurdles lately and was doing it pretty tough. He'd talk to her, line her up to wrap some sort of story around Wiltshire, and then he'd tee up some tame coppers to pull the strings together. They'd bring Darryl Beane into it, just to oil the wheels. It would go like clockwork. Wiltshire would be charged with Ellowe's murder, then the girl would recant and the charge would be withdrawn. But of course the shit would stick. No one would ever believe anything Michael Wiltshire said about the incident again. Baston made it sound so easy. It wasn't until Wiltshire was charged and Sharpey found out a bit more about the case against him that he realised Baston was playing his own game on the side.

Gary Sharpe stomped back to the desk, snatched up the extortion letter from under Daryl Beane's nose and, waving it animatedly, turned back to Baston.

'This bloody letter was sent three months ago.'

A wry smile crept back onto Roger Baston's lips. 'Well, we can't help it if Barry Dougherty was trying to scam some money out of him.'

'That's bullshit and you know it.' Gary Sharpe was hovering over Roger Baston now, yapping accusingly. 'That letter's got "copper" written all over it and no one knows more shonky bloody coppers than you do. Your head's right in the middle of all this, Roger, don't you try and tell me that it isn't. You've been lining this scam up for months. And now you and our shifty bloody lawyer mate here are stringing the whole thing out until Wiltshire pays up, aren't you?' His chubby face was bright crimson as he leaned in closer and bellowed his accusation again for added emphasis. 'Aren't you?'

Roger Baston had come a long way since his copper days. The immaculate silk tie, the gold cufflinks and the elegant Armani suit complemented his short-cropped, grey-speckled hair so seamlessly that even Gary Sharpe could perhaps be forgiven for forgetting who he was talking to. But Roger Baston wasn't the forgetting or the forgiving kind. His face twisted into a vicious scowl.

As Sharpe began to straighten up Baston lunged forward with one of his huge hands, snatched at the politician's polyester tie and wrenched his face forward and down until Sharpe could smell the stale cigarette smoke on his breath. Tightening the noose around the politician's neck until his eyes were popping grotesquely in his head and his constricted breath was rasping noisily in his throat, Baston quietly whispered a hoarse warning.

'You ever raise your voice to me again and I'll peel that ugly face right off your fat fuckin' head. You understand me?' Gary Sharpe nodded frantically, gasping for air as Baston continued quietly and unemotionally. 'You're not dealing with your pissant politician mates now, son, so you just remember your place, alright? I've been doing you a little favour out of the goodness of my heart, and if I want to make an earn on the side for my trouble, that's my business and only my business, you understand?'

He let go of the tie and Gary Sharpe staggered backwards into the middle of the office, clutching at his collar, desperately trying to claw it open, gulping in whatever air he could. The wry smile returned to Roger Baston's face.

'You paid your money to get on this ride, Sharpey old son, and yours truly is driving the bus. So I suggest you sit down and buckle up real tight, because if you fall out you could get very badly hurt.'

CHAPTER TWENTY-FOUR

Slick had her doubts as to whether Eddie was entirely serious about this job. In his crumpled black stovepipe trousers, open-necked mauve shirt, crimson jacket and high-heeled black suede boots, he looked more like a jazz musician than a lawyer. Ever since they arrived at the legal visits area of the prison and settled in around the narrow desk in the middle of the incongruously expansive wooden room, awaiting the arrival of their newest client, Eddie had sat back with his feet propped up, studiously endeavouring to balance two coins edge on edge on each other on the surface of the desk. They had been waiting more than ten minutes now and Eddie had hardly said a word.

Slick knew he wasn't happy. He'd made up his mind that their client was guilty, and that when that fact finally became obvious to everyone Slick was going to get hurt all over again. He'd convinced himself that they were both too close to it and should stay right out of it. But Slick had persisted, and ultimately Eddie had relented. He'd agreed to come and talk to Wiltshire, to listen to his story, but only on the condition that Slick accompanied him to take notes as his clerk. She knew Eddie wanted her to hear the story first-hand. He wanted her to make the call.

When Michael Wiltshire stepped into the room his shock was obvious. Frank Vagianni had told him to expect a visit from Eddie Moran, and when the guards had called him to legals he'd hoped it would be his new lawyer. He knew he'd met Moran briefly years ago and had a vague recollection of him, although the man in the crimson coat and dark sunglasses struck no chord of recognition, and Frank had told him all about the well-known lawyer, embellishing the story with more than a liberal spattering of well-placed lies designed to maximise the overall impact of Eddie's reputation. But Frank had completely omitted to mention anything about Kirsten Foster, mainly because he couldn't quite work out how to break the news to Wiltshire that the girl he'd been paying Frank to hunt out for the past few months was living in Surfers Paradise and employed by his own lawyer. So when Wiltshire laid eyes on Slick for the first time in roughly four years, it hit him like a freight train that came out of nowhere. He stood motionless in the doorway, mouthing words that obviously wouldn't come. Then suddenly he seemed to become conscious of his drab attire, adjusted the waistband of his prison tracksuit pants, then looked up again, pathetically nonplussed.

'Kirsten, what are you doing here?'

His voice was so thin and fragile that Slick had to resist a spontaneous temptation to pity him.

'I'm working for him.'

Wiltshire turned to the untidy-looking man with his chisel-toed boots propped against the desk.

'Really? And who's he?'

Eddie lifted his sunglasses momentarily and looked the prisoner up and down.

'Eddie Moran, pal. Your last hope and only salvation.'

The conference opened predictably enough. Eddie charged out of the blocks like a wounded bull, laying down the rules about his fees: three hundred and fifty an hour plus expenses, paid upfront in instalments to be lodged in the trust account promptly as and when requested. Any bounced cheques, failures or delays and he would pull the pin. The brief was likely to take at least a week to work up and the committal hearing itself would take another two weeks, so he could count on the best part of fifty grand to be chewed up on the magistrates' court hearing, plus probably around another five grand in expenses, and then he was a laydown misère to be committed for trial, and the trial itself could take up to twice as long as the committal, so he had to be prepared to double those figures when it got to the Supreme Court. It wasn't the most subtle attempt Slick had ever seen Eddie make to talk himself out of a job. She'd half expected him to pull a stunt like this, in the hope that Wiltshire would realise immediately what an arsehole Eddie was and have the good sense to sack him there and then before the show got started. But Wiltshire listened attentively, and when Eddie had finished his obnoxious little spiel and had gone back to balancing the two coins on each other, he sat silently for a moment, apparently weighing up what had been said, before he answered quietly.

'Frank Vagianni says you're a good man.'

'Frank's a liar. Haven't you worked that out yet?'

Wiltshire smiled. Whatever else he was, Moran was a straight-shooter. Michael Wiltshire had been in business long enough to know you always do your research before you enter into any deal, and he'd been in Silverwater long enough to do plenty of research on Eddie Moran. His reputation within the prison population was as an arrogant, uncompromising court brawler who did no deals and never took a backward step. What Michael had seen in the past few minutes confirmed everything he'd heard.

'I'm a businessman. I like to budget for my outgoings and I don't like unknown variables. What about a lump sum fee?'

'It's not a Dutch auction, pal. I've told you my terms. You either accept them or you don't.'

The response couldn't have been less diplomatic. It was clear to Michael Wiltshire that Moran had some unresolved issues bubbling somewhere close beneath the surface.

'You appeared at Trevor Ellowe's inquest, didn't you?'

'That's right.'

'You think I'm guilty, don't you?'

'It doesn't matter what I think, buddy.' It wasn't an answer to the question, but the disdainful look on the lawyer's face said all that needed to be said. 'It's the jury that counts.'

Wiltshire nodded thoughtfully. 'So how do I convince the jury?'

Eddie Moran held his gaze grimly. Then he flipped his eyebrows.

'I don't know, maybe you could start by telling them what you know about what happened to Trevor Ellowe.'

'I don't know anything.'

He was looking Eddie directly in the eye. The lawyer smiled back cynically. It wasn't the lie that irritated him so much as the fact that Wiltshire looked him in the eye to tell it.

'Bullshit, pal.' Eddie shook his head wearily. 'That's complete fuckin' hogshit and you know it.' He leaned to one side, clicked open his briefcase, then dragged his folder off the desk and dropped it in. 'Listen, buddy, I didn't come all the way down here for you to give me a fuckin' tap-dancing lesson, okay.'

He got to his feet and clicked the briefcase closed. 'If you want to keep your grubby secrets to yourself that's fine, go for your life. But leave me out of it.'

Eddie was so intent on going through his theatrical routine, he didn't notice that Slick hadn't moved. As he turned towards the door he was surprised to hear her voice continuing the conversation.

'We know from the phone records that Trevor rang you at least three times in the weeks leading up to his death. What was that about?'

She was staring into Wiltshire's face, awaiting an answer. Wiltshire met her gaze and held it for a short time, then dropped his head and dragged his fingers through his hair.

'I didn't know who he was at that time. He was just a voice on the telephone, warning me to stay out of Fred Hunter's business.'

Slick wasn't letting up. 'What business?'

'He didn't say, but it was pretty obvious from what was happening at the time that he was talking about the goings-on at the Enmore branch.'

'How many times did he ring you?'

'Just the three, I think. But they got increasingly more threatening.'

She paused, considering his answers as Eddie circled, listening in.

'He also rang you the night he died.'

'Yeah.' Michael Wiltshire was looking straight into her eyes. He should have told her long ago about the final conversation he'd had with her ex-husband; she deserved to know. But he could see no hint of emotion in her eyes. It was as though she was merely harvesting the facts, not searching for any denouement.

'It was later than the other calls, some time after midnight. He was on about the books that Barry Dougherty had taken. He thought I had them, said Hunter wanted them back. He said he was going to come to my house that night.'

'And did he?'

'I don't know. I left the house.'

Eddie Moran stopped in his tracks and turned

accusingly to Wiltshire. 'At midnight? With a seven-year-old kid in tow?'

Michael Wiltshire looked up at him, a weary grimace wrinkling his face. Then he turned back to Slick. 'Look, it was all getting completely out of hand. I didn't know what to do.'

Eddie wasn't backing off.

'My guess is that means you did something — something that you now regret. Am I right?'

This time Wiltshire didn't look at him. He kept his eyes trained on Slick, looking like a man who was desperately pondering his position. Finally he spoke.

'I rang Gary Sharpe.'

It was an answer even Eddie couldn't have anticipated. Gary Sharpe, the newly appointed federal Minister for Foreign Affairs and, according to many, the heir apparent to the Labor throne, had often been a controversial figure but his name had never featured anywhere in connection with the Ellowe matter. Its mention now drew the same astonished reaction from both Eddie and Slick.

'Who?'

'Gary Sharpe, the politician.' Wiltshire paused again, intently studying his hands as though searching for inspiration. 'He was pretty thick with Fred Hunter in those days. I told him what was going on, asked him to intercede.'

Now Eddie was starting to get interested. An incredulous smirk crept onto his face.

'What do you mean "intercede"?'

'I don't know, ring Hunter, tell him to drop off, I suppose.'

Moran scoffed derisively but Slick pressed on undeterred.

'What was Sharpe's reaction?'

'He said he'd sort it out immediately. He hung up and then he rang me back about two minutes later, said he'd spoken to Hunter and Hunter had agreed to call his man off. Gary told me to get out of the house until the morning, just to give things time to blow over. I threw Simon in the car and went up to the Palm Beach house for a couple of days.'

Slick looked up at Eddie. It was possible. It fitted all the independent evidence. Eddie Moran looked mildly uncomfortable as he started circling again. When he got in front of Wiltshire he fired another question.

'So what do you say happened to Ellowe?'

'I told you before, I don't know.' Wiltshire looked up at the pacing lawyer. 'My guess is Fred Hunter's people dealt with him.'

'That's horseshit, pal. He was Hunter's man. Why the fuck would Fred want him knocked?'

'Like I said, I don't know.'

There was a defeated quality about his voice that gave his response a curious ring of truth. Eddie didn't like it; the prospect that Michael Wiltshire might be innocent hadn't for a moment entered anywhere into his reckonings. It complicated things immeasurably. Slick was gazing at him with a dumb look in her eyes that spelled trouble with a capital T to Eddie. Without another word she turned back to Wiltshire.

'You're after a lump sum deal? We'll do the whole job for a hundred and seventy grand, win, lose or draw, paid upfront on retainer within the next seven days.'

Eddie opened his mouth but the words stuck in his throat. It was more money than he'd ever seen in one hit. He'd pumped the figures up unmercifully to make it all too hard for Michael Wiltshire, but now it looked like he was seriously considering the offer. Wiltshire was facing off with Slick like they were a couple of desperate poker players trying to anticipate the next card off the deck. Eddie held his breath until eventually Wiltshire made his play.

'What about one forty?'

'Make it one fifty and you've got a deal.'

'Done.'

* * *

Darryl Beane loved this restaurant like no other place on earth. The tables were intimate, deliberately spaced with a discretion that allowed one to be seen without being overheard. The settings were immaculate, the food sumptuous and the service unsurpassed. From his regular table he could look out through the glass wall at a two hundred and forty degree vista of the bustling Sydney CBD below, the Harbour Bridge, the Opera House and the glistening blue waters of Sydney Harbour stretching out to meet the Heads. Sometimes he even came up here alone, to dine elegantly and be seen doing so, to savour the view and recharge his batteries, to remind himself how successful he had been, how he owned this town.

Today it wasn't working. As he sipped intermittently at the chilled chardonnay he looked down at the city with a hollow, aching feeling gnawing at his stomach. Today he could see only shadows, dark places where danger lurked. Darryl Beane sensed a serious emerging problem.

'G'day, mate.'

Roger Baston settled into the chair opposite him, sat back momentarily as the attentive waiter slipped a serviette onto his lap, ordered a light beer for starters, then moved forward in his chair and hunched conspiratorially across the table towards Darryl.

'Have you got it there?'

Beane slipped the folded letter from his inside coat pocket and placed it neatly on the table. When Baston opened it out he saw that the contents were short and to the point.

Dear Sir,
 RE: Michael David Wiltshire
 I have received instructions to act on behalf of the abovenamed in respect of his criminal prosecution. I understand that you previously acted on his behalf. Accordingly I now enclose my client's written authority and direction to you to release to my firm all material currently held by you on his behalf. I would be obliged if you would forward the whole of my client's file and all associated documents and other material to me forthwith.

 As you will appreciate, committal proceedings in relation to the charges against

my client are due to commence very shortly and I would therefore respectfully suggest that you ensure that the file is transferred promptly so as to obviate any undue delay in the proceedings or other waste of court time.
   Yours faithfully,
   Edwin C Moran

Baston looked up from the letter, his hooded eyes squinting meanly at the lawyer. Darryl Beane's sallow face had a vulnerable air, and as he fidgeted nervously with the ring on his right finger he looked distinctly like a liability to Roger Baston. Beane had no stomach for tight corners and Baston could see he would somehow have to put a little lead back in his pencil. The lawyer's voice was fragile and pathetic.

'Should I go and see Michael, find out what the problem is?'

'Fuck Michael!' Baston spat the words out loudly enough to make his jittery lunch companion jump a little in his seat. 'He's a smartarse little prick.' He was scowling malevolently at Darryl Beane, intent on spelling out his message loud and clear: this was no time to go to water. 'This is all about the deal, that's all. Wiltshire's too fuckin' tight to shell out, so he's pulled that silly fuckin' Moran in and now he thinks he can roll the charges. Well, good luck to him.'

Beane was unconsoled; the wine glass trembled almost imperceptibly as he raised it to his lips. 'We can't afford to let this go to trial, Roger.'

Baston's lip curled disdainfully. He was sick of dealing with pissants who went wobbly at the knees every time things didn't going according to plan.

'I can tell you now, sure as your arse points to the ground, it won't be going to trial.'

Baston didn't take his eyes off Darryl Beane as the waiter set his beer in front of him and he raised it to his mouth, gulping down several mouthfuls. As he set it down again on the crisp white tablecloth he moved even closer. 'Listen, Wiltshire's all cock-a-hoop now because that Moran clown will be filling his ear about what a genius he is and how he's going to walk him out of the charges. Things'll change bigtime when he gets committed for trial.' He sat back, took another swig of beer and licked his lips. 'These are early days, old son, early days. Softly softly, catchee monkey.' The smug grin that was still settling on his face suddenly evaporated. 'How are we looking for the committal?'

'Fine.' Darryl Beane drew in a deep breath. 'So long as the girl holds up it's a good strong prima facie case.'

'Good.' An air of self-congratulation flooded back into Baston's face and he threw his head back and took several deep swallows of beer. 'She'll hold up alright. And you watch the wind come out of Wiltshire's sails when that magistrate sends him to trial for murder. He won't be feeling so smart then, I'll guarantee you.' He hooked one arm over the back of his chair and sat back, taking in the view. 'The price has just gone up for that smartarse.'

Darryl Beane felt mildly comforted. He knew how well Roger Baston understood this game. When he had his foot on someone his timing was always immaculate. He knew precisely when and how to grind them down into the earth. But this time it was slightly different. Wiltshire was no cheap crook, and two million dollars was a lot of money.

'What if he won't come into the deal?'

'He'll come into it.'

'What if he doesn't?' Darryl sat forward, suddenly alarmed again, as if the sound of his own voice was scaring him. 'We can't afford for this thing to go to trial.'

Roger Baston leaned in close, the corners of his mouth stretched downward in an intimidating glower. His gravelly voice was soft and menacing.

'I promise you, if he doesn't come into the deal, he won't make trial.'

CHAPTER TWENTY-FIVE

'This Dougherty swill's our problem.'

Eddie was mumbling to himself. Slick didn't mind; in fact she preferred it that way. At least with Eddie off in his own world he was too preoccupied to give her crap about her driving. As she steered their Mini hire car through the city streets at a breakneck pace Eddie didn't seem to notice the squealing tyres and screeching brakes. He kept on muttering absently.

'When the jury hears Wiltshire was making cash payments to Dougherty, and that he denied it to the police, and then Dougherty winds up dead, and the coppers find a two-million-dollar extortion letter on Wiltshire when they search him, the whole thing starts to smell like a bucket of stink.' He was chewing assiduously on one index fingernail. 'We've got to get rid of that Dougherty shit. Here!' He stabbed a spindly finger in the direction of the Downing Centre looming quickly on their left and Slick slammed on the brakes, squeezing the little car to an abrupt halt by the kerb.

As Eddie manoeuvered his long legs out onto the footpath he was still summing up the situation. 'Get rid of the Dougherty stuff and it comes down to a straight credibility attack on Bagley.' He held the door open and poked his head back in. 'Now that's a fight we've got some chance of winning.' He started to close the door then returned briefly with an afterthought. 'By the way, you still drive like shit.'

With that he was gone, striding purposefully in the direction of the main stairs of the court complex, leaving Slick to arrive at the only conclusion available to her: that as the lowly chauffeur to The Talented Mr Moran, her job was to go and park the car wherever she could find a place, then come back and somehow find Eddie somewhere in the Downing Centre. Now she remembered why she hated him so much. She pushed the gearstick forward and jammed the accelerator down. 'Arsehole.'

When Bruce Parforth saw Edwin Moran stroll through security into the Downing Centre and head for the lifts he felt a peptic stirring in his stomach. He knew this wasn't going to be a pleasant experience. It never was with Edwin C Moran.

Bruce had felt good about the Wiltshire matter since day one. It was a meaty murder case against an accused who was a man of both wealth and influence, and the fact that the Director had chosen Bruce to lead the prosecution team confirmed in his mind that he was still the DPP's number one strike bowler. The evidence was strong: he had the next best thing to an eyewitness, whose account was corroborated by independent evidence on several critical features, and he had some good strong circumstantial stuff to back it up. But this wasn't just a straightforward confession case; it was an intricate forensic matrix that required a skilled and experienced prosecutor to lay it carefully before the court, and no doubt that was precisely why the Director had entrusted it to Bruce. And he felt very good about it. At least he had, until he heard that the accused had sacked his former solicitor and his very learned counsel Mr Lyle Phillips QC and had retained the services of the difficult and abrasive Eddie Moran.

When Bruce Parforth and his instructing clerk pushed through the door into the compact courtroom it was mainly empty of people, except for a depositions clerk shuffling files in readiness for the arrival of the magistrate, and Eddie Moran, sitting at the bar table surrounded by untidy bits and pieces of his brief and scribbling feverish notes in a pad. Parforth set his folders down on the bar table and nodded to the depositions clerk.

'Morning.'

Eddie Moran didn't even look up. 'Bruce, how the hell do you say this Dougherty charge is joinable with the murder?'

Parforth felt a faint twinge flare in the pit of his stomach as he looked down at Moran, who was still scribbling in his notebook.

'Well, the facts are inextricably interwoven, aren't they.'

Moran suddenly stopped writing and looked up at Parforth, his brow knitted and his lip curled quizzically. The expression made Bruce stumble slightly into his next sentence.

'For instance, the blackmail payments Wiltshire made to Dougherty —'

'Hang on, why do you say they're blackmail payments?'

Bruce Parforth stopped for a moment, to consider the question, then delivered his response.

'Well, you only need to look at the extortion letter Dougherty sent to him to —'

'How do you know Dougherty sent that letter?'

Parforth felt a mild flush of irritation. It was the second time in as many questions that Moran had interrupted him, which was precisely the level of discourtesy he'd come to expect from the man. His answer was curt and direct.

'We say that can be inferred from the blackmail payments.'

'What?' Moran threw his pen down. 'Are you serious?'

As Parforth mentally retraced his words he broke into a stutter. 'No, no, no, no, what we say is —'

'You're not serious?'

'Yes, of course I'm serious.'

Moran was on his feet now. 'So you're seriously advancing the proposition that the fact that Dougherty sent the letter proves they're blackmail payments and the fact they're blackmail payments proves Dougherty sent the letter?' Parforth flicked his eyes to one corner of the ceiling, revisiting the proposition. 'Is that it, Bruce? Is that what you're saying?' Moran was standing almost on top of Parforth, leering at him. 'Doesn't strike you as a tad circular by any chance, does it?'

Parforth was silent for several more seconds before he finally responded.

'No ...' he began cautiously, as if feeling his way. 'No, it has to be seen within the context of Dougherty's murder shortly after the letter was sent.' He looked more confident now. 'We say a jury could infer from those combined facts —'

'Righto.' Moran was suddenly back in his chair, scribbling again. 'Well, your starting point is that Dougherty was murdered.'

'Of course.'

'Fair enough, I understand. Yeah, okay, that makes sense.'

He seemed satisfied that the argument had merit, and as Moran scribbled it down into his notes Bruce Parforth couldn't resist a brief moment of self-congratulation at having so succinctly and effectively enunciated the Crown argument. But Eddie Moran wasn't leaving anything to chance. As he continued writing he summarised the Crown contention aloud, just to make sure Parforth knew exactly what he had to argue.

'You say that provided the Crown can prove Dougherty was murdered, that constitutes a primary fact on which a jury could rely, in combination with the fact of the cash payments from Wiltshire to Dougherty and the discovery of the extortion letter in Wiltshire's possession, to draw an inference that Dougherty was blackmailing Wiltshire over the murder.'

Parforth puffed his chest out proudly. 'Precisely.'

When he finally opened his argument before the magistrate, he got it just about word perfect.

'Your Worship, the starting point of course is that the Crown will prove that Barry Dougherty was murdered. Once that is established, in my submission a jury could rely on that fact, in combination with the cash payments made by the defendant to Dougherty and the discovery of the extortion letter in the defendant's possession, to draw an inference that Dougherty was blackmailing the defendant over his involvement in the murder of Trevor Ellowe.'

Eddie smiled quietly to himself. Leading Bruce into the Valley of Death was always such a pleasure. Eddie wanted all the Dougherty evidence out of the picture, and the best way to do that at this stage in the process was to get the charge of attempting to pervert the course of justice separated out. Parforth knew as well as he did that on its own that charge wouldn't go anywhere: there simply wasn't enough evidence to prove anything. Its only value was that it badly muddied the waters in the murder prosecution. The Crown had to ensure the two charges were heard together because, if they were separated, the charge of perverting the course of justice would have absolutely no legs on its own, and once it was peeled off the murder case would be infinitely cleaner and easier to defend. So Eddie had applied to have the charges heard separately, and the magistrate had agreed to hear the application immediately, in advance of the committal hearing. But he needed Parforth to make the post-mortem medical examination the lynchpin for the whole of the Dougherty evidence, and Bruce had just obliged.

'What do you say about that, Mr Moran?'

Eddie wasn't too surprised to see that the New South Wales chief magistrate, Sue Withnall, had taken the Wiltshire case onto her own docket. It concerned extremely serious charges against a high-profile defendant who, at least at one time, had some serious political connections; the kind of case that warranted a close eye from the top. But more than that, if there was skullduggery going on behind the scenes, and someone was nervous about the possibility of sensitive political issues arising, such as Gary Sharpe's controversial noggin poking up in the middle of it, Sue Withnall was the obvious choice to try and steer it towards. As an ex-Labor lawyer and one-time party staffer, she was universally recognised as a blatant political appointment by state Labor, the spearhead of their affirmative action policy, and her bolt out of the blue from lowly solicitor with an indigenous legal centre in Redfern to the chief magistrate's job had put a lot of legal noses out of joint and got a lot of people talking. Popular opinion was, she owed a big favour to the Labor government and, when push came to shove, she would deliver.

Eddie Moran wasn't so sure about that. From what he'd seen of Withnall she was an intelligent woman and a very capable lawyer, and he guessed she had too high an opinion of her own ability to think she owed anybody any favours. From the little he knew of her legal career she hadn't taken too many backward steps when she was in the trenches out at Redfern and, political appointment or not, she didn't look to Eddie like she was planning to be anybody's lackey now. As he climbed to his feet to answer her question she looked down at him attentively.

'Well, as my learned friend says, Your Worship, the Crown's starting point is that it has to prove Dougherty was murdered. Unless they prove that as a threshold point, the rest's irrelevant. The Crown's problem is their scientific evidence just doesn't prove that Dougherty was murdered: in fact, the post-mortem examination results demonstrate exactly the opposite. Dougherty died by accident.'

Sue Withnall's eyebrows arched as if in mild astonishment as Bruce Parforth clambered quickly to his feet.

'That's not right, Your Worship. In fact I'll tender the report of the doctor who conducted the post-mortem right now on this application.'

As soon as the report was admitted as an exhibit in the application, Eddie looked up matter-of-factly. 'In that case I'd like to cross-examine the doctor, Your Worship.'

Bruce Parforth was certain this was just another stunt by Moran, probably designed to delay the proceedings while they tried to get the doctor down from Queensland, no doubt in the vain hope that any delay would facilitate another bail application. But he congratulated himself in knowing that this time he was one step ahead. The doctor was currently in Sydney, scheduled to attend Bruce's office for conference the following day. When Parforth triumphantly announced that to the magistrate, adding that he hoped arrangements could be made to have the doctor available for cross-examination directly after lunch, Sue Withnall simply nodded once and rose to her feet.

'Very well. We'll hear the doctor's evidence this afternoon. Adjourn the court until two thirty.'

* * *

By the time Slick had driven halfway across the city in search of a parking station that wasn't full, had done three laps of every level to track down what was seemingly the last remaining vacant parking space in the entire building, trekked back across town to the Downing Centre, conducted a thorough manhunt of every courtroom, conference room, witness room and rest room in the complex, and finally tracked Eddie down, the lawyer was sitting all alone in the courtroom, his feet up on the chair next to him, leafing through his copy of the police brief.

'What kept you?'

'What do you think? I decided to do a scenic tour of Sydney's parking stations.'

Eddie looked like he wasn't interested and wasn't listening. He had the brief open on the so-called Dougherty extortion letter and was staring blankly at it.

Slick looked around the empty room. 'Where is everyone?'

Moran didn't answer. He was still staring at the

letter and mumbled absently, 'I don't get it. It doesn't make sense.'

Suddenly he leaped to his feet and bundled his papers into his briefcase.

'Let's get down to the cells. I want to talk to Wiltshire.'

Dressed in his court clothes Michael Wiltshire looked almost the way Slick remembered him from years earlier. His hair was longer now, perhaps a little greyer, the lines in his face more pronounced, and he had a weary, almost haggard expression in his eyes, but his own clothes nonetheless restored to him a semblance of dignity, and a difficult-to-define impression of pride and control had returned to his bearing. As the guard ushered him into the room he smiled gently at Slick, and she felt strangely comforted to recognise some trace of his former self-assurance in his eyes.

Eddie opened up the questioning before Wiltshire even got onto his chair. 'You say this character out at the prison ...' He was flicking through his brief, searching for a name. 'What's-his-name, McPhee, you reckon he claims Baston's behind this extortion letter, is that right?'

'That's what he claims.'

'Whoever it was who wrote it talks about there being witnesses, and says this ...' Eddie underlined the text with his finger as he read aloud to his client. *They know ... why Trevor was on his way that night and who you called to get him sorted out.* He stopped and looked Wiltshire straight in the eye. 'They're obviously talking there about your call to Gary Sharpe, aren't they?'

'It looks like it.'

'Did you ever tell anyone about that call to Gary Sharpe?'

'No.'

'Barry Dougherty maybe?'

'No.'

'Darryl Beane?'

'No. Darryl's never asked me for any detail about what happened on the night.'

'And you never spoke to Roger Baston before he came to see you at the prison?'

'Never.'

Eddie paused again, still holding Wiltshire's gaze intently. 'So how would Baston know about that call you made to Gary Sharpe?'

Wiltshire was looking straight back into his eyes, his countenance unmoved. 'I've no idea.'

They stared at each other in silence for a moment before he continued. 'Sharpe told me he rang Hunter straight after my call. Maybe Hunter told Baston.'

'Why would he?'

There was an accusatory tone in Eddie's voice that clearly troubled his client. Wiltshire's features stiffened with a look of mild resentment.

'I don't know. Maybe he called Baston to help him stop Trevor Ellowe coming to my house.'

Eddie Moran scoffed at the suggestion. 'Why would Fred Hunter need Baston's help for that? Fred was the one who sent Trevor to your house in the first place, wasn't he? All he had to do was ring him up and call the whole thing off.'

Wiltshire blinked and looked down at the creased letter in his lawyer's hands, then back up at Eddie Moran's fixed pupils.

'I'm sorry, I don't know.'

Eddie held his gaze until Wiltshire looked down again uncomfortably. Then the lawyer slammed his brief shut and leaped to his feet.

'Well, you'd better think about it, pal.'

He turned and swung open the door. 'You better have a real good think about it.'

Eddie was out the door before Slick got to her feet. When she rose she heard Michael Wiltshire's voice behind her.

'Kirsten.'

As she turned back to him their eyes met and she found herself looking into the face of the gentle, courteous man she had spent so many pleasant hours with at the Old Priory on the hill at Petersham. It was the first time they had been alone together since that painful last night when she had asked him for the truth and he had told her it was more than he could give her. He smiled at her wistfully now, apologetically, knowing that they were both remembering that night, and as the smile gradually faded on his lips he looked away for the briefest moment, before his eyes returned earnestly to hers.

'I'm sorry, Kirsten.'

Slick's chin began to tremble almost imperceptibly as she blinked and stretched her eyes open again, looking away towards a far corner of the ceiling.

'Yeah well, you know what, Michael?' She looked back at him, now suddenly more composed. 'You should be.'

Throwing her bag over one shoulder Slick pushed back her chair, turned and stepped out through the door.

By the time she caught up with Eddie she had her sunglasses on and she was rummaging through her handbag for her cigarettes, heedless of the strict ban on smoking in the building. As soon as the lift doors closed behind them she lit up. Eddie did his best to ignore her, watching the lights illuminate the floor numbers. He knew from bitter experience that moments like these were not the most opportune for him to offer his views. But he could hear her sucking hard on the cigarette and blowing out the smoke with equal force. Eventually her manic puffing was too much for him.

'I thought you were giving up.'

Slick leaned in his direction and blew a stream of smoke into his face. Blinking the smoke from his eyes, Eddie turned back to the door and continued watching the lights chronicle the progress of the lift. They stood side by side in silence for several long seconds before eventually Slick propped a hand against the lift wall, lifted one foot and stubbed the cigarette out on the sole of her shoe.

'Okay, shithead, so what are you thinking?'

His eyes propped sideways in her direction and then went back to the lights.

'You want the truth?'

'No, Eddie, I was hoping you'd bullshit me like you normally do.'

Eddie smiled faintly. Then he slowly turned to face her, a sad and serious expression in his eyes. Before he spoke he looked at her long enough for her to sense his genuine concern, and as she returned his gaze the venom drained quickly from her face.

'The truth is, Slick, I'm thinking your boyfriend just might be a lying sack of shit.' Slick had an almost resigned look in her eyes and seemed to be ignoring his 'boyfriend' jibe. 'My guess is, no one rang Fred Hunter to call Trevor off that night. If Trevor was working for Fred Hunter, all Hunter had to do was say the word and Trevor would have scurried straight home with his tail between his legs. I doubt he was ever given that option.' He paused to let her soak it in before he added his conclusion. 'If you ask me, the only call anyone made that night was to Roger Baston, and Baston's brief was plain and simple.'

'But why?'

As the lift gently glided to a stop and the doors slid open, Eddie shrugged his bony shoulders. 'I don't know why, kiddo. Not yet.' He stepped out of the lift, leaving Slick to follow like a well-trained lapdog. 'But I'll work it out.'

He was striding across the foyer so resolutely Slick was having trouble keeping up with him.

'So what happens now?'

'Now we go back into court and demonstrate that this Dougherty evidence is nothing but a crock of shit.'

* * *

Dr Mark Dalton was a conscientious, hard-working general practitioner who had operated as the government medical officer in Mackay for nearly twenty years. The son of a Bowen tomato farmer, he was a modest, naturally conservative man whose genuine respect for the law was evident even in the orderly manner of his approach to the witness box. He took his seat in the raised stand, laid his notes neatly in front of him and assumed an efficient, upright stance, waiting compliantly to answer questions.

Dr Dalton had performed the autopsy on the body of Barry Dougherty the day after his death and, as anyone who knew the doctor would expect, his post-mortem report was a highly detailed and factual record of his observations. Accompanying the post-mortem notes was a brief witness statement, prepared by the New South Wales Police Service on the appropriate statement of witness form, annexing the report and summarising the doctor's findings as to cause of death. In its final paragraph the statement neatly concluded that death had resulted from a heavy blow to the forehead of the deceased, and that the fatal wound was consistent with the deceased having been struck heavily with a blunt instrument such as a baton or bar of some description. Eddie noted that Detective Phil Manning had prepared the statement. As he rose to his feet he flattened the statement out with the palms of both hands.

'Doctor, that conclusion you express there — was that something you formulated off the bat as it were, or did you arrive at that formula in response to specific questioning by Detective Manning?'

Dr Dalton was looking at him wide-eyed, as if anxious to assist. 'I'm not sure I entirely follow you there, I'm sorry.'

'Is it the case that, having read your original post-mortem report, Detective Manning posed to you a question along the lines of "Was the wound consistent with the deceased having been struck heavily with a blunt instrument such as a baton or bar of some sort?"'

'Yes, something to that effect.' The doctor looked relieved.

'And you answered "Yes" to that question?'

'That's right.'

'Because indeed the wound was consistent with such a cause.'

'Yes, indeed.'

Eddie put the statement to one side and planted one hand on the bar table.

'But it was also consistent with other causes, wasn't it?'

'Such as?'

'Well, for instance, such as rather than the head being struck by a blunt instrument, the head striking a blunt instrument, or even for that matter a blunt surface.'

Dr Dalton was nodding enthusiastically even before Eddie got the question out.

'Oh yes, yes of course.'

'For example the edge of a cement stair.'

'Well, yes.' The doctor looked almost perplexed, as though the proposition was so elementary it should be assumed. 'Any hard edge or defined linear surface could potentially cause that injury if the head struck it with sufficient force.'

Eddie picked up his brief again and leafed over several pages.

'The deceased had a blood/alcohol content of point two one at the time of death, didn't he?'

'Yes, I think that's quite correct, yes.'

Moran looked at him and flipped his eyebrows cheekily.

'In layman's terms that's a heck of a skinful, isn't it?'

'Well, yes.' Dr Dalton looked a trifle uncomfortable with the lawyer's terminology. 'I would expect him to be quite intoxicated at that level, yes.'

'And of course alcohol has a marked sedative effect on the various groups of nerve fibres within the body that control muscle coordination and movement, isn't that correct?'

'Yes, that's true, yes.'

'It's for that reason that we often see a drunken man stagger and sometimes even fall, because the nerve fibres that control muscle coordination and movement have been impaired by the alcohol.'

'Yes.'

Eddie stopped and waited briefly for effect.

'And the deceased was a very drunken man on the night of his death, wasn't he?'

'He was, yes.'

Now the lawyer leaned over the bar table again, supporting his bony frame on his long arms as he slipped into a relaxed, conversational tone.

'Tell me this, doctor, if a very drunken man of approximately the deceased's height and weight were to fall directly from a standing position onto a hard surface, such as the cement stair we spoke about a moment ago, the momentum of that fall would potentially provide sufficient force to cause that head injury, wouldn't it?'

Dr Dalton looked a little troubled. 'It could, conceivably, yes.'

There was enough equivocation in his voice to prompt Eddie to move on quickly, but before he could get to his next question the doctor qualified his answer. 'Although ordinarily one would expect that normal reflex defensive action would break the fall somewhat so as to very significantly dilute the force generated by a fall.'

The lawyer nodded silently. There was more work to be done.

'You mean ordinarily you'd expect a falling man to put out his hands and thereby cushion the impact.'

'Yes, you wouldn't expect him to fall with full unbroken weight straight onto his face.'

'That's if his reflexes were functioning normally, isn't it?'

'Yes.'

'But alcohol also affects the reflexes, doesn't it?' Eddie wasn't waiting for an answer. He wanted to get this proposition out in its entirety to avoid any room for doubt. 'In physiological terms, it inhibits the passage of electrical impulses down the spinal column from one nerve cell to the next — it slows down messages coming from the brain.'

Once again the doctor was nodding enthusiastically. 'Yes, that's right, yes.'

'And of course the reflex defensive action you talk about is one such message coming from the brain.'

'That's true.'

'So a man with a point two one blood/alcohol reading is likely to react very slowly, isn't he?'

'True.'

'And sometimes not at all.'

'Yes, that's possible.'

Eddie Moran straightened up and stood with his hands held palm-up by his sides, looking nonplussed around the courtroom without saying a word until finally the magistrate looked up from her notes at him. Then he made his point.

'This man could have just tripped on the bottom step leading to his porch and fallen headlong onto the edge of the top step.'

'It's possible.'

That was probably all Eddie needed. But having established the beachhead he moved on.

'Did you ever see the location where the body was found?'

'No.'

'Have a look at these Queensland police photographs taken at the scene.' Eddie handed four black-and-white prints to the court clerk as he continued with his question. 'They show the body in situ, lying in a garden bed at the bottom of three stairs leading to the cement landing at the entrance to the deceased's residence.' He paused briefly while Dr Dalton closely inspected the photographs.

'The front edge of that cement landing is exactly the kind of "hard edge or defined linear surface" that you referred to earlier, isn't it, the kind capable of causing the head wound you saw?'

The doctor looked up from the photographs, squinting inquisitively.

'Yes, I would have to say it is, yes.'

'Thank you.' Eddie clicked open his ring-binder folder and extracted several pages. 'Now I'll hand to you a report prepared by Mr Robert Gall, a forensic scientist with the Queensland Government John Tonge Centre in Brisbane.'

As the clerk delivered the pages to the witness Moran dropped a copy on the bar table in front of Parforth and then turned to the magistrate. 'Of course I'll be happy to formally prove this evidence in due course should my friend so require, Your Worship.' Bruce Parforth was feverishly scanning the document as Moran pushed on with his questioning.

'You'll see from Mr Gall's report that the Queensland police provided him with swabs taken of traces of blood and tissue located on the front edge of that cement landing. He came up with a positive matching of those swabs to Barry Dougherty's DNA.'

Dr Dalton arched his eyebrows in a look of palpable surprise.

'Yes, so I see.'

His voice had the cold, resentful edge of a man who'd been kept out of the loop, and Eddie let it filter through the court before he spoke again.

'You've never been shown that report, have you, doctor?'

'No, I haven't.'

Now Eddie waited again, formulating the question in his mind, knowing that he had to get it exactly right.

'Assuming its contents are correct, and taking into account the deceased's blood/alcohol level at the time of death, would you agree that it's entirely possible that the head wound that killed Barry Dougherty was caused not by an assault with an iron bar or other such blunt instrument, but by an accidental trip and fall, resulting in his head striking the front edge of that cement landing?'

The doctor looked up from the forensic report in front of him, the resentment now permeating his whole countenance.

'Frankly, I'd have to say it's more than likely.'

Bruce Parforth did his best to repair the damage in re-examination, but it seemed the more he pushed the more the doctor dug his toes in, and by the time the witness left the courtroom Parforth was in the hopeless position that according to the Crown's own witness it was 'more than likely' that Barry Dougherty met his death by tragic accident. Without evidence of foul play, the cash payments made to Dougherty meant nothing, and the fact that someone had sent an extortion letter to Wiltshire was irrelevant.

By the time Dr Dalton stepped down from the witness box the chief magistrate's expression made it clear that she was less than impressed with a police investigation that had seemingly withheld important evidence from a crucial witness. Before Sue Withnall heard another word in argument she invited Bruce Parforth to consider his position regarding joinder of the charges, adding that, as currently advised, even if the charges were not separated, on the evidence she had heard so far she would be inclined to rule that there was no prima facie case on the charge of attempting to pervert the course of justice, and she would therefore strike out that charge and order costs against the Crown.

A pale-faced Bruce Parforth requested that the hearing be stood down briefly to allow him to consider his position and confer with the Director, and after a twenty-minute adjournment he returned to advise the court that the Crown had elected not to proceed with the charge of attempting to pervert the course of justice. Ms Withnall LCM dismissed the charge and adjourned the court for hearing of the murder charge alone.

As the court rose to the formal proclamation, Eddie leaned down to Slick and whispered from the corner of his mouth, 'So much for the sideshow. Now, on to the main game.'

CHAPTER TWENTY-SIX

As soon as Fred Hunter lifted the receiver on the intercom the buzzer stopped. He had to squint closely at the black-and-white surveillance screen but even with his failing eyesight he quickly recognised the familiar face of the man standing at the front door. In his raspy, pre-lunch voice he croaked into the receiver, 'Hang on, I'll come up and let you in.'

Hobbling through the empty restaurant towards the staircase Fred called to the bar manager to get someone to set up a table for two and whip them up something edible for lunch. As the manager barked orders in the general direction of the kitchen, the old man tightly grasped the mahogany railing and pulled himself onto the stairs. He loved this restaurant but he hated the stairs.

Fred Hunter had bought the White Whale Restaurant two years earlier, because it was just too good a deal to pass up. The previous owner, Benny Zhou, had built it up from nothing into one of the best lunchtime venues in the city; between the lawyers, the bookies and the politicians it was hard to find a spare seat in the house in those days. But Benny's vicious punting streak had got the better of him in the end, and by the time the halfwit receiver had realised there was no way any restaurant would ever trade its way out of Benny's blister with the bookies, and the liquidator had let the lawyers and accountants get their snouts into the trough, there didn't look to be too much worth saving. Nobody wanted the White Whale any more, but Fred Hunter knew a bargain when he saw one. He knew there were still plenty of people in this town who liked to have a discreet meeting over lunch somewhere a bit private, somewhere they could be assured of getting a good feed, a decent bottle of wine and a bit of a perv at some top-looking sorts serving behind the bar. That was the White Whale, always had been, and the fact that its custom had fallen off a bit since Benny hit his hurdle didn't deter Fred Hunter one iota. He bought it from the liquidator for a song, reopened the doors, and installed his son as maitre d' and manager. Since then the place had never looked back.

Fred spent most of his time at the restaurant these days. After a lifetime of arguing with truckies and bone-brained labourers he'd grown tired of the constant hustle of the transport company, and although he had enough money socked away to retire a rich man any time he wanted to, he knew he wouldn't last five minutes sitting around at home with no one but his missus for company. So nowadays he came into the restaurant almost every day to hide — from his missus, from Hunter Transport and from all the other little dramas and aggravations in his life. Not the least of which was the New South Wales Royal Commission into the transport industry.

'Hello, mate.'

'Hello, Fred.'

As Eddie Moran stepped in through the front door of Fred Hunter's restaurant, the old man pushed a crumpled Royal Commission summons to witness form into his hand.

'They come back on Monday morning with a bluey.' He relocked the door as they headed back down the stairs. 'I got to front the Commission some time next month.'

Eddie Moran had known Fred Hunter for longer than he could remember. Fred and all the boys from Hunter Transport had been regulars at the Oxford Tavern in Crystal Street way back in the late seventies when Eddie's father was the licensee and publican of the thriving Petersham hotel. To an awkward, gangly teenage schoolboy they were all big rough, tough tattooed truckies who worked hard, drank hard and played hardest of all. They were always at the centre of whatever happened to be happening in the public bar, they invariably ate their dinner in the beer garden and then drank it out till closing time and often beyond, and they always had an extra buck or two to throw in the direction of the young lad collecting empty glasses from the tables. Or at least Fred did; he was the leader of the pack, the godfather and benefactor, the dispenser of all largesse. Even then Fred Hunter was known in the inner west as a wealthy man, and even then there were serious questions being asked about his criminal connections. But no one challenged his credentials as a man of the people, one of the boys, a humble son of Marrickville who had dragged himself up by his own bootstraps and who had never turned his back on any of his old mates. Following the crooked little man carefully negotiating the stairs ahead of him, Eddie hardly recognised anything about him but the big ears and the gravelly voice.

As they slid into one of the booth tables Eddie was trying to work out how to delicately broach his current difficulty with old Fred Hunter. Fred had telephoned him on spec a month or so ago to mention he was starting to get heat from the Royal Commission about giving them a statement concerning his association with various shady characters from his not-so-distant past, and Eddie had provided him with general advice about his right to silence and the coercive powers of the Royal Commission, and referred him to a Sydney solicitor just in case the thing blew up. He hadn't expected to hear any more about it so had been surprised to get a call from Fred's son on his mobile phone that morning asking if, while he was in Sydney, Eddie would mind dropping in to see the old man at the restaurant. He'd been surprised because he'd already referred Fred to another lawyer, and also because he didn't know how Fred could possibly know he was in Sydney. But in view of the questions that had been bubbling around his brain all week about the Wiltshire case, it was an appointment he wasn't about to miss.

'You want a lobster? We get the best fuckin' lobsters in town here, mate. Forget that other pooncy fuckin' joint over on the water.' Fred Hunter poked his head out of the booth in the direction of the kitchen. 'Hey Nick, do us up a lobster for Eddie, will you.'

Eddie threw his hands up defensively. 'Whoa, hang on, Fred, I don't want a lobster. Just a cup of coffee will do me.'

The old man squinted back at him incredulously. 'You don't want a lobster?'

'No thanks, buddy.'

'What, you don't like lobster?'

'I'm not hungry.'

'What do you mean, you're not hungry?'

'I'm not hungry.'

'What, you're not going to eat anything?'

'No thanks, pal.'

'You've got to fuckin' eat, mate. You don't eat, you die.'

'Really, I'm not hungry.'

'Mate, no wonder you're fuckin' skin and bone. Look at you. You must be fuckin' starvin'.'

'Fred, it's eleven o'clock in the morning. I've only just had breakfast.'

'But, mate, we've got the best lobster in town here, son. You want to see how beautiful Nick does it up.'

They danced around the subject of a lobster lunch for several more minutes before Fred Hunter finally relented, ordering two cappuccinos from the kitchen instead. As soon as he turned back to the table Eddie jumped in with both feet.

'Do you know why I'm in Sydney, Fred?'

'Course I do, son, course I do.' He was looking at Eddie cryptically and the lawyer wondered just how much he really knew. He didn't have to wait too long to find out. 'That's why I asked you over. When I get into that Royal Commission, the first bloke they're going to ask me about is Roger Baston.'

The name of Roger Baston hadn't figured anywhere in the police brief on the Wiltshire charges, and there'd been no mention of him in the press or anywhere else in connection with the death of Trevor Ellowe, yet Fred Hunter was clearly making the connection. Eddie knew this was Fred's way of telling him that he knew he was in town about the Ellowe murder trial, but more importantly that Roger Baston was mixed up somewhere in the broth.

'You know Baston?'

'I know them all, mate, you know that.' He nodded absently to himself as if recollecting old faces. 'I know them all. Abe, Lenny, English Tony, Flannery, Ned, all of them.'

'Did Baston have anything to do with Ellowe's death?'

It was too direct a question about much too sensitive an issue to expect a straight answer out of Hunter, and Eddie realised it before the words were even out of his mouth. The old man shrugged his shoulders and turned his palms up comically.

'How would I know, mate, how would I know?'

He lifted himself out of his seat, limped to a nearby table and returned with a sugar bowl.

'Listen, let me tell you a story. I grew up on the wharves, right? Things were a lot different in them days. You didn't have no ICAC, or no Royal Commissions or any of that shit, all you had was a whole bunch of battlers and knockabouts living side by side on the waterfront, doing their best.' Eddie sensed he was going to have to hear the old man out, and he waited patiently for him to come to the point. 'The day my old man died I cried like a baby, and big Charlie Grey come up to me at the funeral and says, "If there's ever anything you need, kid, come and see me." I'm like thirteen fuckin' years old or something, mate. What do I need a hitman for at thirteen years of age? But then when I start out on me own a few years later and I'm getting squeezed by the big petrol companies, I suddenly need thirty grand, so I went to Charlie Grey. Thirty grand was a small fortune in them days, mate. You know what Charlie said? "Take sixty — put them arseholes in credit." I said, "Charlie, I don't know how soon I can pay you back." He said, "Forget it, kid, pay me when you get it." So I put sixty in folders on the table and suddenly my word was good for anything I wanted in the industry. That's what really got me started, son.' He looked Eddie in the eye. 'Sure, I know Roger Baston. I know lots of blokes. But their business is their business. I'm just the bloke who carts their furniture for them.'

It was a nice folksy story about the bad old days down on the waterfront, but Fred obviously knew more about the truth concerning Trevor Ellowe and Roger Baston than he was letting out so far, and Eddie wasn't about to let him off the hook with the old 'I don't ask no questions' line. He held the old man's stare and fired his next question at him.

'What was Ellowe's connection to Baston?'

Fred Hunter smiled wryly as the waiter arrived with the cappuccinos and set them down carefully on the table. By the time the young man retreated the smile was fading on his boss's leathery face.

'He was one of Roger's boys.' He slipped a sugar satchel from the bowl and flicked at it idly with his finger. 'I had him on my books for a while there, like I did a lot of blokes back in them days, but I never even hardly knew the bloke. He done collection work for Roger.'

Eddie kept talking, keen to keep the information flowing. 'The phone records show Ellowe rang you the night he died.'

'That's right.'

Fred tore the sugar satchel open and poured its contents into his coffee. He was moving slowly, deliberately, as if to give himself some time to think, time to work out just how much he was willing to reveal and how much he wanted to conceal. Eventually he spoke again.

'Roger just had him do a job for me, that's all. That Wiltshire was causing me all sorts of trouble at the branch so Roger had his man make a few calls for me, try and shorten the bloke up. The kid always rung through a report to me afterwards.' He paused while he stirred the coffee thoughtfully.

'That night Roger sent him round to get me books back for me. That silly Barry bloody Dougherty lifted them from the office and he reckoned he give them on to Wiltshire. So Roger put Ellowe on the job. He rang me to report in as usual, real late it was, like sometime after midnight, said he'd been to Wiltshire's house but the books weren't there. Said Wiltshire reckoned Barry hadn't give them to him after all, which is probably fuckin' right. That was it. Next thing he turns up dead.'

It wasn't much but it was more than Eddie'd ever thought anyone would get from Fred Hunter on the subject. He decided to press on while Fred was in a talkative mood.

'According to Wiltshire, he rang Gary Sharpe for help and Sharpe rang you to call off Trevor.'

'That's bullshit.' The old man's tone was so genuinely dismissive that Eddie didn't doubt for a moment he was telling him the truth. 'I don't know what Gary Sharpe's been saying or why, but if he was going to ring anyone to pull the kid up that night it would've been Roger Baston, not me. Baston and Sharpe were pretty bloody thick at that time don't forget.' The caution was gone now; his crackly voice was laced with emotion. 'I originally put them two together because Sharpey wanted someone to lay some muscle for him, and that was Baston's go in them days. But then after that they got real cosy.'

There was something in the expression that suggested Fred could tell a lot more about the relationship than he was saying.

'How cosy?'

'Mate, you work that one out. That's what you get paid for.' The old man sipped at his coffee then grimaced bitterly. 'All I'm telling you is that's one scrum I never had me head nowhere near. That kid never done no harm to me.'

He dipped his lips back into the coffee, thereby announcing that the conversation on this subject was over. Eddie picked up his own coffee and blew gently onto the hot surface, watching the old man sipping quietly across the table. Fred Hunter hadn't brought him in today to solve his case for him, and their conversation had nothing to do with Fred trying to avoid any sort of liability. He just wanted Eddie to know that, whatever anybody thought, he'd played no part in what had happened all those years ago to Trevor Ellowe and he didn't want the blame laid at his feet. As Eddie watched him drink Fred Hunter suddenly looked back up at him through his bushy eyebrows.

'You sure you don't want to try some of that lobster?'

* * *

Sasha Kelly stepped out of the witness box, straightened her jacket, smoothed her tight, dark skirt, and strutted towards the courtroom door feeling a sense of accomplishment and mild relief. She had known for weeks she was needed to give evidence in the Brisbane District Court on the three-year-old fraud case she had kicked off just before her transfer to Mackay, but she'd had no idea what the defence would try to make of her evidence, and therefore whether she would be in the witness box for two minutes or two days. She had packed her suitcase for the latter eventuality, but fortunately reality had proved closer to the former and that meant Kelly had the rest of the day off to spend as she pleased, perhaps take a stroll down town, maybe do a little shopping, relax and enjoy herself. That was, as soon as she disposed of one outstanding matter.

As Kelly pushed through the door into the foyer of the court the first thing she saw was Frank Vagianni sprawled luxuriously across one of the witness couches, slurping noisily on his thick shake through a plastic straw. At the sight of her his face lit up with mischievous glee.

'Holy shit, Kelly, you look like the accused all decked out in that fancy court clobber of yours.'

Kelly strode purposefully to a nearby conference room and pushed the door open.

'Yeah well, you look a bit like a copper sitting out there on your arse doing nothing, Frank.' She turned to face him. 'I suppose that just shows how deceptive first appearances can be.'

Frank chuckled to himself as he struggled to his feet and limped into the room; he was happy to know he'd gotten somewhere under Kelly's skin. He pulled a swivel chair up to the desk as Kelly closed the door, clicked her briefcase open on the desk, removed a thin manila folder marked 'Confidential', then sat down opposite Frank looking like an auctioneer waiting for the opening bid. Frank stared blankly back at her for several seconds then shrugged his shoulders inquiringly.

'So? Let's see the file.'

Kelly's eyes narrowed suspiciously. 'You show me yours, then I'll show you mine.'

The words had hardly left her mouth before she realised what she'd said. Kelly blushed a bright shade of crimson as a lascivious smirk spread across Frank's unshaven face.

'You know, Kelly, I thought you'd never ask.'

He pulled a folder from his overnight bag and slapped it onto the desk between them, still grinning like a pervert with a pocketful of boiled sweets. Kelly kept her eyes on the folder as she pulled it towards her and flipped it open.

'You're a deviant son-of-a-bitch, you know that don't you, Frank.'

'Yep.' He leaned back into his chair, his hands locked behind his head and his face still beaming with an insolent, toothy grin. 'And loving it.'

Kelly didn't look at him. The blood was still colouring her cheeks as she did her best to concentrate on the text of the documents in the file Frank had just handed to her. They included extracts from the transcript of the separation hearing before Ms Withnall LCM and some of the Coroner's Court depositions, and a copy of all the statements Wendy Bagley had made to the police. Frank had highlighted and flagged the relevant parts for ease of reference, and as Kelly flipped to each successive segment, digesting its contents before proceeding to the next, the flush in her face gradually faded, replaced by her natural healthy hue and the soft rose of her cheeks. A lock of her honey blonde hair had escaped and fallen onto her face, and Frank watched it gently dancing back and forth across her cheek as she scanned the pages one by one. He knew what she was thinking. Kelly had had a bad feeling about Phil Manning and the whole Wiltshire case for a long time now, but she was still a cop and the thought of doing anything that had a chance of weakening the prosecution case on a murder charge didn't sit easily with her. She had to satisfy herself she was doing the right thing. Frank had always known she would. Any copper would, particularly one who was as good as Sasha Kelly. She could be an infuriating pain in the bum at times, but he had to admit, when all was said and done she'd turned into a first-class D.

Finally Kelly looked up from the folder. 'That bastard Manning didn't show Dr Dalton the forensic report?'

Frank arched his eyebrows. 'What did you expect?'

Kelly was hunched forward over the file, looking deep into his eyes. With his peripheral vision Frank sensed her open neckline was revealing much more than she was intending to be on show, and he squinted painfully straight back into her eyes, concentrating desperately on resisting the temptation to look down. When Kelly finally looked back at the page he snuck a quick peek, then snapped his eyes back into place just in the nick of time. When Kelly looked at him again her eyes held a look of genuine concern.

'What do you think's going on, Frank?'

It felt good to have Kelly asking his opinion, showing him some respect like she did back when she was a fresh-faced rookie straight out of the academy. She'd always been smart, she learned fast. She was a good cop.

'I think they're trying to line Wiltshire up.' It was none of her business but something made Frank want to tell her anyway. 'Our mail is that Roger Baston cooked up the extortion letter and, according to Wiltshire, Manning's already put it on him for a sling to make the whole thing disappear.'

Kelly nodded thoughtfully, looking suitably impressed, as though she accepted unreservedly everything Frank had said. He felt unfamiliar pride spark somewhere deep within him as Kelly put one hand onto the file marked 'Confidential' and slid it across the desk. Frank opened it up and flicked through the wad of documents it contained.

'This is good shit, Kelly.' He paused briefly on one of the pages, quickly scanning the contents. 'You know, you could have made a good detective — if only you'd had the right training.'

Kelly smiled wistfully. 'Maybe you should have stayed with us a bit longer, Frank.'

Frank hadn't left the service of his own accord; he'd been forced out, and Kelly knew that well enough. After all, she was mainly to blame for it, or at least that's what Frank had always told himself. But as he looked across the desk at her now, he could tell she was talking about more than just his resignation from the police service. She was talking about what it was that had got him to that point in the first place, and he knew the truth was that he'd found his own way there, without the help of Sasha Kelly or anyone else. Frank had made his own decisions long before the Commissioner tapped him on the shoulder. Somewhere along the way he'd chosen his own path. He smiled back comfortably at her now, almost despite himself.

'Maybe you're right, maybe I should have.'

He thought about it for a moment, and then popped the question. 'You know what? Why don't I buy you lunch? That way you can tell me all about where I went wrong.'

CHAPTER TWENTY-SEVEN

The first witness to be called at the Michael Wiltshire committal hearing was Wendy Glenys Bagley, which didn't surprise Eddie Moran one little bit. Bruce Parforth was nothing if not utterly predictable. He'd obviously convinced himself Bagley was to be the ace up his sleeve, and he was experienced enough to know that it was always smart to lead out with your strongest card. He'd disposed of the formal part of the proceedings as quickly as he could, tendering the various statements and exhibits, dealing with procedural issues and the like, and now that the real show was set to start, it was time to play his trump. He was right about one thing: his whole case now hung on Wendy Bagley, and if she wasn't good enough to do it for them then it wasn't going to get done. But as Eddie sat bouncing one knee maniacally beneath the bar table and cracking his knuckles loudly, to the mild irritation of Ms Withnall LCM, he was wondering if Parforth's trump card might soon look like the two of spades.

As Wendy Bagley strutted towards the witness box he had to admit someone had done a fairly tidy job of dressing her up to look like someone credible. The bottle-blonde hair he'd remembered from the Coroner's Court hearing was now dyed a more sedate auburn and the low-cut top and skin-tight skirt had been replaced with a conservative well-cut navy suit over a cotton blouse buttoned right up to the throat. Someone was determined to make every post a winner.

As she drew level with the dock she cast a contemptuous glance in the direction of the defendant, but then quickly looked away, concentrating on the witness box as she approached and stepped into it. Michael Wiltshire stared helplessly at her, trying to recollect if he had ever laid eyes on her before, desperate to understand what he could have done to make her want to wreak the destruction she had brought into his life. The more he looked, the more he was certain she was totally unknown to him. He noticed Moran whisper something discreetly to Kirsten Foster at the bar table and she rose and stepped towards him in the dock. She moved so close to him that he could smell the sweet fragrance of her skin and felt the soft puff of her breath as she whispered in his ear.

'Do you know this slag?'

'Never set eyes on her before in my life.'

Without another word Kirsten went back to the bar table and whispered the instructions to Moran, who was still bouncing one agitated knee under the table and had now commenced feverishly chewing on a fingernail. He said nothing as Kirsten relayed the message, just kept his eyes fixed on Bagley, as if by looking hard enough at her he would eventually see something no one else could. As Bagley took the oath card in her hands he noticed that the painted nails were still just as long and just as false.

Parforth did his best to mitigate what was always going to be his star witness's most obvious point of vulnerability, eliciting from her upfront some self-serving evidence about how and why she'd given false testimony at the Coroner's Court. Wiltshire had telephoned one afternoon, imploring her not to mention that she and Trevor had driven to his house that night and that she had left him there. Wiltshire had stressed to her how damaging it would be to him politically if that were to get out, and she felt sorry for him. She believed then that Trevor had been accidentally killed later in the night in a car crash in the Cross, so she saw no harm in leaving Wiltshire out of her version of events. He had offered her two thousand dollars to protect him and she had foolishly agreed, not suspecting for a moment there had been foul play. She would never forgive herself for having been so gullible.

Apparently that was supposed to make it all okay. Not in Eddie's book it didn't.

Moran was on his feet even before Parforth had resumed his seat and gnawed voraciously at the end of his biro as he stared at the witness. When all was said and done there was only one fight that had to be fought and won at this hearing, and now was as good a time to kick it off as any.

'You're a pretty practised liar, aren't you, Ms Bagley?'

Parforth's leather soles scuffed frantically on the vinyl floor before he eventually got enough traction to propel him to his feet. He wasn't going to let Moran pull his usual stunt and turn this hearing into a circus.

'I object, Your Worship!' He pushed his glasses back onto his nose. 'My friend is not entitled to insult the witness in that fashion.'

Moran turned on Parforth, grimacing disdainfully. 'That's not an insult.'

'Yes, it is.'

'No, it's not.'

'Yes, it is.'

'It's not.'

'Gentlemen, please!'

The stern voice of the chief magistrate sliced through their confrontation like a razor and seemed to jolt them both back to reality. They stood silently for a moment like two squabbling schoolboys being dangled by the ear by their headmaster, before Moran collected himself and turned to the bench.

'Your Worship, it's a straightforward proposition. I'm simply asking the witness to confirm a simple fact: that she's a practised liar. Obviously it goes to her credit. She can either concede it or deny it.'

Sue Withnall had no problem with the argument but she was clearly unimpressed with the delivery style of Eddie's opening gambit. There was as much threat as imprimatur in the tone of her ruling.

'I'll allow it, Mr Moran.'

Moran shot a final scornful glance at Parforth as he turned back to the witness.

'It's true, isn't it? You're a practised liar.'

'No, I'm not.'

'No?' Moran nodded thoughtfully. 'Well, let's have a look at it.' He stooped and drew from his briefcase a folder marked 'Confidential' and laid it neatly on the bar table beside him. He opened it and flicked through several pages before settling on the document he wanted. 'Your first conviction as an adult was at age twenty-one. You pleaded guilty to fifteen charges of obtaining by deception. True?'

'Yes.'

'You would have had to tell a few fibs to pull them off, wouldn't you?'

'Yes.'

'Okay, then four years later you were convicted of eighteen counts of credit-card fraud under the name Wendy Baker.'

'Yes.'

'And of course even that name in itself was a lie, wasn't it — your name wasn't Baker.'

'No.'

'And I suppose every time you used that dodgy credit card you pretended it was all legitimate?'

'I suppose.'

'And you were lying every time, weren't you?'

'I suppose so.'

'All eighteen times. Then a couple of years later you pleaded guilty to an attempted fraud related to a motor vehicle insurance claim.'

'The Falcon, yeah.'

'That's right, the Falcon. You had a boyfriend steal it for you, isn't that right?'

'I think so, yeah.'

'And you told the insurance assessors it had gone missing from outside your house.'

'Yeah, maybe.'

'But of course all that was nothing more than an intricate, premeditated lie by you to pull the wool over your insurer's eyes to pick up an insurance payout, wasn't it?'

'Yeah, I suppose.'

'And that involved having to lie to lots of people, including the assessors, the police, the insurance company, the hire purchase people, even your neighbours — you even lied to them about it, didn't you?'

'Yeah, I think I did, yeah.'

'And they all believed you, didn't they?'

'They did at first, yeah.'

'It was only when your boyfriend was picked up in the car that it all came out, wasn't it?'

'Yeah.'

'And even then you tried to lie your way out of it. You told the police you knew nothing about it.'

'Yeah.'

'But they found photos of you and your boyfriend in the resprayed car, didn't they?'

'Yeah.'

Eddie looked up from the open file, pausing several seconds for effect before he revisited his opening proposition.

'You're a good liar, aren't you?'

Bagley looked mildly insulted as she swept the hair back from her face and cast around the courtroom for whatever sympathy might be on offer. Bruce Parforth buried his head in his brief, and Ms Withnall LCM stared coldly at her from the bench.

'No, I don't think so, no.' She looked around again, once more in vain. 'No more than anyone else.'

'No?' Eddie flipped his eyebrows theatrically then returned to the file still open on the bar table. 'Well, eight years ago you were convicted of imposition on the Commonwealth, weren't you?'

'I think so, yeah.'

'That related to your fraudulent receipt of unemployment and other benefits over a period of approximately five years, didn't it?'

'Yes.'

'And of course that involved your having lodged regular false returns with the Department of Social Security over a long period, didn't it?'

'Yes.'

'And you lied your head off in those returns, didn't you?'

'I suppose.'

'Each and every one of them.'

'Yeah.'

'Time after time after time. You lied and lied and lied, didn't you?'

'Yes.'

'And they believed you every time.'

'I guess so.'

Eddie paused again.

'You're a very practised liar, aren't you, Ms Bagley?'

'Maybe.'

'You even lie about your own name, don't you?'

'No. What do you mean?'

'You've called yourself Wendy Baker — that was a lie, wasn't it?'

'Yeah, I suppose.'

'Glenys Walters?'

'Yeah, that was for the dole office.'

'Yes, and it was a lie.'

'Yeah, I suppose so.'

'As was Glenys Walker.'

'Yeah, that was the same sort of thing.'

'Another lie?'

'Yeah.'

'And the list goes on and on, I suggest. Wendy Lane, Wendy Glenny, Patricia Walker, Patricia Lane, Patricia Parker — they're all aliases you've used.'

'Yeah, mainly for the dole though.'

'For whatever reason, they're all lies you've told.'

'Yes.'

Eddie paused again and asked the question slowly, articulating every syllable.

'You're a very practised liar, aren't you?'

'Yeah, I said I was.'

She snapped it out indignantly, then turned angrily to Parforth, her crimson lips pursed into a tight pucker, as if demanding an explanation for his more-than-apparent disinclination to rally to her assistance on the point. Eddie waited in silence while she stared down the prosecutor and then redirected her displeasure back to her interrogator. When she did so, he responded with his own ice-cold glower.

'And you've lied about this matter, haven't you?'

'No.'

Her jaw was jutting out resentfully, just waiting to be socked.

'Yes, you have.'

'No, I haven't.'

'You gave a statement to police about this matter immediately following Trevor Ellowe's death, didn't you?'

Her confidence faltered momentarily as she tried to anticipate the lawyer's point.

'Oh yeah, I lied then but that was because Wiltshire told me to.'

Eddie paused again, looking as puzzled as he could.

'Did he?'

'Yeah.'

'According to your statement, he rang you and said there was to be a public inquest and he asked you to lie at the inquest.'

'Yeah, same thing.'

'But the decision to hold a public inquest wasn't made until several months after Mr Ellowe's death.'

'Yeah, so?'

'You made your first statement to the Darlinghurst police the day after he died. That must have been months before the defendant rang you to say there was going to be an inquest.'

'Yeah, it probably was, I suppose.'

Eddie plucked the statement from his brief and waved it in the witness's direction.

'And the statement you gave the Darlinghurst police was effectively the same account you gave in evidence at the inquest, wasn't it?'

Bagley was staring blankly at him, mouthing words that wouldn't seem to come to her. Eddie Moran took the opportunity to reinforce his point.

'Months before, according to your story, the defendant asked you to lie, you'd already told the Darlinghurst police that the last time you saw Trevor Ellowe was when he left your flat shortly before midday heading for the Royal Shield Hotel.' He waited silently as Bagley stared back at him, her mouth gaping comically. 'Didn't you?'

'I suppose so.'

Her answer was little more than a whimper, and Eddie boomed his next question at her derisively.

'Did you lie to the Darlinghurst police too?'

'I must have.'

'Well, why would you do that?'

'I don't know.'

'It wasn't because of anything the defendant said to you, because his conversation with you about the inquest didn't happen until months later.'

'Yeah.'

'So what's the explanation?'

'Don't know. Maybe I was just confused. Like, I was pretty upset about Trevor and that.'

Moran scoffed loudly and shook his head, glaring contemptuously first at the witness and then in the direction of the prosecutor, who quite obviously was doing his best to wholly ignore the irritating defence lawyer's theatrical posturing. When Eddie reckoned that the full force of his disdain had permeated the courtroom he blew out a last indignant sigh and resumed his questioning in a more subdued fashion.

'Anyway, the Darlinghurst police seemed to believe you?'

'Yes.'

'After you gave your account to them, they typed up a statement and you were asked to come in, read it over and sign it?'

'Yeah.'

'And you did that. You read the statement and you told them it was all true and correct and you then signed it as such?'

'Yep.'

'And you say that was all a lie as well, was it?'

'Well, yeah.'

'But they believed you?'

'I guess so.'

'Then when you came to give evidence at the inquest did the prosecutor speak to you beforehand?'

'Yeah.'

'And did you tell him the same story?'

'I think so, yeah.'

'And you say that was a lie?'

'Yeah.'

'But he seemed to believe it?'

'Yes.'

'And then you took a solemn oath to tell the truth?'

'In the court I did, yeah.'

'Just like the oath you took today.'

'Yeah.'

'And then you say you lied again.'

'Yeah.'

'And the prosecutor, and the police, and the lawyers, and the coroner, and everyone else in the court seemed to fall for it hook, line and sinker.'

'Seemed to.'

Eddie straightened up to his full height, gripping the lectern with both hands as he came to his point.

'So, on your story you've lied and lied and lied again, well enough to hoodwink everyone you've ever come into contact with, but now, lo and behold, you're telling the truth, so now we should all believe you all over again when you tell us you were lying then but you're telling the truth now, is that it?'

'I guess so.'

Eddie shook his head again, then slammed shut his copy of the police brief and leaned forward with his elbows on the lectern. He peered reproachfully at the witness, and when he spoke again it was in a quiet, measured tone spelled out syllable by syllable.

'Well, one thing's for certain: you either lied under oath at the coroner's hearing or you lied under oath here today, didn't you?'

'No, not today.'

'Well, how would we know?' He paused as if expecting an answer, but then resumed without waiting for one. 'How would we know you're not lying right now?'

Bagley stared back at him, open-mouthed, as if searching for words, but once again Eddie didn't wait for them to come.

'I mean, the fact is, you're a practised liar, aren't you, Ms Bagley?'

She was still staring silently at him.

'Aren't you?'

She nodded sheepishly. 'Yeah.'

'And you're darned good at it too, aren't you?'

'I guess so.'

'I guess so too, lady, I guess so too. In fact, I guess you're probably a good enough liar to fool all us poor saps seven days a week. Wouldn't that be right?'

'I object!'

Parforth was halfway to his feet, still trying to get traction on the vinyl floor, as Moran picked up the brief again and started nonchalantly leafing through it.

'That's alright, I don't need an answer.'

It was obvious Sue Withnall LCM found Moran's histrionics distasteful, and she glared down at him from the bench as Moran studiously leafed through his brief. Ultimately, her disapproval of the witness seemed to persuade her to overlook the lawyer's insolence for the time being.

'Do you think you'll be much longer with this witness, Mr Moran?'

There was something in her tone that suggested she had already drawn adverse conclusions on the credibility of Wendy Bagley and didn't need to hear much more, but Eddie wasn't yet convinced he was entirely finished with the witness. He needed time to think about a couple of things.

'I could be a little while yet, Your Worship.'

'Very well, we'll adjourn now for the mid-morning break.'

* * *

As Slick followed Eddie demurely into the legal conference room and closed the door discreetly behind her she was straining to contain the elation that was exploding in her brain. As soon as she'd squeezed the door shut her petite face lit up like a beacon and she swiped a lethal right cross into the air.

'Take that, you lying slut!'

Eddie was already hunched over the desk and trying hard to ignore her as she circled him, celebrating enthusiastically.

'You nailed her, Eddie! You nailed her to the wall! I love you, baby. You kicked her big fat butt! She is like totally gone, baby, gone!'

Eddie stopped reading and looked up quizzically, as though he had just heard her for the first time.

'What?'

She stopped circling and stood in front of him, her hands propped against her hips, her face frozen in a look of mild stupefaction.

'She's lying. It's obvious. Even the magistrate can see it.'

Eddie squinted back at her uncomprehendingly. 'Yeah, but why?'

'Does it matter?'

He squinted again and pushed his glasses back onto his nose as he resumed his reading. 'It'll matter to a jury.'

She stood waiting for him to elucidate but of course he didn't. Eddie was off in outer space again, and Slick knew there was nothing she could do but wait until he came back down to earth, if he ever did. She remembered again why she hated him so much. She screwed up her face and poked out a long pink tongue at him. But Eddie wasn't even looking; he was too far out in deep space now to even sense her presence. She flashed a final snarl at him then rummaged through her handbag for a cigarette. Suddenly she needed one.

As Slick slammed the door behind her, Eddie Moran had the typewritten extortion letter in both hands and was studying it carefully. He wasn't reading it, he was looking at it — looking at the way it was set out, the spacing, the wording, the type itself. Why was Wendy Bagley lying about Trevor Ellowe's murder? He knew he'd have to come up with some sort of an answer to that question sooner or later.

He could tell a jury she was lying, and he could show them how utterly unreliable she was, but he knew the first question they would ask themselves was: Why? Why would she lie about it? She lied at the inquest because Wiltshire offered her money, and now she wants to clear her conscience — okay, we can understand that. But why would she come back now and put her head on the chopping block by perjuring herself? What's in it for her? Revenge, money, power — what? Eddie knew that if he couldn't give them some sort of an answer to that question then the chances were they might swallow her story despite her lack of credibility.

He knew what the answer to the question was. It was right there in the document he was holding in his hands. Eddie just had to dig it out and throw it on the table so everyone could get a decent look at it.

CHAPTER TWENTY-EIGHT

As the clerk announced that the local court was now resumed and the parties took their seats, Michael Wiltshire noticed an elegant figure pushing in quietly through the courtroom door. Darryl Beane's usually tanned complexion looked pale and drawn as he settled unobtrusively into the back row of the gallery, his bearing upright and his demeanour respectful. At first his eyes were fixed on the chief magistrate, but then they wandered cautiously around the room until finally they met Michael's, whereupon the lawyer nodded courteously, pleasantly, a curt tug of the corners of his mouth intending to convey condolences, some reassurance and best wishes. Michael nodded back, and both men looked away, to the woman sitting in the witness box waiting to resume her evidence.

Michael had known Darryl Beane since they were both barely out of their teens, young university students fired with a passion for the labour movement and the hurly-burly world of student politics. He had never much liked his highly intelligent, self-opinionated young associate in those days, but he'd never had a reason to suspect him of any kind of treachery. They had moved in the same political and social circles for most of Michael's adult life, and while it was true they had not become close friends, so far as Michael knew they had not been enemies. So what was Darryl Beane's interest now in these proceedings? Was it what Michael hoped: the interest of a long-time associate and colleague genuinely concerned about his old companion's fate? Or was it something far more sinister? Could it be true that the lawyer had some part in a plan to extort two million dollars from him? He had no reason to suspect Darryl Beane of collusion and conspiracy other than the say-so of criminals and convicts. Yet as he glanced at the dapper lawyer perched demurely in the back row of the gallery, he saw something in the pallor of his skin and the tension in his face and neck that said the stakes were high today for Darryl Beane.

'Do you know a man by the name of Roger Baston?'

The question had the impact Eddie Moran was hoping for. The blood drained quickly from Wendy Bagley's face as she nodded blankly at the lawyer.

'Yeah.'

'In what context do you know him?'

'He used to be a copper.'

'That's right, and he arrested you on the fifteen charges of obtaining by deception back when you were twenty-one, isn't that right?'

'Yeah, that's right.'

'And you were fined for those offences.'

'Yeah.'

Moran again picked up the folder marked 'Confidential' and flicked it open. The witness watched him cautiously as he found the document he was looking for and skimmed over it with one finger.

'And then five years later he arrested you again, didn't he, for receiving three stolen video players?'

'Them charges never went ahead.'

The lawyer looked up from his file, a faint suggestion of a cynical smirk forming on his lips. 'I know they didn't.' He nodded silently as Bagley nervously brushed her hair back from one eye. 'And it was just as well for you that they didn't, because by then things were getting pretty serious, weren't they? By then you were on a suspended sentence for the eighteen credit-card fraud offences we talked about earlier.'

'Yeah.'

'And if you'd been convicted of the receiving on top, you'd have definitely gone to gaol.'

'I suppose.'

'But fortunately for you, the police offered no evidence and you were discharged.'

'That's right.'

Moran paused for several moments, then leaned forward on the lectern again and asked his next question in a quiet, confidential manner.

'Why didn't the police offer evidence on that charge, do you know?'

'Don't know.'

'Just lucky?'

'I guess.'

The smirk was back more fulsomely now as the lawyer nodded thoughtfully in response to her answer.

'Well, you had a run of good luck in the next few years, didn't you, all involving Roger Baston.' Once again he pinned his finger on the open file beside him. 'Six months later he charged you with cheque fraud but the charges were subsequently withdrawn. Correct?'

'Yep.'

'Then in the following year he arrested you on a possess cannabis charge but once again no evidence was offered and the charge was dismissed.'

'Yeah.'

'Four months after that he charged you with stealing as a servant. Yet again the prosecution didn't proceed. True?'

'Yeah.'

'And a total of three further prosecutions by Mr Baston over the next four years all ended the same way, didn't they?'

'Yeah, I think so, yeah.'

Moran closed the file carefully and stood up straight, gripping the lectern in both hands.

'He didn't seem to be able to take a trick against you, did he?'

'What do you mean?'

'Why was Roger Baston running dead on every charge he brought against you?'

'I object!'

There followed a heated exchange in which Bruce Parforth robustly advocated that the use of the expression 'running dead' was wholly inappropriate in the circumstances, since whilst there may be some question as to why the various prosecutions had not proceeded, there was no proof that there was anything improper about the decision not to offer evidence in any of the cases. That of course gave Eddie Moran the opportunity to repeat the details of each of the aborted prosecutions by Roger Baston of the witness, and repeat and reinforce his proposition that there was something very smelly about the history of the relationship between the two. Bruce Parforth didn't let it go; he fought hard on the objection and the discussion thrust and parried back and forth longer than perhaps it should have. By the time Ms Withnall LCM finally ruled that the question should be rephrased, Eddie's point was clearly and firmly cemented in the mind of every person in the courtroom.

When he resumed he seemed to have forgotten all about the question that remained unanswered.

'Several months ago you were charged by Manly police with possession of goods which were suspected to have been stolen or otherwise illegally obtained.'

'That stuff wasn't in my place, it was all in a storage shed.'

'Yeah, a storage shed you rented.'

'Well, yeah.'

'That charge was also dropped, just a very short while before you made your statement to police about this matter, wasn't it?'

'Yeah, I suppose.'

'This time it was dropped because you were able to come up with a statement by someone who swore to having legally sold you the items in your storage shed, isn't that right?'

'Yes.'

'And that someone was Roger Baston, wasn't it?'

'Yes.'

'So Baston makes a statement saying all the items in your storage shed are property repossessed through his mercantile agency and sold legitimately to you, and the police drop the charges against you. Then within a matter of days of Roger Baston helping you out, you're back in the police station giving your own statement about the defendant in this matter. Is that how it went?'

'I guess so.'

'Thank you. No further questions.'

Eddie was already back in his seat, scribbling in his notebook. So far, so good. He'd achieved what he'd wanted to. He'd chopped up Wendy Bagley's credibility, and that was the primary mission accomplished. He'd also managed to get Roger Baston onto the radar screen, and that meant that suddenly there was a murky connection between the Crown's star witness and the controversial ex-policeman. Eddie could almost hear the cogs spinning in Sue Withnall's brain trying to work out where Baston fitted into all this. That was good, that was very good. He had no idea how he was going to answer the question, but it was good that at least the question was being asked.

At the other end of the bar table Bruce Parforth was feverishly whispering to his arresting officer, Detective Senior Sergeant Nick Phelps. Parforth could see that Moran was going to try his usual trick of distracting the hearing with irrelevances and red herrings designed to cloud the issues and confuse the magistrate.

Nick Phelps had prepared a written statement dealing with his part in the investigation, but Parforth hoped a few well-placed questions would quickly dispel Moran's back-handed suggestion that the police had done some sort of deal with Bagley to convince her to make a statement against the defendant. After announcing his intentions, Bruce Parforth called Phelps to the stand, had him formally adopt the contents of his statement, and then moved quickly to his killer point.

'Senior Sergeant, were you aware of any connection between Ms Bagley and Mr Roger Baston?'

'No.'

'How did you first come into contact with Ms Bagley?'

'Originally she made a couple of anonymous calls to the uniformed police at Marrickville. She didn't want to give her name, but she told them she had information about the murder of Trevor Ellowe. She claimed she knew who done it, but she wasn't willing to give any names until she spoke to the detective in charge of the investigation. The Marrickville police got hold of Detective Phil Manning because his name was on the original coroner's job, and I think Phil referred them on to me. So next time she rang Marrickville they plugged her through to me.'

'So did you have any correspondence at all with Mr Roger Baston about the matter?'

'Absolutely not.'

'Did you have any knowledge whatsoever about that "goods in custody" charge Mr Moran mentioned?'

'None at all.'

'So Ms Bagley came to you completely out of the blue, as it were, of her own accord?'

'Yeah, completely.'

Bruce Parforth looked up at the bench with an aspect of sublime self-satisfaction.

'Thank you, Your Worship.'

He pulled his chair in neatly behind him and sat down.

Moran jumped to his feet, leaned across the lectern and nibbled absently on several fingertips curled into his mouth. He was staring blankly in the direction of the witness box as he finished processing Phelps's evidence through his mind. What did it mean? Bagley had originally made an anonymous call to the police, and Manning had kept it all at arm's length, referring the Marrickville police to Phelps. It seemed a strange way to proceed if Manning was in the loop. But then again, maybe it wasn't so strange, maybe it was pretty clever. Eddie lifted one spindly finger and pressed his glasses back to the bridge of his nose.

'When the Marrickville police plugged this anonymous caller through, you were in your office, were you?'

'I was, yeah.'

'Was that just fortuitous, that she rang when you were in, or were you expecting her call?'

'No, it was just luck that I happened to be in the office at the time she rang.'

Moran nodded thoughtfully and took another nibble at his fingernail.

'Was Manning there at that time as well?'

'Yeah, I think he was actually.'

'Yeah?' Eddie paused briefly again, mentally evaluating the response. 'So what happened?'

'She said she knew who had killed Trevor Ellowe, and she was convinced the same bloke had just organised a hit on Barry Dougherty up in Queensland, because Barry knew about it all as well.'

Bruce Parforth smiled privately at the mention of the Dougherty allegations. They had been excluded from the hearing and wouldn't even have been mentioned if Moran hadn't opened up this line of questioning. It was his own fault — if you're going to ask the question don't complain about the answer you get. The crazy thing was, Moran didn't even seem to appreciate his blunder. He was continuing the same line of questioning, apparently oblivious to the response.

'Did she give a name?'

'No, she said she would only give anonymous information, she was too frightened of Wiltshire to go on record.'

'What changed her mind about that?'

'Well, actually we traced one of her calls back to her residence and we went out and spoke to her.'

Moran dropped both hands down onto the lectern and arched his eyebrows, as if he had been shocked out of a slumber.

'You traced her call?'

Nick Phelps seemed equally surprised by the reaction he had drawn from the lawyer and looked cautiously towards the prosecutor before proffering his answer.

'Yeah well, we had a fair idea who she might be. We'd obviously discussed the possibilities, and Phil Manning told us he'd always suspected Ellowe's girlfriend knew more than she let on at the inquest.'

'So did Phil Manning trace the call?'

'Well, he organised it to be done, yeah.'

'So it was really Detective Manning who led you to Miss Bagley?'

'You could say that, yeah. In the end it was.'

Eddie smiled despite himself. 'I see.'

It had a nice symmetry. Baston gets Bagley to make her first call anonymously so it's unconnected with anyone in the whack, and meanwhile Manning's working as his man on the inside, ferreting away to make sure the police investigators are eventually steered in her direction. That gave it all a nice independent look in case anyone eventually came sniffing around asking questions. It also made it a pretty safe bet to Eddie Moran that Detective Nick Phelps wasn't in the loop, and that was good news as well. If he was on the up and up, and if he was any sort of an investigator, he would be sure to have looked into Bagley's story pretty closely.

'Did you check out her story?'

'As best we could I did, yeah. Her description of the house matched up alright, and the phone records corroborated what she said about Ellowe ringing the defendant before the incident. In fact, the defendant himself corroborated that during our interview.'

Eddie now had Bagley, Baston and Manning all swimming around somewhere in the same cesspool. There was just one more name that he wanted to see added to the mix, and this was his opportunity to drop it in.

'Mr Wiltshire actually complained about getting threatening calls at the time, didn't he?'

Nick Phelps glanced sheepishly in the direction of Bruce Parforth, but the prosecutor kept his head down.

'Well, he claimed he told Mr Gary Sharpe about them.'

The mention of the name caused the magistrate to look up from her notes. During his interview at the Sydney Police Centre, Michael Wiltshire had told the police that he had reported the threatening phone calls to Gary Sharpe, but the claim was buried deep in the transcript of the police interview and otherwise figured nowhere in the police brief, and it was clear that the mention of Sharpe's name had hitherto escaped the attention of the chief magistrate. She watched the witness carefully as he completed his answer.

'But our inquiries didn't bear that out.'

'What do you mean by that?'

'Mr Sharpe couldn't recall any such conversation.'

Eddie Moran stood up straight and looked around him quizzically, as if the proposition was preposterous.

'Well, is there a statement from this Mr Sharpe?'

Bruce Parforth leapt to his feet, struggling with the ring-binders on his brief.

'Yes, Your Worship.'

He quickly freed a one-page document and waved it triumphantly in the direction of the magistrate, delighted to be able to summarily dismiss another of Moran's attempts to delay and frustrate the proceedings.

'I'm happy to tender that if my friend so wishes.'

It was a two-paragraph statement by Gary Sharpe saying he was a long-term associate of Michael Wiltshire, that he had known him well during the relevant time, but that he did not know of Trevor Ellowe and could not recall the defendant ever mentioning the name. Likewise he had no recollection of the defendant ever complaining of having received any threatening telephone calls from a Mr Ellowe or anybody else. Once Eddie had read it, Parforth handed it up to the presiding magistrate and it was admitted into evidence in the proceedings. Eddie made a mental note as he turned back to resume his questioning of Detective Senior Sergeant Phelps.

'At some stage you became aware, did you not, that someone had sent an anonymous blackmail letter to the defendant demanding two million dollars in connection with the death of Trevor Ellowe?'

'Yes.'

Parforth looked incredulously at his opponent. He couldn't understand why Moran would want to introduce evidence about the extortion letter; it could only reflect badly on his client.

'Did you ask Wendy Bagley if she'd had anything to do with such a letter?'

'I did actually. She denied any knowledge of it.'

'Did you check her story out?'

'Sure.'

'How?'

'Well, for one thing I arranged to have a search done of her premises.'

'What for?'

'Anything that might be connected to the case: letters, correspondence referring to Wiltshire, newspaper clippings maybe, drafts —'

'Drafts of what?'

Eddie was leaning forward on the lectern again, supporting his chin in one hand as he stared at the witness. Nick Phelps looked a little hesitant.

'Drafts of anything that might be relevant, I suppose.'

'Drafts of the extortion letter, for example?'

'Maybe.'

Eddie could understand why Nick Phelps was being a little coy. Like any investigator worth his salt, Phelps had had questions in his mind about a witness whose claims were diametrically opposed to her previous sworn evidence, particularly in circumstances where someone was trying to set up the supposed culprit for a two-million-dollar sting. But he'd checked her story out and it had seemed to hang together, and whatever lingering reservations he might have now, she was all he had to hang his murder charge on, so he wasn't going to give Eddie Moran any more assistance than he needed to.

'You were looking for drafts of the extortion letter because it wasn't beyond the realms of possibility that Bagley might have been involved in the extortion attempt, was it?'

'Anything's possible, Mr Moran.'

Eddie wasn't going to let him get away with that. He pressed the point.

'Yeah, and one of the possibilities was that Bagley was part of a plan to blackmail the defendant.'

Phelps delayed his answer for a moment, struggling with the proposition put to him.

'It was possible; pretty unlikely though, given she'd already made a statement to police. But, like I said, anything's possible.'

'So you searched her premises.'

'That's right.'

'Have you got a copy of the search warrant there?'

'Yeah.'

'Could I see it, please?'

'Sure.'

Phelps rifled through his narrow briefcase until he found the document he was looking for and handed it over to the lawyer. Moran skimmed it quickly then leaned forward on the lectern once again, holding the warrant out in front of him in both hands.

'According to the warrant one of the items you were searching for was, quote, *any electric typewriter or other typewriting equipment of any description, including typewriter parts, accessories, ribbons, or other equipment of any kind whatever.* The extortion letter you found had been written on an old-style electric typewriter, hadn't it?'

'That's right.'

'So you were specifically looking for an electric typewriter or anything to do with an electric typewriter when you searched the house?'

'Amongst other things, yeah.'

'Did you find any such thing?'

'No. I think I specifically asked Ms Bagley and she told me she'd never owned a typewriter.'

'But you searched for one anyway.'

'Oh yeah, all the guys that went to the house that day were fully briefed on what we were looking for. There was no typewriter or anything connecting her to the letter found on the premises.'

Moran looked unconvinced.

'Is that right?'

He looked back at the warrant, nodding absently. 'Alright, thank you.' Just as he turned to resume his seat he seemed to be struck by an afterthought.

'Oh, by the way, I take it Detective Manning knew in advance that you were going to search her premises?'

'Of course.'

Moran nodded again and sat down.

* * *

Darryl Beane slipped out through the back door of the courtroom shortly before the committal proceedings were adjourned for the day. He didn't want to be around when the court rose. So far he'd avoided any direct contact with Michael Wiltshire or any of his legal team and he preferred to keep it that way. As he walked out onto the steps leading down to the footpath he punched a familiar number into his mobile phone. Roger Baston didn't have to ask who was calling.

'How's it going in there?'

'Hard to say.' Darryl Beane was trying hard not to sound nervous. 'They've finished with the girl at least, but that Moran's been asking a lot of questions about the letter.'

Baston barked angrily into the phone.

'He's a little fuckin' smartarse, that bloke. Someone should've had him tidied up a long time back.'

Darryl pressed the phone hard against his ear and glanced around, hoping Baston had not been overheard. When he was satisfied no one was listening in, he cupped one hand over his mouth.

'I don't know that he's making too much progress overall though.'

'Course he's fuckin' not!'

Darryl hated the blind confidence of Roger Baston, but at the same time he loved it. It always calmed the nervous beating in his chest. All they had to do was hold their nerve, and no one held his nerve like Roger Baston.

'Listen, mate, I told you — this is a credibility case, right. Once the sheila says he's done it, then it's a matter for the jury — he gets committed for trial, that's all there is to it.'

He was right, Darryl Beane knew that. All the magistrate had to decide was whether or not there was some evidence on which a jury would be entitled to convict, and once there was eyewitness evidence implicating an accused, no matter how lacking in credibility the eyewitness was, then it was for a jury to assess the credibility of the witness and of the evidence, so the accused had to be committed for trial. Sue Withnall was going to put Michael Wiltshire on trial for murder in the Supreme Court.

'And as soon as he's committed we go back and pay him another visit, son. That's when we get him by the short and curlies and give those orchestras of his a gentle squeeze.'

CHAPTER TWENTY-NINE

Detective Senior Sergeant Phillip Manning had looked uncomfortable all day. Eddie Moran spent the morning cross-examining him about his original investigation on behalf of the coroner, the evidence he had given in the Coroner's Court, and the process of reinvestigating Trevor Ellowe's death consequent upon the recent statement of Wendy Bagley. Over the course of a lengthy cross-examination like this one, witnesses could sometimes become distracted — casual, relaxed, even bored. But Phil Manning never looked in danger of becoming any of those things. He was like a cat on a hot tin roof, and when Eddie Moran finally got around to the subject of Roger Baston he responded as if he'd been expecting it all day.

'You're an associate of Roger Baston, is that so?'

'I worked with Roger Baston about ten years ago, alright?'

There was too much vigour and more than the appropriate degree of venom in the witness's response, and Eddie paused long enough for its effect to be felt throughout the courtroom.

'Were you aware that Wendy Bagley was an associate of Baston?'

'Was she? I wouldn't know.'

Manning was staring belligerently at the lawyer, accentuating his obvious desire to dissociate himself from both Bagley and Baston, and so playing directly into Eddie hands.

'Really?'

'Yeah, really.'

The answer came back quickly and so patently aggressive that the magistrate peered at Manning over her spectacles.

'That goods in custody charge against Bagley which was dropped not long before she came forward to make a statement in this matter, that was handled by the Manly detectives, wasn't it?'

'How would I know?'

Eddie smiled benignly, resisting for the time being the witness's obvious challenge to cross swords with him.

'Well, you were involved in that investigation, weren't you?'

'No.'

He was still staring coldly at Moran, more than prepared to take the fight up to him. But Eddie preferred to bide his time. He methodically selected one of the folders marked 'Confidential' from the pile beside him on the bar table and began leafing through the contents.

'We've heard the charge was withdrawn after Roger Baston swore a statement that he sold the property to Bagley for value.'

Eddie looked at Manning who stoically returned his gaze, and they faced off in silence for a time before Manning finally responded insolently.

'Is that supposed to be a question, is it?'

Eddie smiled faintly again and shook his head.

'No, I'm just telling you that's the evidence we heard here yesterday. Do you agree Roger Baston provided such a statement?'

'Well, how the hell would I know?'

'How would you know?' Eddie was suddenly alive again as he slapped the vinyl folder down on the lectern and leaned accusingly towards the witness. 'How would you know?' He threw the folder open again and flicked the pages over. 'Well, that one's easily answered, isn't it? I mean, there's been a few mysteries in this case, but that's not one of them.' When he reached the document he was searching for he pressed the folder fully open. 'You'd know, witness, because you organised the statement, didn't you?'

Suddenly Manning's confidence was gone. He looked wary and uncertain, like an odds-on favourite caught off-balance by a rank outsider.

'I don't …' He faltered for a moment, wondering just how much the lawyer knew, before quickly re-establishing his composure. 'No, I don't recall having anything to do with that matter.'

Moran ripped two pages out of the folder. 'Have a look at this document.' He waved it in Manning's direction until the clerk took it from his hand and dutifully delivered it to the witness. 'Isn't that a copy of the statement Roger Baston signed to get Bagley off the hook on that charge?'

Manning hadn't seen the document in months, and obviously wasn't expecting to see it now. As soon as it was set before him his countenance hardened and he curled his lip churlishly at his interrogator.

'Yeah, that's it.'

'It's typed on a standard New South Wales Police witness form, isn't it?'

'Yep.'

'Signed by Mr Baston next to the word "signature" on the bottom of each page.'

'That's right.'

'And witnessed.'

'Yeah.'

'And that's your signature appearing beside the word "witness", isn't it?'

Manning paused and took a deep breath in, swallowing his animosity towards the lawyer.

'Yeah.' His voice was lighter now, palpably conciliatory. 'I'd forgotten I took that statement actually.'

Moran scoffed disdainfully at the witness.

'Completely forgot that a matter of days before Bagley contacted police about the Wiltshire matter you got a statement from the controversial Mr Roger Baston exonerating her on a serious criminal charge!'

Manning was sorely tempted to snap back, but managed to maintain his equilibrium.

'Looks like it, yeah.'

The lawyer shook his head theatrically, scoffed again, then squinted at Manning with a look of comically exaggerated incredulity. Suddenly the whole ugly Eddie Moran Show was back in full swing.

'Just completely slipped your mind, did it?'

'I'd say so.'

'Are you serious?'

'Yes.'

'You're seriously telling us you just forgot?'

'Yeah.'

'You can't be serious, surely?'

'Yes, I am.'

'You can't be.'

'I am.'

'You're not. You can't possibly be.'

'I am!'

'You can't be!'

'I object!'

Before Bruce Parforth could get to his feet, Moran had already announced that he would not be further pursuing the point and had no further questions for Detective Manning, and announced to the chief magistrate that he wanted Wendy Bagley recalled for further cross-examination. At the other end of the bar table the prosecutor stood open-mouthed for several seconds, trying to decide whether he should be arguing his original objection, objecting to the question having been asked and then withdrawn, or addressing the new application Moran had just thrown unheralded onto the table. In the end he stumbled into the final option.

'With respect, Your Worship, I can't see how recalling Ms Bagley could possibly advance these proceedings. What does it matter that Detective

Manning took a statement from her about a completely different charge?'

Eddie Moran smelled the opportunity to make a little speech from the bar table to neatly summarise for the magistrate where they'd been so far and where they were going. He slapped his hand palm-down on the lectern.

'It matters, Your Worship, because in my submission this whole relationship is just a little bit too cosy. The Crown's central witness, Bagley, gets charged with a dishonesty offence, so ex-Detective Roger Baston goes to Detective Manning and gives him a statement to get her off the charge, then Bagley promptly reciprocates by giving Detective Manning a statement implicating the defendant in this charge. Meanwhile, someone's trying to blackmail the defendant, and at least Detective Phelps suspects that someone might be Wendy Bagley.'

While Eddie was delivering his speech the magistrate was nodding in apparent agreement. She'd heard enough to be convinced that there were plenty of unanswered questions about the relationship between the Crown's star witness, her arresting officer and one of the most notorious ex-policemen to ever grace the front page of the *Sunday Truth*. She wanted to know more, and it was obvious even before Moran had finished his first sentence that she was going to order that Wendy Bagley be recalled. As soon as he concluded she made the order promptly and concisely, sending Parforth into a flustered whispered conversation at the end of the bar table with Detective Senior Sergeant Phelps. Seconds later they emerged from their confabulation, Phelps scurrying from the courtroom and Parforth rising to his feet to announce to the magistrate that Bagley was still in the precincts of the court and would be recalled presently.

They waited in silence. In the dock Michael Wiltshire could almost hear his heart beating in his chest. He was still struggling to fully digest what had happened so far, but he understood enough to know that Moran had just turned the whole hearing on its head. Now Manning and Bagley were the ones under suspicion; now questions were being asked about their motives and their connection with the shadowy Roger Baston. He had no idea where it was leading, or whether any of this meant the case against him could be faltering or not, he only knew it felt good to see the woman who had told so many lies about him embarrassed and discredited, and the arrogant, abrasive Detective Manning sweating and fumbling with his words. Michael looked across the courtroom to where Eddie Moran sat hunched over the bar table, bouncing one knee and munching abstractedly on his fingernails. He was an obnoxious, infuriating man, but Michael was pleased he had him sitting in his corner.

As the minutes ticked over on the courtroom clock, Eddie was going over in his mind what he had so far, and what he needed. It was obvious that something was going on between Baston and Bagley, and clearly Manning had his head in the scrum as well. He had them all in bed together, now he had to show what they were doing beneath the sheets. He carefully planned his line of questioning, preparing himself for the next round. This one had to be decisive, he had to get it just right. He wasn't interested in a points decision; he was looking for a knockout.

Wendy Bagley sashayed back into the courtroom with a curious mixture of trepidation and disdain splashed across her face. She kept her nose high in the air as she passed the bar table then stepped up into the witness box, haughtily brushing strands of hair back from her face. She glared defiantly at Moran as he rose to his feet.

'Ms Bagley, I want to ask you some further questions about that property the police found in your storage shed.' Moran opened the folder on the desk beside him and flicked over several pages until he settled on one which he pinned down with his finger. 'When you were first asked about it you told the police it was property you'd accumulated over a number of years.'

'That's right.'

'Baston later made a statement claiming he sold it to you in one hit not long before the police raid. Was that true?'

'Yeah.'

'Well, why did you initially give the police a different story?'

'I don't know.'

'Why didn't you tell them you'd bought it all from Roger Baston?'

'I thought they might think I was lying.'

'Why?'

'I don't know.'

Eddie Moran paused briefly, smiled cynically at the witness, then flicked to the next page in his folder.

'Why did you hire the storage shed in a false name?'

'That was just a name I used.'

Moran looked up from the page.

'I gather that, but why?'

'Why?'

'Yeah, why? If this was just a shed you used to store your property, why have it in a false name?'

'Just did, I guess.'

He kept his eyes trained on her, nodding thoughtfully.

'Anyway, in that shed was all the gear the police confiscated — yes?'

'Yes.'

'Did you have any other storage sheds?'

'No.'

'So what did you do with the property when the charge was dropped and the police returned the property to you?'

'I just kept it all at home.'

'Have you sold any of it, or otherwise disposed of it in any way?'

'I haven't had time. I've been in witness protection for the past two months.'

'So it was there when the police came to search your house?'

'Should be, yeah.'

'All of it?'

'Yeah.'

Eddie Moran paused, staring silently at the witness. At first she met his gaze with palpable truculence, her lips pursed tightly and her brow knitted in a determined frown, but as the silent seconds ticked away her stern demeanour faltered by degrees, replaced by increasing uncertainty, until eventually she looked nervously around the courtroom, searching for reassurance and support. The magistrate was looking at Moran, waiting for him to continue, and finally even Parforth looked up at the defence lawyer, wondering what was going on. When Eddie had everyone's undivided attention he asked his killer question.

'Including the electric typewriter?'

Bagley's mouth dropped open slightly.

'What electric typewriter?'

'The electric typewriter that's clearly noted on the property seizure record.' Moran ripped two photocopied pages out of his folder and held them up. 'And on the indemnity receipt you signed when it was returned to you. Do you not remember the electric typewriter?'

Bagley closed her mouth, grimacing slightly.

'Oh yeah, that's right, I think there was an old typewriter there, but it was just a heap of junk.'

'Well, where was that heap of junk when the police searched your house?'

'Oh, I think I give it away to someone.'

'Who?'

The witness's face was now drawn and pale.

'Geez, let me think.' She dropped her head forward and stood for several silent seconds gazing straight down at the floor, then threw her head back again and brushed the hair back from her face. 'No, actually I remember now — I just threw it out.'

'Threw it out where?'

'Just in the rubbish. I'd say the garbos would have collected it.'

'When?'

'Oh, it would've been just before the cops come round.'

'Why?'

She faltered, struggling painfully for a response.

'Why?'

'Yeah, why? Why did you throw it out just before the police came around?'

Bagley's mouth opened and shut several times before she finally found her voice.

'I got it out one day to write a letter and it didn't work so I thought I may as well just chuck it out.'

'Is that right?' Moran was glaring at her. He pulled the lectern in towards him and leaned forward over it. 'Well, when the police came to your house they specifically told you they were looking for an electric typewriter, didn't they?'

'Yeah, I think they might have, yeah.'

'And you told Detective Phelps you'd never owned a typewriter of any description, isn't that so?'

Bagley hesitated, screwing her face comically to one side.

'Yeah, I probably did.'

'Why'd you tell him that?'

'I don't know. I just did.'
'I know you did, but why?'
'Don't know.'
'You must know, surely. Why would you tell him something like that?'

Bagley opened her mouth but nothing came out. Moran waited a moment then pressed on.

'What was the big secret about this typewriter?'

Her mouth was open slightly, her chin trembling almost imperceptibly as she struggled to shape an answer that wouldn't seem to come. Every eye in the courtroom was trained on her now and as each silent second ticked over the agony of her dilemma became more palpable. When he was convinced her silence had achieved its maximum effect Eddie quietly rephrased his question.

'What was it about the typewriter that you had to get rid of it in such a hurry before the police arrived to search your house?'

Bagley looked down at the floor and then up again.

'Can't remember.'

Her voice was little more than a pathetic whimper now, and her eyes dropped sheepishly again. When she eventually looked back up Moran was staring accusingly at her.

'Was that typewriter used to type a letter to Michael Wiltshire late last year?'

Bagley was shaking her head vigorously from side to side before he even got the question out. 'No way.' There was a look of near panic in her eyes. 'I never had nothing to do with no blackmail letter.'

Moran straightened, a look of feigned surprise stretching his face. 'What blackmail letter?'

She faltered again, casting her eyes desperately around the courtroom.

'Well, that letter you're talking about.'

'How do you know it was a blackmail letter?' The witness looked like a cat frozen in headlights. 'It's a simple question, witness. How do you know the letter I'm talking about is a blackmail letter?'

She was staring back at him, fumbling awkwardly with her words.

'Well, I don't know, I just... I don't know.'

'You haven't been privy to the prosecution brief, have you?'

'What's that mean?'

'No one gave you any of the police witness statements or the evidence to read?'

'No.'

'Well, how would you know a blackmail letter was sent to Michael Wiltshire?'

'I just guessed, I suppose.'

It was a beautiful answer. Eddie just loved it.

'What? Are you serious?'

'Yeah.'

'You guessed?'

'Yeah.'

From the corner of his eye Eddie noticed the chief magistrate shaking her head and arching her eyebrows sceptically. Now was the time to move in for the kill.

'You had a hand in the preparation of that blackmail letter, didn't you?'

'No.'

'Did Roger Baston dictate that letter for you to type on your old electric typewriter?'

'No.'

'Or was it perhaps Detective Manning?'

In a rustle of papers Bruce Parforth leapt to his feet.

'I object to this, Your Worship!'

Ms Withnall LCM turned calmly to the prosecutor.

'On what grounds, Mr Parforth?'

Parforth looked almost affronted that the magistrate had asked him the question, and began stuttering and stumbling to formulate an argument before Withnall mercifully interrupted him.

'Mr Moran, I suppose at least if you're going to pursue this line of questioning the witness is probably entitled to a warning.'

Even if he'd had grounds to oppose the magistrate's proposal Eddie wouldn't have bothered. He'd got all he was ever likely to from Bagley, and it was all he needed: the damage was done. Sue Withnall recited to the witness the formal warning pursuant to the provisions of the *Evidence Act* that she was not obliged to answer any question asked of her if she feared the answer might incriminate her in the commission of a criminal offence. Bagley didn't have to hear the warning twice. She quickly declined to answer any further questions about the letter that was sent to Michael Wiltshire. The magistrate turned to Eddie Moran.

'Mr Moran, are you willing to accept that blanket refusal, or do you want to take it question by question?'

The magistrate's disgust with the witness was painted all over her face and Eddie was feeling great. On the inside he was jumping up and down, cracking champagne corks, but he tried hard to maintain a deeply troubled countenance.

'What's the point, Your Worship?'

'Indeed.' Withnall cast a final disdainful look towards the witness.

As the parties rose to adjourn proceedings for the day, the mood at the prosecution end of the bar table seemed positively bleak, as though things couldn't possibly get worse. But Eddie Moran had one last piece of bad news for them.

'Your Worship, earlier today my learned friend tendered a further statement, being the statement of Mr Gary Sharpe. I'd like Mr Sharpe to be available for cross-examination.'

* * *

As soon as Moran got out of court he turned on his mobile phone and jabbed in the number for his office.

'Kenny, in the bottom right-hand drawer of my desk there's a list of my press connections. I want you to do a ring-around to all of them this afternoon. I've got a red-hot story for them tomorrow.'

CHAPTER THIRTY

'Hello, stranger.'

Sue Withnall looked up from her morning cup of coffee at the smiling face leaning in through the door to her chambers.

'Hello, Don!'

She was genuinely pleased to see the State Attorney-General, big Don Bollard. She had known the affable lawyer ever since she had first left university to take up articles of clerkship with a small firm in the same city building where he worked. In those days Don was a young, hard-working solicitor with a solid practice in personal injuries law and a passion to follow his father's lead into local Labor politics. They met at a local branch meeting and became friends, and thereafter Don was something of a mentor to her through those early years of her professional career. In return she had been a strong supporter of his bid for pre-selection for a state seat, and she had helped man the polling booths at his first-ever election. Even after he was elected to state parliament they met regularly at party functions and had remained close friends. When Don

Bollard was appointed Attorney-General in a state Labor government committed to affirmative action, Sue Withnall's stakes as a prospective candidate for appointment to the bench soared in legal circles. Of course she publicly disavowed all the predictions, but privately she hoped Don might just throw her name into the hat for a spot on the District Court. In that sense her appointment to the magistracy had come as something of a disappointment, but when the elevation to chief magistrate quickly followed, she was seen by all and sundry as a rising star. And she knew she owed it in no small part to Donny Bollard.

As Sue rounded her desk to greet her old friend she noticed that he closed the door behind him as he entered. She offered him tea or coffee, both of which he cheerily declined, and they settled comfortably on the couches at the far end of her room. They had been friends for a long time, but the Attorney-General didn't drop by too often for a social chinwag with the chief magistrate. Don was here on business, and Sue had always been a girl who liked to get straight to the point.

'So, to what do I owe the pleasure of this lofty visit?'

Don Bollard laughed a little more heartily than the question warranted and, when he finally got around to answering, the self-conscious half-smile on his face looked curiously out of place.

'Well, actually I just dropped in because I got a call from someone down at Gary Sharpe's office last night. Apparently the DPP are chasing him to give evidence at this Michael Wiltshire hearing.'

Sue Withnall took a sip of her coffee. She had been so troubled by what she'd been hearing about the relationship between police and Crown witnesses at the committal proceeding over the past two days, she had forgotten for the time being that these proceedings also had a potentially political flavour. The Wiltshire name had once been a familiar one in New South Wales state Labor circles, and although the press didn't seem to have made the historical connection yet, it was understandable that the party might be sensitive about what evidence came out. As she swallowed down her coffee she was trying to anticipate what Bollard might have on his mind.

'Yeah. I think they're calling him this morning.'

'No, well, that's the thing see.' Bollard sat forward in his seat, rubbing the palms of his hands together. 'Apparently he can't do it. See, federal parliament's still sitting. Sharpey's in Canberra at the moment.'

Sue Withnall felt herself relax slightly. Don had simply come to sort out a practical difficulty regarding Sharpe's attendance. A member of parliament was excused from answering a court summons if he or she was required in the house. The committal hearing would have to be adjourned and resumed when the current sittings of parliament had concluded.

'When does parliament rise?'

'Well, shit, who knows?' Bollard was shaking his big head, looking everywhere but at the magistrate. 'But, you know, I really don't think Sharpey wants any part of it, you know what I mean.' He paused, finally looking her straight in the eye. 'I mean, Jesus, Sue, it's awfully bloody messy that thing.'

'That's an understatement, Don.' A look of concern clouded her expression. 'In fact I'm thinking of referring some of the evidence to ICAC or the PIC for investigation.'

Sue Withnall searched the face of her old mentor, looking for some guidance in her difficult dilemma. But none was on offer. Don Bollard just looked anxious and uneasy.

'What?' He shifted nervously on the couch. 'Well, shit, you can't pull Sharpey into something like that. For God's sake, Sue, the press'll bloody slaughter us if they get wind of it.'

She felt a sudden stab of exasperation.

'I'm not pulling him into anything, Don. The Crown tendered his statement, and the defence want him for cross.'

'Well, tell 'em to get stuffed.' Bollard was on the edge of his seat again. 'It's just a denial statement anyway. It's got no relevance to any bloody thing.'

Sue Withnall was surprised to hear that Don Bollard actually knew what the contents of Sharpe's statement were, and now she wondered whether this was all about the fact that Sharpe was being called or what he had to say.

Bollard leaned in earnestly towards her. 'We've got a federal election this year, Sue, and the press are already all over us about this stupid bloody Hutton affair. All we need is for Gary Sharpe's name to be tied in with a murder bloody case!' A thin film of sweat was glistening on his forehead. 'It's got nothing to bloody do with him anyway, for God's sake.'

Sue Withnall needed time to think. The statement had been tendered and if it was material to the proceedings the defence had a right to cross-examine it. She had a job to do and she wasn't about to let her politics get in the way of that. On the other hand, the last thing she wanted was to give the media a free kick at the Labor Party in the lead-up to a federal election. This was a crucial time for the nation and they had to get Labor across the line. A scandal that dragged the Foreign Affairs minister into a murder prosecution could be devastating to their chances. She knew Gary Sharpe. She'd met him once or twice over the years. He had his enemies, plenty of them, both outside the party and within, but she had no reason to think he was anything but a true-blue son of Labor who had nothing but the best interests of the party at heart. She wasn't about to let one of her own get savaged for no reason.

'I'll see what I can do.'

As Don Bollard headed out the door he gave her a warm peck on the cheek and squeezed her elbow confidentially.

'Listen, you're doing a great job down here. I'm hearing some real good things about you.'

'Thanks.'

He leaned in a little closer and gave her a knowing wink.

'We could do with someone with your admin skills up in the District Court, I'm telling you.'

* * *

When court convened that morning the first thing Sue Withnall noticed was the line of journalists packed untidily into the press gallery. She walked onto the bench with her eyes hooded in deep concern, painfully aware that the stakes had already been raised. Someone had tipped off the media that Sharpe was summoned to appear, and that meant what happened from now on would dictate just how damaging the exercise would be for the Australian Labor Party. She listened solemnly as Bruce Parforth advised that overnight inquiries had revealed that Mr Gary Sharpe was currently unavailable due to parliamentary commitments in Canberra, and in the circumstances the Crown made application to withdraw his statement. Predictably, Eddie Moran opposed the application, correctly pointing out that since the statement had been tendered and admitted it was now part of the evidence in the proceedings. But that wasn't the end of it as far as Sue Withnall was concerned; not all statements in committal proceedings could be cross-examined as of right.

'Mr Moran, why do you say it's necessary for you to cross-examine the witness at these proceedings?'

Eddie had come prepared to meet some opposition and he laid out his argument logically and concisely. The Crown case was that when Wiltshire was faced with threats made to him by Trevor Ellowe, he took matters into his own hands and arranged for someone to assault and ultimately kill the deceased. When police put that allegation to him Wiltshire told them that, on the contrary, as soon as he received the threatening call from Trevor Ellowe he rang his friend Gary Sharpe and told him all about it. The Crown had sought to put that vital assertion by Wiltshire to lie, by calling evidence from Sharpe that no such call was made. The issue of who Wiltshire called consequent upon his receiving threats from the deceased that night, and why, was absolutely crucial to the factual matrix upon which the Crown case was founded. Moran produced a long list of decided case authorities on the legal principles to be applied by magistrates in determining whether a witness should be called at the preliminary hearing, all of which strongly supported his position. He handed a photocopy of each case to the clerk who dutifully delivered them up to the magistrate.

On the bench Sue Withnall trawled through the cases with a knitted brow then looked at the prosecutor.

'Mr Parforth, when does federal parliament rise?'

'This Friday, I believe, Your Worship.'

She scribbled a quick notation in her court diary.

'Very well, I'll adjourn the proceedings until ten o'clock on Monday morning. Mr Sharpe's attendance will be required at that time.'

* * *

As they stood alone together in the elevator Slick could see that Eddie was cooking something up inside his head. He had that spaced-out look he got from time to time when he was about to cause someone a lot of trouble.

'Eddie.'

'Mmm.'

'What's going on here?'

'What do you mean?'

'Why are we chasing this Gary Sharpe guy?'

Eddie didn't answer. He was looking at the lights illuminating floor by floor. She could tell that he was trying to ignore her.

'We both know once you got rid of the Dougherty stuff, Bagley was the only witness that mattered.'

'Maybe.'

'So what are we still doing here?'

Eddie kept his eyes trained on the little lights. He was thinking about his next move. Slick was right. Bagley was the only crucial witness for the Crown and she had been totally discredited. Wiltshire might be committed for trial on murder, but the charge would never stick. Not unless they somehow came up with something new, and that wasn't going to happen. Sooner or later Wiltshire was going to walk. That was what Eddie got paid for: to see his clients walk, guilty or not. But this time it wasn't quite that simple. There was a lot more at stake in the Wiltshire case than just the fate of Michael Wiltshire. This time it wasn't simply a matter of beating the charge and watching the client ride into the sunset. This wasn't just another case, this one had strings attached. Which was precisely why Eddie didn't want to touch it in the first place. Slick had insisted, and he knew why. It was for exactly that reason Eddie knew he had to finish this job, right down to the last question. When Slick dragged him into it she said she had to know who was in on Trevor's murder. Now was the time to find out.

As the lift doors slid open on the ground floor Eddie pulled the car keys from his pocket and held them out to Slick.

'You go get the car. I'll meet you out the front in twenty minutes.'

Slick had known Eddie most of her life. She also knew that nothing she could say now would change anything. She took the keys and headed for the main doors.

* * *

When the warder ushered Michael Wiltshire into the legal interview room Eddie Moran was already pacing back and forth on the other side of the glass panel. As soon as the door closed Moran held up a copy of the blackmail letter.

'See this letter, pal? See what it says?'

Wiltshire eyed him wearily before answering.

'I know what it says.'

Eddie Moran poked a finger at the page, underlining the text as he read it out. '*You thought there were no witnesses but there were. They know all about your dirty little deal and why Trevor was on his way that night and who you called to get him sorted out*. That's what it says.'

The lawyer obviously had something on his mind. Michael pulled the chair out from the desk and sat down, waiting for him to come to his point.

'Whoever wrote that letter was trying to squeeze two million dollars out of you, pal, and to do that they had to scare the fuck right out of you. They had to make you believe they knew enough about the skeletons in your closet to bury you ten feet underground.'

Michael Wiltshire was staring blankly back at him like a poker player with a handful of nothing. The lawyer dropped both palms onto the narrow desk and leaned forward until his face was almost up against the glass.

'That's why they were telling you they knew you'd done a "dirty little deal" and they knew Trevor was on his way to see you about it, wasn't it? Because it was true — you did do some dirty little deal. And whoever wrote this letter knew about it and they wanted you to know they knew.'

Eddie was looking straight into the eyes of Michael Wiltshire, who held his gaze unflinchingly. They remained like that, staring defiantly at each other through the glass, until finally Moran straightened up and slipped the folded letter back into his pocket.

'You keep whatever skeletons in your closet you want to, pal, but one thing's for certain: whatever you told Gary Sharpe that night about why Trevor was coming to see you persuaded him that the bloke to get the job done was Roger Baston, and Baston only had one brief — to put Trevor Ellowe in the ground.'

He reached back and took hold of the door handle.

'We're only going to get one shot at Gary Sharpe, pal, and that's next Monday morning. That's when I get to ask him all about that dirty little deal of yours, and why he needed Roger Baston to sort it out for him.' He pulled the door open with one hand as he poked a spindly finger at his client with the other. 'So it's your call, buddy, it's your call. If you've got any kind of story, you've got till Monday morning to come up with it.'

* * *

Some gifts keep on giving. Some mistakes you pay for all your life.

As Michael Wiltshire stood against the cold wall, waiting for the prison officer scribbling his details into the security register to usher him through to the legal visits area, he scoured his mind to try to recollect where and how things had gone so very wrong. His memories of his wife's illness and her tragic death were now like some horrific nightmare that had long since faded, and all that was left was a kind of dull ache unaccompanied by any detail whatsoever. He realised now he had survived on autopilot throughout most of those months, taking very little in. Even after Jane's death he had struggled for a long time, living one day at a time, just trying to keep it all together for him and for his son. But time heals all wounds and eventually, gradually, Michael's wounds began to heal. He had found himself fighting back, regaining his old confidence, lifting up his head again, looking around him, planning for the future. The return to Sydney was part of it: a new beginning, new ventures, a new life. He would put the real-estate development skills he'd learned in Queensland to good use in Sydney and realise the potential he'd long known was there in abundance in the inner-city suburbs. Perhaps he would also revisit his now long-faded passion for Labor politics, go back to his roots, follow in his father's footsteps as so many in the ALP had once hoped he would.

It was a hopeful, exciting time for Michael Wiltshire. His old friend Gary Sharpe had welcomed him back to Sydney and back into the Labor bosom like a prodigal son — Charlie Wiltshire's brilliant boy, returned to take his rightful place at the party table. The future seemed unbounded. Together they would carve up the city, and reshape the face of Labor in the inner west. Gary Sharpe had it all planned. He had all the answers.

'Righto, through you go.' The warder nodded towards the wooden walkway leading to the legal interview rooms.

Michael had been thinking about what Moran had said to him ever since their meeting in the cells below the court two days ago, and he was looking forward to continuing the discussion now. Eddie Moran was a lawyer who had already been paid his full fee and who was required to follow his client's instructions. So why was he now running in his own direction, apparently without any consideration of the best interests of his client? Why was he insisting on calling Gary Sharpe for cross-examination when, as far as Michael could see, the prosecution case already had been very effectively dismantled through the cross-examination of Wendy Bagley, and calling Gary Sharpe could only introduce dangerous uncertainties that might undo all the good work? Michael wanted answers to those questions from Eddie Moran.

When he got to the verandah outside the interview rooms he saw the brash young prison officer Phallon standing outside one of the closed doors.

'You're in here.'

It was unusual to see any warders in this area, and there was something unfamiliar about Phallon's demeanour that produced a sudden twinge of nervous tension in Michael's chest. Phallon was pointing to the door next to him, and as Michael approached the warder opened the door with one hand and directed him in. When he stepped through the doorway and the door closed firmly behind him Michael Wiltshire was shocked to see the face of an old friend across the room.

'G'day, Michael.'

Gary Sharpe had an affected smile spread across his pockmarked face, but his discomfort was patently evident in the flush of his skin and the taut stretch of his mouth. As Michael moved towards the narrow desk Sharpe shifted in his chair, as if about to rise to greet his old friend, but in the end he just held out his right hand.

'How's things, mate?'

Michael Wiltshire looked down at Sharpe's outstretched hand, then at the crisp white cuff of his shirt sleeve and the silver-and-pearl cufflink. A sudden flood of nausea welled in his stomach and he felt his heart thumping painfully in his chest as emotion flooded into his throat and mouth and eyes. He looked down at his crumpled green prison-issue tracksuit, then back at Gary Sharpe.

'Crook, mate.' He swiped a strand of lank hair back off his forehead. 'Things are crook. Real crook.' He dragged the wooden chair out from the desk and flopped onto it, his eyes glistening as he stared incredulously at the man opposite him. 'Crook as Rookwood.'

It was the language of their boyhood, the language of the past, of what was lost and gone forever and would never be recovered. Gary Sharpe knew what message his old friend was trying to sell him, but he wasn't buying. Loyalty and old time's sake was strictly for old-timers. Michael Wiltshire hadn't been worried about old time's sake when he threatened to go to the police about the death of Trevor Ellowe. He'd been ready to tip a bucket on Gary Sharpe, but he got beaten to the punch. He got what he deserved. As the two men sat staring across the wooden table at each other Gary Sharpe felt nothing but disdain for

Wiltshire. His face was drawn and unshaven, his greasy hair was plastered back behind his ears, and his clothing was ugly and unkempt. His bloodshot eyes looked vulnerable and a tiny tremor was tugging at the corners of his mouth. He looked so pathetic Sharpey felt like laughing. Michael Wiltshire, the handsome, swashbuckling prima donna who'd once had it all, the man who was everything Gary Sharpe had wanted to be himself, had hit a major hurdle. He'd thought he could walk over Gary Sharpe. He was wrong. He had taken Sharpey on and lost.

'Why'd you do this to me, Gary?'

Michael's voice was so ridiculously plaintive Sharpey couldn't help but smile and shake his head. At last Wiltshire understood that no one got the drop on Gary Sharpe. No one. As he looked back at the prisoner the smile faded quickly on his lips.

'Because you wouldn't listen to reason, Michael. You just wouldn't fucking listen.' He beat out the last three words on the surface of the desk. 'If I'd let you go to the police you would've dragged my whole political career down into the dunny, everything I've worked for all my life.'

The emotion drained away as Michael nodded silently. He understood the equation; deep down he had always understood. Everything Gary Sharpe did, everything he had done, was done for Gary Sharpe.

'Why are you fucking around with this thing, Michael?' Sharpe was leaning forward on the desk now, speaking in a hoarse whisper. 'We both know there's a deal on the table.'

He paused, waiting for some reaction. Wiltshire stared blankly back at him.

'You're a rich man, Michael — all they want is money.' He paused again, looking deep into the prisoner's unfailing gaze. 'It doesn't have to be two million. I can get it down from that. Way down. All you've got to do is offer them some sort of a decent sweetener and they'll go away.'

A bitter smirk crept onto Michael Wiltshire's lips. For Gary Sharpe the solution had always been so simple. You paid what you had to pay, dealt with whoever was at hand, walked over anyone you had to. You did whatever was required to get the job done, so long as you came out a winner in the end. That was all that mattered. It was what had made him such a success; what made him so admired, and so despised.

'So you're in that loop too, are you?'

Sharpe curled his lip angrily and bared his teeth like a rabid dog. 'Of course I'm bloody not!'

The anger disappeared quickly, replaced by something that looked more like desperation. 'But I don't control this thing any more, they do. And the only way it's going to go away is if they kill it off.'

The cynical smirk still tugged at the corners of Wiltshire's mouth. He could see the desperation clearly now, the panic in his old friend's eyes. Gary Sharpe was grappling with the same problem that had plagued him all along, the problem that had created this whole horrific nightmare. Sharpey thought he had all the answers, but he didn't. He thought he could control every situation, but he couldn't. He thought the solution was simple, but it never was. Gary Sharpe controlled nothing. He had dragged them both down into murky depths, and now they were struggling together to keep their heads above the water. As Wiltshire stared silently across the desk at him, Sharpe could see in his eyes the recognition that now the stakes were equally high for both of them.

'Don't be a fool, Michael — take the bloody deal, for God's sake.'

The smirk disappeared from Michael's face.

'Why should I?'

Sharpe blinked and looked down at his hands where they fiddled nervously on the desk in front of him, then he looked back up.

'Trust me, Michael, you don't know these people like I do.' He held Michael's gaze for several long seconds. 'If you don't take this deal you're a dead man.'

* * *

Michael Wiltshire stood in the telephone line for nearly forty minutes that afternoon. There was someone he had to call.

As he neared the head of the line yet another tattooed and scowling prisoner shouldered his way ahead of him and, as always, Michael stepped back and said nothing, meekly accepting that in this world the weak deferred to the strong. He waited patiently, and eventually his turn came.

When the last prisoner hung up the receiver and sauntered away, Michael stepped forward and punched the number into the telephone. His heart was beating nervously as he listened to the ringing at the other end, hoping there was someone home.

'Hello.'

It was good to hear the sound of her voice.

'Kirsten, it's me, Michael. I need you to come and see me urgently.'

'Why? What's wrong?'

She sounded genuinely concerned.

'I just need to talk to you as soon as possible.'

'What about?'

Michael teetered on the edge a moment, then jumped in.

'Kirsten, I told you once that I wanted you to know the truth about Trevor's death. You wouldn't listen to me then. Now you have to.'

CHAPTER THIRTY-ONE

Gary Sharpe wore a bemused smirk on his face as he stepped briskly up the stairs leading to the court complex and shouldered his way politely through the throng of media collected outside the main doors. He looked almost as though he knew something everyone else didn't. And he did. Sharpey knew that he was smart enough to stay one step ahead of all these dopes seven days a week.

No doubt all his enemies, including the halfwit pinko Labor lefties as well as those numbskull Tories, would be rubbing their hands together at the prospect of his being publicly embarrassed by association with a murder case, but that just proved how out of touch they were. John and Mary Citizen didn't care two parts of three-quarters of bugger all who was called to give evidence at the Michael Wiltshire committal hearing. Even if they did read about it in the paper, most of them wouldn't understand what it was all about and those that did wouldn't give a square root anyway. After all, Sharpey was there to give evidence for the Crown. He was on the good guys' side, and even if the media did try to make something of his association with a murder suspect, so what? It was just another storm in a teacup that would blow over in about five minutes flat. As usual, today's front page would be tomorrow's fish-and-chip wrapper. Sharpey had been in politics long enough to know that.

He'd been under the hot lights plenty of times in his political career. It was like water off a duck's back to Gary Sharpe. No one handled the tough questions like he did. There wasn't an investigative journalist or television interviewer in the country who had the clout to lock horns with him, and he certainly wasn't going to have any trouble with some half-baked country-town solicitor. He couldn't be pinned; his evidence would be straightforward and uncontroversial. He couldn't remember getting a call from Michael Wiltshire on the night in question, but hey, it was five years ago — who could be certain? He was reluctant to call Michael Wiltshire a liar on the point, but for the life of him he couldn't recall ever having fielded such a call, and obviously it followed that he couldn't comment on any detail of any alleged conversation between them. How could he comment on a conversation he just couldn't recall? Of course anything was possible, but it was curious he had absolutely no recollection of it. Wiltshire might be telling the truth, maybe he did make the call and maybe Sharpey had inexplicably forgotten all about it, but that of course would seem incredibly unlikely, and maybe Michael Wiltshire was just a guilty man doing his best to shift some of the heat off himself.

As Sharpey strode confidently past the press gallery he felt a warm thrill of excitement in his chest. He loved being in the limelight, even when the light was hot, and he was going to enjoy demonstrating yet again to all these imbeciles that there was no better operator in the game than Gary Sharpe.

* * *

'Mr Sharpe, do you know the defendant, Michael Wiltshire?'

Bruce Parforth was standing bolt upright, phrasing each of his questions clinically and concisely.

'Yeah, I know Mick Wiltshire. I think we were probably in sub-junior together back in the old De La Salle College, Bankstown days.'

A snicker of recognition rustled through the public gallery while Bruce Parforth carefully constructed his next question.

'At the time of Mr Ellowe's death were you and the defendant on friendly terms?'

'Ohh ...' Sharpey's head was tilted to one side, a conflicted grimace contorting his expression. 'Friends? Yeah, I guess you could say we were friends. Yeah, sure. I mean, as I say, I've known Mick Wiltshire since we were at school together. I haven't seen much of him in the past twenty years or so, but yeah, I mean, on the odd occasion I've run into him we've always been on good terms, yeah.'

Sharpey stretched out comfortably and rested one arm on the edge of the witness box. He was proud of that answer. It set the tone perfectly. He'd met Wiltshire back when they were schoolboys together. Old schoolmates were like relatives — you couldn't help who they were and you couldn't be blamed for knowing them. And there was no shame in De La Salle, Bankstown — it was Labor heartland, and the Brothers had turned out everyone from criminals to cardinals. The fact that Sharpey was happy to recollect his old school showed he was a man of the people, and the fact he wasn't about to disown an old schoolmate in trouble, even though they hadn't seen much of each other in twenty years or so, showed what an all-round good bloke he was.

Parforth's examination-in-chief of Gary Sharpe went as predicted, with the prosecutor's concise questions being answered by the witness with good-natured, homey responses which were never damning or dogmatic but always open to the possibility that the defendant might just be mistaken or confused in his recollection, or perhaps even Sharpey's memory was faulty, although personally he found that difficult to accept. In any event, he had absolutely no recall whatsoever of having received any call from Michael Wiltshire on the night of Trevor Ellowe's death.

When Bruce Parforth eventually sat down, Sharpey cast an eye towards the press benches, where several of the journalists were now sagging in their seats, their earlier anticipation flagging noticeably. When he looked back to the bar table, Eddie Moran was climbing to his feet, shuffling together a jumble of handwritten notes. He asked his first question without looking up, still leafing through the pages on the lectern in front of him.

'At the relevant time, was your home phone number listed in the telephone directory?'

Sharpey adopted a comical expression of feigned horror and turned to the press gallery.

'I don't think so!' The journalists erupted into guffaws of laughter in accompaniment with Gary Sharpe's staccato cackle. When he'd composed himself he turned back to the magistrate. 'Once you've taken a few calls in the middle of the night from irate conservatives wanting to complain about the state of the nation, Your Worship, you pretty soon get over that caper, I can tell you.'

Sue Withnall smiled cautiously back at him as a new wave of laughter filled the courtroom. Only Moran seemed to have missed the humour in the response; he stood squinting quizzically at the witness from the bar table.

'Well, I take it then you don't receive too many phone calls in the middle of the night?'

'If I did my missus would soon have something to say about it, I promise you.'

A renewed round of chuckles in the public gallery seemed to intrigue the defence lawyer, who turned to take it in, before swinging back to face the witness, a faint bewildered smile now tickling the corners of his mouth.

'So if someone did ring you at 1:18 in the morning you'd remember it?'

There was something about the lawyer's expression that made Gary Sharpe feel suddenly uncomfortable.

'As I've just said, Mr Moran, I've racked my memory but I can't recall receiving any such call. It could have happened — I mean, the old brain isn't getting any younger, that's for sure.' He shot a cheeky glance in the direction of the gallery. 'But I think I'd remember if I had.'

Moran nodded silently as he weighed up the reply. Sharpey could see there was something dangerous about this man. He wasn't as stupid as he looked — which would have been a tall order in any event. His instincts told him the lawyer thought he had something up his sleeve, and sooner or later he was going to pull it out. Sharpey would have to step warily all the way.

'You said earlier the defendant was a friend of yours. Was he a good enough friend that he might want to ring you in the middle of the night for help?'

Gary Sharpe smiled at the lawyer. If this was his trump card he was as stupid as he looked after all.

'Like I said before, Mr Moran, a lot of people want to ring me in the middle of the night. That doesn't make them my friends.'

Someone in the gallery chuckled lightly but the lawyer kept his eyes trained on the witness.

'I suggest he did ring you to tell you that an unnamed man, the man we now know to be the deceased, Trevor Ellowe, the man who had been calling him on and off for several weeks, making threats on behalf of Mr Fred Hunter, was on his way around to his house that night.'

'Not that I recall.'

Sharpey was shaking his head sadly like a disappointed man who couldn't understand how or why his old schoolfriend would lie so blatantly about such things.

'And you told him you'd contact Mr Fred Hunter immediately to sort it out for him.'

'Fred Hunter? No. If he'd told me what you just said, I would've told him to call the police.'

All Sharpey had to do was stick to his line. He had no recollection whatsoever of any such call. It was his word against that of an accused murderer desperate to save his miserable bacon. That was the beauty of it. There were no records and no witnesses. Sharpey just couldn't be pinned.

'I suggest that only minutes later you rang him back and told him you'd rung Hunter and sorted out the problem, and that in the meantime he — Wiltshire — should vacate the house to allow things to, in your words, "blow over".'

'What? Turn it up!' Sharpey scoffed. He turned incredulously towards the press gallery. He had to ramp it up a little now. 'I don't remember anything like that.'

'Do you deny it?'

'Of course I do.' He shook his head dismissively at the suggestion, but for the first time there was a faint hint of apprehension in his countenance. 'In fact, if you'd done your homework you'd know the police have spoken to Fred Hunter and he's already confirmed he didn't speak to me that night.'

From the corner of his eye Sharpey could see some of the journalists noting down his answer. *Wiltshire's story was obviously a fabrication — the police had already checked it out and found it wanting.*

'I didn't say you spoke to Hunter. I said you told Mr Wiltshire you'd spoken to him.'

'No.' Sharpey shook his head again. 'Why would I be ringing Fred Hunter to mediate between him and Michael Wiltshire?'

'Because you and Fred Hunter were as thick as thieves in those days, weren't you?'

Bruce Parforth was halfway to his feet with an objection but didn't get a chance to open his mouth before Sharpey snapped back indignantly, 'No. I hardly knew the bloke.'

'Really? You'd had financial dealings with him, hadn't you?'

A nervous flutter sprang into Gary Sharpe's chest.

'What financial dealings?'

'Well, had you had any financial dealings with him?'

The lawyer was obviously fishing.

'No.'

Eddie Moran stooped and sifted through the pile of folders alongside the lectern. When he found the one he wanted, he leafed through it, removed several pages and held them out for delivery by the court clerk.

'Would you please have a look at these documents.'

The clerk took them from his hand and walked them to the witness box.

'That's a company search detailing the directors and shareholders of a company called Melrosa Pty Ltd. It was a two-dollar shelf company of which your wife, Lainie Sharpe, and Mr Hunter's wife, Marjorie, were the sole directors and shareholders.'

'That was my wife, not me.'

Sharpey shot a cautious glance in the direction of the journalists who were feverishly scribbling notes of the details of this apparently sensational link between the Foreign Affairs minister and the shady transport industry heavy whose name was currently featuring in the Transport Royal Commission. From the fervour of their note-taking none of them seemed too focused on the distinction Gary Sharpe was drawing between his wife's financial dealings and his own.

'Anyway, that company never traded.'

'It bought and sold property though, didn't it?'

'It bought one piece of vacant land years ago, for about eighty grand or something. That company's been wound up more than ten years.'

Gary Sharpe suddenly looked a little flustered as Moran leafed through his folder once again.

'The piece of land it bought was directly opposite the site of the new International Soccer Stadium, wasn't it?'

'Not when we bought it, no.'

'No, when you bought it the government's decision on the stadium site hadn't been announced.' Moran looked down at his folder, apparently reading from the contents. 'You bought the site in the January for a purchase price of ninety-seven thousand dollars, the whole of which was paid by Hunter Transport cheque, correct?'

'I don't know. Could be right, I suppose.'

'Then in April the state government announced it would be developing the soccer stadium site, and all the surrounding sites saw a corresponding rise in value.' He paused and looked up at the witness. 'So much so that in August you were able to offload the property for a whacking four hundred and sixty thousand dollars.'

'Not me, the company. I didn't offload anything.' A light film of perspiration was shining on Gary Sharpe's forehead. 'I wasn't even a shareholder in Melrosa.'

He flashed a quick glance at the press gallery again then turned back to the lawyer.

'Don't forget too that everything in Sydney was going up around that time.'

Moran was now bent over the lectern.

'I thought you said you didn't have any financial dealings with Fred Hunter.'

'Yeah, and I haven't!' Gary Sharpe's voice sounded shrill, almost panicked. He cleared his throat and tried to compose himself. 'I told you, that's my wife. You seem to be having some difficulty hearing me or something.'

'Well, you personally haven't had any financial dealings with Mr Hunter?'

'That's what I've been telling you.'

He laughed dismissively and looked to the gallery, but for the first time no one was laughing back. When he turned back to the lawyer, Moran was again removing pages from his folder.

'Would you have a look at this document, please.'

Sharpe waited anxiously for the document to be delivered to him. He quickly scanned it then shook his head.

'Oh God, this is nearly fifteen years ago. This is ancient history.'

'It's a mortgage document relating to a second loan you took out on your home, isn't it?'

'Yeah, about fifteen years ago.'

'And the mortgagee is Fred Hunter.'

'I needed money at the time to put a pool in and Fred agreed to help me out, that's all.'

'He lent you eighteen thousand dollars.'

'Yeah, something like that.'

'Interest free.'

'Yeah, probably. Look, it was small change for Fred.'

'And three years later he forgave the debt entirely.'

'It was small change.'

'I thought you said you'd never had any financial dealings with Fred Hunter.'

'That was so long ago I'd forgotten all about it.'

Moran shut the folder and leaned forward on the lectern once again.

'But on the night Trevor Ellowe died, you were still pretty thick with Fred Hunter, weren't you?'

'In what respect?'

'Well, for one thing your wife, Lainie, was employed by his company, Hunter Transport, wasn't she?'

A pregnant silence settled momentarily on the courtroom before Sharpe answered.

'Yes.'

'In fact, your wife first went on the payroll of Hunter Transport as a typist eleven years ago.'

'Yes.'

'Does your wife have any formal qualifications as a typist, Mr Sharpe?'

'Not that I know of.'

'Did she ever go in to work at the Hunter Transport office?'

'She was on call.' Gary Sharpe shifted uncomfortably in his seat. 'I think the arrangement was that they could send work out for her to do at home.'

'How often did that happen?'

'How would I know?'

Moran opened the folder again and began reading from the contents.

'Your wife remained on the Hunter Transport books, receiving a weekly wage, until two weeks before the current Royal Commission into the transport industry was announced last year, at which time she appears to have retired —'

'Your Worship, what's this got to do with anything?'

Gary Sharpe was angrily facing the magistrate, both hands propped against the arms of his chair as though he was about to jump to his feet and run out of the courtroom. He had to get onto the front foot right now and close down this line of questioning. It had nothing whatsoever to do with the case, but it could cause him a world of pain in the press.

Sue Withnall LCM turned to the witness and waited several seconds before she finally spoke. 'I think Mr Moran is concerned to test your assertion that you hardly knew Mr Hunter.' She paused, looked down at her notes, then continued, 'Which I must say doesn't seem to me to sit well with the fact that he employed your wife for more than a decade, Mr Sharpe.'

Gary Sharpe sat wide-eyed in the witness box, staring back at the magistrate. Her response wasn't what he had expected. Sue Withnall was supposed to be a friend of the party. She had no known allegiances to the Labor left. So why wasn't she backing him up? These questions had no relevance to the Wiltshire case. Couldn't she see this kind of muck-raking was just giving the press a free run at the party, playing right into the Tories' hands?

'On the night of Trevor Ellowe's death, Michael Wiltshire rang you at home at precisely 1:18 a.m., didn't he?'

'I've already told you, I don't remember.'

'Would you look at this document, please.'

The very words set off another nervous flutter in his chest. Each time Moran uttered them he seemed to come up with an even more damaging bombshell to drop. Sharpey quickly scanned the document delivered by the clerk as Moran put the question to him.

'That's a printout of Mr Wiltshire's telephone records. If you follow them down until you come to 1:18 a.m. you'll see a call, the duration of which is said to have been two minutes and eleven seconds. See that?'

The flutter in Sharpey's chest became a painful thump. He didn't like this. Where were all these documents coming from? This was supposed to be just his word against Wiltshire's.

'Yes.'

'That number there that he called, that was your home telephone number, wasn't it?'

The witness swallowed hard before he answered.

'Yes.'

'He rang to tell you that the man who had been threatening him was coming to his house that night.'

'Maybe.' Sharpey needed time to think. 'I'm struggling with my memory, I really am.'

'And you told him you'd ring your mate Fred Hunter and sort the whole thing out.'

'Maybe.'

'Do you know a man called Roger Baston?'

The name hit him like a punch in the face.

'Who?'

'Roger Baston.'

Gary Sharpe was desperately trying to organise his thoughts. How did Roger Baston's name get into any of this? What did Moran know about Baston? Where was he heading with all this?

'I've read his name in the papers. I think he used to be a police officer, wasn't he?'

'Well, you're a bit better acquainted with him than that, aren't you?'

'What do you mean?'

'Would you look at this document, please.'

The words set a wave of nausea washing over him as Moran plucked a document from his folder and handed it to the court clerk. The clerk politely took it from the lawyer's hands and walked towards the witness box. As he approached, Gary Sharpe stared at the papers, trying to decipher what they were. When they were handed to him his heart sank into his stomach.

'It's an application by a company called Midas Investments to rezone a two-thousand-square-metre site in Marrickville from residential A to multiple dwelling.'

'Yes.'

'Midas was a joint venture between your family company and Michael Wiltshire's development firm, wasn't it, the idea being you would join forces to acquire the site, get it rezoned and then develop it for units?'

'That's right.'

'Mr Wiltshire's company put up all the money, and your job was to consult on the town-planning issues.'

'Yes.'

'Because you had very strong contacts in the Marrickville shire council.'

'So? There's nothing wrong with that, is there?'

The response was palpably defensive, but Moran pushed on regardless.

'And the other part of your role in the joint venture was to get contracts on the various house lots that comprised the site, wasn't it?'

Sharpe hesitated for a fraction of a second; when he answered his voice was hedged with caution.

'That's right.'

'But tying up the house lots turned out to be a tougher ask than you'd expected, didn't it?'

Now he knew exactly where Moran was going. He had to think quickly, realign his strategy. He had nothing to hide. It was a legitimate commercial deal. He'd done nothing wrong.

'No. It was pretty straightforward really. For the money we were offering, people were falling over themselves to sell to us.'

'Most of them were, but the last few dug their toes in, didn't they?'

'Oh, a couple of them were trying to hold out for a few extra bucks.'

'So without reference to Mr Wiltshire, you hired someone to help persuade them to your line of thinking, didn't you?'

Sharpey felt a dull ache gnawing in the pit of his stomach. He swallowed painfully before he answered.

'I'm not sure I'm with you.'

'Would you look at this document, please.'

This time he knew what to expect. There was no law against hiring who you pleased.

'Oh yeah, I think we did get Roger in to do a little bit of consultative work on that job, yeah.'

Eddie Moran arched his eyebrows quizzically.

'By "Roger" you mean Roger Baston, do you?'

'Yeah.'

When the clerk delivered the document to him

in the witness box Sharpe gave it no more than a cursory glance.

'That's a copy of your family company's tax return, isn't it?'

'Yeah, that's right.'

'In which you describe Mr Roger Baston as a, quote unquote, contract negotiator for your family company.'

'Yes.'

'What's a contract negotiator?'

'Just what it says — someone who negotiates contracts with the vendors.'

Sharpe had an agitated half-smirk on his face and was shifting nervously in his seat.

'Why did you need an ex-police security guard and debt collector to negotiate with your vendors?'

'Roger had a lot of experience in the police force.' Gary Sharpe's forehead was now shining with sweat as he looked up at the magistrate. 'He had very good inter-personal skills.'

'Inter-personal skills?' Moran barked the words so forcefully the witness swung back immediately to face him. 'Roger Baston was nothing but a thug you hired to stand over reluctant vendors, isn't that so?'

'No, it's not.' Sharpe shouted the answer back far more robustly than he had intended, and the vehemence of his own voice seemed to surprise him. He quickly collected himself before continuing. 'I made it clear to Roger that I wanted everything done legally and above board.'

There was an audible rustle in the gallery as the journalists scribbled down the response. Gary

Sharpe turned to them open-mouthed, fixated by their reaction. Things were slipping out of his control. This lawyer was trying to make him look bad and the press were swallowing it hook, line and sinker. He had to do something. He had to rethink his strategy immediately. He had to turn this thing around.

'Do you know a man called Thomas Attwell?'

At the mention of the name Sharpe turned back to the lawyer, his face flushed with trepidation.

'Roger Baston's only instructions were to sign up Tom Attwell at whatever price he'd sell for.'

Sharpe's voice was rash and belligerent. In contrast, Moran remained unemotive.

'But it didn't work out that way, did it? Mr Baston got a little heavy-handed in his sales-negotiation technique with Mr Attwell, didn't he?'

'I wouldn't know,' Sharpe snapped back defensively as he squirmed in his seat. 'There were rumours going around at the time, but all I know is Roger's instructions from me were very clear.'

'The rumours that you're talking about were to the effect that Roger Baston went into Mr Attwell's house and violently assaulted him.'

'I don't know what he did.'

Moran flipped open a folder on the bar table beside him and used his finger as a pointer as he scanned down the page.

'Thomas Attwell was attacked in his home and suffered a broken cheekbone and a fractured jaw, did he not?'

'So I believe.'

'He sold out to your joint venture within days after the assault, didn't he?'

'Yeah.'

'And he died only a matter of weeks later, didn't he?'

'Tommy Attwell died of a heart attack, nothing to do with that bashing.'

The answer was barked back so aggressively that the lawyer paused and looked up from his folder. He waited patiently as the answer permeated the silence of the courtroom.

'But of course if the rumours that were going around ever got out, they could have been extremely damaging to you, isn't that so?'

'It had nothing to do with me.' Sharpe's voice was now paper-thin. 'The rumours were about Roger Baston.'

'You were a high-profile officer of the New South Wales Labor Party at the time. Allegations of this kind would have been devastating to your political ambitions, wouldn't they?'

'I just told you, it had nothing to do with me.'

Moran paused again.

'On the night Trevor Ellowe died, Michael Wiltshire rang you and told you that the man who had been making threatening calls to him for the past several weeks had rung again.' The lawyer's voice now had the slow, hollow beat of a funereal drum. 'Only this time he wasn't doing Fred Hunter's business. This time he was on a mission of his own. He'd come across information implicating you and Michael Wiltshire in the death of Tommy Attwell. And he said he was coming to the house that night to spell out to Michael Wiltshire what he wanted in order to keep quiet about it.'

'None of this had anything to do with me.' The politician's voice was almost a screech. 'I never even met Tom Attwell.'

'Mr Wiltshire asked you who Tom Attwell was, because he'd had nothing to do with the acquisition of any of the lots.'

'Neither of us had anything to do with Tom Attwell.' Gary Sharpe cast his eyes towards the gallery and then at the magistrate. All he could see were accusing faces. His heart was thumping painfully in his chest and the sweat was collecting on his upper lip. He wasn't going to cop this. He wasn't going to be the one to shoulder all the blame. 'That was Roger's job. That's why I hired him in the first place.'

'You told Wiltshire you'd ring Fred Hunter and get the whole thing sorted out.'

'Wiltshire said the bloke had been ringing him for Fred, so I said I'd talk to Fred about it.'

'But you didn't ring Fred, did you?' Moran snatched the folder from the bar table and plucked a page out of it. 'You rang Roger Baston.'

Gary Sharpe started to mouth an answer, but it didn't come. He stared at the lawyer hunched over the lectern, clutching the single sheet of paper in one hand, and his thoughts darted frantically from one point to another. What was the document fluttering in the lawyer's hand? Would it prove that he had rung Roger Baston that night to get Ellowe sorted out? As he struggled to collect his thoughts Moran poked a spindly finger at him and barked his accusation.

'The moment you hung up the phone, at 1:21 a.m., you rang Roger Baston.'

'Tom Attwell was Roger Baston's problem, not mine!' The answer leapt reactively from the politician's mouth and lay in the silent courtroom like a cold cadaver. 'I wanted nothing to do with it. Roger created the bloody mess, he was the one who had to clean it up.'

Moran stood motionless, his eyes trained cruelly on the witness, who was puffing fitfully as though he had just run up a flight of stairs. Silent seconds ticked over on the courtroom clock as the significance of the answer seeped into the consciousness of everyone there. When the lawyer finally resumed, his voice was dripping with disdain.

'Well, he cleaned it up alright, didn't he?'

'I don't know.' The Foreign Affairs minister's sweaty upper lip curled resentfully. 'I haven't got a bloody clue what he did.'

'Well, I have, Mr Sharpe, I have.'

Eddie Moran scrunched the page in his hand into a paper ball as he turned to face the magistrate.

'I have no further questions of this witness, Your Worship.'

* * *

'Jesus, Donny, all bloody hell's broken loose!'

The Prime Minister sounded uncharacteristically rattled, even through the telephone line. It was no wonder. The events of the past two days would have been enormously damaging at any time, but in an election year they were catastrophic. Don Bollard had a sick feeling in his stomach. The news reports of Gary Sharpe's evidence at the Wiltshire murder committal were bad enough. Despite the torrent of letters Sharpe's lawyers had sprayed around the country threatening injunctive action and defamation suits, every front page, radio bulletin and television current affairs program in Australia had carried the story as its main headline, complete with an ugly, blow-by-blow account of the minister's revelations about his relationship with underworld identities and his murky involvement in the death of a small-time drug addict and cheap crook in the Cross five years ago. But the decision of the magistrate had made things ten times worse.

If Sue Withnall had committed Wiltshire for trial, it might all have blown over, at least for the time being. They could have avoided being dragged into the controversy on the basis it was sub judice and therefore any public comment was inappropriate, and that way the whole thing could have been put to bed until after the election. That would have given them time for Gary Sharpe to announce his retirement so they could put some distance between him and the party before the matter came to trial. But for some reason Withnall had had a brain explosion and refused to commit Wiltshire for trial. She'd ruled that although a bare prima facie case was made out on the evidence, applying the second limb of the committal for trial test, the evidence was so weak and tenuous that no properly instructed jury would be likely to convict, and therefore the defendant should not be sent for trial. Who would have thought Sue Withnall of all people would pull a stunt like that? Donny Bollard should have seen it coming when she flatly ignored his express wishes not to require Gary Sharpe for cross-examination. He should have known then she had her own agenda. She'd keep. The party had a long memory.

'What do you think, Don, could we maybe present an ex officio?'

It was an option. Notwithstanding the magistrate's decision not to commit for trial, the Crown could always present an ex officio indictment to the Supreme Court, which meant the matter would then go to trial, unless a Supreme Court judge ordered otherwise. If that happened, the whole thing would go onto the back burner until the trial, the sub judice rules applying to gag any further pre-trial press reporting. But it was a risky strategy. That smartarse Moran character was sure to challenge any ex officio indictment that the Crown put up, and even though the chances of a Supreme Court judge ordering a stay of the indictment were pretty slim, the whole process would draw the government intimately into the mire. From what Don Bollard had read of the evidence in the Wiltshire case over the past two days, this was one house of cards that was going to fall down in a messy heap eventually, and anyone who was anywhere near the scene of the accident when it happened was likely to get trapped under the rubble. The further the party stayed away from this one, the better.

Don Bollard shook his head and blew a weary sigh into the telephone.

'Too dangerous, mate. This one's got an awful smell under it.'

'You don't think Sharpey could really be involved in it, do you?'

The long pause answered his question.

'Could be.'

There was another hollow silence before the Prime Minister eventually whispered his reaction.

'Shit.'

The head of the ICAC had already publicly announced that Commission investigators had launched a full-scale investigation into 'allegations of murder, bribery, corruption and conspiracy to pervert the course of justice against one former police officer and one currently serving Sydney police detective, two prominent Sydney identities, and other persons'. It was no secret that they had already executed search warrants on Roger Baston's office and home, that Phil Manning had taken indefinite stress leave from the police service, that Wendy Bagley had absconded from the witness protection program and her whereabouts were presently unknown, and that Darryl Beane was currently 'assisting investigators with their inquiries'. The big question was: what was Gary Sharpe going to do?

Whatever it was, it was bound to be ugly.

'So how do we ditch him without hurting the party?'

EPILOGUE

A spring haze had settled over the deep blue waters of the Brisbane River and now a late-morning breeze sprang into life, wafting gently up the hill and rustling the leaves and early-season bursts of purple that were already blooming on the jacarandas. Kirsten Foster slid further down into the canvas of the squatter's chair and smiled at the little boy sitting cross-legged against the verandah railing opposite her, munching contentedly on his chicken sandwich. Simon Wiltshire could hardly contain his excitement; his dad was coming home.

'Want to play another game on the Xbox?' His words were barely decipherable through the mouthful of sandwich.

'I already kicked your butt.'

The little boy smiled back at her playfully.

'Yeah, two out of three.'

The day had started awkwardly. Kirsten had hardly spoken a word to Michael Wiltshire since their painful, teary conference at the prison, when he had finally confessed to her the truth about that fateful night. He'd told her that when Trevor called him, accusing him and Gary Sharpe of arranging to have Tommy Attwell bashed, he had no idea what Trevor was talking about. He'd contacted Sharpe immediately, knowing nothing more than that Trevor had been threatening him on behalf of Fred Hunter. Sharpe claimed he didn't know what Trevor was talking about either, but he would ring Fred Hunter to have him intervene. So when Michael subsequently learned of Trevor's death, he feared the worst: that Hunter's intervention on their behalf had been lethal. But he'd had no way of knowing that for certain. He went to the coronial hearing hoping the evidence would dispel his fears, but it merely confirmed the possibility of foul play, in which Michael feared he might be intimately implicated. He found himself on the horns of a desperate dilemma. To go to the police with his concerns was to risk being charged himself. The repercussions would be devastating, not least of all to his cherished son, who had been through so much already, and the equation was further complicated by the revelation that Trevor Ellowe was the ex-husband of a woman for whom he had developed a deep affection. What could he tell the police anyway? What did he really know? Nothing. Except that Trevor Ellowe was obviously a violent man, who might have met a violent end for any one of many reasons. So Michael had said nothing, and when Kirsten Foster asked him the question on their last night together in the Old Priory, he lied to her.

He lied to her. Slick still hadn't forgiven him for that. She wasn't sure she ever would.

Michael Wiltshire had paid a hefty price, and maybe he had got what he deserved. But the one person who hadn't deserved any of it was the beautiful young boy sitting opposite her munching his chicken sandwich. She had agreed to take the early-morning flight back to Brisbane to be at the house when Michael's sister dropped young Simon home. Eddie and Michael had to finish off one more conference with the ICAC investigators before they could finally leave Sydney, but they expected to be back by lunchtime. In the meantime, she had found herself unexpectedly nervous about meeting the little boy she had not seen in four years, and when he politely shook her hand on the driveway of Michael Wiltshire's sprawling mansion, she wondered just how difficult the day would be.

But as Simon moved around the house, reacquainting himself with his home, the questions had gradually begun to flow and they were soon deep in conversation about all that had happened to his father and what was happening now. She told him all she knew. After all, the kid deserved to know and Slick was nothing if not direct.

When the magistrate dismissed the case his father was released immediately, but agreed to remain in Sydney long enough to provide statements to the Major Crime Squad and the DPP about his knowledge of the assault on Thomas Attwell, and to ICAC about the death of Trevor Ellowe. The Mackay police had found copies of Fred Hunter's books amongst the possessions located in Barry Dougherty's house and Detective Kelly had handed them on to

ICAC, but according to Eddie they weren't much interested — it was small-time stuff and too long in the tooth. The Transport Royal Commission might be interested, and if they were Simon's dad might have to go back to Sydney to give a statement to the Royal Commission about what Dougherty had told him. But there would be no further charges. His father had done nothing wrong. The nightmare was over; his dad was coming home.

Kirsten Foster sat up, squinting mischievously.

'Two out of three, ay?'

Young Simon nodded with delight.

'Okay, let's do it.'

As she struggled from the chair she heard the familiar rattle of a loose manifold and Frank Vagianni's Falcon swung into the driveway. Simon leaped to his feet excitedly and peered over the verandah railing to the front gate.

'They're here!'

With that he was gone, leaping down the stairs by twos and threes. By the time Slick got to the front door, Michael Wiltshire was climbing from the rear of the Falcon, pulling a leather travel bag from the back seat. He looked up as the boy dashed across the front yard towards him.

'Dad!'

They came together with a thud and the father hoisted his son up in a bearhug and buried his face into the boy's neck.

As Kenny Takahashi pushed the selector into park, Eddie slid forward on the back seat and leaned over Frank's shoulder to see Michael

Wiltshire and his son wrapped in each other's arms. Farther down the driveway his best mate's kid sister was stepping tentatively towards them, her eyes glistening with tears, and as Eddie watched her fumbling for a tissue he felt an unfamiliar hollow ache in his stomach.

'Awful lot of hormones happening around here.'

Frank nodded absently. 'Mmm.'

Eddie slid back on the Falcon's vinyl seat.

'Why don't we go and grab some lunch, come back and collect Slick later?'

Kenny's eyes lit up. 'I've got a mate who's just opened a Jap restaurant in the Valley.'

'What do you reckon, Frank?'

'Can we get a beer there?'

'Yeah.'

'You got me.'

A TRIP TO THE BEACH.
TWO MISSING KIDS. A MOTHER'S NIGHTMARE.

GONE
CHRIS NYST

A gripping legal thriller from the bestselling author of COP THIS!

Other gripping novels by Chris Nyst:

GONE

A crime which burns into the mind and heart of every Australian

On a hazy summer's morning in 1965, nine-year-old Michael McCabe and his four-year-old sister, Catherine, kiss their mother goodbye and set off to the beach. They never return.

As a junior police constable, Bill Keliher was there when the McCabe kids went missing. Now, thirty years later, the respected senior police inspector is still enslaved by the mystery. For others, it's a riddle that will never be solved. But Bill Keliher knows better. He knows that no secret can be buried so deep that sweat, toil and tears won't eventually bring it to the surface. And he's going to be there when it happens. He has to be. It's his secret too.

> "fans of Grisham et al may well turn their allegiances to this first-class home-grown product. I dare you to put it down after the first chapter." *Sun Herald*

> "A fine Australian crime novel that mixes dry wit with moments of real poignancy and sadness." *Canberra Times*

A highly charged, hard-hitting legal thriller
from Australia's John Grisham
COP THIS!
CHRIS NYST

COP THIS

In 1969 a home-made bomb explodes in the sleazy heart of Brisbane's Fortitude Valley, killing eleven people and igniting a controversy that could threaten the government itself. When small time criminal Johnny Arnold is charged, his fight for justice sets two men — father, then son — on a collision course with the state's most powerful men.

Nyst's powerful tale of corruption, idealism and personal courage, spans two decades of dark political intrigue and sensational courtroom drama.